BELOVED ENCHANTRESS

"Know you this—when you are mine, I will not allow you to run wild."

Sunniva's blue eyes narrowed. "Is that so? Well, then, mayhap we should not drink the wedding ale after all. I will not be ruled by you or any other man!"

Raven marked that she was lovelier than ever in her fury. He feasted his eyes on the dewy softness of her mouth and on her shapely breasts that thrust against her kirtle, rising and falling with each angry breath she drew. She was adorable. He pulled her into his arms.

"Beast! Stop it."

He laughed and his kiss was so hungry it left her gasping for breath. He plunged his tongue into her mouth in a way that left no doubt she was his. She met it, eagerly, hungrily, as a delicious warmth spread through her body, a thing she had never experienced before. She melted against him, her lips parted. She wanted to stay in his arms forever.

"A brilliant new talent!"—Sylvie Sommerfield

JOAN VAN NUYS

BELOVED ENCHANTRESS

LEISURE BOOKS NEW YORK CITY

I dedicate this book with love and admiration
to my daughter, Carol.
Your adventures in Norway started it all.
Tusen takk for alt.

A LEISURE BOOK®

March 1990

Published by

Dorchester Publishing Co., Inc.
276 Fifth Avenue
New York, NY 10001

Printed in the United States of America

PROLOGUE

September 1006

WAVES OF PALE LIGHT FLICKERED ACROSS THE BLACK northern sky as the first snow of the season began to fall. Silently and quickly it covered the dwellings and fields of Lilleby, and covered the two lads and the young maid with its thick feathery flakes.

"If this keeps up, Ulf, we ski tomorrow," Raven said.

"Ay, and about time."

Ulf Mellby was blond and blue-eyed, not quite as tall as his best friend, but as strong-built as a young bull. Sunniva Mellby, skipping happily between her brother and Raven Trondsson, laughed and caught snowflakes on her pink tongue and with her red-mittened hands. She was as excited as they.

"We can go through Solby Wood to Strande," she cried. "'Tis all downhill, and we can take our time about coming back. We can carry foodpacks and dig a snow-cave for sleeping. Oh, I hope it snows all night!"

1

"'Tis a fine idea, that," said Ulf, "but not for you, Sunniva. 'Tis doubtful our father would allow it."

His sister's blue eyes flashed. "Why not?"

"Be reasonable, Sunni. Strande is a long way and you are but twelve winters old. And you are a girl."

Sunniva gave him a look of pure outrage and turned to the boy at her left. "Raven, you know I ski well. You taught me, after all. Tell my father I can hold my own!"

Raven chuckled. He was a gray-eyed lad with thick ebony hair that was dappled now with snow. At eighteen winters, he was over six feet tall, and his slender body was hard as granite, his shoulders broad and muscular. He was well on his way to powerful manhood.

"You have coaxed me into many things, little vixen, but not this time. Nay." He gazed down at Sunniva, his long-lashed eyes narrowed against the wind-driven ice crystals. "What if you broke a leg or fell into a tarn and froze your feet?"

Ulf chortled. "If you can guarantee either, then I say she goes. At least 'twould keep the little pest out of our hair for a while." He scooped up a handful of snow and threw it at his sister.

"Troll!" She punched his arm.

Sunniva liked her brother well enough most of the time, but now that he was sixteen, he had grown far too bossy. Always had she wished that Raven were her brother instead, and she wished it now more than ever. He was generous with his compliments and gentle with his criticism, and he never laughed at her, only with her. And when Ulf and her father had not the time to teach her to ski, it was Raven who showed her. Every winter he worked with her regularly.

"How about going through the wood to Nybling tomorrow instead of Strande?" he offered. "'Tis plenty far enough for the first run of winter. What say you, Sunniva?"

"Ay!" Her pretty face lit up. "Will you race me?"

Raven's smile shown white against his naturally dark skin. "Just try and stop me." Seeing Ulf's sudden gravity, he touched his friend's arm. "Now what, man? Does this not suit you either?"

Ulf looked uncomfortable. His little sister was a trial, wanting to go everywhere with them and do all that they did, but he did not crave to see her unhappy. He said quietly:

"You will not be allowed, Sunni."

Sunniva blinked her big eyes at him. She had the same striking attractiveness and coloration as her brother, but while he, like Raven, was close to manhood, she had an appealing childish softness about her—round pink cheeks, a full rosy mouth, eyes blue as cobalt framed with long gold-tipped lashes, flaxen hair hanging down her back in two plump, girlish braids.

"Not allowed? What mean you, Ulf Mellby? I have always been allowed." She watched as the boys exchanged a long look. "What is't? Tell me."

Ulf shrugged. "'Tis just that—you are almost a woman now, Sunniva."

Sunniva's face grew hot despite the frosty air. It was embarrassing enough to face that fact when she bathed and saw herself, but for Ulf to say such a thing in front of Raven—! She was so mortified, she was speechless.

Seeing her stricken face, Ulf added gently, "Women do not go dashing off on ski about the countryside with men, Sunni."

Sunniva glared at him. "This one will."

Ulf shook his head. "I think not."

Sunniva bristled, pink-faced. "I will!"

"Nay," he said stubbornly.

"You're not men yet anyway," she taunted them.

Ulf ignored that. "Our father says 'tis time you thought about sewing for your bride-chest and other such woman-things."

"Sewing! I hate sewing," Sunniva cried.

"Bride-chest?" Raven laughed. "Odin's bones, Ulf, the little troll is but a baby yet. What mean you, bride-chest?"

"Baby? Raven Trondsson, I hate you. I hate both of you! And why would father tell this to you, Ulf, and not to me?"

"Calm yourself, Sunni. He said naught to me. I happened to overhear him and our mother talking one night." Ulf made a ball of the wet snow, aimed for the front door of their dwelling and hit it squarely. "Our mother likes it not that you play sports so much and broider and bake so little."

Sunniva pulled in such a deep breath of icy air that her lungs ached. "What else said they?"

In her anger, she had all but forgotten the excitement of the first snowfall and the waves of color rolling and flickering across the sky. She, too, packed the wet snow into a ball, aimed for a distant birch and let fly. She put her arm into it, the way Raven always told her, and watched, satisfied, as the snowball thudded solidly against the dark trunk and clung. There! She could throw every bit as far and as hard as Ulf. She felt Raven's arm go across her shoulders.

"Let us walk a little, you and I, Sunni. Ulf, I would talk with your sister."

"Ay. I want to check my gear for tomorrow anyway."

With Raven's comforting arm about her, Sunniva's anger began to fade. Ever since she was small, he had been her best friend, her safety and happiness, her harbor in a storm. And he had not really meant she was a baby. That she knew.

"Know you, Sunniva," his deep voice was far above her head, "that your parents love you well."

"Ay."

"And they do only what they think best for you."

"Ay."

"Then does it not follow that, for your own good, they want you to be a proper young lady?"

"I will not be a proper young lady."

"Come now, they would never ask you to give up all the things you love."

"Nor could they make me," she said, pouting.

Raven sighed. Well did he believe it. Sunniva Mellby was not at all like other maids. No other girl in the valley, in all of Norway probably, was like Sunniva. Her eagerness to taste and to take all that life offered had always tugged at his heart. He could not refuse her when she begged to learn those things every Norse lad took for granted—riding and swimming and skiing, even war-skills. Things maids were never taught. Now he wondered, had he harmed more than helped the imp by giving in to her every wish?

The two walked in silence about Arn Mellby's large, prosperous steading overlooking the Strandefjord. They passed his large wooden manor house with its overhanging balconies on all sides, passed the lesser dwellings of the serving folk, passed the brewhouse and the weavinghouse and kitchenhouse and the long row of storehouses standing on their high wooden legs. Through the thickly falling snow they walked, as the canopy of pale shifting lights streamed far above their heads.

"Frey is making rainbows for the springtime," Raven said, his voice coaxing. He hoped to brighten her mood, but she made no answer. Finally he tilted her chin so that their eyes met. "Come, Sunniva, 'tis not as bad as all that."

"Hah! 'Tis little you know." Her lower lip thrust out in another pout. "Lucky you are to be a man, Raven Trondsson."

"And lucky you are to be a woman, Sunniva Mellby. Man's work is from sun to sun and season to season with never a rest in between."

"So is woman's," she muttered, sulky. "And women work long past sundown, just ask my mother. And men get to rule the world."

"Oh, ay, but the women rule the men."

"Hah!"

Silence returned as they toured the outer court-yard, where the various barns and animal houses stood. At that hour, all the animals were slumbering in sweet, dry straw.

"I trow you have forgotten, Sunniva," Raven said gently, "that when wars come, as they always do in this land of ours, 'tis man-blood that spills, not woman-blood. Mine will spill, as will the blood of my unborn sons spill for some unknown king." He looked down at her and cocked one black eyebrow. "Would you still be a man?"

He watched as her head snapped up, her eyes wide. He stared. Always had he thought her a comely child, but he saw now that her fairness was turning to extraordinary beauty. When had it happened? Or had her eyes always been that amazing color, a deep purple-blue, and her skin so creamy and flawless?

"Oh, Raven, nay! Say you will not go to war and spill your blood!" She flung her arms about him wildly and hugged him close, her snow-covered head pressed hard against his red wool tunic. "Never go to war! Promise me. Oh, Raven, I could not bear to lose you, to never see you again. . . ."

Astonished by the depth of her anguish, he said low, "There now, Sunni. Shhhh."

He continued to hold and comfort her, not daring to remind her that he trained daily for war. Every man did. He was the son of a chieftain who had gone bravely to Valhalla, and all in the valley knew that when war next came, he would go, a chieftain himself.

"I refuse to think about war," she said, sniffing, her voice muffled and her face still pressed against his hard chest. "Everything is going to stay the way it is. I want naught of war nor a bride-chest nor a stupid husband. I want to ride and ski and have fun."

His arms tightened about her childish body. "Shhh, little one, 'tis all right."

"And I want you to teach me more things. Will you, Raven? Please?"

"Ay. As long as I am here, I will teach you things, anything your heart desires."

"Will you teach me to throw a spear?" Her nose was still buried against his red tunic.

"Ay." Seeing the heavens brightening and the waves of color intensifying, he said, "Sunniva, look at the sky! Just look!"

Sunniva lifted her damp eyes at his bidding and gazed upwards to where wide ribbons of pink, lavender, foam-green, and pale lemon were playing about, streaming and surging across the velvety blackness, their long fingers raying outwards and shooting higher and higher into the zenith. She gasped at the shimmering beauty.

"'Tis wonderful! Think you that Frey really is making rainbows for Spring?"

"Ay. I suspect he really is. Especially for you."

Sunniva threw back her head and laughed at the wonder of it, her troubles forgotten on the instant. Her laughter was silvery, minding Raven of the sounds of a harp had they been frozen and then scattered about the frosty night. He thought suddenly, unexpectedly, that it would be a lucky fellow who got Sunniva Mellby when that time came.

"Tomorrow we ski to Nybling!" Sunniva cried. She began hopping about, unmindful that she looked like a snow-tumbled bear cub in her woolly brown cape and hood and the soft leather boots tied about her feet.

Raven chuckled. "We do, do we?" His gray eyes played over her affectionately.

"Ay. For no matter what Ulf says, I know my father. If I sit on his lap and put my arms 'round his neck and bawl a bit, he will let me go."

"Little troll." Raven gave her a swat on her small flat rump. "'Tis as I said, Sunniva, the women rule the men."

"Ay!" She tossed him an elfin grin over one shoulder and began trotting toward the manor. "Race me, Raven?"

CHAPTER 1

May 1012

SUNNIVA CHOSE THE LONG WAY HOME FROM THE SOUTH
field, where she had been haying. There were more
creeks and fences to jump that way, and she loved the
sensation, the power of soaring upwards with a
mighty horse beneath her, as though she were floating with invisible wings. She flicked Sooten's reins
and nudged his glossy barrel with her bare heels. He
responded immediately, stretching his ebony neck
and his long ebony legs to canter across the flower-
filled meadow.

Sunniva was unaware that men and women alike
stopped their haying to watch her fly past on the great
stallion. She seemed a warrior-girl with the face of an
angel, excitement shimmering in her expressive dark-
blue eyes, her masses of silky flaxen hair lifting in the
wind as freely as the stallion's flowing mane, her
lavender kirtle bound high so that her long legs
gleamed whitely against her mount's jet blackness.
She laughed with the joy of it as Sooten stretched,

lifted, and effortlessly took the jump over Solby Creek. She still could hardly believe he was hers, a gift from her father on her eighteenth birthday last week.

Sooten whinnied, shying suddenly to the left, and it was only Sunniva's natural skill as a rider that prevented her from losing her balance and being thrown off his bare back. She had automatically tightened her calves and thighs around his barrel as she gently applied the reins.

"Easy easy easy," she crooned, sounding as calm as she could manage, but her heart was galloping. What was it that had frightened him so?

Stopping at a safe distance, she swiftly removed the bow slung across her back and notched an arrow into it. She waited, her steady gaze fastened on the thick stand of bushes bordering Solby Wood. There was a deep growl, and as Sooten nickered and pawed the ground, Sunniva raised her bow.

"Easy, Sooten," she whispered, sighting down the arrow. "Steady, old lad, easy."

A large silver-gray wolf came out of the woods, his head high to sniff the wind. He gazed at Sunniva, his great plume of a tail twitching. It would be easy to drop him where he stood, but he was so beautiful, so majestic. She hoped with all her heart that he was no threat. When he finally blinked his green-gold eyes at her and returned to the woods, she sighed, relieved.

Thinking once more of all the chores awaiting her, she returned her bow to her back and signaled a gallop to Sooten. She gave herself to the warm wind and the sun then, racing headlong beside sprouting fields, past waterfalls and bounding over more creeks as she neared Lilleby. With the serving-folk in the hayfields most of the day now, she and her parents had servants' work to do in addition to their own, and

Sunniva wanted her chores all done before eventide. She was going to meet Raven.

A smile curved her rosy mouth at the thought of him. He and Ulf had been at sea, home-bound from an overlong cruise, during her birthday celebration last week. But now they were here and neither had forgotten her big day. Raven had brought her a gift from Dublin, a lovely ivory comb studded with shining deep-blue gems. But had he yet another gift for her now? she wondered. Why else did he want to meet her in the orchard at the sunset hour? She had questioned him, but he would only grin, his gray eyes teasing.

Arn Mellby was bringing his herd in for milking when his daughter galloped up the road and into the courtyard as though a fury were chasing her. She was a vision—her long, silken, spun-gold hair blown by the wind about her beautiful face, cheeks rosy, eyes the color of larkspur, slender body erect, hands in complete command of the great black beast.

Although he watched her deft handling of the stallion with admiring eyes, Arn's mouth was tight. What meant the girl, pulling her skirts up so high that every man in the valley could feast his eyes on those creamy rounded limbs of hers as she galloped by? Was this how she rode Sooten? Half-naked? By the gods, the girl sometimes showed no sense at all.

Her high spirits always had been a problem, and now her ever-blossoming beauty was another. Not that he regretted it—nay, she was the treasure of his life. In fact, he was over-proud of her fairness, but these past several years, it had become a grave concern. Every bachelor and widower in these parts wanted her to wife so that there had come hard feelings between neighbors over her, and bitterness toward himself, although it was Sunniva who refused them.

He watched his grown child dismount gracefully, shaking out her lavender kirtle and tossing back her long mane of hair. He noted, curious, that not only were her cheeks rosy, but her face and arms, usually so white and luminous, were pink and glowing too. And her eyes sparkled. Doubtless it was Sooten's doing, he thought with great tenderness. He minded not at all that she might possibly love him less than the great beast he had given her.

He pulled in a deep breath. For certain she would love him even less when she learned he had finally betrothed her and that Sooten was a gift of conciliation, a bribe for her good behavior. Ay, it was what many fathers did, this giving of their young maids to men without the maids' consent, but it had always been distasteful to him, a thing he himself had hoped never to do.

But he had been in such a bind, what with Sunniva's turning up her nose at all who asked for her and his neighbors growing angry, that last month he had taken the matter in hand. He had given her to an old friend of his in Bergvin. Holy Thor, he thought hotly, what else was a man to do? The maid was well past the age of betrothal. By rights, she should have had a babe or two by now.

"Papa! Hello!"

Arn managed a smile. "How goes it, my treasure?"

"Oh, father, 'tis still hard to believe Sooten is mine. I can never thank you enough. A thousand thanks!"

Sunniva raised her white arms and gave him a hug and a kiss on his bearded cheek, just as she had when she was tiny. But those days were past, Arn thought sadly. His masculine eye saw the lush swells beneath her coarse wadmal kirtle, saw the soft rounded perfection of arm and throat, the tenderly curved cheeks and chin, the gold-fringed eyes beneath the sweetly-arched golden brows, the graceful feminine body.

He sighed. Sunniva's beauty was of the sort that men seldom saw. He himself had rarely seen her like in all his travels, and of late he had begun to worry that it was a beauty men might kill for. Rolf Gunnarsson leapt to mind. Not that the Northland chieftain had actually threatened him when he was refused Sunniva's hand. Nay, the fellow was far too wily a bird for that, but the fury in his eyes had chilled Arn to the bone. It was but one of the reasons he had gone ahead and chosen a husband for her.

Eirik Paalsson was a wealthy Bergvin merchant of forty-two winters, a comely man, tall and strong, and he would protect Sunniva well. And he would rule her, thought Arn. Gently, of course, but rule her he would, more than her father ever had. And although Arn felt a woman needed that, especially a strong-willed maid like Sunniva, his heart was burdened by the thought. He had brooded long over his April meeting with Eirik in Bergvin where the latter's fleet of merchant ships nearly filled the harbor.

"You say your maid is fair, old friend?" Eirik had asked.

"Ay. In truth, Eirik, I have seen none other who can compare with her."

"Methinks 'tis a proud father speaking," Eirik had answered drily.

"Nay. Sunniva is a true beauty, man, I swear it."

"Is she healthy?"

"Ay. She bursts with health. She fairly glows with it."

"But you say she has a mind of her own. 'Tis not a good thing in a woman, that."

"I wish 'twere otherwise, but 'tis the way of it, man. I cannot lie about it. But she responds well to kind treatment. She has known naught but kindness, Eirik."

"I am not one to mistreat women, Arn, you know that, but I do expect obedience. No maid feels my hand who knows I am master."

"Ay." Arn had nodded glumly.

"Is her breath sweet? And are her hips broad enough to bear children?"

Arn had stiffened. "Man, this is my daughter we are discussing, not some damned heifer for sale."

Eirik had neither apologized nor backed down. "These things matter to me, old friend." His voice was gruff. "I want sons this time, having naught but daughters, and my first wife had black teeth and breath that made me puke."

"Sunniva's breath is sweet, I trow," Arn had muttered, struggling to suppress his anger, "and I trow she can give you as many healthy sons as you crave."

"Good."

Arn had felt sick to his stomach while they discussed the dowry and a wedding date, and when they finally struck hands, sealing the bargain, he was sick all over. But the man was a good one, he assured himself, and being comely into the bargain was a boon. Sunniva was sure eventually to appreciate that. And basically, Eirik was a kind man at heart. He would be good to the maid as long as she minded him.

Arn sighed deeply. Now he himself needed the heart and the courage to tell Sunniva and her mother what he had done. Jesu's Blood, he would have to choose the moment wisely.

"Papa, are you all right?" Sunniva gazed at her father curiously, concerned by the sudden change in his mood.

"'Tis just that I am behind in everything, what with

the servants in the fields all day. How goes the haying?"

"'Tis near done and, if the weather holds, 'twill dry fast. We do the east field tomorrow."

"Good."

"Shall I help you with the milking after I dry Sooten?"

"Nay, these maids are help enough." He indicated the daughters of their serving-folk.

"Well, then, I will be in the kitchen-house with mother after I finish." She turned Sooten's head toward the barn.

"Sunniva . . ."

She looked back and saw him frowning. "Ay, father?"

"Mind you lower your skirts when you ride, girl." His voice was sharp. "'Tis not proper, the amount of leg you show, a high-born maid like you."

Sunniva gave a merry laugh. "Papa, who would notice?"

"Every man in the valley with eyes in his head," Arn growled. When Sunniva sniffed her disdain, he added, "Were you to meet a band of those damned rogue Danes, they would think you naught but a common wench they could toy with."

At that, Sunniva grew solemn. "'Twould be amusing to see them try. Sooten can outrun anything, and no one dares toy with this—or this!" She patted the delicate but deadly jeweled dagger at her belt and indicated the bow slung across her back.

"Perhaps so, but I am master of this steading, lady, and I say lower your skirts from now on." He looked so stern that Sunniva blinked in surprise.

"Ay, father," she said quietly, sensing it was no time for teasing. "I always do. 'Tis just that my mind was—on other things."

15

It had been on Raven and on his mysterious command that she meet him later. What was it all about, she wondered again, turning Sooten's head toward the horse-barn. She dismounted, took up a wadmal rag and began working it in vigorous circles over Sooten's steaming black coat.

Her thoughts were filled with how wonderful Raven looked after his long weeks at sea, so tanned and strong and handsome. She smiled at the memory of his black beard. He always grew one on cruise and she was not at all sure she liked it. But he was home safe, that was the main thing. Her heart pounded harder. O, she was so glad he was home . . .

As Sunniva greeted her mother in the kitchen-house, she wondered if she herself would ever be such a woman as Anna Mellby, giving orders for this to be put into the oven at such and such a time, for that to be prepared just so, and the floors swept thus and spread with rushes, and the boards to be placed on the trestles and decked. The competent, contented mistress of her own manor.

Raven had given Sunniva a talking-to one snowy night long ago and ever since, she had tried hard to be a better daughter, diligently working at her spinning and weaving and sewing and such. The chores had bored her then and they bored her now, but her doing of them so pleased her parents that she had decided it was well worth it. Perhaps she would enjoy the chores more when she had a beloved for whom to do them.

"Sunniva, your cousin is fetching more onions from the storehouse," her mother said. "Run and fetch more carrots, too, and some turnips, and mind you help with the peeling."

"Ay, mother."

Sunniva lifted her skirts and ran. No one dallied

when Anna Mellby issued a command, and soon the
two maids were settled on a bench by the back door
with a basket heaped with vegetables between them.
Although her cousin lived close by, it seemed to
Sunniva that Inge was at Lilleby more often than she
was home.

"Sunni, why are you not yet betrothed?" the girl
asked, of a sudden.

Sunniva was taken aback. Inge was a mere babe of
twelve winters. How could she possibly be interested
in such things—or had she heard folks talking?

"A maid gets betrothed," Sunniva said gently,
"when she finds the man she loves, Inge. I have not
found such a man yet."

"My mother says love has naught to do with it. She
says a maid and a man must wed when their families
wish it."

Sunniva shrugged. "Mayhap with some maids that
could happen, but not with me. My father has promised I will have a say in the matter. He knows I would
never wed a man I did not love."

Inge's eyes were like blue saucers. "What if you get
so old and wrinkled waiting for the man you love that
he will not want you when you find him? Then what
will you do?"

Sunniva's laughter rang out. "'Tis hardly likely,
Inge, but 'twill be time enough to worry if it happens."

For a certainty she could not—nay, she would
not—marry the sort of man who thus far had asked
for her. Last month alone there had been three she
could not abide: one with a fat red face and piggy
little eyes, one so hairy he minded her of a bear, and
one who had squeezed her breasts and kissed her on
the mouth when they were alone. He was a chieftain
from the Northland, a man of great importance and
glorious to look upon, but he had frightened her so,

she had smacked his face hard. She shuddered at the thought of waiting in her bridal bed for any of the lot of them.

"Methinks I will do the same as you, Sunni," said Inge. "Methinks I will not wed 'til I fall in love. My man must have yellow hair and blue eyes and a nice hard backside. I could not abide a man with a fat behind."

Sunniva threw back her head and laughed again. The imp was positively precocious. "I agree, except I want my man to be dark."

"And tall?" Inge's eyes were dreamy.

Sunniva nodded. "Certainly tall—and lean. A hard lean man. Methinks I could never be happy with a soft plump man," she said, scraping a carrot.

"Nor I," Inge sighed, working at a turnip. "My man will be tall and lean and hard and broad-shouldered."

"Oh, ay, that sounds even better."

"What color of eyes, Sunni?"

Sunniva thought for a moment. "Gray, methinks."

"Like an eagle's!" Inge was enthusiastic. "Fierce gray-gold eyes. Such a man would protect you well from any marauding Danes, Sunni."

When had the child become so interested in men? Sunniva wondered, amazed. What a romantic little thing she was, and what a contrast to herself at the same age when she could think of nothing but horses and skis and bows and arrows. Caught up in the spirit of the game, she added:

"My man will have black, silky hair, I trow. Blue-black and gleaming."

"Like a crow's wing," breathed Inge.

"Not a crow's wing, silly, a raven's wing."

"A raven's wing then. Mine will have silky hair, too, only 'twill be yellow. Like cornsilk. Have you ever run your fingers through a man's hair, Sunni?"

18

"Nay," Sunniva murmured, nor had she ever wanted to, but now she grew quiet thinking of the possibility.

"Sunniva!" her mother called from within the kitchen-house. "What is keeping you two with those vegetables?"

"We are just finished, Mother."

"Good. Get them in here and get them to boiling and ladle out that first batch. We will have a crowd of hungry folk here before you know it. Inge, help get the boards down."

As they obeyed, Sunniva heard Inge's high-pitched chattering and laughing, heard her mother's voice going on about decking the boards and slicing the bread, but it was as if she herself were moving through a sea of syrup. She placed the vegetables in the bubbling vat, ladled the cooked ones from another vat and got the dishes and cups from the shelves. She tried to place them on the boards, but she was slow and clumsy. She kept seeing silky black hair and far-seeing gray eyes and a tall, lean body.

Raven . . .

She was shocked. Raven was her dear friend, her almost-brother, her happiness-maker, her teacher, her confidant. It was easy enough to understand why she might want the man she wed to look like him, for Raven Trondsson was a handsome devil and a chieftain. But there were more things to consider than good looks and bravery when picking a mate. Her beloved must be gentle and kind and tender with her; he would laugh ever so easily and not mind her independence and her silliness and . . .

Sunniva blinked and sat down abruptly on the corner seat, her heart thumping so that it was hard to breathe. Was it possible? Was it Raven Trondsson whom she loved?

19

"Sunniva! Whatever ails you, child?" Anna Mellby exclaimed. "Here they all come now, in from the fields. Did I not tell you to get the boards decked? Inge, take those platters away from your cousin and deck the boards. Tch! I cannot imagine what ails that maid . . ."

CHAPTER 2

May 1012

THE CHESTNUT STALLION AND ITS TALL RIDER MOVED slowly along the dirt road that divided the greening fields of Marvik from the blue waters of the Strandefjord. The sun's rays gleamed long and low and red-gold, burnishing the animal's coat, the man's thick black hair and beard, and the silver scabbard holding the sword Gildor. They transformed his royal-blue tunic to purple, his gray eyes to gold; their shadows deepened the clefts on either side of his tautly held mouth, a mouth that was usually generous and quick to smile.

Raven Trondsson had just returned from an extended cruise to the Norse-occupied lands to the south where, for the past seven months, he and his men had been conquerors—commanding, demanding, suppressing, ever on guard. It was never an easy thing for him to return to everyday living and the running of Marvik after a cruise, and this time his homecoming held yet another reason for discontent.

He was in love. He was painfully, hopelessly, deeply in love.

It was a unique experience and one he had never sought; he enjoyed his freedom too much. Worst of all, the object of his unexpected insanity was Sunniva Mellby. Little Sunniva! He shook his dark head in disgust. She was but a child, the baby sister he never had. A child? He hurled derisive laughter at the red-streaked pewter sky. Come now, man, no child she! Not any longer. She had grown tall and slender and softly curved this past year, the fairest maid in Norway's land.

Halfway through his cruise, somewhere on the Irish Sea between Maun and Ireland, the thunderbolt had hit him. He wanted her. He wanted Sunniva Mellby and none other, and from that moment on, his fevered brain could think of nothing but her. She had sailed eager and laughing by his side. She had shared his food and drink and wondered, wide-eyed, at the strange new sights he pointed out. She had slept, soft and warm and sweet-smelling in his arms when he slept.

Every time he thought of her, his skin prickled and his blood surged, pushed by a wildly soaring heart. He had been driven half-mad by his need for her and by the worry that she might be given to another by the time he returned. He had had no women the remainder of the cruise, nor had he desired any. He was weary of conquered female flesh, trembling maids who were terrified of him no matter how gently he treated them. Would Sunniva, too, fly from him like a frightened dove—not because she feared him, but because he was who he was? The one she would have chosen as a brother?

His manhood stirred at the memory of her joyous greeting two days past, her soft body pressing against his, her rosy lips on his cheek, her breath sweet and warm, and her eyes starry. He groaned and undid the front of his tunic to let his heat escape.

He had planned on confessing to her this night how he felt, yet the closer he drew to Lilleby, the wiser he knew it would be to move slowly on this and not frighten her away with his eagerness. Ay, this evening he would tell her only of the good news that had been awaiting him upon his return from the sea. He would bide his time with her, but as Odin was his witness, he meant to have her.

He marked Sooten grazing in the orchard before he saw Sunniva herself. His breath caught in his throat. She was clad in green—a green kirtle and a forest-green cape with a hood covering her shining hair so that she blended in with the trees and the deep grass. She could have been an elf maiden standing there with that mysterious little smile on her lips, beckoning him, luring him to some unknown but enchanting fate.

"Hello, Raven." Her voice was so soft, almost shy, that his eyes narrowed.

"Hello, imp." He forced himself to be casual. He dismounted and gave her a kiss atop her hooded head. "Is all well with you?"

"'Tis fine."

The hood slipped back, freeing her hair that was as yellow as wheat. Her skin showed white and soft against the dark green of her cape and, in the fiery twilight, her eyes seemed as deep and fathomless as a forest pond. She was a lily, a rose, the most perfect blossom on this earth. Why had it taken him so long to notice? He was hard-pressed not to take her into his arms then and there and cover her with kisses.

"Is't well with you, Raven? You—you look at me so strangely."

He laughed, swiftly gaining command of himself. "It seems you have become a young lady while I was

23

gone this time. And a very pretty one." Pretty? She was a goddess, an enchantress who had bewitched him! He could not tear his eyes from her breathtaking beauty.

Sunniva turned pink. Rarely did Raven comment on her appearance and before she could think of a suitable reply, she marked a tell-tale muscle working deep in his jaw. It usually meant he was annoyed. She bit her lower lip, wondering if he sensed her new feelings for him. If he had, it would be terrible! She would never be able to look him in the eye again.

Raven gave her a brotherly smile. "'Tis said you had several suitors while I was gone."

"Ay."

From his mother's gossipy account, he had heard it was an astounding number. And he had heard that Rolf Gunnarsson, who thought he owned northern Norway, had actually stroked her breasts and kissed her mouth as though she were already his. Arn should have floored the damned scut. He himself certainly meant to deal with the bastard when next he saw him.

"They were trolls, all of them," Sunniva said.

Raven's eyes danced over her. "Surely not all of them."

"All of them. Mayhap I will never marry, Raven. Mayhap my bride-chest will go to Inge and 'twill be the convent for me."

He laughed at that and cocked one black eyebrow. "I doubt any convent would take such a warrior-woman as you, Sunni."

Sunniva, too, laughed—in relief. He suspected nothing, and she therefore could behave with him as she always had, as though her whole world had not been turned upside down such a short time ago. She gazed at him hungrily, devouring with her eyes his wonderful long-lashed eagle eyes under those straight black brows that signaled his emotions so readily; the thick black hair that fit his head like a gleaming helmet; his tall, disciplined warrior's body in the familiar blue tunic and brown trews; the wide hard-muscled shoulders; the . . . She frowned.

Seeing where her eyes lingered, Raven gave her a wicked grin and stroked his clipped glossy beard. "Do I not pass muster?"

Sunniva sniffed. "As if it mattered what I thought."

She decided she hated the beard. It outlined his square jaw before creeping halfway down the dark pillar of his throat. It made him look savage. Only when he wore a beard could she imagine Raven Trondsson as the chieftain he was, for she had never seen him in battle gear. Of a sudden, she imagined him in chain-mail, his tall form moving with that proud arrogance that came of great strength and confidence, his narrowed eyes watchful and icy, his hand atop Gildor's silver haft as he led his men ashore from Odin's Raven, his warrior ship. And how that great drekar must frighten folk with its blood-red sail and the gilded dragon on its iron-clad prow.

Sunniva blinked. The Raven she had just envisioned was only a part of the whole man, for all in the Solby Valley said that Raven Trondsson was as fair and just a man on cruise as he was on his own steading. Never would he abuse a conquered people simply to show his power.

"Where did you go this time?" she asked.

"Where we always go. Ireland, England, Maun."

Those lands had yielded long ago to his forebears but always were there uprisings to be quelled and tribute to be collected and governing to be done.

"You were gone so long, I missed you." Sunniva blushed. "That is—we all missed you."

"The fall storms came early and we deemed it best to winter in Dublin." Seven months instead of the usual three; half of them sheer torture, thinking of her and yearning for her.

He saw now that biding his time in telling her of his love was not going to be an easy matter. He could not pull his eyes from her mouth, full and red as a ripe plum against her soft white skin. He yearned to sample and explore its sweetness for the first time.

"'Tis lucky you are, Raven, getting to see so much of the world."

"Ay."

Odin help him. He was on fire. He turned so she would not see his need and pretended to examine the pale new leaves sprouting on the nearest apple tree. Sunniva lay a hand on his arm.

"Why did you want to see me, Raven?" If he had another gift for her, she wanted it. He had dallied long enough.

"Mind you my uncle who lives in the Southland?" he said, forcing his breathing to remain steady.

"At Nydahl?" Why was he acting so peculiar, Sunniva wondered. And when had he ever been so interested in her father's orchard? She was growing impatient with him.

"Ay. His news was awaiting me when I got back." He turned to her then, his smile coming easily. "He has married an estate down there and he has deeded Nydahl to me."

"No!" Sunniva gasped. She gave an excited little skip and clapped her hands. "Oh, Raven, how wonderful!"

"Ay," he laughed, "'tis wonderful."

But she did not know how wonderful. With the acquisition of Nydahl, he was now a man of vast property and Arn Mellby need have no hesitation about putting her welfare in his hands.

"I know that the running of estates are of small interest to you, Sunni," he began, "but—"

26

"Oh, Raven, not where you are involved. Oh, 'tis glad I am for you!" Innocently, joyously, she threw her arms about him as she always had when there was cause to celebrate. She stood on tiptoe and kissed his cheek.

Feeling her body's softness and her kiss, light as the wings of a butterfly brushing his cheek, Raven tossed all prudence aside. He had only a glimpse of her wide, startled eyes as he pulled her into his arms and kissed her mouth. She tasted as he had known she would all those long, hard, lonely weeks he had dreamt of her. Sweet as honey. Nay, she was sweeter than honey. She was rose nectar and her lips were petal-pink and petal-soft, moist and yielding.

Unable to stop himself, he showered her mouth with kiss after kiss, its dimpled corners and full lower lip, the adorable peaks of her upper lip, finally covering both fully and deepening the pressure until Sunniva murmured beneath him. He freed her lips but continued to hold her close. She kept her face hidden against his chest, much as she had when she was small.

"Sunniva . . ." he said, low. He felt her trembling.

"Ay?" she murmured, still burrowed against him, her arms still about his waist.

"Did I fright you?"

He had kissed many maids in many lands but none as hungrily as he had kissed this one who trusted him so completely to do her no harm. What was he thinking, giving in to his hunger so fully? Although guilt stung him, he kept her softness pressed against him.

"Sunniva . . ." No answer. He lifted her chin. She kept her eyes downcast. "Sunni, are you angry? Look at me."

When she obeyed, his heart beat harder. He had held her in his arms many times, but only to comfort her. Never had he gazed so closely at the perfection of her luminous, glowing skin or the wine-flecked depths of those dark blue eyes. He kissed her thickly fringed eyelids, unable to resist. Her lashes were as soft as sable.

"If I frighted you, I am sorry."

"Nay, I am not frighted, Raven." She was shocked. And delighted. Her heart was pounding so hard her voice sounded faint in her ears. "And I am not angry. Nay."

How strange it was. He had always been the one in command and she always the one doing the begging —begging to learn how to swim or ski or throw a spear or a ball; begging to tag along whenever he and Ulf had places to go and things to do. Always begging. Now her woman's instincts told her that things were very different indeed. She leaned back lazily against his cradling arms and gazed up at him, her smile teasing.

"Actually, 'twas rather nice, Raven Trondsson. I rather liked it." His deep laughter sent a thrill through her heated body. So did the tightening of his arms about her.

"You rather did, did you?"

"Rather."

"Well, then, little troll, let us do it again."

She put her hands on his chest. "I think not."

She wanted him to kiss her again. And again and again and again. Her lips were tingling and her whole body was flaming, but she dared not surrender to her yearnings. That day when she first became a woman, her mother had warned her that men and women must not kiss with such passion unless they were handfasted. It was wrong and could lead to greater wrong.

"My parents would be furious if they knew."

"Then why tell them? Sunniva, never would I hurt you."

"I know that."

He was the dearest person in her world and never would he intentionally hurt her, but she had learned that men were different from women. Men tended to take lightly what a woman might give her whole heart and soul to—and her body. She knew Raven had had women. So had Ulf. She had overheard them talking one night. At the time, she had felt nothing but curiosity, amusement even, but now it was different. Now it hurt even to think of Raven and other women.

"I trow it would make a difference," Raven said softly, "if we two were betrothed?"

Sunniva searched his face with startled eyes. "What?"

Holy Odin, the damned words had just sprung off his tongue, and now she would want to dash off like a scared rabbit. Well, he would not let her. He had started this thing and he would finish it. He tightened his hold on her.

"You heard, little enchantress."

Sunniva's lovely face grew pink. Little enchantress? Betrothed? What had come over him? He was gathering her closer, his arms hardening, tightening about her, his chest and thighs pressing against her like rock. Flattered but flustered, laughing in her confusion, she put both hands against his face to keep his hungry mouth from taking hers again.

"Raven, behave! I just may call for help!"

He laughed down at her, his gray eyes hot. "Come, little wench, I only want to kiss you. 'Tis not so fearsome a thing, surely. You may as well yield for there are none here to save you."

"Indeed I'll not yield, you knave! Not until you tell me what this is all about. What mean you, betrothed?

And when have you ever called me aught but troll, pest, wart, imp, scamp, vixen, wench—" She could go on and on. "Since when am I an enchantress?"

"Since I have known I loved you."

Her silvery laughter rang out. He was teasing her. He was a chieftain. He had sailed all over the world and had done everything there was to do. He had tasted all life had to offer while she herself had never even left this valley where she was born. What could she give to such a man? Seeing his suddenly grave face, she grew very still.

"Raven, you—you cannot mean it," she whispered.

"Nay?"

He took the small white hands pressed against his face, kissed the palms, and then gently forced them behind her, imprisoning her in his arms. With his strong dark fingers, he tenderly traced her lips and the soft curves of her chin and cheeks and throat. He stroked her pale silken hair.

"Then why is't I want to wed you, Sunniva Mellby? Why can I think of naught but you day and night?"

His words seared her like lightning, leaving her body strangely weightless and without strength. Had his arms not been around her, Sunniva knew she would have fallen to the ground.

"Wed?" she whispered. "You would wed—me?"

"I want no other. Will you have me, Sunniva?"

"O, Raven—"

Seeing the joy and the excitement on her beautiful face, Raven laughed. It seemed she loved him as much as he loved her, and all of his worrying had been for nothing. He swept her off her feet and up into his arms, cradling her, hugging her, delighting in her delight and in her softly curved body clinging so tightly to his. He would make her the happiest maid in Norway. He would protect her and cherish her the rest of his life. Ay, he would give her the world.

"How about that kiss, imp? Do you yield or do I take it?" He bent, laughing, to her glowing up-turned face.

"I—I yield me, Raven." It was a shy whisper, but invitation smoldered like blue flame in her half-closed eyes. She lifted parted lips to him.

He took them gently, brushing, teasing them, returning the love-nips her small white teeth were inflicting on his chin and throat, all the while holding under fierce rein his desire to fill her with himself, with his tongue and that hot, tortured shaft throbbing inside his trews. But, nay, he would not harm nor frighten her for all the world.

Eyes closed, he nibbled at her sweetness. She was so soft and smooth in his arms, her flesh so fragrant and creamy. If only he could thrust himself deep inside her, claim her and carry her off, ignoring all the betrothal proceedings, the bargaining and the contract-signing and the drinking of wedding ale and all the other damned endless customs of the land. It was a sore temptation, that, stealing her by the stronghand and carrying her off in Odin's Raven to a place where they would never be found.

He banished the thought as it was born. It was the blood of his forefathers stirring in him, men who had cared for nothing but satisfying themselves, no matter what the cost to others. It was a battle he himself had met and fought and won long ago. There was more at stake here than his own hunger and yearnings; there was Sunniva's happiness and trust. Her honor. He raised his head, having drunk of her tantalizing freshness until he was almost dizzy. He saw the worship and adoration in her eyes.

"I love you," she whispered, slipping her fingers

through his hair. "Methinks I've always loved you, Raven Trondsson."

"And I love you. Never will I let you go, Sunniva."

More than his own life he loved her. She was his treasure. His hungry eyes glittered over her face and breasts and white rounded arms and throat. Holy Odin, he loved her. She was a woman to die for. Overwhelmed by his good fortune, he threw back his head and uttered a hoarse cry that had never before been heard in the Solby Valley—the victory cry of a Viking.

CHAPTER 3

SUNNIVA HAD NEVER KNOWN SUCH HAPPINESS. AS SHE raked the long grass in the east field alongside her father's serving-folk the next day, she thought over and over of the wondrous thing that had happened to her. Raven loved her. He had said he would have none other and would never let her go. He wanted to wed her! She had relived it a hundred times.

She gazed about the meadow, sniffing the air and drawing into her lungs the fragrance of fresh-cut grass and black earth, of sprouting blueberry bushes and pussywillows. The sun was hot on her braided hair and fair skin and the sky so piercingly blue her eyes ached to look at it. Was the day so magical because she was in love? she wondered, shaking the grass onto the fence to dry.

Hearing the soft coaxing call of a black grouse, Sunniva stilled her rake in mid-air and listened, her ear cocked toward the old smithy whence the sound had come. When it came again and yet again, the strange whistling of a bird that had never been known to mate in these parts, she laughed in delight. It was Raven. She stood her rake against the fence, hurriedly bound up her kirtle and leapt onto Sooten. She did not stop to explain where she was going, nor did any among the serving-folk dare to question the young mistress of Lilleby.

When Raven saw Sunniva astride Sooten and flying straight for him, he was minded of a young Valkyrie out of Valhalla. Blue kirtle, flaxen braids flying, her face intent yet holding an undeniable joy. He almost burst with the pride he felt. She was beautiful and she was his. And what a rider she had become! Always an apt and eager student, she had attained an effortless control since he had last given her a lesson. But he did not like it that she still raised her skirts to ride. When she was a little thing, it had been all right, but now her naked thighs were far too white and tempting against Sooten's ebony barrel.

"Raven! Hello!"

Sunniva jumped off the great beast, threw her arms about Raven's neck and kissed him on the mouth, driving from his head all but how she felt and tasted. He rubbed his lips hungrily against hers and discovered her tongue-tip resting between her teeth. He met its small velvet point with his own tongue, circling it, darting at it, finally catching it between his teeth and nipping it gently before kissing it. He heard her small gasp, felt her yield and soften further as his loins grew hot and eager.

"Do you love me still?" she whispered.

"Can you even doubt it?" he laughed, but a black jealousy was growing inside him.

It was clear she had kissed before—someone had taught her about tongues. And it seemed she knew nothing of the dangerous waters in which she trod, tempting men, himself even, with her rosy tongue and white thighs. His jealousy surged. Combined with his possessiveness, it soon overwhelmed him.

Raising his mouth from hers, he said gruffly, "'Tis surprising your father lets you ride about half-naked like that."

As he spoke, he scanned the road and the hills around them. There were always armed men about, both Norse and Dane, and he knew what a prize she would be. Holy Thor, she would be passed from man to man for gold!

Sunniva looked up at him, startled, and then down at her bare legs. Her face was fiery as she unbound her kirtle. The skirt fell to her ankles.

"I was in such a hurry to come to you, I forgot." Her eyes flashed angrily. "And I hardly consider this half-naked, Raven Trondsson. You have said naught of it before! Do my legs displease you so?"

"Displease me? Don't be a little fool, Sunni."

"Ah, so now I am a fool?" She drew herself taller. "Know you this—if men did not make such silly rules and women could wear trews to ride horses, I would not have displeased you so, but no, 'tis against *your* rules. You keep us hobbled and helpless in these stupid long kirtles!"

"Well you know, little hellion, that most women know naught of riding horses, nor do they care to, and besides—"

"Ah, now 'tis little hellion. What happened to little enchantress?" she taunted, hurt to the core. "And who taught me to ride in the first place?"

"Damn me, Sunniva, I will not have every cursed wadmal-farmer and goatherd gawking his fill of you as you ride by! Your father should not allow it." Did Arn not know the terrible harm that could befall her?

35

He wanted to spank her. "Know you this—when you are mine, I will not allow it."

Sunniva's blue eyes narrowed. "Is that so? Well, then, mayhap we should not drink the wedding ale after all. I will not be ruled by you or any other man!"

In her fury, Raven marked that she was lovelier than ever. He feasted his starved eyes on the dewy softness of her mouth and on her shapely breasts that thrust against her kirtle, rising and falling with each angry breath she drew. She was adorable. He pulled her into his arms.

"Beast! Stop it. Raven, I mean it. Stop!" Sunniva pounded his chest with her small fists until she was crushed so close to him she could not wiggle a finger. "Beast!"

He laughed and his kiss was so rough and hungry it left her gasping for breath. He plunged his tongue into her mouth in a way that left no doubt she was his. She met it, eagerly, hungrily, as a delicious warmth spread through her body, a thing she had never experienced before. She melted against him, her lips parted. She wanted to stay in his arms forever.

"Sunni, I am angry only because I love you," he murmured, his mouth against her silken hair. "No harm must come to you."

"I—I promise to be more careful from now on." She was limp, throbbing all over. What was it they had done with their tongues? What had happened? Never had she done or felt such a thing before. "And I will wed you, Raven. Oh, I love you so much. I love you, I love you." She looked up at him, her eyes wide and eager. "Will you speak with my father soon?"

"This day. I will go to him after evening-food."

"And I will tell my mother—she will be so pleased! She has always loved you."

* * *

It was sunset when Raven sought Arn Mellby in his hayloft. What a strange thing, this, he thought, entering his friend's large cowbarn and climbing the loft-ladder. Never had he expected to ask for any maid's hand, much preferring his freedom, and now to be asking for Sunniva Mellby. . . . He had come unannounced and without formality, bringing no band of richly clad kinsmen to plead his cause, nor was he himself finely clad. Arn was such an old and dear friend that anything but simplicity would have been awkward.

"Raven! Greetings, lad," Arn welcomed him. He was sweeping his loft, making space for his new straw and hay.

Raven took a broom. He was primed and eager to say why he was there, but it would not do to blurt it out. There were rules to follow, and for what seemed an endless time, he forced himself to work in companionable silence.

"I'll want to hear about your latest adventure when the haying is over," Arn said finally.

Raven nodded. " 'Twas a good cruise."

"Did your father ever tell you how we two once had to winter in the Orkneys?"

"Ay." Sensing Arn was about to launch into a long tale of his own Viking days, Raven said, "Arn, I would speak with you about Sunniva."

"Sunniva?" Seeing the other's serious eyes, Arn sat down on a heap of straw and mopped his sweating brow. Always had Raven come as her defender. "What has the maid done now, lad?"

"We want to wed, Arn. I am asking for her hand."

"Wed?"

"Ay."

Arn blinked up at the young master of Marvik, astonished. Always had he thought of Raven and Sunniva as brother and sister, nothing else. Raven was more brother to her, in fact, than Ulf ever had been.

Raven got immediately to the business at hand. "As my extra-gift, she will have half my tribute from this last cruise. 'Tis considerable, Arn."

"Well I know its worth, Raven," Arn muttered, dread weighting his body.

"—and for my morning gift, I mean to proffer her Nydahl. 'Tis mine now." Raven felt a glow of satisfaction as Arn's eyes widened.

"Holy Jesu, Raven, I congratulate you. I had not heard. Your uncle has done the right thing finally, seeing how 'twas your father's in the first place and—"

"So what say you, Arn?" Raven interjected impatiently. "Can we strike hands on it and work out the date and the other details later?"

Arn rose and began pacing his loft. "Raven, I wish this could be. . . ."

Raven laughed. "It can be, old friend. Just unbend your back a bit. I know you think of me as a brother to Sunniva, but those days are gone."

"Raven, I—" Arn shook his head, filled his lungs.

Raven's gray eyes narrowed. "What is't, Arn?"

"'Tis impossible, lad."

Raven was stung. He said quietly: "Is't that you think I crave naught but sailing and wenching?"

When Arn did not answer but looked instead at the floor, Raven felt the blood drain from his face. He was hurt. Nay, he was crushed. Did Arn not know him better than that? In a fury, he grabbed the older man's arms and spun him to face him.

"Say what you think, man." His white lips scarcely moved. "I would hear it."

"Come, Raven, loose me," said Arn gently and Raven's hands dropped to his sides. "Know you, lad, had I but heard this sooner, gladly would I have welcomed you as son-in-law, but—" He could scarce speak the words.

"But what?" Raven growled.

"I have given her to another."

Frozen in the awful unblinking gaze of the other's ice-gray eyes, Arn was unaware that he made the sign of the Hammer. Where had he last seen such a bone-chilling look? Then he remembered. It was on the battlefield, on the face of Raven's father as that Solby chieftain had coldly, methodically, cut the blood-eagle on the chest of a screaming Dane.

"Damn you!" Raven's voice was thick with his fury. "Who is it? You promised Sunniva would have a say in this."

Arn held up a warning hand. "Hush, man. I hear the women below and I would not have them know this yet."

Raven glowered at him. He would say nothing at this time, but only because his wrath was so huge it would only worsen matters. He watched as Sunniva ascended the loft-ladder, followed by her mother. Anna Mellby was as bright-eyed and pink-cheeked as Sunniva herself.

"Have you two talked yet?" Sunniva asked. Seeing Raven's anger-darkened face and her father's scowl, she cried, "Papa, what is't?"

"We will talk of it later."

The life and color drained from her face. "You mean—you have said nay?"

"Later, Sunniva," Arn said sternly.

Sunniva's frightened eyes flew to Anna Mellby. "Mother! Do something!"

"Calm yourself, child."

Anna Mellby was a faded replica of her daughter, a tall, slender, strong-willed woman who was a decided force in the running of Lilleby. Now she fastened cool blue eyes on her husband of twenty-two years.

"For two winters," she said, "Sunniva has refused all who have asked for her. Now she says she loves Raven and he loves her. If he cannot have her, why not? I would hear it, husband."

Arn straightened his shoulders and stroked his sandy beard. There was nothing for it but to confess and face the angry onslaught of the three of them. Thor's bones, he had done what he thought he had to do! Why had the damned lad not told him earlier that he wanted Sunniva?

"Father, I love Raven and he loves me." Sunniva's dark eyes were large and begging. "We want to wed. 'Tis as simple as that. You have but to say yes." She threw her arms about his neck and clung to him. "Say yes, Papa. Please?"

Arn removed her white arms, held them at her sides and busked himself for his ordeal. "Sunniva, I—have betrothed you to another."

"What!" She leapt back as though stung.

"Arn Mellby!" It was a screech from his wife. "You have betrothed our daughter without consulting me?"

Sunniva gasped, "You—always said I could make my own choice! Father, what have you done?"

Arn did not yield. "I had no idea then how many men wanted you, Sunniva, nor how bitter was the rivalry between them. You saw how many there were."

"But you promised . . ."

"Who is this man?" Anna demanded. "I would know something of him."

"His name is Eirik Paalsson, wife. He is a widower, an old friend from Bergvin."

"So far?" she cried.

"Well you know how things are, woman," Arn growled, on the defensive now. "There is bitterness here over Sunniva, and I deemed it best not to give her to a valley man. I must needs keep peace with my neighbors. Bare is a neighborless back."

"And cold is a loveless bed!" Sunniva cried. She yearned to weep, but could not. She was too enraged, too sick to weep.

"You will like Eirik, Sunniva. Mayhap you will even grow to love him. He is comely and I know he is kindly, for I have known him long. We were guardsmen together in Earl Haakon's court."

Wanting to hurt him as she herself had been hurt, Sunniva cried, " 'Tis an ancient man you are wedding me to then?"

"Forty-two is hardly ancient," said Arn stiffly, for he himself was forty-two. "Eirik is wealthy and powerful. He will keep you safe from men like Rolf Gunnarsson."

"Raven can keep me safe from such beasts." Sunniva's rosy mouth was sullen and her eyes held lightning that seemed about to strike.

"We need to think on it, Arn," Anna Mellby said. " 'Tis so sudden."

"There is naught to think on, woman. 'Tis agreed! We have struck hands."

Sunniva made a small, strangled sound and Anna gave her husband a disbelieving look. What she intended to say to him could not be said before Sunniva and Raven. There was nothing else to do now but support him.

"Sunniva," she said, trying to sound calm, "if this Eirik is a strong, comely man who will be a good provider and a protector of you and your children, mayhap 'tis for the best."

"Ay," Arn said eagerly. "He has already raised one family, so he'll not be wearing you out. A young bull would have you lying in the birthing straw yearly. I

41

trow three or four sons would satisfy Eirik." He hoped to Holy Jesu it was true.

At that, Sunniva lashed out. "I will not have him, nor will I have any mewling babes for him. I hate the damned scut! I want Raven!" For the first time, she looked at her beloved. His dark face was impassive but watchful.

"Sunniva!" Anna was shocked by her daughter's coarse language.

"Watch your tongue, my fine maid," Arn growled, reddening. "You are still small enough to go over my knee."

"Try it!"

"Sunni, let it be," Raven said, low, and put his arm around her.

"O, Raven . . ." Sunniva buried her face on his chest. Feeling the hot sting of tears in her eyes, she blinked and swallowed hard. She would not weep. To weep meant that she had surrendered and was without hope. And that she was not.

Raven could have slain Eirik Paalsson. He could have slain Arn himself, for he saw no way out of this. If the two had struck hands, Arn was bound to the contract more firmly even than if he had done it in writing. His honor was at stake.

"I hate him," Sunniva wailed. "And I hate you!" she flung at her father.

"Silence!" It was an explosion from the master of Lilleby.

She met his furious blue gaze, so like her own, with her head high, but inwardly she quaked. She had never seen him so angry, his face all red and the veins on his temples standing out like great red worms.

"Damn me if you will not wed the man I have chosen, Sunniva. All in the valley have said I was ever too lenient with you and now methinks they were right. From this instant forward, you will obey me. You will go to the husband I have chosen for you, and you will obey him. Hear you?"

Numbly, Sunniva nodded her head. She knew her mother dared not interfere, nor would Raven. No man would criticize another on his own manor ground.

"You will wed Eirik Paalsson and you will show him the respect you never show me."

Sunniva gulped. It was not that she did not respect him! "Oh, Papa, I—"

"—and you will give him as many children as he craves. Hear you what I am saying, woman?" She nodded. "And if your lady mother has told you naught of how babes are made, I suggest you learn immediately."

"Arn!" Anna shot him an outraged look.

"Silence, woman. We have raised a disrespectful, willful daughter whose stubbornness and waywardness will surely lead to naught but her unhappiness. She must learn that 'tis woman's lot to be ruled. I see well that she has yet to learn what beseems a good wife, and before the wedding ale is drunk, she—"

Sunniva had heard enough. Without another word, she turned and climbed down the loft-ladder. Her parents called after her, but she paid them no heed. She knew Raven was behind her as she fled the barn and ran out into the peach-tinged twilight.

"Sunniva, wait!" he called.

She neither waited nor answered but ran, weeping, into Solby Wood. When she was exhausted and could run no further, she dropped beside a deep-green tarn whose still waters reflected her blue kirtle, ashen face, and the golden cloud of her hair.

"Sunni . . ."

"I will throw myself in," she gasped, winded from her flight and her desperation.

"Nay." Raven sat down beside her and put an arm about her.

"I will. I refuse to marry that ancient troll. My father had no right to g-give me away. . . ."

"He had every right. 'Tis the way of things in this land of ours."

"He promised . . ."

"Ay, little one." Raven held her close, tucking her shining head under his chin and smoothing her hair back from her hot, tear-streaked face. "My precious treasure . . ."

"I will not throw myself into the tarn," Sunniva murmured, "but neither will I go to that man, Raven. Our wedding ale will never be drunk."

Raven already had promised himself that. His growing bitterness over the situation was forcing his thoughts in a direction that was against everything he believed in—against law, order, discipline.

"I mean to run off."

"You will not!"

"I will wear Ulf's old clothes. I will cut off my hair and I will take Sooten. None can stop me, not you, not anyone."

"Damn it, Sunniva!" Raven cursed himself to Valhalla and back for teaching her how to defend herself and to ride like a man. But on the other hand, would he have wanted her helpless? "Do naught that is foolish," he growled. "Leave this to me."

Seeing the grimness of his bearded face, his lips compressed into an ominous slash, eyes like slate, the tell-tale muscle leaping in his jaw, Sunniva felt a chill. He frightened her when he looked so. He was every inch a Viking chieftain.

"What will you do?" she quavered.

"Naught that men have not done before."

"You would not slay the man?"

Raven laughed. "Nay, Sunni, I will not slay the man. But know you this—he will never drink the wedding ale with you."

Sunniva studied him with grave eyes. "Raven . . ."

"Ay, my treasure?"

"You must not."

He looked as innocent as a babe in its cradle. "Must not what?"

"Take me by the stronghand," she whispered.

She knew him well, Raven thought. While it pleased him that she saw so easily the workings of his mind, he did not want to fret her. The less she knew of his dark, gathering plans, the better.

"Raven, you must not."

"Hush, Sunniva."

He tried to kiss her but Sunniva would have none of it. She looked at him with frightened eyes. The penalty for woman-stealing, she knew, was outlawry. There would be a price on his head and, for the rest of his life, he would be fair game for any man.

"Raven, you will be slain! I am not worth turning outlaw and dying for, no woman is."

"You are not to worry." He stroked one white arm, raised her small soft hand to his lips, kissed the pink tip of each finger.

"Say you will not use the stronghand," she ordered, frantic for his safety. "Promise me!"

He chuckled. "'Tis a fine idea you have given me, Sunni."

"Beast, you were thinking it already." She punched his arm. He caught her fist and kissed it, too.

"Little hellion."

His tenderness melted her. "Promise me. Oh, Raven, please, promise me . . ."

He kissed her mouth, the sweet ivory hollow at the base of her throat, a lock of her hair. He grew serious then.

"I can promise you only one thing, my Sunniva—I will never let you go. Had I the choice, know you that I would never turn outlaw. But now we have gone past that point."

CHAPTER 4

RAVEN WASTED NO TIME. ALL IN THE VALLEY THOUGHT he had gone to the mountains to look in on his summer farm there, but in truth he was rallying his men—those strong, hard, single young bucks who craved adventure and the booty it brought and who went on cruise with him. He sought each of them in turn, giving each the chance of helping him take Sunniva by the stronghand. He did not judge any who said nay, for those who went with him could never return to Norway's land. They faced outlawry.

The three days he was gone, one thought bedeviled him: Should he ask Ulf? Did he have the right to put him to such a terrible test, choosing loyalty to his parents or to his best friend? He decided there was but one answer. Ulf had to know. Raven found him fishing on that evening he returned from his quest.

"How were things up at your seter?" Ulf asked. "I mean to visit ours next week and lie there several days. Come along with me, the game is good now."

Joan Van Nuys

"I was not at my seter," Raven answered quietly.

Seeing his friend's unsmiling face, Ulf knew instantly what he had been about.

"You were rallying the men?"

"Ay." Gray eyes met blue. "Know you what I mean to do?"

Ulf nodded. "You have no other choice. Does Sunniva know?"

"Nay, she would be wild with worry. 'Twould show."

Ulf sighed and put away his rod. "You've thought this all through, I trow?"

Raven's eyes glittered. "I am not asking your advice, man, nor am I asking you to come. I was obligated to tell you."

"Ay."

"My men will arrive before the week's end. It would seem we are taking the ship to the race over in Veldoy."

Ulf grinned. "And you will steal Sunniva during the night, ride through the wood to Veldoy, and board ship there." When Raven nodded, he said, "I trust my little sister will go willingly?"

"Nay, but I will take her no matter." Seeing Ulf's eyes narrow, Raven added, "Man, she will balk only because she fears for me. I cannot let that stand in my way."

Ulf sighed as he rose and collected his gear. "Nor should it. So, where are we bound, old friend?"

Seeing that Ulf had made his decision, Raven clapped him on the shoulder. "Sunniva must decide. For myself, I would head for far places—Maun, the Orkneys, the Hebrides—but she might prefer Denmark or Sweden."

"Ay, she will want to meet with the folks now and again."

48

It was a subject to which Raven had given much agonized thought. He had not a hope of receiving a grace-deed, being a known enemy of the present kings who shared the throne, but he was certain Arn would forgive Sunniva and himself in time. Never would he disinherit her or have their children declared illegitimate, but Ulf—Raven shook his head. On Ulf, Arn might go harder.

"Mayhap you should think again on this before you decide, Ulf," Raven said. "You have been hasty with your answer. You will be losing not only Lilleby but your parents as well. 'Twill be hard on them, losing a daughter and a son." There would be a price on Ulf's head as well as his own.

"Man, I have thought on naught else ever since this happened. 'Twas clear to me you would take her."

"Does Arn suspect?"

"Nay."

Raven's pensive eyes went to where his great drekar rocked gently on the blue-gray waters of the Strandefjord. Never had he thought he would be unfurling her red sail and starting on another long journey so soon. Especially a journey of this sort.

"Know you, Ulf," he said low, "that I would never ask you to do this for me, to give up everything. Your home and heritage and country."

"And know you, brother mine, that I am a fighting man, not a farmer like my father. If ever I must make the choice, I will go to Valhalla by your side rather than die on Lilleby-land with a plow in my hands."

As they struck hands, Raven felt a swell of love for his friend. "So be it then. We will talk on this later."

Sunniva passed her needle in and out of the snowy linen on her broidery hoop, one tiny finely formed golden bud after another taking shape on the chemise that she would wear on the night of her wedding. Only five days had passed since she had learned of her betrothal, but to Sunniva it seemed an endless number of sunsets had dragged by.

She had gone about her spinning and weaving, deceptively quiet and docile, but beneath her placid bearing ran a steely resolve. She was not going to wed Eirik Paalsson, although even her mother now accepted the inevitability of it. Anna Mellby had prodded her all week to sew for her bride-chest and already her father was sending forth greetings and invitations to kinfolk from afar to come and drink her wedding ale. She had been forbidden to see Raven.

Sunniva had rebelled at that and stamped her foot, whereupon Arn Mellby had declared that if she would not obey, it was an easy enough thing to escort her to the Solby Convent, where it was certain she would not see him. She could make up her own mind as to which it would be. She had been frightened enough by that to obey. But it frightened her even more that Raven might take her by the stronghand and be outlawed before she could decide on what to do.

She threw down her hoop and sat herself before the loom. She tried to thread the blue and green balls of wool in and out of the warp, but it was useless. She could not sit still, nor could she concentrate. She must think, plan. . . .

"Sunni, may I come in?" Inge stood in the doorway to the weaving room. Her blue eyes, always big, were huge as she gazed at her cousin. "Are you all right?"

Sunniva smiled and beckoned her in. "I'm fine. Not happy, but fine."

"I just wanted you to know, methinks 'tis horrible what has happened." There were tears in her eyes.

Sunniva was so touched, she hugged the child.

"You are sweet to care." Sweeter by far than her own folks, she thought bitterly.

"When is the wedding?"

"August fifth."

Sunniva wanted to blurt to Inge that she need not fear, her big cousin would never drink the wedding ale with an ancient troll she did not love. But she dared not. Inge might unwittingly say something.

"Think you," Inge whispered, "that Raven might carry you off by the stronghand?"

"Nay. Besides, never would I let him," Sunniva said. "He has too much to lose."

But he would forfeit it all for her, she brooded, trembling as she always did when she thought on it. He would face outlawry for her. Death even. Oh, surely those stranger-kings on Norway's throne would grant him a grace-deed! Surely they would. What king could be so cruel as to punish a man whose only crime was loving too well? And it was not as though she herself were unwilling to be borne off. But dared they take a chance on royal leniency?

The answer was no. Neither Raven nor her father supported the men who were now in power, which meant that she should flee before Raven did anything rash. And knowing him, his plans were doubtless already made. She must escape tomorrow, perhaps even this night. There was simply no more time for her to think on what to do. She must act.

"Are you cold that you shiver so?" Inge asked, her eyes wide with pity. "Oh, poor Sunni. Oh, 'tisn't fair!"

The very thought of flight filled Sunniva with terror. Where would she go? How would she live? Since childhood, her head had been filled with the terrible things that could happen to an unprotected woman. But then, doubtless Raven would find her before she got far and would bring her back anyway.

51

"Sunni, you fright me when you look so. I thought you said you were fine. What is't?"

Sunniva blinked. Raven would find her. Of course, that was it! It was so simple, she could scarcely believe she had not thought of it sooner. She would flee, ay, but beforehand she would tell Raven exactly where she would be. He would come for her and from there they would escape to wherever he deemed it safest to go. When he did not return with her to Lilleby, all would think he searched for her still and never could he be accused of the stronghand. Oh, that was it!

"Sunni, what is't?" Inge had begun to weep she was so frightened.

"Honey, 'tis all right. Everything is finally all right. Listen, I want you to do something for me! Will you?"

"Ay," Inge said, weeping still. "Anything."

"They have forbidden me to see Raven but please, tell him to come to the cowbarn at moonrise. We must talk. Will you do that?"

"Ay. Oh, ay!"

Sunniva was edgy for the remainder of the day, and by evening she could scarcely sit still. For the third time, she put down her broidery hoop, stepped over the sleeping hounds, and poked at the spitting hearthfire with a fir root. Her father, gone in drink, slumped on the fireside bench, eyes closed, while her mother worked at the board on a great pile of sewing. Anna Mellby looked as fresh as she had that morning, her coif crisply white and her apron and kirtle almost speckless. It seemed she could go on for hours and Sunniva was ready to fly out of her skin.

"Sunniva, you should be abed. 'Tis late."

"I'm not sleepy, mother. The room is so smoky, methinks I'll go outside for a little."

Anna was careful to keep her eyes on her work lest they betray the happy secret she was keeping from her daughter.

"All right, but mind you stay within earshot, child. There are strangers about at all hours. Take the dogs."

"Nay, they are sleepy. I will stay close, never fear." Sunniva settled her green wool cape over her shoulders and pinned it shut with a copper brooch. "You must be tired, mother. I will do some of that mending in the morn."

"Ay, 'twill still be here, most of it. But run along now." After the door had closed, Anna smiled. She drew in a deep breath of contentment. All was well. Somehow she had known it would be, and tomorrow Sunniva would learn of it.

It now stayed light all the night long after a hard winter of snow and wind and endless dark days. As Sunniva hurried to the cowbarn to meet Raven, she thought on how mysterious it always seemed at this new turn of season. So strange and quiet with the sun a cold pale globe hanging just above the horizon, birds not chirping nor animals stirring and all the serving-folk abed. She wondered suddenly if Inge had remembered to give Raven her message. Disappointment rushed over her, thinking that he, too, could be abed and sleeping. But nay, here he was, his tall form suddenly by her side. His arm went about her waist.

"Hello, my treasure."

"Hello . . ." Sunniva blushed, looking up into his dark handsome face. She was unused still to such love-words from him.

Raven led her into the barn before pulling her close and kissing her mouth. She felt the fast heavy thumping of his heart against her breasts as he pulled her into the shadows of an empty stall and drew her down into a strawheap. They exchanged a long kiss and then she cried softly:

"O, Raven, I have such good news for you!"

His eyes danced over her in the half-light. "I have some news myself. But I would hear yours first."

He listened, intent and grave-faced as she put forth her plan of how they might flee together with impunity. He was impressed with its cleverness, thinking it might well have worked had they needed it. As luck would have it, they did not.

"It has great merit, Sunni, but—"

Sunniva frowned. "You will not use the strong-hand. I forbid it absolutely."

He laughed. What a Valkyrie she was. "What say you, little troll, to drinking our wedding ale right here at Lilleby in early July with hundreds of guests looking on?" With his finger, he traced the adorable pink circle her mouth had formed. "What say you to a magnificent wedding train for me and a bridal bed for you such as has never been seen in the Solby Valley?"

Sunniva giggled. "Methinks you are mad."

"Nay, not mad," Raven laughed, nuzzling her throat and kissing her sweet mouth over and over. "Arn has received strange tidings from Bergvin this eventide. It seems your venerable betrothed is missing, Sunniva."

"What!"

"The all-powerful Eirik Paalsson has disappeared in Dublin on a trading trip."

Sunniva was shocked. "Nay!"

"Ay. He may have been abducted or gone off mysteriously on his own." Raven's gray-gold eyes danced. "None seem to know what has become of the poor fellow."

Thinking of her parents sitting so calmly back in the hearth room, her father sleeping, her mother sewing, Sunniva cried, "Mean you that my folk knew of this, yet said naught to me?" She stamped her foot at the unjustness.

Raven chuckled and pulled her closer. "Unruffle your feathers, chick, for 'twas done at my bidding. I wanted to be the one to tell you."

Sunniva's hopes soared, winged, only to crash immediately. "But how can such a thing be? 'Tis too easy, surely. What if he returns tomorrow—or next week? Am I not betrothed to him still?"

"Nay. Arn is angered. He says if Paalsson has gone off without a word to any, he is irresponsible. And if he was carried off against his will, he is no fit protector of his daughter." Raven pressed her back into the straw and stroked her hair and her cheeks. His mouth brushed hers. "You are mine now, Sunniva."

"I—I can scarce believe it, 'tis so sudden," she murmured. Now she would not have to flee, nor worry about the stronghand nor outlawry.

"Believe it."

"But what if he does come back? What if he holds my father to the handsala?"

"Then he will have me to deal with," Raven said. He stretched out beside her and nestled her head on his shoulder so that he could easily kiss her lips.

"You are my own sweet, betrothed maid now, Sunniva." He covered her hands with his. "It took me over-long to realize I loved you—never can I forgive myself for that—and then I lost you to another, but now—now I have you again." His kiss was so rough and hungry it burned her lips and his beard bruised her tender flesh. "I swear by holy Odin, I will never lose you again."

It was the first day of June, a month before the bridal, and all of Lilleby was caught up in preparation for it. With more than two hundred guests expected to drink the wedding ale, there was such a flurry of brewing and baking and cooking going on that it sometimes dizzied Sunniva to be in the midst of it. One afternoon, she carried her spinning gear to the cherry orchard to find a bit of peace and to dream a bit.

How could she be so lucky? she mused. Lucky that poor Eirik Paalsson—she wished him no harm—had disappeared; lucky that Raven loved and wanted her; lucky that she was to have such a grand wedding. It seemed she was the luckiest maid in all of Norway. She was about to sit down and spin when a male voice came from close behind her.

"Greetings, mistress."

Sunniva spun about, startled. She had neither seen nor heard the man's approach, but now she saw his lathered horse tethered to a distant tree.

"Greetings, sire." He was dark-haired, dark-skinned, and dressed in farmer's clothes. She could not place his accent, but she knew it was not from these parts. She gave him a polite smile. "Can I help you?"

"I seek Arn Mellby."

"My father is not at the manor right now. You will find him in the north meadow washing and shearing sheep."

"How far is't from here?"

He stepped so close that Sunniva could smell the odor of beer and sweat that clung to him. She took a step backward.

"Just down the road a bowshot," she said, coolly. Too late, she realized the odd look in his brown eyes meant danger. His fingers closed painfully about her upper arm.

"Let's have a sip of your honey, little wench."

"You tread dangerous ground, oaf! Unhand me." She tried to free herself but could not. He laughed, his hot eyes sliding over her.

"My lord was right," he said gruffly. "You are a beauty."

In an eyeblink, Sunniva was crushed against him and his wet bearded mouth was clamped onto hers. Outraged, she pummeled his shoulders and head with her fists, but he was undeterred. He bent, suddenly, clasping her about the thighs and lifting her. She shrieked.

"Pig! Let me go!" When he ran toward his horse, she knew he was going to carry her off. "Stop! Beast!" Again she screamed but none heard. They were too distant.

"Keep your lips sealed, wench, or I will have to hurt you." His big hand covered her mouth, effectively stifling her cries. "Ah, God's bones, what a honied little bitch you are. Mayhap I'll keep you for myself."

He threw back his head in a triumphant laugh, exposing the ugly bony knob in the center of his throat to Sunniva's terrified eyes. She acted swiftly and automatically, giving it a sharp crack with the edge of her hand. The man went down like an oak. As the air whistled through his lungs and he gasped for breath, she leapt onto Sooten and raced toward the north meadow to tell her father. Arn Mellby and his men immediately galloped back to the orchard seeking the stranger, but he was gone.

From that moment on, Sunniva's life was changed. Raven and her father met, and long and long into the night they talked. Early the next morning, she found herself astride Sooten and on her way to Solby Convent. She was fuming. She had had no say whatsoever in the matter, and now she was a prisoner. Raven rode by her side, Sooten's reins in his hands, and all about her was a veritable shield-burg of his serving-men armed with swords and pikes. Raven alone wore a corselet and hauberk of chain-mail over a body-shirt of black silk. His shield was slung at the ready on his mount's crupper while Gildor, thin-lipped and thirsty, lay to hand in a heavily embossed silver and gold sheath. Sunniva herself was covered from head to toe in her father's great gray cloak. Any looking on would never know that a soft young maid rode in the midst of those fighting men.

In her heart, Sunniva knew that never had she seen Raven look as handsome as he did in his battle-gear, but she was so wroth it did not matter. She was furious with him, with her father, with everyone, herself included. How foolish to have said anything at all about that clod when she was well able to take care of herself. Had she not proven it by downing him?

"How long am I expected to stay in this convent place?" she asked, stiffly.

"'Til we wed," Raven answered, equally stiff.

Sunniva shot him a look of exasperation. "But I am needed at home, what with all the preparations!"

From her father's serving-wenches, she had heard terrible tales of the convent. It was said to be filled with loveless women who wore gray wadmal and ate nothing but gruel and bannocks, and the only men there were the guards who protected them from the Danes.

"Raven, 'tis the silliest thing I ever heard, this putting me in a convent. What a pother over nothing! Please, take me back home."

"Nay."

"Beast!"

She was tempted to snatch the reins, give Sooten her heels and lead them all a merry chase. None but Raven would ever catch her, but when he did . . . She sighed. He would be so angry, she could not even imagine what he might do.

"I should think you would want to feel safe," Raven said, his voice low. " 'Tis a serious thing, this, Sunniva."

She laughed. "Come now, some boor wanting a kiss?"

" 'Tis a powerful man who wants you, Sunniva, one whose servant calls him lord. The boor was but an underling sent to fetch you. 'Tis likely the man is some chieftain or king in one of the thousand valleys in this land." When she looked disdainful, he growled, "Is't what you want then? To belong to some bastard who will keep you hidden away and have his will with you?"

Seeing he had sobered her, he added, "We have not seen the tail of this beast, Sunniva. Arn and I suspect he will try again, so let me hear no more foolish talk of your returning to Lilleby. Understand you?"

Sunniva nodded, now thoroughly subdued and remembering what she had tried to forget. The fellow had very nearly carried her off, and she had been horribly frightened. It was just luck that she had had the chance and the wits to hit him where it had done some good. Ay, it was luck and well she knew it.

Seeing her so quiet and pale and young-looking, Raven reached over and caught her hand. "All will be well. You are not to worry, Sunni."

"Ay." Her small white hand remained nestled in his the remainder of the journey.

Solby Convent stood like a gray, treeless mountain beside the River Solby. Having been a fort in times long gone, it was encircled by high stone walls, the only entry a solid oaken door in the front wall. Two strong, tall men in chain-mail and fierce-looking helmets guarded the building from without, and within, the courtyard was patrolled by two more men in similar garb. All carried shields, swords, and battle-axes. Raven knew the Abbess and, after explaining their plight, his band was given entry. He accompanied Sunniva to the small, clean cell where she would stay.

" 'Tis a good safe place for you, Sunni," he said. His heart was light, for he saw that she would be secure there until they were wed and she was under his complete protection.

" 'Tis ridiculous!" Sunniva's eyes flashed angrily as she looked about her.

The room was hideous, nothing but a gray stone closet. It held a narrow cot, pillow and featherbed, a stool, and a tiny table on which was a fresh candle. The barred window was too high to see through.

"I hate it! I—I cannot possibly stay here, Raven. What will I do with myself for the next four weeks?"

Raven slipped his arms around her waist and smiled down at her, his eyes dangerous, hungry, in the shadowy light. "You will think of me, my Sunniva."

"Indeed I will. I will be hoping a troll takes you!" she snapped, and then, "I—I didn't mean it. Oh, Raven, please, take me home. . . ."

"Nay, Sunniva." He cradled her beautiful face and kissed her soft mouth, stilling her. He felt her tremble. "Methinks you could put this peaceful time to some good use."

She shook her head, despairing. " 'Twill be a complete waste."

"Nay, not if you sew on those lacy broidered things

you are making." His voice was husky. "The ones you will wear in our bridal bed." At the thought, passion seared his loins and he took her mouth again, a long deep kiss that left her breathless. "Not that I will take much time to observe them. . . ."

She blushed as his starving eyes feasted on her mouth, her silken skin and blue-violet eyes, luminous and gold-lashed. The eyes of an elf maiden, he thought, so innocent, yet tantalizing and mysterious beyond belief. Hungrily he took her parted lips and tasted their sweetness, felt the shudder that swept her slender body. Holy Odin, he was tempted to take her here and now. How easy to spread her heavy cloak and the featherbed on the floor, draw her down, lift her skirts, part those long white silken legs, slip his shaft between them and then plunge into her deeply, ever so deeply. . . .

"Raven, what is't? Why are you looking like that?"

"Like what, my heart?"

"Your eyes are so strange—all glittery."

He laughed, kissed the end of her nose. "I will tell you on our wedding day."

Now it was Sunniva who laughed. "I see. Be warned then, Raven Trondsson, that I may give you precious little time to talk then."

Her eyes held that same smoldering invitation he had seen in them once before. Filled with delight, Raven caught her closer.

"Temptress."

But nay, he could not wile away the day holding and kissing and stroking her, much as he yearned to. His men were receiving hospitality in the kitchen-house, but even so, he could not keep them waiting longer. There was much work to be done back at Marvik. He released her.

" 'Tis time I left, Sunniva."

Unexpectedly, panic gripped her. Sunniva dropped to her knees and threw her arms about his legs, imprisoning him.

"Nay, Raven, please! What will I do here amongst all these grim, praying women? There is a limit to how much sewing I can do!"

Gently Raven freed himself. "We are needed in the fields, Sunni, but I will come again soon, I promise." His voice was firm. "On Friday. Two days from now."

Seeing that argument was fruitless, Sunniva drew a long breath and rose. Very well, she would stay. She would do so well at Solby Convent, perhaps she would not even want to leave when that time came. Perhaps she would just stay and become one of the holy sisters. Then he would be sorry.

Raven noted with relief the proud straightening of her back and shoulders, the lifting of her small chin, the cool, determined smile on her lips. On the other hand, he feared to know the cause of it.

" 'Til Friday then," he said, kissing her.

"Ay. 'Til Friday."

Wordlessly Sunniva moved by his side through the dark narrow corridors to the dirt courtyard where the men of Marvik were already mounted and waiting to depart. Watching Raven effortlessly mount Baldur, she felt of a sudden that she would burst with pride. He sat head and shoulders above the others, his coal-black hair and mail shirt glimmering in the sun. How she loved him. And he loved her! It was the only reason she was here, and she was being horrible about it. Childish and vindictive.

" 'Til we meet again, Sunniva." He donned his helmet and touched his sword to it, honoring her with his salute.

Sunniva made her mouth form a smile. " 'Til we meet again. And may luck and gladness ride at your side."

Her heart leapt, soared, melted. Never would she love another as she loved him, and if he wanted her here, then here she would stay until he took her home. She would do anything in the world to please him. She watched as he replaced Gildor in the sheath, watched the opening of the great oaken gate. And then the men of Marvik struck spurs and were gone.

CHAPTER 5

June 1012

FOR TWO DAYS, A WARSHIP HAD WALLOWED IN THE slow gray seas north of the Strandefjord. She was a large vessel, dark blue with a great square wadmal sail of deep purple, and she carried a crew of one hundred and twenty men. Her sides bristled with burnished shields and her iron prow was studded with spikes, the better for ramming. The dragons carved on her stem and stern wore a fine coat of gilt that glittered magnificently in both sun and moonlight.

She was the Landwaster, the pride of Rolf Gunnarsson of Hedeby, and on her deck men sprawled about restless, eager to be on the move. None knew why they were at anchor off Norway's westland, when booty lay to the south and west in Britain and Ireland. None dared ask. They knew that, while their chieftain showed no emotion on his face, he was in a black mood as he awaited the return of Heller Orm, his kinsman.

The Lord of Hedeby played neither draughts nor chess with his crew as he sometimes did, nor did he listen to the songs and the sagas of his skald. Instead he prowled the deck, stony-faced, his pale eyes constantly seeking the misty shore. His men stayed out of his way. He minded them of a distant tempest that might sweep over them all. Nothing could be seen nor heard of it, yet was the air filled with great tension. When Heller Orm came aboard at sundown the second day, all learned what this was about. A woman.

"Where is she?" Rolf growled.

"My lord," Orm's brown eyes avoided his chieftain's, "the maid was nowhere to be found."

"Nowhere to be found?" Rolf's eyes, blue and merciless as flame, burned over his cousin.

"Nay, my lord," Orm said, as the crew crowded about to hear. "Yesterday I watched Lilleby from dawn 'til dusk. 'Tis a large and prosperous steading, as you know, and 'tis possible I could have missed her, yet I dared not ask any of her whereabouts. Today I observed several nearby steadings also, thinking mayhap she was visiting"—his red tongue flicked nervously across his lips—"but nowhere did I see such a beautiful maid as you described."

Meeting his kinsman's cold gaze, Heller Orm knew that Rolf Gunnarsson knew he was lying. There was nothing that the Lord of Hedeby did not know, being the closest thing to a god that there was on this earth. He even looked like a god. He stood far above six feet and his face and his lithe, fair-skinned body were things of great masculine beauty despite their many battle scars. His hair and his beard were full and golden, as was the fine curly fur that covered his chest and sinewy limbs. Ay, he was a god. It had been a grave mistake to lie to him, but how could

Orm admit he had been bested by a woman—and a young maid at that?

"My lord, could we speak alone?" he said low.

The blue eyes narrowed. Rolf yearned to tie the bastard to the mast and give him a lashing he would not forget, but he dared not treat any of his men so. They were not his friends—nay, for he had no friends, not even this cousin of his—nor did he crave friends. Rather they were his bodyguard, his army and his navy. They were indispensable to him. He needed their good will. In turn, they took pride in his valor and fearlessness. He led them to great booty and adventure and if his wrath frightened them, what matter? Did he not treat them as royally as any king between times?

"Ay, we will speak alone," Rolf said tightly. The two went below deck to the only private space in the vessel. Rolf took off his cape and swordbelt, lowered himself to his mattress, and offered half of it to Heller Orm. "Sit you, Orm, for I would hear this tale from the beginning."

Orm took the plunge. There was nothing to do but get the ordeal over with. "She was there, sire," he muttered. "I had her, but she escaped."

Bastard, Rolf thought, raging but hiding it. The trolls take him.

"Ah. You had a soft, weak maid in hand but she escaped?" His lip curled.

"She caught me off guard, my lord. I was carrying her to my horse when she struck me a blow on the windpipe and fled. Never did I expect a maid to know that trick."

"So she actually bested you?" Rolf asked softly, feeling himself swell with arousal. Greatly would he like to see the little bitch try to best him.

"Once, my lord, but never again would she have

such a chance. I would lay her low immediately and then carry her to you."

"And why did you not try that next, kinsman?"

"Because after she fled, there came a great hue and cry with armed men all over the steading. This morning at dawn, she was taken under heavy guard to Solby Convent, where she will be kept until she is wed."

It was a hammer-blow to Rolf's gut. "Wed?"

"Ay. The first day of July, Raven Trondsson takes her to wife."

Rolf's face remained masklike, but a firestorm swept through his body. Raven Trondsson had been given her when he himself had offered her marriage and the honor of bearing his name and children and been refused? He ground his teeth at the outrage but his icy eyes expressed only curiosity.

"I would hear of this coming bridal, Orm. Tell me all you know, but first, tell Halfdan to steer a course for Hedeby."

As Heller Orm spoke, Rolf Gunnarsson's keen mind was sifting over hidden aspects of the situation that Orm had not even begun to suspect. It seemed he himself had benefited them all greatly by his murder of Eirik Paalsson. The Bergvin merchant had not been beloved by any of them, whereas Raven Trondsson was. The Solby chieftain was the man the maid truly loved and the man her father favored. The man Rolf had long yearned to see dead. . . .

After Orm was gone, Rolf lay on his mattress in the shadowy hold, his eyes gleaming and his heart thudding. The gods were smiling on him this day. Even that dolt Orm's stupidity would work to his own advantage in the long run. His revenge would be one hundred times sweeter when it was Raven Trondsson who lay in the dead straw, for he meant to slay him as surely as he had slain the Bergviner. He would slay any who stood between him and Sunniva Mellby.

He shook his golden head. But for the damned wench, he would not have turned murderer. Her beauty was so great, and his desire for her so huge, that he had vowed to have her. And when legal means had failed him, he had turned to illegal doings to possess her. But it was of slight importance. Never would he admit to killing Paalsson before the Thing, nor would he make reparation to the fellow's family as was required by law. Nay, he would pay no wergeld for the slain because all would remain secret.

And now it was Raven Trondsson he must think on. The bastard had become a mighty force amongst the westland vikings, and he had been a thorn in Rolf's side for some time. His jealousy and hatred for the Solby chieftain had come to a full head last spring in Dublin when two of his own men deserted his band to join Trondsson's. Immediately, Rolf had taken his two berserkers to slay the traitorous scuts. Trondsson anticipated his move and, with his own berserkers, had slain the Hedeby lord's prize warriors.

Now Rolf smiled as he lay in the dark damp hull of the Landwaster, listening to the familiar sound of water rushing past his head. He was an impatient man, but he knew full well that revenge was sweetest when it was long in coming. And that time was growing close to hand. He rose from his mattress, carefully groomed his luxuriant hair and beard, and strapped on his swordbelt. He returned his cape to his broad shoulders. There was much planning to do but it would be done at Hedeby at his leisure. Now would he celebrate the good fortune the gods had bestowed upon him. He went on deck and called for his skald.

"Einar!"

"Ay, my lord Hedeby, what is your pleasure?"

"I would hear the song you made for my victory over Con Cory of Maun."

"Ay, sire." When his skald hurried off to fetch his harp, Rolf summoned his crew. "Gather you 'round, men, and for all, extra ale. Knut, bring the keg."

On land, the fierce warriors of the Landwaster were men of importance and influence who had great respect for law and tradition. Once back in the Vaaga Valley in the Northland, they turned eagerly to their homes and families and the ordering of their farms and their businesses, usually with the help of the high-born English and Irish men and women they had taken as thralls during their cruises.

Rolf Gunnarsson cared nothing for farming and business. He was a warrior-king and the running of Hedeby was beneath him. Such was the work of servants and thralls, and these did it well, for who would dare shirk the duties assigned them by the Lord of Hedeby?

Rolf himself dwelt much on war and seafaring, both honorable occupations. Never had he acquired by sweat and work what he could take by blood and the sword. It was the way he had come by those vast tracts of land he owned in the Vaagaland. It was the way he had become king there. War was critical to his very existence. His status and importance, ay, his very honor depended on the number of his followers and the splendor of their equipment. To maintain them, he was ever obliged to wage more wars for booty and money. Since he could no longer do so in Norway, where the land was all taken, he waged it in distant lands. Already had he conquered the northern portion of Maun, a large island off western Britain, and soon would he be king there in addition

70

to being the Vaaga-king. It was to Maun that he planned to carry Sunniva Mellby.

Upon reaching Hedeby, Rolf's days were filled with the athletic games he played with his new berserkers, two fierce giants he had acquired in Denmark, who accompanied him everywhere. The three of them wrestled, swam, ran, jumped, leapt and practiced their balancing and climbing in addition to their constant war-games—fencing and archery and spear-play. But it was the nights Rolf enjoyed most. Nights, he made his plans to steal Sunniva Mellby by the stronghand.

Always he preceded his planning with his memories, the ever-simmering memories of the humiliation he had suffered at the hands of the so-proud Mellbys. His first meeting, a long talk with Arn Mellby alone, had gone well enough. He had been dressed in his finest, silks and velvet-lined fur with thread of gold, and behind him stood his band of kinsmen, all men of wealth and power. There was every evidence that the master of Lilleby had been impressed by them and by Rolf's vast holdings and wealth and bravery and high standing at Earl Erik's court.

Rolf had discovered the maid alone on his next visit and spoken with her. She had been cool, which served only to amuse him—most maids strove to flatter him. She had refused to meet his eye and given polite but icy answers to his questions, but if she had meant to chill his ardor, she had not succeeded. It made her more intriguing to him than ever. He was unable to keep his hands off her.

So confident was he that she would be given to him, he had seized her, squeezed one plump white breast, and kissed her forcibly on the mouth despite her struggles. And then the bitch had struck him in the face. No woman had ever dared strike him before, and it lit a fire within him such as he had not felt in a long time. It was then that her father had appeared and sent her from the room.

"'Tis a feisty maid you have there, sire, and a beauty to boot." Rolf had longed to taste and feel her softness again, but it was unwise to show too much eagerness.

"I am sorry you chanced to see Sunniva. I did not intend that." Arn Mellby's eyes lingered on his red stinging cheek.

"So." Rolf straightened his shoulders so that his rich garments and awesome height could better be appreciated. "Let us get down to business. I am satisfied that our families are well-matched in rank and wealth."

Although never could the Mellbys match the Gunnarssons in the matter of birth and powerful connections, he thought. But then, what matter? He wanted this maid for one reason and one reason alone and it was not to extend his influence in Norway's land. Thinking of shoving himself into her beautiful, soft white body whenever he chose heated him unmercifully. He had to have her, and despite his resolve not to appear eager, he had said:

"I am prepared to pay whatever mund you ask for her, sire, for never have I seen such a beautiful woman. I am willing to pay above and beyond what we discussed our first meeting. . . ."

"My lord, I cannot give her to you."

Rolf had felt his blood run hotter still at the challenge. "What mean you, you *cannot*?"

"I have had strange tidings from the Northland since last we met." Arn straightened his own broad shoulders. "I have heard a waif word of your strange doings with women, my lord."

"Strange?" Rolf had laughed at that. "I trow that our customs in the Vaaga Valley could be considered different from your customs here in the Westland, but I doubt me they could be considered strange or sinister, sire."

Arn stood firm. "My lord, I am sorry. . . ."

At that, Rolf had spoken softly but his wrath was great. "A waif word is hardly cause to deny me your daughter, sire. I demand further reason for such insult."

"Very well." Arn had met his gaze directly. " 'Tis said the whole Gunnarsson clan are a wild-tempered, lecherous lot. 'Tis said that your own father dishonored your wife more than once, and then there is the boorish manner in which you recently divorced her. Further, there are tales of the wenches and thrall-wenches at Hedeby who have borne your bastards. Know you this, my lord Hedeby, you may be powerful and friend to the kings that now rule our land, but never will I surrender Sunniva, my most precious treasure, into the hands of a man who cannot rule his own passions."

Bastard!

Rolf poured more ale into his horn from the keg beside his bed and laughed aloud. It would have pleasured him to kill the fool on the spot, but he had learned never to act hastily. Never would the man surrender his most precious treasure, eh? Well, now he would never have to, for she would be stolen from under his very nose. On her wedding day. He had spent much time thinking on it and now his plan was ready. He would use the holy sisters' treating of the sick at the Solby Convent to gain entry to the fortress.

Throngs of the ill arrived each morn early, and he would send several of his band in with them. It would be an easy enough thing to disguise them as old feeble men in rags such as always roamed about the countryside begging food and shelter. Once in, they would overpower and kill the guards and take the maid; his men without would take the gate-guards. Sunniva would then be carried to where he waited in the nearby wood. From there they would ride to the river where two of his burden vessels would be anchored. From thence they would row to the open sea where the Landwaster waited to sail for Maun.

Rolf smiled and poured himself another horn of ale; never had he honored the Viking rule of not drinking alone. Hedeby was as cold and damp as ever, but he was warmed by drink and satisfaction. It was a good plan. His handsome face was flushed and his pale eyes glittered. Never would the bitch's proud father want her back after she was filled with his growing seed—and it was Arn Mellby's own doing. He had refused great mund for her and had reviled the name of Gunnarsson of Hedeby. Now, instead of the respect and honor the wench would have had as his wife, mistress Sunniva of Lilleby would be just another thrall who would bear his child.

When her shame was visible to all, then would he seize Raven Trondsson and bring him to her, and then would Rolf slay him before her eyes. It was a plan of perfection—the Solby chieftain's seeing the depths to which his handfasted maid was sunk and helpless to change any of it; the proud wench's realizing her plight was hopeless and seeing her betrothed slain; the satisfaction of Arn Mellby's grief and rage. . . . Thor's bones, but life was good. He had much pleasure ahead of him.

Not the least of it was that the maid was high-born and had spunk. Rolf's blood ran hot and fast at the thought of besting her, of bending her completely to his will, whatever and whenever it might be. His revenge would be satisfied as fully as his lust for her.

He rose and went to a window. It was light beyond

the narrow slit, the sun riding the treetops, but it was well past midnight. All of Hedeby slept. His berserkers slept on skins before his door, guarding it. Rolf strode to the door, unbarred it and woke them.

"Fetch my skald," he commanded them.

He would hear Einar sing of his many victories in battle, and afterwards, he would pleasure himself with the Englishwoman he had taken on his last cruise. She was white-skinned and soft and her breasts were still swollen with milk for the brat she had been suckling. He smiled. She was so frightened of him, he could smell and taste it when he took her. He liked that. . . .

CHAPTER 6

28 June 1012

SHE HAD BUT TWO DAYS TO WAIT, SUNNIVA THOUGHT, slipping on a lavender kirtle in the pale gray light of dawn. Two more days and then would Raven and his men come for her early in the morning, and in no time at all she would be home at Lilleby. How she had missed it. She could hardly wait to see all the preparations that had been made, and to see her kindred who had come from afar to drink her wedding ale.

A bell echoing through the winding stone corridors of Solby Convent interrupted her thoughts. She must fly, for if one was late for meals here, one did not eat. She quickly drew on her stockings, tied on her shoes and donned a rose-and-white striped apron, fastening it at the shoulders with bronze pins as she hurried to the kitchen-house to break fast with the others.

There was fresh-baked bread and fresh butter and eggs and cheese and Sunniva ate of it all heartily. Her father's serving-women had been wrong about many things regarding Solby Convent. The food there was almost as good as at home, and while the sisters did indeed wear gray wadmal, Sunniva herself could wear whatever she chose. And while it was true that they prayed overmuch for the world, they also laughed and talked as they worked and they were warm and friendly with her. Sunniva had come to love every one of the twelve and had invited them all to her wedding.

She was helping to wash up after breakfast when one sweet but plain-faced young sister came to her.

"Your Raven is here," Hildigunn whispered. "I trow, Sunniva, never would I have taken my vows had such a man asked for me."

In the visitor's room, Sunniva found Raven waiting for her impatiently. His darkness and height, his dangerous eyes and the breadth of his shoulders made the room seem ever so small and prim and holy. Laughing with surprise and pleasure, Sunniva went into his arms.

"Never did I expect you today, my love, but 'tis glad I am to see you!" She frowned then. "Is aught wrong?"

"Nay, all is fine." Raven kissed her lips. "'Tis just that I wanted to hold you close."

He said nothing of the strange fears that had goaded him there, the dark feeling that she was in danger. He wanted to pick her up and cradle her, cover her face with kisses, but the damned place was so open—no doors on the jambs and whisperings and soft footsteps forever echoing in the murky corridors. For certain, he thought, annoyed, it was not the place for lovers.

"I'm going to take you into the countryside for a little, Sunniva. I have told the Abbess."

Sunniva quickly threw off her apron and then,

hand in hand, the two walked to the courtyard where Baldur stood waiting. Raven lifted her up into the saddle and mounted behind her. Seeing the respect and admiration for him on the guards' faces, Sunniva felt wonderfully important. She belonged to a Viking chieftain! She felt small and safe, compressed snugly between his hard body and the saddlebar with his arms about her, his strong sun-darkened hands controlling the reins. Never had she felt so safe. When the convent was left behind them, she lifted her lips to his.

"Know you how much I love you, Raven Trondsson?" she whispered.

He laughed. "I wager 'tis probably half of my love for you Sunniva Mellby."

"'Tisn't! No one has ever been loved the way I love you, and know you—"

His kiss interrupted her protest, a deep, long, hungry kiss that lasted until they reached a cool dell. Raven dismounted, and as he lifted Sunniva to the ground, he took care that she saw nothing of his strong arousal. He muttered:

"Methinks we had best not kiss like that again 'til we wed, Sunniva."

"Why ever not?"

She blinked her beautiful eyes at him in all innocence, but she saw that his breathing was heavy and there were tiny droplets of sweat on his forehead. She hid a smile. What a strange and wondrous thing it was, this power she had over him. But then he exerted the same enchantment over her. She could no more live without him than she could live without air to breathe or water to drink. He had become her life, her heart.

Raven spread his cloak under a large birch and drew her down onto it. She lay on her back, her golden head in his lap.

"Just let me look at you," he said, smoothing back a tendril of silky hair that had escaped the braid trailing down her back. "Have you been as happy here as you seem, my heart?"

Sunniva shrugged. "'Tis not home—but ay, I am happy. There is much to do and I love the sisters. Hildigunn, especially. I have invited them all to drink our wedding ale with us."

"Good. We will bring extra horses when we come for you."

"Sister Ulvhild told me something nice. . . ."

Raven gazed down on her animated face. Never had he seen such beauty or such exquisite skin. It glowed as though light were emanating from within her. Her cheeks were rose pink, her mouth soft and red and full from his kisses, and there was her incredible mane of wheaten hair and those purple-blue eyes with their thick fringe of sable lashes. Her modest lavender dress served only to accentuate her pink and white blondness. She was the loveliest maid alive.

"Tell me what the sister said, Sunni. I would hear it."

"Mind you that she thought I was quick at learning to brew herbs and such for medicine?"

"Ay, I mind."

"Well, this morn she said I may have a calling. She said if ever I should decide, someday that is, that I wanted to enter the convent"—Raven gave a snort at that—"that I would be good at treating the sick. She says I have a natural bent for it."

"Ah." Raven smiled his encouragement. "'Tis wonderful, that."

What the good sister didn't know was that Sunniva Mellby had a natural bent for all manner of things. She was expert with the spear and the bow, she swam like a seal and rode like a fury, she could read and write and ski and snowshoe—and she could drive a man out of his mind with wanting her.

Seeing the scowl on Raven's face, Sunniva quickly changed the subject. "How go things at home, my love? I would hear everything."

How stupid of her, Sunniva thought, talking of entering the convent when she would be Raven's wedded wife within two days! And, too, he did not care for the new religion of the White Jesus which her father had embraced and which the convent espoused. Always would Raven belong to Odin.

"I trow Lilleby is near ready for you now," Raven said, lying back in the grass. He pulled Sunniva close beside him, his arm about her and her head on his shoulder. "The great hall has been scrubbed and given fresh straw, the lofts are all cleaned and aired for the guests, beds put 'round the walls in all the other rooms, and your mother and my mother have hung every tapestry and broidered cloth they own on the walls."

Sunniva giggled at the thought of Lilleby bedecked so grandly. "And the gold and silver candlesticks and plates?"

"All polished and in full sight on the boards that are already placed. And ale is brewing and bread is baking and so much sewing is going on that Arn dares not go near his own manor for fear of dirtying the grand fabrics. He stays in the barns or the fields. Did I tell you?—he's hired a harper and a fiddler."

"How wonderful! I trow there will be no horse fights."

"Nay, no horse fights."

Sunniva's eyes grew wet suddenly, thinking of her mother and cousins and aunts working feverishly on her bridal room. Always had Anna Mellby promised that her bridal bed would be heaped with the best skins and furs and pillows, and the timbered walls of the bride-room would be draped with tapestries and there would broidered hangings forming a tent about her bed. Now it was all coming to pass and she was not there to help prepare it and share in the excitement. It wasn't fair.

"Sunni?" Raven's arm about her tightened. His lips pressed the top of her head.

"Ay?"

"What is't? You are so quiet."

She swallowed the tears sliding down the back of her throat and dabbed her eyes furtively. Had she not just said how happy she was here? It was just that she had not allowed herself to brood on things until now.

"Have my aunt and uncle arrived from Finnmark?"

"Ay."

Her heart thumped at that. Soon would the great golden bridal crown of her mother's Finnmark kindred sit on her head and she would be decked in her mother's own scarlet bridal robe and silver brooches. Soon. But for now she was here and far away from it all. It was as though it all were happening to some other maid.

Realizing suddenly that the shoulder of his tunic was wet with her tears, Raven rose on one elbow. He tilted her chin and scowled down at her streaked face.

"Sunni, what is't?"

She shook her head. "Nothing. 'Tis just that I'm a—a bit homesick."

"My little heart . . ."

Rarely had he seen her weep. His big hand gently caressed her cheeks, wiping away her tears, and then his lips brushed her wet lashes, her temples, her fresh mouth.

"Oh, Raven, I—I know 'tis best for me to be here, 'tis just that I'm missing everything. 'Tis as if I am a guest at my own wedding. . . ." Her wretched tears gushed anew.

"Nay, my little one. No guest you, but my very own betrothed maid." He pulled her closer still, so close that his long hard body was pressed against the whole length of hers. "Soon will we be together, Sunniva."

He covered her lips with his, gently at first, and then passion exploded in them both as his tongue met hers, subdued it, and explored the hidden velvety recesses of her mouth. She gasped at his boldness, at the sweet glow beginning to burn deep between her thighs. What was this magic that happened to her when she was in his arms? It made her his thrall, more bound to him than she ever would have thought possible.

Their mouths still sealed, Sunniva slipped her arms about his waist and tried to wrap her legs about him in a wild effort to get closer but her long skirts were in the way. How strange she felt, how wonderful to be on fire for him. His lips sought her throat and pressed kisses upon it and on her mouth and her breasts as his hands stroked and loved her everywhere. He lifted her skirts, caressed her stockinged legs, held them against him so that he was gripped all the tighter between them.

"O, Raven, I love you so," she whispered. "I—I want you closer. . . ."

"Sunni, we must wait. . . ." he muttered, his hungry mouth dipping to one taut little nipple thrusting against her dress. Holy Odin, never would he dishonor her, but to kiss her so was not dishonor, not when she would be his in but two days.

He unfastened the metal pin that held her dress together at the neckline, exposing the curves of her full white breasts and the deep valley between them. When he took one silky pink nipple in his mouth, she whimpered, thrusting herself against him so that her entire breast was offered to his hungry mouth for the taking.

"Sunniva . . ."

He buried his face in her lushness, lifted and pressed and kneaded both soft, creamy globes, covered them with a hundred kisses, took each blossoming nipple between his teeth and nipped, sucked.

Why was she weeping, Sunniva thought, when it felt so wonderful? Her tears would not stop and she heard herself murmuring his name over and over and over. She was wild, frantic for his kisses and his touch, writhing, arching against him, wrapping her legs about him, hugging him. She was disgracing herself, and he was laughing! In between his chuckles, he was kissing her everywhere, his hands moving all over her body, gentle, protective, comforting, soothing, yet exciting her so much that she could scarcely bear the delight of it. Soon he would be hers, all hers, but how could she wait to lie in his arms in her bridal bed when she felt so fire-filled now? O, dear Jesu-Mary, O, holy Thor and Odin, help me. . . .

Raven's big, dark hands stroked her long legs, his swollen shaft throbbing, thirsting to drive home between them as his eyes glittered over her fairness. She was his, his, and she was melting in his arms, her soft body yielding, begging for him to take her. He knew suddenly that this was right. All the gods, all the laws of the land be damned. Good days fell to wise folk, ay, but the best days of all fell to those who sometimes dared to be unwise. Was not a betrothed woman's virtue so carefully guarded in order that her husband not be cheated and her children be his? And was he himself not the groom and his bridal only hours away? And she wanted him as much as he wanted her.

"Sunniva—?" His voice was low, questioning, but he saw that words were not needed. She understood.

"Oh, ay, Raven, Oh, please . . ."

Well he knew the difference between a maid's weeping with need and one weeping with fright or pain. He removed her long stockings and her underthings, smoothed her white, silky legs, gently parted her thighs.

"Hush, my treasure, 'twill be all right." He spoke to her as he had when she was a young thing flown to his arms for comforting—only then she had never wept. "Hush now, my love. Shhhh . . ."

He removed his own clothing and pulled her to him. They lay on their sides, the full length of their bodies touching, naked, for the first time, their mouths drinking of the other's sweet nectars. She was so soft against him, so smooth and sweet and fresh that he craved to take her instantly to sate his fierce desire for her.

Instead, he slipped his engorged manhood between her thighs. It lay there pulsing as he played with her breasts, kissing and cupping and licking them. He turned her onto her back. How fair she was, a vision, white and pink and gold, her breasts the most beautiful he had ever seen, her satiny little woman's mound and rounded belly just waiting to be pressed, ay, crushed against him. . . .

"Part your legs for me, little one."

Sunniva's eyes glowed, yet she hesitated. "Is't all right, think you, Raven?"

"Ay, Sunni, 'tis all right. 'Tis love between us, and we are handfasted."

She relaxed her legs then, lowering them to the sides so that her hidden beauty was opened before him, pink, glistening, and deeper still, barely revealed, the tiny red jewel of her womanhood. He knelt, longing to kiss and fondle her there, but nay, not this first time. They had their lives ahead of them to taste and enjoy and explore.

" 'Twill hurt some this first time, Sunniva, but only for a little."

Sunniva was breathing hard, her eyes half-closed, her rosy lips parted. Again and again he kissed them as he touched himself to her cleft, parted it with gentle fingers, touched the head of his shaft to her tiny jewel that grew hard and peaked even as he gazed on it.

"I care naught if it hurts," she gasped, "Oh, I care naught, Raven, just do something. . . ."

Remembering the screams and cries of her father's mares and bitches, Sunniva was prepared for great pain. It was woman's lot, after all, and she so wanted to please Raven. And surely, when he entered her this unbearably sweet, hot pressure growing so deep within her would stop. Surely it would. He was circling her secret parts with the head of his shaft, rubbing her, teasing her and suddenly she felt a gush of wetness, as though she were honey-filled and it was seeping out of her. It was at that instant that he drove into her, hard and fast. Before she even knew it had happened, his manhood was thudding against the back of her very womb.

She screamed, a small shriek of pain and surprise, which she stifled instantly. It did hurt, it did! She was mortified that she had cried out, but it seemed that already he had forgotten it. She was so crushed beneath his weight that it was difficult to breathe. Her breasts spilled out across his chest, so tightly was she pressed beneath him. He rolled onto his side then, still moving within her, his eyes distant, glazed, his face a mask of near-pain—never had she seen him so—as his slow, deep, easy plunges touched her very depths.

It was all so strange, so new, this being filled so fully with his hardness and possessed by him so completely. For the first time in her life, Sunniva felt soft and powerless, swept along by a mighty force from which there was no escape. And she liked it. She loved it. She loved it because it was Raven who was making her feel this way.

The heady warmth that had been seeping through her body turned fiery suddenly, fanning out to every part of her and consuming her with its pulsating heat. She gasped as his kisses grew deeper, more passionate, his tongue plunging, piercing her mouth in the same wild rhythm as the shaft that was rubbing, stroking the sensitive walls of her sheath. She closed her eyes, moaning, experiencing once more that sweet hot rush as if honey were flooding out of her.

It was wonderful and terrible all at the same time, as though something inside her were growing and swelling, ready to burst into—into she knew not what. She had never felt such a thing before. She yearned to squeeze her thighs together to capture and hold him, but fearful of hurting him, she strove not to move. It was impossible. She had to move. On its own, her body writhed, squirmed beneath him. She whimpered, feeling the innermost part of her tightening about him. She arched her soft body then, causing her belly and her breasts to thrust against him. The movement drove his shaft into her more deeply still.

She felt him moving faster within her, almost frenzied, his eyes closed, his dark face a sweat-glistened mask of pleasure-pain. It was Odin himself riding her, she thought, near to swooning with the delight of it. It was Odin's fire and lightning within her, his starbursts flaming through her limbs and centering, exploding in that hidden cavern deep inside her. . . .

It was done. Sunniva was drained, weak as a kitten, her release as sweet as had been her hunger, the valley as beautiful as the mountain top. Her beloved sighed and gently released her damp, relaxed body so that she could lie close by his side. She put her head on his shoulder and gazed at him through sleepy, wondering eyes. His handsome face was dark-flushed, his own eyes closed and their long black lashes brushing his cheeks. His hands moved over her slowly, soothing now, comforting. No longer did he ride her or possess her. Long and long they lay in each others' arms, dazed and wordless, exhausted by the pleasure that still pulsed through them, teasing, reminding them of how it had been. Sunniva's fingers went to his chest, playing with the thick mat of black curls there.

"Never have I felt so," she whispered.

He kissed her rosy palm, kissed the tip of each precious finger. "Nor I."

"I—made you happy?"

She blushed. She knew she had. It was just that she wanted to hear it from his lips.

"'Tis the greatest pleasure I have ever known, little one."

He spoke the truth. Tenderly he kissed her pink mouth, kissed each white breast that thrust upwards so charmingly. Feeling himself stiffening again, he sat up. Nay. No more for now. He had used her more roughly than he had ever intended, but her body was so beautiful, so yielding, and her love-juices so thick and plentiful, that he had not been able to rein in his fierce passion. He stood up, his back to her as he gathered his clothing so she would not see that he was newly aroused.

"'Tis time we returned before they send the guard for us, Sunni."

He began to dress, watching as Sunniva gracefully rose and began donning her own garments. He was unable to tear his eyes from her. She was a treasure beyond compare, far beyond mere gold or silver or precious gems. And she was his. The thought filled him with both triumph and trepidation. The fear that had brought him to her this day returned in full force. He must guard her well, for men would ever be wanting her and trying to steal her from him. He had many enemies who might venge themselves that way. Even had he not enemies, she was a prize. Kings would want her; he feared one already did. He helped her mount and sprang up behind her, turning Baldur's head toward the convent.

"Do you love me still?" Sunniva asked quietly.

"Do I act as if I don't?"

"'Tis said if a man gets free milk, 'tis witless of him to—to buy a cow."

Raven chuckled. He kissed the back of her neck where it was softest and whitest.

"Know this, little enchantress. I love you more than I love my own right arm, more than I love my life. Were you to leave me, I would not rest 'til I got you back. I would go to the ends of the earth to find you, Sunniva Mellby."

Sunniva sighed. She was well satisfied. "And know you, Raven Trondsson, that I would be waiting for you." Nestled in his arms, she was soon fast asleep.

CHAPTER 7

1 July 1012

AFTER WEEKS OF MOILING AND TOILING, LILLEBY LAY in readiness for the wedding of Sunniva Mellby and Raven Trondsson of Marvik. There was food and drink aplenty for three days of festivity for the two hundred guests gathered, and Lilleby itself glowed with the silver and gold and pewter and rich tapestries and broidered cloths that Anna Mellby had removed from the storage lofts for the special event. Lilleby was ready, ay. All that was lacking was the bride, and that was soon to be remedied.

A strong party of twenty armed men and ten extra horses was already en route to Solby Convent while the wedding guests, housed all about the valley as well as at Lilleby and Marvik, were still sound asleep. Raven and Ulf Mellby rode abreast behind the standard-bearer. Above their heads fluttered Raven's red banner on which was the black raven beloved by Odin. Ulf threw a devilish grin at his best friend.

"'Tis a far cry, this, from the stronghand, man," he spoke low so none could hear.

Raven grinned back. "'Tis a happy thing for us all. Never did I want the other, but if losing Sunniva were the alternative, I had no choice."

"But now you have followed all the rules and she is yours, fair and square."

"Ay."

He had spoken the words of espousal before witnesses; he had ringed her and bought her with mund, and this day would they wed. The two of them would be put to bed with a joyous celebration rather than in the shadow of the arrow going out across the land declaring him outlawed, and his sons would be inheritance-born, not bastards. Raven sighed. It had been a close call. He had been about to carry her off.

"Never have I seen my father so light of spirit as last night," Ulf said.

"Ay." Raven smiled at the memory.

It was a gladsome thing, thought Ulf. His father's terrible mistake reversed and his dearest friend and his sister so joy-filled. Never had Ulf seen a bridegroom take so good-naturedly the coarse jests that were broken on Raven's head last night. Well could he imagine that Raven might never again be impatient or unhappy now that he had Sunniva. As for Ulf himself, he was happiest when those he loved were happy. The three had visited until the early hours the many guests housed about the valley, and at every steading, there had been ale to drink and tales to tell. Now, a very few hours later, they were up and on their way.

"I feel like a rag," Ulf muttered, "and I taste worse. What sense I ever had, I drank away last night. Wake me when we get there."

Raven nodded, chuckling. He himself was wide awake and fire-filled. He had made Sunniva his already, ay, but from tonight forward, she would be his forever. But there was much to be gotten through before then. They would be at the convent before cock-crow, and if the women were ready, they could start back with just a short rest for the horses. It was not a long journey between the two places, but it was a stiff one, hilly and with the paths not always cleared. It was why they had brought horses instead of carts for the ten holy sisters who would be returning to Lilleby with them.

His mind spun. He and his men should be back at Marvik well before noon, after leaving Sunniva and her party at Lilleby. What with Arn's wanting the wedding in a church, matters were slightly complicated, but only slightly. The wedding train would begin its journey at Marvik with the priest leading it, followed by Raven's groomsmen, his mother, his kinsmen and the guests staying there.

At Lilleby, Sunniva and her party would join the train with her parents, kin, bridesmaids, and all the other guests who would have gathered there. Between Lilleby and the church, he had ordered their way to be strewn with sprigs of rowan-berries and pine branches and any flowers the serving-wenches could find. He had promised Sunniva it would be the grandest wedding train ever seen in the Solby Valley, but now he decided it would be the grandest ever seen in the whole Westland for its length and the number of standards flying.

He had given careful thought to his clothing. A dark-green silken coat slashed at the sides to show his finest leaf-brown trews, the narrow gold-bossed belt he had bought in Dublin and from which Gildor would hang, the dark-red velvet cloak in which his own father had been wed. He was uncertain yet about the hat his mother wanted him to wear. It was of dark green silk, which was fine, but he was not sure he liked the wings on either side of it nor the two long streamers trailing from it. It was French and considered fashionable, but he scowled thinking of it. He did not want to look a fool on this of all days.

It was her wedding day, and Sunniva was so excited she could not sleep. Hearing a noise, she sat up.

"Sunniva . . ."

Sunniva saw Sister Hildigunn's little round face above the candle she held. The nun wore a plain wadmal wrapper over her nightshirt.

"What is't, Sister?" Sunniva rose on one elbow and stared up at her.

"I heard you stirring," Hildigunn said, "and I hoped you were awake. Oh, Sunni, I am too excited to sleep!"

Sunniva laughed, sat up in bed, and stretched her arms above her head. "I, too. I've not slept one wink all night long."

Hildigunn closed the door and put her candle on the small table.

"Tell me more, Sunni," she pulled the stool close to the bed and sat upon it, "and mind you start from where you left off last night. . . ."

Sunniva had come to love the little sister in the few short weeks she had been at the convent. Hildigunn was blond, blue-eyed, and young, scarcely older than Sunniva herself. And she said what she thought. She minded Sunniva greatly of Inge.

"Well, let me see now—where was I?"

"The bridal bed," said Hildigunn, without hesitation.

"Ah." It was Sunniva who blushed. "Well, now—"

"You said 'twould be in the bride-room in a loft."

Sunniva hid a smile. "So I did. Well—"

"You said 'twould have fine hangings about it and be heaped with silken pillows and rugs and furs."

"Ay—and over all of that will be a broidered silk coverlid. A blue coverlid." When Hildigunn sighed, Sunniva went on. "And my mother and kinswomen will have hung the loft walls with rugs and tapestries and the benches will be heaped with more pillows."

"And what will you wear?"

"My mother's scarlet bridal robe and—and her jewelry."

Sunniva feared that, in a way, she was making Hildigunn unhappy. Never would the young nun have such a wonderful thing happen to her, for she would never leave the convent. She was alone, without parents or family. There were none to give her such a wedding.

"What jewelry?" Hildigunn's eyes were dreamy.

"Oh, silver brooches and golden armlets and such. Neckchains . . . rings . . ." Sunniva shrugged. "Nothing all that important."

But the fact that they were her mother's was important, and it was important that she had a wonderful father who had taken such good care of her and could give her such a grand wedding. Only since coming to the convent and seeing droves of the poor and homeless had Sunniva realized just how fortunate her family was. Always had she known Lilleby was a great steading wholly befitting a man who had once been an esquire bearing arms to King Haakon. Arn Mellby, a man of means, had been careful in his undertakings and was a careful husband of his goods. Anna Mellby herself had brought wealth to the union.

"You talked of a crown. . . ." Hildigunn murmured.

"Ay." Sunniva nodded.

She wished now that she had said nothing of it, yet it was excitement and happiness she saw in Hildi's eyes, not regret or envy. Her heart lightened.

"'Tis the bridal crown of my mother's Finnmark kindred."

"Is't gold?"

"Ay. 'Tis beautiful. 'Tis set with emeralds and rubies and little diamond clusters." When Hildigunn clapped her hands, Sunniva laughed, adding, "I wear it for the mass, then 'tis taken off for the feasting and drinking and dancing—my father has hired a harper and a fiddler. And then there will be the gifts to look at and then Raven must read aloud all the deeds and what not—"

"Do you wear the crown again, ever?"

"Ay." Sunniva was feeling as intoxicated as if she had already drunk her wedding ale. "After we greet all our guests and dance around the bonfires, then will I wear my bridal crown again."

The women would lead her to the bride-room and remove her scarlet robe, leaving only the linen shift she wore beneath it—the shift she herself had broidered with thread of gold. Then they would help her into the bridal bed and put the heavy crown on her head, and Raven would come. It would be his hands that would remove it and her shift, his hands that would take the silken bindings from her hair and pull her close against him.

Seeing Hildigunn's suddenly grave face, Sunniva whispered, "Sister, have I made you unhappy?" It was what she had feared.

"Nay, Sunni, 'tis just that 'tis said no man must see his betrothed on their wedding day 'til she is led forth in her bridal robe. Does that not worry you?"

"It cannot be helped. I am sure that—"

Hildigunn leapt up, startled. "Did you hear that?"

"Hear what?"

"Methought for a moment 'twas a—a man's voice. . . ."

Now Sunniva rose hurriedly and donned a wrapper over her nightshirt. "Mayhap, 'twas. Mayhap Raven and the others have come early!"

Hildigunn caught up her candle, opened the door, and stepped into the hall. She rushed back in.

"I was right!" she gasped. "'Tis a man coming. A stranger! Oh, Holy Mary Mother of God, protect us!"

"A man?" Sunniva put an arm about her. "Why, Hildi, surely 'tis one of Raven's men come looking for me. . . ." She took the candle from Hildigunn.

"Nay, Sunniva, do not go out there!" Hildigunn gasped, but already Sunniva was in the dim corridor.

Even as she held up an arm and hailed the man, Sunniva felt a sinking sensation. It was a stranger, and, too, Raven knew where her small cell was. He himself would have come for her. She fled back into the room and both women leaned against the door, which had no lock. Hildigunn's eyes were closed, her lips moving in ceaseless silent prayer. Sunniva's eyes were opened wide. Who was he? What did he want and how had he got past the guards? What man prowling about the dim corridors of a convent hours before dawn was up to any good? She must protect the two of them—she must and she would! The door flew open, kicked by a powerful foot. Sunniva froze, seeing his face in the flickering candlelight. She knew him. . . .

"So, mistress Sunniva, we meet again." Heller Orm laughed as his dark eyes moved over her lightly clad form.

Sunniva's heart pounded in her ears. She was outraged that he should have tracked her down, but the fact that she had no weapon to defend herself and Hildigunn frightened her. When he reached out to grasp her, she retreated. She felt a steely barrier raising itself in her mind the way Raven had taught

97

her, a barrier between her fear and the job that had to be done. She must down him and flee. She must flee and hide until Raven got there.

Heller Orm's hot eyes measured the beautiful woman he had come for. Again he laughed. The bitch would not escape him this time. Glancing at the plain little nun in the corner, he saw that she watched him with white lips and terrified eyes.

"You!" he snarled, "crawl under the bed and stay there, face-down." Trembling, Hildigunn obeyed. "And you, mistress," he took another step toward Sunniva, "you will come with me."

His arm shot out and grasped her wrist. When she did not resist, he was instantly wary, and when he felt himself being jerked toward her, he knew what she was about. The sly little bitch was going for his groin. What a Valkyrie! He sidestepped her quickly upthrust knee which would have laid him low and twisted his arm about her neck, forcing her to gasp for breath.

"Nay, nay, mistress. 'Tis a naughty thing for a maid to do to a man."

He quickly tied her wrists behind her, stuffed a rag into her mouth and threw her roughly over his shoulder. She was carried swiftly, silently down the dark corridor to the front hallway. While she could not see about her, flung as she was over the man's shoulder like a sack of potatoes, Sunniva could hear the weeping of the women and the deep rough voices of stranger-men. She knew then that the holy sisters had been routed from their beds in the search for her and her heart sank. Had any of them been harmed?

"I have the bitch," said her captor, "so let us be off. You nuns," he growled, "'twould be wise to remain within these walls 'til cockcrow if you would stay alive."

As she was carried out into the courtyard, Sunniva

glimpsed the guards, all four of them, lying in pools of blood on the flagstones. She closed her eyes, sickened. They looked so still, and there was so much blood. She was handed up to a man already mounted, and within minutes the band was stealing quietly through the sleeping town. Once out of the village, they galloped northward through a dark wood, carrying her to what place, what fate she could not imagine. She knew only that try as she might to be brave, she was afraid. She was numb with fear. And she grieved for Raven, for her parents and for those men lying so quietly in their own blood. . . .

Raven could not still the uneasiness that gnawed him as they neared the convent. Having felt it many times before, he had learned to heed it. Now it was about Sunniva that his inner alarm was clamoring. Something was wrong.

"Ulf!" he spoke sharply to his best friend, who was asleep in the saddle. "Wake up, man!"

Ulf's blue eyes opened. "Are we there already?"

"I want to take a stiffer pace."

"And break the beasts' legs?" Ulf asked. "I know you crave to make her yours, man, but you can do naught about it 'til after midnight." Seeing Raven's icy gray eyes, he stifled any further coarse jesting. "Holy Thor, Raven, what is't?"

"I don't know. I know only that we must hurry."

They arrived in the town just as the gray smoke of cooking fires was curling toward the pale sky. When Raven saw, from a distance, that the door in the convent wall was unguarded, he grew cold. He was too late. Sunniva was gone. His scout raced ahead to open the door and the Marvik men pounded in at a gallop. Within the courtyard lay the four guards in their own congealed blood, their throats slit. Raven burst open the door to the convent.

"Sunniva!" he roared. The great front entry hall was empty, and from somewhere within came the sound of muffled wailing.

"Abbess!" When there was no answer, he bellowed, "Woman, in the name of Odin, come forth! 'Tis Raven Trondsson of Marvik."

At that, the hall filled with weeping women, red-eyed, white-faced.

"Oh, sire," the Abbess cried, "we are so sorry!" She got no further for weeping.

Raven harshly grasped her thin shoulders, forcing her to face him. "Who did this—and when?" He was ready to slay, to rend the fort asunder and lay waste the whole countryside.

"'Twas in the middle of the night," she wept. "We—we all slept. . . ."

"We heard naught," cried another, "and then they —burst into our rooms, pulled us from our beds—"

"There were many?"

"Ay."

"How many?"

None knew, nor could they describe the men. They knew only that they would have been killed had they resisted.

"And Sunniva?" A swell of fury was rising, pounding in Raven's head. There was more wailing. "Damn it!" he roared. "Someone speak. Someone tell me what has happened."

"Sire—" A young nun stepped into the hall just then, trembling so that it seemed she might fall down. "'Twas a man Sunni knew who took her."

Raven's fierce gray eyes narrowed, devouring her pinched face. "How know you that?"

"I—I was in the room with her. We were talking of her wedding," Hildigunn gulped and wiped her brimming eyes. "The man was dark and tall with a black beard, and he said, 'So, mistress Sunniva, we meet again.'"

Raven and Ulf locked angry eyes. Seeing the girl was near collapse, Raven asked softly, "And then . . . ?"

"He ordered me under the bed, but I heard all. Oh, sire, she was so brave! She would have fought him, but he—he began choking her. . . ."

Raven had managed to control his emotions somewhat, not wanting to frighten the holy sisters further. Now a gate opened within him and a red fury roared through him unleashed, pumped by his heart into his brain and his veins and muscles. He wanted to hew the ribs from the bastard's backbone, tear out his still-pumping lungs and still-beating heart to flutter and die in the cold light of dawn. Never had he cut the blood eagle on any man, but now his own heart screamed for revenge. He felt Ulf's hand grip his shoulder.

"Easy, man. . . ."

He took a deep breath. "Ay."

Raven steeled himself then. He must turn off his rage and emptiness and his great fear; they would not find Sunniva for him. And he would learn no more from these weeping women. Nay. It was time to comb the countryside and knock on doors and ask questions. Somewhere, someone had seen or heard something and he had not a moment to lose.

CHAPTER 8

SUNNIVA COULD NOT STOP SHAKING. SHE WAS STILL bound and gagged and, aside from her fright, she was chilled to the bone. It was unseasonably cold and she wore only a wadmal wrapper over her nightshirt. But her thoughts were not on her discomfort. They whirled, dark and frenzied, over what had happened and what was going to happen. And she grieved for her parents and for Raven. How they would suffer when they learned she was gone! And the convent guards—surely they were dead? And the holy sisters had wept and wailed so, Sunniva feared greatly for them and for their chastity. Oh, why was she being taken by the stronghand on her wedding day, of all days? To whom were these grim, silent, green-clad men taking her?

The one man she had seen before—ay, the clod who had tried earlier to carry her off—but the other seven were strangers. Two of them frightened her so, she dared not raise her eyes to look at them. They were big, handsome men with shaggy blond hair that fell past their shoulder blades, and their hot wild eyes seemed to see beneath her clothing. Always they stared at her. Sunniva feared they could easily overpower the others and have their way with her, for both were near to seven feet tall and powerfully built.

The man in whose arms she rode held her impersonally. It was as though he were made of granite and ice, and for that she was grateful. She must be thankful for any blessing now, she thought bitterly, as she was carried through the dark wood, swiftly, silently, endlessly. It was the only way she would get through this awful time. Her hopes soared as she saw up ahead a band of mounted men blocking their way. Perhaps when they saw her plight, they would free her! But then, perhaps they themselves would seize her and treat her more shamefully than those who held her now.

Her eyes widened as a tall golden man on a golden stallion came forward to meet them. His pale blond hair flowed into a darker beard and he wore a brownish-green cape and trews, as did the other men. He was magnificent to look upon and by his very bearing, Sunniva surmised that he was a chieftain. And then she recognized him. Oh, no. No, no, no . . .

"We took her unseen by townsmen, my lord Hedeby," said her black-bearded captor. "The guards we slew."

"Satisfactory," said Rolf Gunnarsson, his impassive eyes barely acknowledging his captive.

He had given Heller Orm the chance to rectify his earlier blunder and the man had done well, learning that the holy sisters were attending the wedding and that no sick would be treated that day. Accordingly, Rolf had changed his strategy, his men storming the convent during the night. It seemed the new plan had been a success.

"The wench will ride with me the rest of the way," he said gruffly.

Sunniva was immediately handed up into his keeping and sat upon his rock-hard thighs. She was compressed tightly between his chest and the saddlebar with his arms on either side of her. Her face flamed. Rolf Gunnarsson! The scut! If he thought to wed her after this, he was in for a disappointment. And the poor guards slain, just as she had suspected. She wanted to fall a-weeping in her anguish but she would not let him see her so. She went rigid as his hand slipped inside her wrapper and closed about her left breast. When he squeezed it, chuckling at her discomfort and humiliation, she vowed that if Raven did not find and kill him, she would do it herself.

"Nay, woman, do not glare so," Rolf whispered, his lips against her ear sending chills throughout her body. "You are mine now. I will do with you as I wish."

His hand roamed over her midriff and abdomen, exploring his new possession. He then caught the hems of her nightshirt and wrapper, lifting them so that her legs were exposed. He ran a dark hand over her thighs, testing the silky texture of her skin before slipping his fingers between them. Still bound, Sunniva steeled herself, commanded herself not to shudder. He spoke suddenly, sharply, to the two blond giants riding on either side:

"Unless you are prepared to lose an eye each, keep them straight ahead." To Sunniva, he said, "It seems my berserkers want you."

He continued stroking her thighs thoughtfully, as though not even thinking of the silken flesh beneath his fingers.

"Know you, woman, I will give you to them if you attempt to escape, and I guarantee you will not like their lovemaking." He removed the gag from her mouth then. "You will not cry out." He caressed her throat and, as a warning, his long fingers compressed it briefly until she gasped for breath.

Never had she been so frightened, but she knew she must obey and not cry out—he could suffocate her or break her neck without half trying. But when they arrived at their destination, she would attempt escape. She had to. And if she could slay him first, she would.

"You will never get away with this," she spoke between clenched teeth.

He gave a wolf's smile. "'Twould appear I have."

"Mayhap for now, ay," she muttered, "but my betrothed will never rest until he finds me. And my father and brother and my kindred—all will be searching for me."

"They will not find you." Rolf's fingers moved between her throat and her breasts, stroking, stroking her satiny skin. She had the most exquisite skin of any woman he had ever possessed; soft, silken, white, its scent so tantalizing of itself that he wanted to sink his teeth into it. . . .

"But they will!"

"Nay, abandon such hope, wench. My men are expert in the use of woodcraft. They are concealing our passing, and in this spear-wall of brush, none will find a trace of us. Should they, we will slay them." He laughed at the thought. "But then, I prefer to wait on that. I would rather they saw you as you will soon be, Sunniva, not as the haughty maid you are now. Your proud father will have no cause for pride in you before long, I promise you. He will not want you back."

Sunniva hid her terror as she wondered what he meant. Her fear intensified as his hands continued searching roughly over her body. His mouth took hers hungrily again and again. Holy Thor, what manner of man was this . . . ?

"'Twas a grave mistake," Rolf said, low, "your father not giving you to me. His influence and power would have been extended greatly. Know you that I am king in the Vaagaland?"

Sunniva knew that men did not get to be kings without great power and wealth and the killing of many enemies, but never would she let him know how much that frightened her. She said coldly:

"There are petty kings aplenty in Norway's valleys."

"Rolf Gunnarsson of Hedeby is not a petty valley king."

Sunniva lifted her chin. "So you say."

"You have a sharp tongue, wench."

Sunniva said nothing. When he had asked for her hand earlier in the year, she had marked well that he was vain and arrogant. If she showed her disdain, it would anger him greatly.

"Know you, Sunniva, that 'tis for my pleasure I now possess you, and I do not like a woman with a sharp tongue."

Good. She would sharpen it on him. She would speak only words that were scathing. But even as she thought it, his fingers gripped her throat, again pressing against her tender flesh until her mouth flew open. As she struggled for breath, his tongue leisurely explored the sweet darkness of her mouth. She was dizzy when he finally lifted his head.

"You are mine, Sunniva, and you will obey me. You exist for me. . . ." She sat, numb and trembling, as his arms tightened about her. She had thought she was going to die when he pressed against her windpipe.

"I would hear you say it, my beauty," he whispered into her ear, his fingers still about her throat.

"I—cannot." It was the truth. Always had she existed for herself, and now she existed for Raven. She could not force such disgusting, sickening words past her lips.

"You exist for my pleasure, Sunniva. Say it." His fingers began closing.

"You are an animal," she gasped. "Nay, you are worse than an—" She had no breath left with which to speak. Her throat was closed by his fingers. The blood pounded in her head and sang in her ears. All grew black.

"Say it, my beauty."

When the terrible pressure eased, she gulped in the blessed cold air and choked: "I—exist for your—pleasure."

"You are mine."

"I—am yours. . . ." She hated him! Never could she have imagined such hatred. Oh, her throat ached so horribly. . . .

"You will obey me."

"I will obey you," she whispered. But only until she could think, make some plan to escape.

Rolf chuckled. Her fear of him was now a palpable thing that fired his blood as much as did his passion for her.

"Remember it well, Sunniva, for I am not a patient man. The next time you displease me, I will give you to Helgi and Bjork for a day or two."

"That—will not be necessary, my lord Hedeby."

Remembering how the two berserkers had undressed her with their hot, cruel eyes, she knew that she was in grave peril. No woman would be safe from them. She must give this man her total obedience until that moment when she would escape him.

Rolf fondled her again, kissing her lips and her throat, and there was nothing she could do about it, even had her hands and feet been unbound. She closed her eyes, gritted her teeth, and thought of Raven.

"Know you, Sunniva, that I craved you even before I made suit for you. For five years I have waited for you."

Sunniva felt his teeth on her flimsily clad shoulder. When he gave her a rough bite, she did not cry out. She forced herself to speak.

"How can that be, my lord, when I met you for the first time this year?"

"'Twas in Bergvin I saw you. Your father had come on business to the Thing and you were with him."

Sunniva's skin crawled. "Sire, I was but thirteen years old then!"

"Ay, and the most beautiful thing I had ever seen. I vowed then that I would possess you."

Now Sunniva was not only frightened and cold, she was sick to her stomach. To think, this terrible dark cloud had been hanging over her all this while and none had known it. What normal man would have noticed a child in the first place? And to have harbored such hunger for five years. . . .

O, Raven, she prayed, *find me, beloved, but be careful. Odin guide and guard you, for this beast is a manslayer.*

She sat silent, eyes closed, her thoughts holding to Raven. Never did she doubt that he would soon find her and they would be wed as they had planned. Then her dreams were interrupted by an unexpected sound, men's voices that rose abruptly in a cheer. Opening her eyes, she saw two squat ships moored to posts on a muddy shore and men running to greet them.

"Where are we going?"

"It matters naught to you, woman. You will go where I take you."

Never had Sunniva dreamt she would be carried

off on a ship! But then Rolf Gunnarsson lived so far north, she reckoned it would take less time to go by sea than land.

"Load the horses quickly," Rolf commanded his men. "We have no time to lose."

Sunniva was carried to the woods' edge and unbound. As she tended to her needs, she considered an escape attempt, but she knew it was bootless here. She would be caught and given to the berserkers. She walked back slowly to where Rolf's golden stallion was being driven through shallow water to board one of the ships.

Ignoring the stares and grins of the men, she scornfully studied the vessels. Both needed but few oars and few men to man them. If these were the best the mighty master of Hedeby had to offer, Raven's great dragonship would easily out-distance them. She felt leaden nonetheless, for Raven would have no clue as to which direction to look. And she had been stolen many hours before he ever would have arrived at Solby Convent.

"Into the boat, woman," Rolf commanded her gruffly. When she gave him a look of loathing, he growled, "Move!"

"You will not get away with this!"

She lifted her nightshirt and wrapper to her knees, waded into the icy water in her bare feet, and then stepped over the low freeboard and down into the leaky ship. Within minutes, sails of pale blue wadmal were raised, the men took their places, and the two vessels were rowed out into the fjord.

Sunniva despaired, seeing how deserted it was. There were no other ships in sight, no steadings nor burgs, not one lone dwelling along the coast. And they were headed toward the open sea. She yearned to shout her rage at Rolf Gunnarsson, but she dared not open her mouth.

She studied him with bitter eyes as he stood speaking with his helmsman. He was tall, wide-shouldered and narrow-hipped in his brown-green cloak and trews; the sea wind whipped his blond hair about his handsome sun-darkened face; golden bands ornamented his muscular forearms on which many white scars showed; gold glittered on the haft of the great sword at his belt.

The giant berserkers by his side no longer stared at her, but Sunniva knew it was only because they feared the Hedeby lord as much as she herself did. She sat on a coil of rope and clung, shivering, to the freeboard. She looked about her. What a shabby vessel it was—a helmsman, a lookout, two men bailing and the others manning the meager oarbank and the sail. Twelve crew in all. The cargo area was so laden with barrels, skin bags, and tubs that she feared they would sink before they ever got as far north as the Vaagaland.

The sun had been overhead for some time when she saw the berserkers pointing southward. The crews of both ships gave a glad shout. Following their gaze, Sunniva felt her heart sink. It was the largest vessel she had ever seen, and she understood at last what was happening. Any who chanced to see the great gold-beaked, purple-sailed dragonship that was gliding so swiftly toward them would remember the sight forever. The Hedeby chieftain therefore had taken no such chance. They were far from landfall when he threw Sunniva roughly over his shoulder and carried her aboard. His men howled their approval. Sunniva was pink-faced with wrath as he dumped her onto the deck and grinned down at her.

"Scut!" she cried and slapped his face.

There was sudden silence. Only then did Sunniva remember the terrible promises he had forced her to make and the equally terrible consequences if she disobeyed. She stood stiff as a statue, afraid to move, to breathe, even to swallow. What had she done? Would he now give her to Helgi and Bjork before all these men? When he merely laughed, she grew so weak with relief that she nearly dropped to the deck.

"'Tis a fine, spirited wench you have, my lord Hedeby," someone called.

"Ay, 'twill be a pleasure to break her to spur and saddle," Rolf answered.

Sunniva, her eyes cast to the deck, was forced to listen as the jesting grew coarse and thick, and her every aspect—her legs, breasts, skin, hair, teeth, and eyes—were discussed as though she were a mare for sale. She grew pinker and more humiliated by the second. No man she had ever known would have indulged in such insulting talk about the woman he meant to wed.

"'Tis enough," said the Master of Hedeby at long last. "I hunger for this woman now." He looked at his berserkers. "Helgi, come with us. Bjork, stay on deck."

With that, Sunniva was lifted like a feather in Rolf's arms and carried through an opening in the foredeck down into the tarry black hull of the ship, where a mattress lay. She was so frightened, she was ill. And she was confused. Her last glimpse of the outside showed the vessel bearing the horses was sailing north, whereas the Landwaster and the other burden ship were moving southward. Where was he taking her? Her mind reeled with questions as he tossed her roughly onto the mattress on her back. She quickly sat up.

"M-my lord Hedeby," her teeth were chattering, "it surprises me that you treat so roughly a m-maid you wish to wed." As her eyes adjusted to the dimness, she saw Helgi move to the curved hull and sit himself down cross-legged. He was but an arm's-length away.

Rolf removed his swordbelt and cape and sank to the mattress beside her. The sword he put close to hand.

"Wed?" He gave her a mocking look and held up a foot for Helgi to tug off his boot. "Nay, wench, not wed. The time for drinking the wedding ale is past."

Sunniva stared at him as Helgi removed his other boot. "Not wed?" she whispered. "Why then have you stolen me if—not to wed me?"

Rolf's pale eyes were icy as the northern sea in winter. "'Twas time Arn Mellby learned who 'tis he scorned for son-in-law. 'Twas time he felt a like sting. Helgi, band her."

As the berserk approached, Sunniva leapt to the farthest corner of the mattress. "Pig! Don't come near me!"

She screamed and kicked as Helgi caught one slim white foot between his huge hands. It took only a moment. Pressure, a click, and then he quickly withdrew, leaving Sunniva to tug at the wide bronze bracelet on her ankle. It appeared seamless and fit so snugly she could not even get her fingers beneath it. Her heart thumped. She cried:

"What is this for?"

"You are my thrall, woman."

"Thrall?" She had heard of those vikings who were thrall-catchers, slave-users, but never had she known any such despicable men. Her fury boiled up. "You bastard, take this off. I demand you take it off!"

Rolf laughed. "Nay, 'tis not going to come off, not ever. My men will be pleased no longer to draw lots to prepare the food. You will do it, as well as any other thing I require of you." His eyes moved over her body. "Now I would hear the words I taught you, wench."

Sunniva's rage left as quickly as it had come for Helgi sat watching her and she saw that he burned for her. The hated words Rolf bade her speak seared her brain. She would say them, ay, but only because she must survive until Raven came. She did not doubt that this wretch would give her to his berserkers, nor that their brutal passion might kill her. As hideous as the prospect of surrender was, she knew she must yield to this man.

"I am not used to waiting, woman," Rolf growled. "I would hear the words."

Sunniva lowered her eyes so he would not see the hatred glowing in them. "I—am yours, my lord Hedeby," she said low, the words nearly choking her, so bitter were they. "I will obey you. I—exist for you. . . ."

"Very good," Rolf Gunnarsson's voice was as soft as her own. "Now, take off your clothes, Sunniva."

CHAPTER 9

SUNNIVA DID AS SHE WAS TOLD, REMOVING HER LONG wrapper slowly and with some difficulty, for she was sitting on the mattress still. She avoided looking at Rolf Gunnarsson, but she sensed that his intent gaze never left her. When she finally struggled free of the garment, she folded it carefully and laid it beside her. Only then did she meet his eyes.

What she saw in their blue depths was not only lust, but vanity and arrogance. It was clear that the Vaaga chieftain thought highly of himself. He was vastly handsome in face and form and he was, after all, a king in his own part of Norway's land. Sunniva suspected he was a man whom no woman had ever denied, nor would dare deny. And she had slapped his face twice now, once when her father had rejected his suit for her, and now in front of his men.

She saw well that he craved her admiration as much as he craved her body. He wanted her to be as

115

impressed by him as he himself was; as awed by him as were his subjects; as overwhelmed by his appearance and masculinity as were the other women he had conquered. Well, she was not impressed, nor would she ever be—but for now, she must pretend. Realizing suddenly that she might use this weakness of his to manipulate him, she felt a small bud of hope opening within her.

Ay, perhaps she could turn this mighty Vaaga king into a flopping fish hooked on her line. Too late would he discover that she was made of sterner stuff than he had ever reckoned on—but not yet. She did not know how long it would take, but she feared she would have to be very patient. And very brave.

"Come, wench," Rolf growled, "take off your nightshirt. I would see the beauty I have but imagined thus far."

He grasped her arm so harshly that Sunniva clenched her teeth to keep from crying out. For all the scorn she felt for him, the fact remained that she was terrified. She was in a hopeless situation and in his power completely. And if she pushed him too far, he would give her to Helgi, who sat hunched against the hull. The berserker did not look at her, but Sunniva knew he was waiting, waiting for her to make the one wrong move that would deliver her into his hands.

Oh bright elves, Sunniva prayed, help me this day. . . .

With trembling hands, she began to work her nightshirt upwards, pulling it above her knees and thighs, kneeling on the mattress then to pull it up over her buttocks and her slender waist. She hesitated, the wadmal fabric bunched beneath her breasts.

The Vaaga king watched her humiliation with icy

eyes, his mouth twisted into a smile. All that was lacking for his greater pleasure was for her father and her betrothed to see her thus.

"You are slow, wench. Perhaps you need Helgi to assist you."

"Nay!"

Sunniva blinked frightened eyes at him and hurriedly finished disrobing. Then she folded her nightshirt and lay it atop her wrapper—the only two things in this world which she could call her own now. She had no kirtle, no shoes, not even a comb for her hair. And she was property—a slave with a band on her ankle, Rolf Gunnarsson's thrall to do with as he chose. As her nakedness brought the full impact of the horror rushing over her, her whole body grew pink with the shame of it. Just moments before she had been almost hopeful, but that was before the eyes of the two men glittered over her bare flesh.

Hearing strange noises, Sunniva looked at Helgi, startled. The hair rose on her neck as she realized what he was about. Overcome by his hunger for her, he was relieving himself against the hull. The Vaaga chieftain chuckled, amused by her wide-eyed horror.

"Ay, Sunniva, you are indeed a beauty. My man has but to gaze upon your naked charms to spill his seed." His eyes grew narrow as they studied her. "I am well pleased, but I do not like it that you huddle so. Lie down on your back."

Sunniva had been sitting with her knees drawn up, her arms pressing them against her breasts. When she hesitated, he snapped:

"Helgi, I would inspect her."

"Nay!" Sunniva gasped. She tried to scramble back from the berserker's coarse hands, but Helgi caught and stretched her out on her back, arms above her head.

"Enough," the Hedeby lord growled. Helgi obeyed, squatting once more with his back against the hull.

Rolf pulled off his own clothing and lay down beside Sunniva. Raised on one elbow, he ran a practiced hand over her breasts and belly. She was a rare find. He had had more women than he could count, but never had he seen such perfection of skin, nor such beauty of face and form. She was fine-boned and slender, yet her breasts were beautifully full and her limbs soft and rounded. There was not a sharp angle on her body, and that skin. . . .

He put his lips and tongue to her breast, tasted her sweet flesh and drew in her fragrance. Exquisite, by the gods. His eyes and hands burned over her. Perhaps when he tired of her, although he doubted such a time would ever come, he would sell her to one of the Far Eastern princes he had come to know, or perhaps to Kemal Attibak. They, more than most, lusted for such white, silky skin, and more important, they alone had the price he would ask. It would not matter to them that she was not a virgin.

"Ay, you are a treasure, wench. It is to your father's great woe that he did not give you to me when I asked him in all honor. Now will he suffer, as will you."

Rolf's dark hand grasped one of Sunniva's breasts, lifting it into a peak and squeezing it so that the pink nipple hardened into a taut bud above his fingers. He touched his tongue to it, sucked and bit it. Sunniva could not hold back a gasp of pain and revulsion. Gone was her vow to be obedient and subservient to the devil.

"Filthy scut!" she hissed.

With all the strength and fury she possessed, she attempted to claw, kick, and bit her tormentor. But she was at a disadvantage, being on her back and already pressed down. The lord of Hedeby subdued her with a swiftly, cruel blow to her ear that made her head ring. He was wroth at her rejection of him, and although she no longer fought him, he roughly thrust her from him.

"She is yours, Helgi."

"Ay, my lord."

"My lord Hedeby, nay!" Sunniva shrieked. "I beg of you, sire. Please. . . ."

Her anger was gone; fear consumed her. She had hoped eventually to reach the Vaaga king through his vanity, but the berserker could not be led, that she knew. Behind his pale eyes, she saw only lust and cruelty.

"Please! O please, my lord, do not do this! I—I will be obedient."

She was near weeping, realizing how she had jeopardized everything—her life, Raven's happiness, her parents' happiness. Why had she not allowed Rolf to fondle her, painful and disgusting though it was, for it was nothing compared to what would happen to her now.

Oh Holy Thor, be with me, she prayed. Thor and Odin, holy Frey and Freyja, Hel and Heimdal, Ran and Aegir and Jesu-Mary-Holy Ghost, Oh hear me, all you gods. . . .

Rolf muttered to Helgi: "In the mood I am in, I would kill the wench. I want her softened, frightened, but you will not damage her or take her, understand you?"

"Ay, sire."

"My lord Hedeby, I beg of you. . . ."

Helgi wetted his lips as his eyes moved over Sunniva. Already his short, raspy breathing showed his intense excitement, and in the time it took his master to don his trews, he had torn off his own clothing and was beside her on the mattress. Sunniva

119

had breath for only one scream before his mouth seized hers.

When Rolf Gunnarsson appeared on deck wearing only his trews, the eyes of his men met in amusement. All knew what it meant. Soon he would enjoy the new thrall himself, but for now she was being punished. After being bedded by either of the berserkers, the wench would welcome her master with open arms. Ay, and open legs, too. A bull would be preferable to those two.

The sun was high in the sky when the lord of Hedeby finally returned below deck. His thrall, naked still, her face impassive, sat in the middle of the mattress, her arms and legs crossed. Helgi, fully clothed, sat crouched against the hull, his head between his legs. Rolf hid his surprise. But then, why should he be surprised? For the bastard to have such a luscious wench in his arms and not be able to claim her completely would be torture.

"Leave us," Rolf growled.

Wordlessly, the giant rose and disappeared through the trap. In the bright sunlight that poured through it, Sunniva saw that Rolf Gunnarsson was removing his trews again. She shuddered. Was this all that life was to hold for her from now on? Being used by men? Men—hah! These were animals, not men. And at least she had taught that swine, Helgi, a lesson.

Knowing he was forbidden to harm her, Sunniva had acted swiftly once the Vaaga chieftain was gone. She had given him several agonizing knee-blows to the groin and a hammer-blow under the nose with the side of her hand so that he had lain a-groaning most of the time his master was on deck. She knew he would say not a word of the humiliation that had befallen him at the hands of a mere maiden—him, a berserker in his prime. Never would his masculine pride allow him to speak of it. Rolf Gunnarsson, on the other hand, she must deal with in another way.

Sunniva made no protest when he lay down beside her and pulled her into his arms. He immediately took her mouth in a long, drinking kiss, and as one powerful arm bound her to him, his hand roamed over her breasts and the cleft between her thighs. Still she made no protest. He lifted his lips from hers and laughed.

"How docile you have become, wench. Helgi's passion tends to do that."

She wanted to shout that Helgi was a stinking boar that she had tamed. Instead, she lowered her dark eyes so that he would not see the rebellion simmering there.

"I am glad to be in your arms instead, my lord," she said quietly.

"It doubts me not. I hope I am preferable to my berserkers."

As Rolf Gunnarsson explored her body, Sunniva's thoughts were on Raven. He would be looking for her, she knew he would, and it was her job to stay alive until he found her. She would never again do anything that would place her in the hands of the berserkers—Helgi, especially, for he would be wary the next time, and vengeful. Feeling Rolf's rough hands seeking her private parts, pinching her nipples, expertly forcing open her jaws so that his tongue could claim her fully, Sunniva knew she must put her plan into action.

"You are very strong, my lord," she gasped, for he was pressing her to him so closely she scarce had the breath to speak.

"Stronger by far than my berserkers," he muttered. "Stronger than Raven Trondsson. In addition, I command more men, I come from a more powerful family, and I am looked upon with favor by the present rulers of our land." He kissed her fresh mouth again. "'Tis a pity your father rejected my suit for you."

When her lips were once more her own, Sunniva murmured, "Ay. I had not realized you were so . . . very handsome. . . ."

Rolf knew a moment of uncertainty. He had expected such words from her after she had been in Helgi's unwashed arms. Why, then, should he doubt that she spoke anything but the truth? There was not a wench alive who did not seek to flatter him, either because of fear or because she was smitten by his virility and his face and form.

"You seem a great and powerful man, my lord—" Sunniva whispered as his mouth and his hands began moving over her more urgently. If she protested, she would again be given to Helgi or Bjork, yet the Hedeby lord himself was going to take her soon if she did not prevent it. "For that very reason, I know you will not force me."

Rolf scowled and raised his head from her breasts. He had been suckling them, wishing they were milk-swollen like those of his English thrall.

"You are mine, wench, and I will possess you, never doubt it. But whether it be by force or not depends on you."

"Whence I come, my lord Hedeby, men do not use force." She spoke softly, her heart pounding. "Not real men."

Rolf laughed, not a pleasant sound. "Whence I come, real men take what they want. They do not acquire by sweat or begging or politeness what they can take by force or blood."

Sunniva's heart left her throat and sank to her stomach. "My folk call such men weak. Cowards . . ."

"Cowards?"

"Ay . . ."

She did not add what they both knew: When it was learned he had stolen her, the arrow would go out across the land declaring him outlawed. He would be fair game for any man just as Raven would have been had he stolen her. But then—what if none learned it was he who had taken her? And she had not forgotten that he stood in good stead with those kings who now ruled Norway's land—Sweyn Forkbeard and the two sons of Earl Haakon. It would be an easy thing for him to procure a grace-deed. He had borne her off by the stronghand and probably would rape her, but he would receive but a tap on the wrist for punishment if indeed he ever was caught. How unfair it was.

Rolf's fury was great. He had wanted to impress this wench above all others, and now she had intimated that he was a coward. Weak. And weak meant effeminate. There was no greater insult. Perhaps he would kill her. He raised himself to a sitting position and glowered at her.

"I commanded a Viking fleet when I was fifteen winters," he growled. "I was blooded in battle and reckoned a man at twelve. I took my first woman at thirteen. And you call me weak?"

"Mayhap the word does not fit, sire," Sunniva answered, hiding her fright. "Soon will I know. . . ."

His pale eyes blazed so fiercely and he was so wroth, his many scars standing out white as death on his dark face and body, that Sunniva thought her last hour had come. He was going to slay her. She, too, sat up. She crossed her arms over her breasts.

Long and long Rolf Gunnarsson sat, staring at his thrall and collecting his thoughts. He smiled then. In the half-light, it passed for a smile. He would not kill her, nay. He had waited far too long to own her and she was too valuable a prize for him to do anything as foolish as killing her or marking that satin skin and reducing her value. Rather, he would ignore her for now while punishing her in a way she could not have dreamed of, and soon she would come to him. He knew women, and this one was no different. They could not resist him. This wench had just been wrested from her betrothed—that accounted for her actions—but before long, she would come to him willingly. Ay, more than willingly.

Sunniva's surprise and relief were boundless when the Vaaga chieftain began to clothe himself. She saw that her words had stung him badly, but now what? Was she to be given to the berserkers? She could not believe she was out of danger. Doubtless she had merely postponed the inevitable, and soon Rolf would be after her again. She watched silently as he pulled on his long, soft boots, bound them to his muscular legs, strapped on his sword and settled his cloak over his shoulders.

"I require you on deck now." His voice and eyes were icy.

"Yes, my lord."

Sunniva hurriedly tugged on her nightshirt and wrapper and, heart racing, mounted the four steps to the foredeck. She stood a moment, overwhelmed by the vastness of the Landwaster and its great purple sail now unfurled. The steersman faced her, his feet propped to push against the heavy steering oar. Spying her, his dark face took on a leer. The rest of the crew, sprawled about the deck playing draughts and letting the wind do the work of the oars, then noticed her. The wind chose that moment to lift her long flaxen hair and wrapper and seal her nightshirt to her body. There came calls and jeers; the coarse jesting began. Sunniva drew a deep breath and busked herself for whatever ordeal was to come. She had not long to wait.

"Wench!" Rolf was directly behind her.

She spun. "Ay?"

"'Ay, my lord Hedeby,'" he instructed her. His men laughed.

Sunniva swallowed a sharp retort and thought of Raven's searching for her. He would search the world until he found her, and the thought gave her strength.

"Ay, my lord Hedeby," her voice rang out.

She stood straight and proud, shoulders back, not attempting to cover her breasts which were outlined so plainly beneath her night garb. Let them gawk. Let them see that she was not defeated. Her eyes locked on Rolf's, defiant. What a shame, she thought, that a man who looked so like a god should have the black soul of a devil. He was handsome and strong—virile, ay, but what mattered that when his mind and body craved cruelty?

"My men are hungry, wench," he said. "You will serve them now."

Sunniva did not show her dismay. A quick glance showed her there were more than one hundred men there.

"Under the half-decks," Rolf pointed, "you will find the food. Begin now."

"My lord," her eyes flashed. "'twill be the sunset hour before the last man is fed."

"So be it."

He turned, a path opening for him as he strode to the prow. He stood beside the stone anchor there, his arms folded across his chest, his hostile eyes watching her.

No path opened for Sunniva as she made her way to the half-deck. The first man who lifted her skirt to run his hands up her legs, got a surprise.

"Scut!" Sunniva hissed. She grasped both his ears and nearly twisted them off his head.

She had been commanded to obey the chieftain,

not his scum of a crew, and until she was told differently, she would defend herself. She held Raven in her thoughts as, head high, eyes straight ahead, she made trip after trip, her great basket heaped with smoked fish, dried swineflesh, and hard bread. When they had filled themselves with that, she bore water to them in skin bags. They continued to harass her with their unclean talk and jests, but none touched her again. She passed through them as if they were a cloud of gnats.

She had been right. It was near the sunset hour when all were fed and had drunk their fill of water. She was so weary, she could have dropped where she stood. The wind blew colder, and both her body and clothing were damp now from the constant spray. Her feet were freezing and wet from the water that forever sloshed underfoot, and she wanted nothing so much as to curl up somewhere—anywhere—and sleep.

Rolf Gunnarsson was keenly disappointed in his new thrall. It was not that she had disobeyed him in any way, nay. She had fed his men efficiently and tirelessly and had borne their unclean talk and jeers like no wench he had ever seen before. It was only that he had expected, had craved for her to fall a-weeping with fear and frustration and weariness. She had not. Never did he doubt that she felt all of those things, but not once did it show on her face or in her proud bearing.

"Wench!"

"Ay, my lord Hedeby?"

Sunniva was clinging to the rail, the men gathered round ogling her. So many of them were bedeviling her now, laughing, tugging at her hair, and lifting her skirt to stroke her legs that she knew not where to strike first.

126

Rolf saw that her eyes still blazed defiance and that she thought them all cowards. By Thor, before night fell, he would have the wench on her knees begging for mercy! He had marked well that she was near dead on her feet with weariness.

"We will drink now," he ordered. Ah. He saw the first sign of dismay in her eyes. "The beer-kegs are on the half-deck along with the food. The horns also are there."

Sunniva swayed. She clutched the rail until the dizziness passed and her balance returned, and then she obeyed. There was nothing else to do but pick her way back to the half-deck and begin serving the men who now clustered about her bawling for her to hurry. Wordlessly, patiently, she dipped horn after horn into the kegs. She ignored the mounting insults until one man, overcome with lust, lifted her off her feet, crushed her against him and kissed her on the mouth.

It all happened so quickly, she could not even scream. Her clothing was soon ripped off and she kicked and clawed them, cursed them, as their hands moved greedily over her bare flesh. And then she heard Rolf Gunnarsson's bellow:

"Bastards! I gave you no leave to rape her!"

Suddenly he was there, sword drawn, eyes blazing in the half-light. Helgi and Bjork knocked heads and sent men sprawling to the planking. Rolf yanked Sunniva to the trap and thrust her into the gloom below-decks where she went to the mattress and sat trembling. Her heart was going so fast she thought she might swoon. It had been a close thing. He had been at the prow, drinking and yarning with his berserkers while she had been at the other end of the ship. To boot, he was drunk. It had taken him a while to realize what was happening.

127

Sunniva could not stop shaking. Not only was she frightened, she was freezing. She was still shaking when Rolf came below carrying a lighted candle and a bundle under one arm. Bjork bore a second bundle. Sunniva watched, sullen, as they were thrown onto the mattress. They were sleeping bags, leather on the outside, fur within.

"Crawl in before you take a fever and die on me," he muttered.

"Your animals have ruined the only clothing I have," she lashed out, unable to curb her tongue no matter what the consequences. "Now what am I to wear?"

"Get in," he snarled.

It was a command she had no wish to disobey. She crawled into the sleeping bag and was in instant paradise. The fur was warm and soft against her chilled skin. Even so, she knew she would not sleep a wink with this thrall-catcher beside her. She watched with suspicious eyes as he handed the candle to Bjork, untied his boots and pulled them off. He then unstrapped his sword, pulled off his trews, and crawled into the other fur-lined bag. The sword he placed on the mattress between them. Seeing her skeptical eyes on him, he said:

"I will not cross over this blade, wench." To Bjork, he said, "Blow out the candle."

So. She had won; she had bent him to her bidding. Sunniva's smile of triumph was hidden in the sudden blackness. As the pale light from the night sky shone through the trap, she could make out Bjork's humped form and Rolf's long figure on the other side of his sword. She contemplated plunging it into his throat as he slept.

"If you think to use my blade on me, abandon the thought. Bjork is a light sleeper and Helgi waits on deck by the trap. I trow you would not want to be at the mercy of either, or of my crew. Nay, Sunniva, abandon the thought. . . ."

CHAPTER 10

Sunniva wakened and was instantly alert. She was alone. And after being so certain that she would not sleep a wink, it seemed she had slept like a stone the whole night through. Now she lay rigid in the oiled sheepskin bag, her eyes shuttered. What fresh horrors would this day bring? she wondered. Looking toward the trap, she saw a gray, cold-looking square of light. Morning. Misty and gloom-filled. As she gazed at it, a sound struck her ears, a sound different from that of the ship slapping waves as it was pulled through the sea by wind in its great sail. This was rhythmical and jolting. She realized then that it was the oars striking water. Where was he taking her? she brooded, and how much longer before Raven found her?

She shrieked as she was suddenly, roughly dumped from her warm cocoon onto the mattress. Bjork grinned down at her.

"Your master says to come, wench." His pale eyes moved over her naked body, still warm and rosy from sleep, but he did not touch her.

As Sunniva's hands flew to cover herself, she spied beside her the garb that had been torn from her the night before. She glared up at the berserker. "I will dress first."

After he left, she hurriedly examined her clothing and found that her wrapper was still intact. The nightshirt was in shreds. Tearing two strips from it, she quickly knotted them together and belted the wrapper tightly to her body. On deck, the men sat at the oars, two on each bench, muscles straining to the limit with each great sweep of the long oars through the dark, foaming water. Seeing Rolf Gunnarsson at the helm with his berserkers, Sunniva went to him.

"You wished me, my lord Hedeby?" She met his eyes, which then flickered over the wrapper bound so closely to her body.

"Feed my men," he ordered, "and henceforward, you will be the first to rise and the last to bed. This is not Lilleby."

Bitch. This was not at all as he had seen it in his imaginings. He doubted not that there was great woe amongst her family and friends, nor did he doubt that the Solby chieftain was searching for her far and wide, but the wench herself was a disappointment to him. Why did she not scream and tremble and fall to her knees a-weeping? Why was she not terror-filled? She should be too terror-filled to lecture him about what *real* men did or did not do.

But her beautiful face was without emotion. There was only the merest tightening of her soft mouth as she turned toward the half-deck to do his bidding. He wanted to crush those rosy lips under his, bite them, crush her body to him and ravage her, but the more he abused her, the more she would think him a coward. Weak. Inwardly he raged, watching her heap the basket high with smoked fish and bread. Outwardly he showed nothing of his turmoil. Never would he let her suspect that things were not as he wished them nor let his men suspect that he had not taken her.

But it was agony. Never before had it been necessary for him to control his hunger for a woman. Always had his needs been met instantly and abundantly. A muscle jumped in his jaw beneath his golden beard; his hands bunched into fists. But nay, none must guess that his passion for her raged within him so that he could think of nothing else. He calmed himself, drew a deep breath, loosed his fists. He was still in command. No one and nothing ruled him. It was he who ruled.

Sunniva served the Vaaga chieftain and his berserkers before the others. Helgi, sullen, did not look at her whereas Bjork wet his lips and stared at her breasts. Rolf's eyes frightened her so that her hands shook; they minded her of the terrible words he had forced from her. While he had not yet claimed her, the battle was far from over. It was but a small skirmish she had won for now. She knew the Hedeby lord meant to possess her completely, body and mind. She was just as determined that he would not.

As she moved from bench to bench, serving the food and sour milk which broke the men's fast, their eyes told her they remembered yester-eve. She recognized the clod who first had caught and kissed her, but she knew not which other greedy hands and mouths had sought her. As she moved amongst them, their hands again stole up her legs and grabbed at her breasts. Always was she spinning about, ready to defend herself, but never did she see which were the culprits. She saw only their grinning faces.

Rolf, in the prow with his berserkers, looked on but

remained aloof. Sunniva realized then that, short of rape, he would not intercede. It pleased him to see her tormented. Very well—it would please her to ignore them all. She made not one word of complaint to the Vaaga lord when she returned the empty basket to the foredeck. She said only:

"Our stores are low, my lord Hedeby. There is but food for one more meal."

"The burden ship behind us is well stocked. Also, we will make landfall soon. There we will take on more supplies."

Landfall? Her heart gave a leap. What landfall, and would she be taken ashore? Perhaps she could escape or find someone there to help her. But the fact that they were taking on supplies worried her. It could mean that they were going on a long sea voyage. Rolf Gunnarsson's face was closed and Sunniva knew better than to question him.

The Landwaster lay two days at Aggersborg in Denmark. Aggersborg was one of four great Viking military camps where men about to go west-viking in England laid over to gather strength and stores for the long dangerous voyage ahead of them. As they exchanged tales and quaffed beer, they honed their weapons, oiled their leather and mended shields. Skalds sang and chanted poetry. When drink and fatigue finally took their toll, the men went to their barracks, wrapped themselves in their cloaks and slept as the embers died.

Of the Vaaga Vikings, Heller Orm was awake still. He sat on the earthen bench before the rock-lined open hearth in the middle of the room watching the smoking fire, quaffing ale, and listening to the chanting of the skald. Rolf Gunnarsson also was wakeful, drinking and glooming down his long legs into the dying flames. Orm watched his kinsman with guarded eyes. The mood upon his cousin was as black now as it had been when first they came to Aggersborg. The merriment had not touched him.

"What is't, kinsman, that makes you so glum? You own the most beauteous wench in Norway's land or any other, and we will surely see battle and take booty in the next few days. What more could you want?"

"To be left alone," Rolf said, and gave Orm a stare filled with venom. He owned the bitch, ay, but the fact that he had not yet possessed her rankled him mercilessly.

"Ay," muttered the other, draining his horn. He wrapped his cloak about him, stretched out on the bench and closed his eyes. To hell with the bastard.

The Hedeby lord continued to gaze at the fire, the rage that was forever simmering in his blood now ready to erupt in a gout of fury. He was angry with everything and everyone this night. With his men who, for these two days his ship was being repaired and taking on supplies, had swilled beer as fast as their gullets would take it. With Heller Orm, who annoyed him increasingly as the years went on. With the mother who had put him out to die by exposure. With the stepmother he himself had slain. More and more, all of those things set his blood to boiling when he thought on them, and more and more he thought on them. Most of all, his black wrath centered on Sunniva Mellby.

For five years he had planned on having her, never doubting that she would be given to him. He had even divorced his wife abruptly at a feast one night when he learned the wench had come of an age to wed. And then she had spurned him, and her father had nothing but scorn for the Gunnarssons of Hedeby. Now, even though the bitch was his possession, she still was not his, for he had yielded to her damned importuning. By the gods, never had he given in to a man before, let alone a woman, yet he had yielded to her. But the more he brooded on it, the more he saw that it was his own wisdom he was heeding, not anything the bitch had said. His passion for her must not be allowed to overwhelm him. If he became weak in that respect, other weaknesses could follow. He smiled. Ay, this was but one more test of his great strength. He would have her, but in his own good time.

Sunniva had been chained below-deck while the men of the Landwaster were ashore. The whole first day they were gone, she had struggled until her fingers bled to free herself. She could not. The heavy chain, attached to the band on her ankle, was fastened at the other end to a great rusty ring imbedded in an oak beam supporting the deck above. She realized finally that she must remain exactly where Rolf Gunnarsson had left her. It was heartbreaking and disgusting and infuriating, but things might have been even worse.

She had a sleeping bag, a mattress, a bucket. She had hard bread, smoked fish, water—and she had her dreams. No one could touch them or take them away from her, and night and day she dreamt of Raven and of her family. Raven. Where was he now and what was he thinking and doing? Had he somehow discovered it was Rolf who had taken her? But was he headed for the Northland while Rolf carried her south? That worried her. So much time would be wasted.

And her parents. Well could she imagine her father's wrath and her mother's grief. Doubtless her father had a large band searching for her, too. She imagined he would command the land search while Raven roamed the seas for her. Time and again when her spirits wanted to sink, she would think of him and of that moment when she would spy the blood-red sail of Odin's Raven on the horizon. And then her sun would rise again. Ay, she would not stop dreaming. It was the only thing that would get her through this nightmare.

At dawn the third day, the crew returned, supplies were brought aboard, and the Landwaster set sail. Sunniva was released. She did not know where they had been nor where they were going, only that it was ever southward, ever farther away from Lilleby and Norway.

As Rolf Gunnarsson had ordered, she now rose before dawn when most everyone, excepting those at oar and sail, still slept. After a day of fetching, bailing, serving food and drink, mending clothes and turning out the sleeping bags of one hundred twenty men to air, Sunniva crawled into her own sleeping bag at night exhausted. She slept little, although the Vaaga chieftain's sword remained between them on the mattress. Always did he let her know that she was his, and each morn, as his grinning men watched, he carefully examined her.

Clenching her teeth, her face burning, Sunniva submitted to his hands moving over her, tilting up her chin, stroking her cheeks and throat and bared forearms. He liked it not when he marked the darkening effect of the sun upon her. He instructed her to keep herself covered henceforward as he would not tolerate her soft white flesh turning tough and brown.

Nights, the skald never ceased his singing and she was up ladling out the beer while the men drank and told bawdy stories. She feared the nights most of all. She feared Rolf would take her in his drunkenness, or his men would and he would know nothing of it until it was too late.

She marked the days as they passed, scratching

with her fingernails on a bit of soft wood. When two weeks had passed from their last landfall, she heard the shout that land was near. Seeing the mist on the horizon, she wondered if they had reached their destination—or was it just another stop to take on supplies? If that were so, she was sure to be chained below deck again so none would see her.

She realized then that they were nearing land for another reason. The Landwaster was about to attack! The berserkers bawled for her to fetch them beer. She hesitated, for they had drunk the whole night long.

"Wench, make haste!" Rolf shoved her toward the half-deck where the kegs were. "Give them all they require."

"Ay, my lord."

She decided it was a good idea at that. If the two were drunk enough, perhaps they would be slain in the attack. She dipped out a horn for each of them and they gulped it down as the others in the crew donned leather helms, corselets and hauberks of chain-mail. As she dipped their horns in again and again, she began to hear the boom of surf and smell the aromas of the countryside—rich earth, the strong odor of sheep, even cooking smells.

It brought her such strong memories of home that tears stung her eyes. Perhaps after the berserkers had drunk their fill, she could creep below deck and in the excitement, be forgotten. When they landed, perhaps she could escape while the fighting was going on. She was so desperate to get away from Rolf and his men that even the unknown, dangerous as it might be, was preferable.

But the berserkers continued to drink. While the others were gathering and testing their weapons—spears, javelins, lances, axes and double-edged swords—Helgi and Bjork began to tear off their clothing and foam at the mouth. Sunniva stared at them, astonished.

"Keep their horns filled," Rolf growled from behind her.

"Ay, my lord."

Sunniva hastened to do his bidding, marking that now the two giants trembled so that most of the brew spilled onto their naked chests rather than down their throats. She recoiled as they snatched up their shields, which had been mounted on the sides of the Landwaster, and began gnawing the rims. Their eyes rolled in their heads and they growled and roared like animals. Their faces grew purple and swollen.

She minded then what Raven had told her of berserkers: Their battle-madness gave them the strength of angry aurochs, strength that no ordinary man could withstand, and when it was upon them, neither fire nor weapons could injure their skin. They were known to change into animal shapes. It was horrifying. She was brooding over the prospect when the ship was beached and Rolf and his howling berserkers leapt over the sides. The crew scrambled over next, followed by the skald chanting his weapon song in a loud voice. The lur horn was sounded.

Sunniva clung to the mast. Those poor folk in the village were going to die; there was no escape for them. Nor would there be any for her. She had not been left alone on the Landwaster. Fully one third of the crew remained aboard, doubtless to guard it from any reprisals. It seemed as though no time at all had passed before they all returned, howling still and carrying chests filled with their booty. After the chests were stowed aboard the burden ship, the two vessels once more headed south, leaving the village in flames behind them.

Sunniva was sickened to the heart, but the crew was filled with great merriment. They lay sprawled about the deck still in their chain-mail, laughing, jesting, waving their bloody weapons, and calling to her for food and drink. Rolf Gunnarsson grabbed her arm.

"Methinks you are too slow and far too sullen for a celebration such as this, thrall. Aegir and Ran have been good to us. We have fair booty and none slain or wounded."

Sunniva's eyes burned with her anger. Never had Raven nor her father used the sea-gods' help to burn, kill and plunder. "Methinks you are a band of murderers and robbers," she said.

In front of them all, she dashed a horn of beer in Rolf's face. He struck her hard, the impact of his huge hand on her cheek sending her reeling. She fell to the deck, and for long moments it seemed as if all the stars in the heavens were exploding within her head. She felt herself lifted to her feet by his one hand grasping the front of her wadmal wrapper. The next instant, it spanned her throat.

"What said you, wench?" His fingers tightened and his eyes held a menacing blue flame.

He was going to slay her and Sunniva did not care. She was not afraid to die. It was living without Raven that frightened her so. She thought of him and her folk then, of how they would be grieving and mourning for her, waiting to have her back once more. And how awful if the red sail should appear on the horizon just as she drew her last breath! She must rein in her temper and let him think he had conquered her.

"What said you, my thrall?" Rolf insisted, giving her a shake. "I would hear it." He compressed her throat until she gasped and then parted her clothing and kissed her breasts before them all. There was a low growl of approval from his men. "I am waiting. . . ."

Sunniva could not hide the hatred burning in her eyes. Never had she hated anyone as much as she hated him. She looked down at the deck. "I—exist for your pleasure, my lord Hedeby."

"Look at me and say it," he rasped, his hands crushing her arms as though they were in a vise.

"I exist for your pleasure." And for the pleasure of pushing a dagger through your heart, she thought, her face flaming.

"Continue."

"I am yours. I—will obey you."

Rolf was satisfied, though he marked that the bitch wanted to slay him. He nodded. "Continue serving my men, and no scowls nor spills, hear you?"

"Ay." She decided to blunt the dagger before she used it on him.

"See that you serve my berserkers most tenderly after they have recovered from battle."

Following his gaze, Sunniva marked for the first time that Helgi and Bjork sat in the prow sagging against the stone anchor. They were pale and they shook and trembled without cease. How long, she wondered, would it take them to return to their normal repulsive state?

"Hear you, wench?"

"Ay, my lord Hedeby," Sunniva answered softly.

But she was pondering what she had seen. After battle, the two giants were weak as babes. It seemed a goodly thing to remember. . . .

CHAPTER 11

THE RAID THAT SO UPSET SUNNIVA WAS BUT THE FIRST of many. Daily now the men of the Landwaster sharpened their weapons and donned their battle gear. As the skald chanted his weapon song and sang of the Hedeby lord's earlier victories, the berserkers foamed and gnashed their teeth and grew frenzied. Sunniva wanted to flee to the lower deck and pull shut the trap over her head, but she was made to wait upon them and see that they had their fill of beer. And then when their battle-madness was ended, no matter what the hour of the day or night, it was she who brought them food and water and bathed the sweat and foam from their naked, weakened bodies.

On that day when booty overflowed from the burden ship onto the deck of the Landwaster itself, Rolf Gunnarsson found his luck changing. Sunniva did not know what land it was he attempted to ravage next, but the arrow had gone out and its defenders were waiting for him. This time there was no booty and he left dead behind. Seeing the injured brought aboard, Sunniva hardened her heart. She turned her back on them as they lay atop their sleeping bags on deck.

She went about her chores, serving meals, mending clothes, bailing, forever bailing, but eventually their groans drew her to them. It was not in her to be cruel, and when she marked that little was being done for them, she grew indignant. In the Solby Convent, there had been medicinal herbs at hand and clean cloths and water could be boiled, but here— what was here but the ever-moaning sea and wind? She sought the chieftain.

"Why is so little being done to help your wounded?" she demanded.

He answered stiffly, "The one who could treat them lies dead in the Hebrides."

"Then I will treat them," Sunniva said.

Rolf Gunnarsson laughed, but his eyes narrowed. Nothing this wench did would surprise him any longer. He shrugged.

"Do as you wish, but the rest of your work you will do also."

Sunniva was about to ask who had done the chores before she was forced to do them. Seeing his ever-angry eyes, she bit her lip instead and went to the men.

Rolf's resentment and hunger for her burned as strongly as ever. These past days, he had fought long and fiercely and after a man battled, he needed a woman. He deserved a woman. He was easy in his heart on that account and in no wise did he consider himself weak because of his hunger. Nay. But she would, if he took her against her will. Night after night, she lay on the other side of his sword, this woman whose beauty smote him in the gut every time he looked on her. Night after night he wrestled with himself.

Why did it matter to him if she thought him weak? He did not know. He knew only that he abhorred the thought. It filled him with more heat than when he dwelt on her lusting. There were none as strong as he or as brave as he, and by the Hammer, the wench would know it. She would know it soon, or he would take her, no matter.

He watched as Sunniva moved from man to man, five in all, kneeling beside them, her fingers gently testing, pressing the flesh about their wounds, feeling their foreheads. When she rose, the pink was gone from her cheeks. She was grave-eyed as she faced him.

"Know you that they are very ill?"

"'Tis plain to see," he growled.

"What exactly is being done for them?"

Rolf called to a crewman at the oars. "Poul, talk with this wench and show her the medicines." He strode away then.

Sunniva was not surprised that the Hedeby lord's interest in a man vanished once his usefulness was ended. Doubtless he would have preferred leaving the five on the battlefield, except their mates would have taken that greatly amiss. She had seen that he craved their good will. She turned to the crewman.

"Have you been tending these men?" she asked.

"Some."

"What mean you, some?" Her anger flared. "'Twould seem as if you have done naught at all for them!"

He looked at her with insolent eyes. "You are but a woman, and a thrall at that. Mind how you speak to your betters."

When he made to touch her breast, Sunniva caught his thumb, lightning-swift, and bent it backwards.

"I would just as soon break it as look at you, scut," she hissed. "Now, where be the medicines? Or will your mates see that a woman, a thrall at that, has bested you? Which will it be, scut? Quickly!" She applied more pressure.

"On the half-deck," he gasped. "To the right of the bread in a—a cask. . . ." She released him. "Thrice-cursed bitch," he muttered, but she was already moving toward the half-deck.

The cask was there, a goodly-sized pinewood cask bound with worked silver. Sunniva opened it and rapidly sorted through its contents, sniffing, some-times tasting what was in the various pots and jars and pouches. Salsify, swallow-wort, lyngwort, fox fat and goose grease, wild comfrey, horseradish, nettles —it was a good collection. She had seen them all before, both at Lilleby and at the convent. She had even used some of them with success, but here it was so different. And here there was no boiling water.

She carried the cask back to where the wounded lay, fetched her torn nightshirt and a bucket of seawater. As she knelt beside the most severely injured of the men, she trembled at the undertaking that lay before her. Eyes closed, she whispered: *O, holy Jesu, and thee, Aegir, god of the sea and your good wife, Ran. These be your men. Help me to heal them.*

She busked herself, shutting her mind to all defeat in the warrior-way, telling herself that she could do this thing and she would do it. She had to; there was none other. Her face impassive, all of her horror and fear turned to steely resolve, Sunniva tore her night-shirt into strips, dipped one into the seawater, and began. As the sun traveled across the sky, she dipped, wrung, wiped away dried blood and pus, stanched the gouts of blood, smeared the ointments, packed the wounds with the healing herbs, and finally placed on them dry cloths.

For two days and nights, Sunniva nursed the men in addition to her other chores. But the poison had been in them too long. Four died. The fifth hung on, the very one whose hunger for her had nearly caused her to be raped. She nonetheless watched over him, bathing and comforting him, watching fearfully as the red swelling spread to his limbs. In the convent, the holy sisters would have long since used leeches, but of leeches Sunniva had none. She went to Rolf Gunnarsson, tired and disheartened by her failure to save his men.

"Svip needs to be bled, my lord," she said.

Rolf gazed long at her white face and the dark smudges beneath her eyes.

"You would have my dagger?"

"You yourself may prick his veins. Otherwise he will die."

"Know you, Sunniva, that he will die anyway. All were doomed to die before ever you started. They were death-fated."

"Death-fated?" She gave a bitter laugh. "'Twould seem an easy way to avoid caring for them. Will you bleed him or not, sire?"

Seeing that his men watched with curious eyes, Rolf stalked to his fallen warrior and touched dagger point to those swollen fiery places Sunniva indicated. Svip's life's blood gushed out. She quickly bathed it away, sealing the pricks with a mixture of ointment and herbs. She then gave him a sleepy-drink of lyngwort. He smiled up at her through drowsy, pain-glazed eyes.

"Be you Freya, mistress?" he whispered.

"Ay," Sunniva answered, thinking to please him. Surely he was dying, thinking she was a goddess.

"Methinks I see Valhalla in the distance, lady."

"I trow you do, Svip. You are as brave a warrior as any."

"Ay, 'tis Valhalla. . . ." Svip's voice was so weak Sunniva could scarce hear it. "'Tis just the way I heard 'twould be. Bright and shining and the ceiling adorned with spears and shields . . . armor on the walls. . . ."

"Ay, Svip, so I have heard." She took his hand.

The Viking smiled, his eyes on some distant point far beyond her head. "The Valkyries are coming for me, Freya."

"Are they bearing food and drink?"

"Ay. . . ."

Sunniva squeezed his hand. "They will take good care of you, Svip."

Suddenly he went rigid, his death-filled eyes full of fright. "My lady, be we still at sea?"

"Ay."

"Holy Thor," he muttered, "I must have gold before I go." He tried to sit up but could not. "In my pocket—a gold coin," he gasped. "Quickly . . ."

His urgency moved Sunniva to search frantically in the pocket of his trews. She had just remembered, if he did not cross Ran's palm with gold, the sea-goddess would not let him into Valhalla. Ah, there, there 'twas! She had found it! Quickly she pressed it in his cold palm and closed his pale fingers around it.

"You have your gold, Svip," she murmured as he closed his eyes for the last time. "Go in gladness. . . ."

She watched his leavetaking, knowing that after the maidens had plied him with food and drink, then would he go directly to battle. How strange it all seemed, but thus was the way of it. Daily would he fight, kill, maim, and be killed, just as he had on earth. Nightly would he awaken, whole and un-scathed, and return to a hero's welcome in the Val Hall. How strange it was. . . .

* * *

After Svip had drawn his last breath, he was sewn into his sleeping bag along with his dagger and axe and sunk beneath the waves. None seemed to mourn him or the others who had gone on before him. It was as though they had never existed, Sunniva brooded, except for the five empty places on the rowers' benches, and except in her own memories of nursing them day and night between her other chores, comforting them, being with them when they died. . . . She did not know those same memories were burned deep in the mind of the Vaaga chieftain.

That day when Heller Orm had come to him and admitted, shamefaced, that Sunniva Mellby had escaped from him, Rolf Gunnarsson had known she possessed more than remarkable beauty. She was clever and she was bold. And since he had borne her off by the stronghand, he had marked her bravery and her stoicism as well. But her taking command of his wounded was a different matter entirely. She had bested one of his warriors to do it, and had then nursed, to the end, his dying men, one of whom she had every reason to despise. Never had he known such a woman before and it had started him thinking. . . .

He would wed her after all. He could make better use of her as a wife than as a slave. There were places other than his own bed where such a woman could be used. There were other beds. For certain she would be an asset at court where highly placed men would see her and lust after her. He smiled. Ay, that beautiful body of hers was going to gain him more power and riches than he had already.

There was revelry aboard the Landwaster. The night air was filled with song as the skald chanted a saga of old. The men cheered, booed, chanted along or were rapt, silent. The beer flowed freely. Not until all were drunken and could hold no more brew was Sunniva allowed to retire. The moon rode high as she stepped over Bjork, lying on deck by the trap, to descend to the lower deck. Helgi, too, she had to step over, lying as he was at the foot of the mattress like some huge shaggy dog. The master of Hedeby had turned in long since and lay motionless in his sleeping bag. Sunniva hoped that he slept. She had never ceased to fear him, even though the sword still lay between them at night.

She wiped her ever-wet feet on those bits of wadmal still remaining from her nightshirt, and prepared to crawl into the warm welcoming fur of her sleeping bag.

"Hold, Sunniva . . ."

Sunniva stiffened. Why was he not sleeping?

"Ay, my lord?"

"I would have you sleep in my bag with me tonight."

Her eyes flew to the gleaming blade between them. Her heart hammered. "Even though the sword be there, sire?"

"The sword be damned." Rolf removed it, put it on the other side of him. "Take that thing off and get in." When she hesitated, his fingers closed on her wrist. "In, I said, and face me."

Sunniva obeyed. He could break her bones if he had a mind to, and it would not help her cause to be maimed. She untied her wrapper and slid into the double sleeping bag beside him. Her body turned to ice as her nipples brushed his hard furred chest, and his arms and legs went about her.

"I have naught but scathe for you," she muttered.

For long moments he explored her mouth greedily, his hands roaming the smooth skin of her back and buttocks. He craved to fill her with himself, but he would not. And not because of the scathe she might think or feel for him; he cared nothing for her damned scathe. Nay, he would prove to her, as he had to himself, that he was not under her spell. He was Thor-Rolf Gunnarsson, beloved of Thor, king of the Vaagaland, lord of Hedeby, and friend and confidant of kings. He was the future king of Maun. He was not in thrall to any wench, no matter how bewitching.

His arms tightened about her soft body, punishing, bruising her. He tasted blood in his mouth and did not know if it were from her lips or his own. She made no sound. When he released her and held her by his side, both of them unmoving, she still made no sound. When he had command of his breathing and his voice, he spoke:

"Know you, wench, that I am not like other men. I do not spill my seed when I but cast my eyes in your direction. 'Tis spilt when I desire to spill it and that time is not now. That I have not claimed you is my choice, 'tis not of your doing." When she made no answer, he angrily turned her face to his. "I would have you act as though you heard me, woman."

"Ay, my lord, I hear you." Sunniva's thoughts had been on that day when they reached land and she would slay him and flee.

"I tire of your poor manners. 'Tis time you mended them."

"Ay, my lord."

"And henceforward, you will share this sleeping bag with me."

Feeling her shiver, his fury leapt anew. Double damn the witch! Any other woman would have surrendered herself to him willingly long ago. He yearned to smash her, choke her, shove himself into her and gore her 'til she screamed for mercy, but because he craved it so deeply, he steeled himself against it. Nay, he would not yield to such pleasure. He was strong.

"Turn your back to me," he muttered. When she obeyed, he pulled her body close, clasping a breast in each hand. "You are mine, Sunniva. Never doubt it."

"Ay, sire." If such lies lulled him, then she would lie.

"Know you, woman, I have decided we will wed when we reach Maun."

Wed? The word seemed to explode within her head. And Maun was their destination? They had come so far? Both thoughts took her breath and sent her spinning down into a dark tunnel of despair. She remembered then that she must answer him or he would be more wroth than he was already.

"If it pleases you, my lord."

He kneaded her breasts, his shaft pressed between her buttocks. He was not hurting her, not harming her, and she was certain now he would not rape her, but she could not shake free of the darkness into which his words had plunged her. As his thrall, she might have received help and support in fleeing him. Not all folk took kindly to thrall-catchers or to the idea of thralldom. But as the wife of a powerful Viking chieftain, a king, who would dare help her? More likely, they would return her to him if she fled. And she could not legally separate from him unless she declared her reasons for doing so before the Assembly—the Thing.

But she must not dwell on these things. Raven would be coming. She knew it as she knew that day followed night, and it was her job to be unwed and awaiting him when he arrived; her job to forestall or destroy any plans Rolf Gunnarsson might make. If he thought for one instant that he had but to say, "I wed thee, woman," before witnesses to make her his, he was wrong.

She would insist on a priest, just as her father had for her wedding to Raven. And if no priest lived on Maun, why then there would be no drinking of the wedding ale, it was as simple as that. Even if there were a priest, he could not force her lips to say she would take him for her wedded husband. She would bite his fingers off if he tried it!

"I know what you are thinking, wench. You are thinking Trondsson will find you." Rolf stroked her breasts, her belly, now his long fingers found the deep crevasse between her thighs. She gasped, tried to clamp them together, but there was no escape. He laughed and his hot breath fanned the back of her neck. "Well might he find you, Sunniva, but never will he have you. I will slay Raven Trondsson as surely as I slew Eirik Paalsson."

CHAPTER 12

SUNNIVA PRAYED SHE HAD FALLEN ASLEEP AND WAS dreaming. Once more she dug her nails into her palms. But it was no dream. She had heard the lord of Hedeby aright. He had slain Eirik Paalsson. The Bergviner had been tall and strong and comely and he had wanted sons. And she had hated him and actually rejoiced when he had disappeared. Now he lay dead. Murdered. Because of her. And Raven, too, was to be slain. It was almost more than she could bear.

Oh, why did Rolf Gunnarsson crave her so? Surely such a man could have any woman he wanted, so why must it be she with whom he was obsessed? Was it because she had refused him and he wanted that which he could not have? Did he want to show his power that way?

Sunniva lay unmoving, afraid to blink or swallow or breathe. She stared into the blackness wide-eyed until she heard the chieftain's deep, steady breathing, felt his hands relax and no longer clasp her. He slept, but his arms were about her still. She knew she must stay there, pressed close to him, for the slightest sound or movement on her part could awaken him.

Despite the warmth of the bag and the heat of his body, she was chilled to the bone. All through the night her thoughts churned, a kaleidoscope of jagged black and gray—fear, horror, grief, guilt, hatred. The man was a monster. A thrall-catcher, a woman-stealer and a man-slayer. Yet he was an honored chieftain in Norway's land because he was great in battle. How could she, a mere maid, prevent him from wedding her, and how could she save Raven from death at his hands?

She knew the first step. One she had vowed over and over to take, but had failed. Obey him. Not anger him. But it was impossible, she thought, catching back a sob that might have wakened him. But then, Raven had taught her that nothing was impossible. A warrior did whatever had to be done. Once again, Sunniva shut her mind to despair and dwelt on the thought of her beloved. He was dark and shining, sun a-glitter on his black hair and chain-mail, his banner raised high above the red sail of *Odin's Raven*. Her heart thrilled to the picture, it was so real. He would come for her soon, she knew he would. Until then, she must do whatever had to be done to keep herself safe for him.

All of Sunniva's senses were suddenly alerted. Something was different, but what? Rolf had slept long and long, his breathing deep and easy. Helgi was curled at the foot of the mattress still, but as she raised her head cautiously to gaze at him, he rose and ascended to the deck on silent feet. Hearing clearly his low voice mingled with Bjork's, she realized finally what the change was. The silence. She could hear him because all was silent. The oars were at rest and no wind buffeted their sail. The sea was no longer rushing past the hull, a sound that was always close to her head as she lay on the mattress.

Even as she pondered what it meant, Rolf stirred and was instantly awake. Ignoring Sunniva, he crawled from the sleeping bag and hurriedly dressed. Sunniva waited until he had gone on deck before she donned her wrapper. She, too, went on deck then and found it aswirl with mist.

"Is't Maun?" she asked Heller Orm.

"Ay." He paid her no further heed, nor did the others.

When the mist chanced to thin, Sunniva saw that the Landwaster was anchored in a bay with a ramp of wooden slats joining it to the shore. Already the men were unloading the booty from their strikes in addition to the remainder of their food and drink. Tied alongside them was their burden-ship. It, too, was being unloaded and the contents transferred to waiting carts and wagons. When it began to rain, Sunniva turned to run below deck, but Rolf called to her:

"Come, wench, we are home." He started down the ramp.

"Ay, my lord."

The lord of Hedeby, flanked by his berserkers, strode from the beach toward the village. Sunniva silently followed behind, catching only ghostly glimpses of fields and dwellings as the chieftain was greeted on all sides by his men who clashed their spears on their shields. Sunniva felt their eyes on her, and no wonder. She looked like a troll-woman, her long pale hair dirty and matted and her filthy wrapper hanging in shreds. She looked straight ahead, her chin high and her back straight. She heard the sounds of sheep and cattle, heard women calling to one another. Thank Thor and Jesu, there were women here. . . .

They came to a great stone building with a circular tower, its large oaken doors banded in iron. The berserkers opened the doors and the four of them entered. Sunniva stared. They were in a hall which minded her much of the great hall at Lilleby, except here the ceilings were high and vaulted. There were benches along the walls, and a high seat for the master of the house. Three walls were hung with rich tapestries, while the other held overlapping shields. There were two doors, just as there were at Lilleby— one for men, one for women—and both were covered with ironwork and runes.

But there the resemblance ended. At Lilleby, all was bright and shining and clean-smelling. Thorhalla, for that was the name above the high seat, had about it a look of gloom and darkness, and it smelled of sour beer and mold. In the shafts of pale, misty light that pierced the slit windows, Sunniva marked that the bosswork on the shields was dingy and that dust lay thick everywhere. Cobwebs hung from the walls and torches, and there was soiled, ill-smelling straw beneath their feet.

A lump rose in her throat as she was minded of her mother and father, of the wonderful, clean, comfortable home they had given her and the good care they had lavished on her. She saw now that she had never truly appreciated it. O, how thankless she had been. . . . She turned as a woman spoke from behind them, one who had approached them on cat feet.

"Welcome back to Ballageay, my lord Hedeby." Her words had a foreign accent and there was no welcome in her green eyes, only hostility.

Sunniva marked that she was tall and slender, the

way a forest creature was slender, all wiry tendons and taut muscles beneath its glossy coat. Her wild mane of hair was a burnished dark red, a color Sunniva had never seen before, and while she was not pretty, she was strikingly handsome. Sunniva gazed at her admiringly—at the lovely long neck, high cheekbones, eyes up-tilted at the outer corners, short straight nose, and mouth that looked as though it never laughed—or cried. She wore leather leggings bound to her long legs and a green tunic of coarse wadmal. Sunniva instantly coveted her clothing.

Rolf Gunnarsson did not return her greeting. His eyes moved over her coldly, as though she were something he might step on.

"There will be feasting tonight," he said. "See to it."

"Ay, my lord."

"This is your new mistress—we are to be wed. See that she has suitable quarters and attend to her bathing and fresh garments."

"Ay, my lord."

Sunniva was ashamed to meet the woman's eyes. She needed none to attend her once she knew where things were. She would tell her when they were alone.

"Send word to Brother Asmund that we require his presence at the celebration tonight."

"Brother Asmund left two weeks since for Rushen."

"Rushen?" The chieftain's handsome face remained impassive but for a slight darkening of hue.

"An old friend of his in the Abbey there lay dying. He left to be with him."

Sunniva could not have been more pleased. All she needed was time. Perhaps this would give it to her.

Rolf turned to Helgi. "Send someone to fetch him. Instantly."

"Ay, sire." Helgi left at a run.

The Vaaga chieftain and his other berserker departed then, leaving Sunniva and the stranger-woman to gaze at each other.

"You need only show me where I am to sleep," Sunniva murmured. "You need not wait on me."

The green eyes swept over her with disdain. "'Twas never my intention to wait on you."

When the woman strode off ahead of her, Sunniva knew it was a deer she resembled, with that gleaming red-brown hair and those long graceful legs. They mounted narrow stone steps to a second floor where they trod a long dark passageway filled with doors. Behind one of the doors was the room Sunniva was to use. Her eyes widened. It could have been her small cell at the convent: a cot, a straw mattress, a little table with a candle on it, a stool, a slit of a window sliced in the stone, and—how wonderful!—a bar on the door. She felt those green eyes, chilly as an ice cave, studying her.

"'Tis wonderful," Sunniva said. "I am grateful."

The other gave a snort. Did this wench expect to be believed? While it was odd that she wore rags and had no chest of clothes with her, any who looked on her could see that she was high-born and used to the finest of everything.

"If you will but show me where the water is for bathing," Sunniva said, "I will fetch it, and if any can spare some clothing . . ." Her eyes went wistfully to the woman's handsome leggings and tunic.

"You have naught at all?" she asked suspiciously.

"Nay." How Sunniva wished for a spark of warmth in that cool gaze. "Nor have I shoes. . . ."

She lifted her foot for the other to see. In the thick

silence, the slave band gleamed on her ankle. The woman stared.

"You are a thrall . . . ?"

Sunniva was shamed. Her face reddened. "Ay."

Long and long the other gazed at her. Finally, she sat down on the stool and stripped off one legging. On her ankle was a thick bronze band. She drew the legging back on.

"It seems we are sisters," she said, low, meeting Sunniva's astonished eyes. "I am Calla macLir." She rose and offered her hand.

Sunniva grasped it, more grateful than she could say. "I am Sunniva Mellby." Calla's eyes minded her not of an ice cavern now, but of sunlight striking a forest glade.

"These Vikings, they are your people?" Calla asked.

Sunniva shook her head. "I come from Norway's land as do they, but nay, these are not my people. I knew naught of these men before I was seized."

Calla had seen that Sunniva's hands were rough and workworn and her feet bruised and calloused. And no shoes. It did not surprise her that Rolf Gunnarsson would ill-treat such a tender maid from his own land, but it was all to her own advantage. At last she had found the ally she yearned for. But she would say nothing of it just yet. She must tread carefully and be certain. She had meant to make Sunniva fetch her own water from the stream and bathe in it cold. Now they were comrades.

"I will heat water and bring it to you. I will fetch all that you need."

"Thanks for that." Once more Sunniva's eyes went longingly to Calla's clothing. "Think you that you could find me leggings like yours? And another such tunic?"

"Methinks Hedeby would not approve."

Sunniva could not hide her disappointment. "You wear them."

"'Tis all I have ever worn. Besides, you he intends to wed."

Sunniva nearly shouted that she would never wed the bastard; she was going to flee the first chance she got. But caution made her hold her tongue. Perhaps Calla could not keep a secret.

"You are spent," Calla said. "Rest yourself while I fetch the things. I will return soon."

From the moment Raven left Solby Convent, his search for Sunniva was begun. His men he sent fanning out over the countryside to knock on doors and ask those in the fields if they had seen anything amiss. Raven himself and Ulf had made haste back to Lilleby where all awaited the bride and the beginnings of a happy day. Instead there was grief and weeping amongst the women and rage amongst the men when they heard of the fair young maid borne off by the stronghand by man-slayers. It was a horrifying thing to contemplate.

The serving-men of both Arn Mellby and Raven Trondsson had been sent out immediately with pikes and shields to scour the land. Shortly after, the menfolk of the entire Solby Valley began searching the woods and dales far and near, asking all they came upon if they had seen the maid and her abductors, but none had. Betimes, Raven and Ulf had sailed far north to the Vaagaland, sensing that Rolf Gunnarsson was the culprit. Nothing came of it. None had seen him for months and word was that he was in the Baltic. On their way back down the coast, they made a search of every river and fjord and hailed every vessel they met for questioning, with no results.

Two weeks from the morn Sunniva was stolen, Raven stood at the prow of his ship, his taut face and burning eyes showing his rage and frustration.

"In the name of Odin, where is she, Ulf? Who has her and where has he taken her?"

Ulf shook his tawny head. "I know not which way to turn. She seems to have vanished without trace."

"I keep thinking of Gunnarsson," Raven muttered.

"As do I, even though all say he is gone a-viking to the east."

Raven scowled at the setting sun. "'Twould be the smart thing to say to throw any off his trail. I keep thinking of the lout saying 'my lord.'"

"Remember you, my father turned down three others with titles."

"All were gentlemen and law-abiding. Nay, those three did not do this thing. More and more this stinks of Gunnarsson."

Ulf nodded, his face dark with worry and anger. "So where did he take her if not Hedeby? He has a place in Italy, one in Constantinople, three or four strongholds on Maun. The gods alone know where all else . . ."

Raven raked his hands through his flying black hair and then turned and shouted to his steersman: "Turn her southward. We are going to Aggersborg."

"Mayhap 'tis what we should have done in the beginning."

"What we did seemed right at the time."

"Ay. Never would I have believed she could vanish so completely."

"Nor I," Raven said glumly. "I expected to find her long before this."

"Come, man," Ulf pushed him back toward the half-deck where the kegs were stored. "Let us have some mead to keep up our spirits. I wager that if the

163

Landwaster has visited Aggersborg, we will hear of it. And if the bastard has Sunniva, we will hear of that, too. I trow 'tis too good a secret for some to keep.''

Great was the feasting on Sunniva's first night at Ballageay. It was not like those feasts at Lilleby where the food was good and plentiful and ranged from ox, whale, and grouse, to apples, nuts, and honey. At Lilleby, the ladies dressed in their best gowns and jewelry, children tumbled about laughing and playing and the men, no matter how many kegs were broached, never lost their manners—nor their dinners—to drink.

At Thorhalla, all was different. The great hall was as filthy as ever, and in the dim light of smoking torches, Sunniva saw that no woman other than herself was at table. The Celt women were there only as serving-wenches and the guests were warriors and chieftains from other Viking settlements. When Sunniva saw that there was more drink than food— food that was nothing but everyday bread and cheese and smoked fish and sour milk—and when she saw that weapons were not left in the foreroom, but were allowed at the table, she grew fearful.

Rolf sat in the high seat at the bench facing north, his berserkers behind him with their swords drawn. He called for the skalds to chant, and as their voices rose in song, the beer flowed freely. The laughter, talk and singing, running all together with the clashing of cups and drinking horns, grew so deafening it was like the surf breaking over their heads.

Sunniva could not hear herself think, but then she decided it was just as well, for her thoughts were frightful ones. These men were wilder and more unruly than any she had ever seen. They leered at her with hot eyes and vied for her attention like so many silly loons, springing about, cracking jokes, somersaulting, some even standing on their heads, their legs waving in the air. Fools.

Sunniva was bathed and perfumed, and she wore a deep-blue kirtle that complimented her eyes. Her freshly washed hair tumbled over her breasts like a golden cloak to below her waist. Even so, Rolf Gunnarsson rarely looked at her, although he had escorted her to the south bench facing him, a seat of honor. He had commanded her to smile, but she was to say nothing to anyone. The last part was easy. There was no one to whom she wanted to speak, but it was impossible to make herself smile with lips that had long since gone stiff. Now the drinking was growing heavy and there was jostling and quarreling as the men gathered about her, grinning, staring at her. She was becoming frightened and wished Rolf were by her side instead of across the table.

"My lord Hedeby," Sunniva raised her voice, "may I please go to my chamber?"

Rolf did not hear; he was deep in talk with another. Now a black-haired chieftain, who had been staring at Sunniva ever since the meal began, shouted to him above the clamor:

"Who is this beauty, Gunnarsson?"

"My thrall," Rolf answered brusquely, "but not for long, Kol. I mean to wed her. The priest is being summoned and I was about to make known the news. Poul, open more kegs!"

Suddenly, Haftor Kol leapt onto the table, knocking trenchers and forks every which way. He was a big man, and his black hair was so long that he wore it fastened under his sword belt. His face was red with drink and his black eyes glittered.

"I declare myself divorced from Idris, my wife," he bawled. "You are a witness, Heller Orm, and you three—Poul, Gardar and Naakkve. Witness this, I am divorced!" He raised a fist to heaven and spat onto the unclean straw on the floor of Thorhalla. "I claim this wench for my wife." He reached down, seized Sunniva's arm and jerked her to her feet.

Too astonished at first to protest, Sunniva could only gape at him. This could not be real; it could not be happening. Men did not behave this way. She struggled then, for his fingers were bruising her arm. She cried, "Nay, you pig!" Her free hand cracked against his hairy cheek as Rolf jumped up.

"Damn you, Kol, she is my banded thrall. I own her."

"Your band be damned, Gunnarsson, my hand is on her now. I claim her." He insolently tossed a pouch down onto Rolf's trencher. "I trow you will not turn down gold for the wench. Hror, Kaapi, get her!"

Two strange giants appeared on either side of Sunniva. She screamed as one lifted her into his arms and bore her toward the men's door. The other, brandishing sword and ax, followed. But Bjork and Helgi blocked their way. Rolf joined them. The air rang with cries and curses and the clang of blade on blade. As quickly as it began, the fracas was ended, and Rolf Gunnarsson's long arm was about Sunniva's waist. She watched numbly as Haftor Kol and his berserkers were carried from the great hall on shields taken from the wall. All bled from many wounds.

"Now then, drink," Rolf called out to the rest of his guests, "for the evening is barely begun. I trow the rest of you are not as ill-mannered as yon Kol. Know you, he lives only because I chose not to kill him this night. You, skalds, we would hear more of your songs, and you wenches, bring more food and drink." He laughed, seeing that one guest was bearing off a screaming serving-wench. "Ay, 'tis all right, man. Take her, but bring her back when you are through and share her. 'Tis what these Celt wenches are for, after all. But be warned, all of you"—he stroked Sunniva's pale cheek—"this wench is mine. For any who have not yet heard, she is my banded thrall, soon to be my wife. The next man who touches her will lie in the dead straw this night."

CHAPTER 13

SUNNIVA WAS SO ACCUSTOMED TO RISING BEFORE dawn that it was difficult to lie abed the next morning. When the sliver of sky beyond her window turned a pearl gray, she arose, splashed water on her face, and pulled on over her chemise the dark-blue kirtle she had worn to the feast the night before. The feast. She made a face. It was the most disgusting spectacle she had ever witnessed in her entire life. All of those hairy men cavorting and prancing before her like so many silly little boys wanting attention and acting as though they had never seen a woman before.

She bristled, remembering Haftor Kol leaping onto the table to declare himself divorced—and then having the gall to claim her for himself. Her! Now she felt the full outrage which had escaped her last night, for then she had felt mostly shock and fear—and disbelief that such a thing could be happening. As she combed and braided her hair into two thick golden ropes, she remembered overhearing her parents discussing Rolf Gunnarsson's suit for her. Arn Mellby had received a waif word from the Northland that the Hedeby lord was no fit husband for her. Among other things, he had divorced his wife in a disgraceful manner.

Had he, too, leapt onto a feast table, named witnesses, and declared himself divorced? Sunniva wondered. Even worse, had he divorced the poor woman because of her? In truth, she did not want to know. She pulled on stockings, tied on the shoes Calla had brought her, and then stole through the passageway and down the narrow steps. She did not know where Rolf slept, nor if his berserkers were about. She wanted only to get out into the fresh air and away from the damp, musty-smelling gloom of his manor.

She went through the kitchen-room, dark and cold and empty, and found a back door. It creaked on its hinges as she opened it, causing several women passing by to stare at her. Sunniva smiled and greeted them. When they turned away, ignoring her, she flushed. She was not used to being ignored. She nearly marched after them to confront them, to demand to know why they were being so rude. She reminded herself then that these were conquered women, torn from their men and their families to serve Viking warriors. And she was the enemy. They did not know that she, too, had been torn from all whom she held dear.

The sun was not shining, but at least the mist was gone, blown away by wind that keened across the land. Sunniva walked slowly about Ballageay studying everything—the bay; the narrow headland rearing up to the right of it, like a hatchet with its head buried in the green sea; the red cliffs stretching south from there; the herds of cattle and flocks of brown woolly sheep grazing in hedge-rowed fields; thatched cottages settled low in the earth, each having beside it a kiln for drying corn in addition to small huts and pens for animals. And on a rise overlooking all—village, sea, fields and headland—was Rolf's great manor house. Sunniva was gazing at it when Calla came upon her.

"You seem impressed," Calla said drily.

"Never have I seen such a manor," Sunniva said.

"Ay. 'Tis splendid."

To Sunniva's eyes, Calla herself was splendid. The wind whipped her wild, dark-red hair about her face; her up-tilted eyes matched the forest-green of her tunic. Sunniva thought she had never seen a more beautiful woman but she said nothing, sensing it would embarrass her new friend. She returned her gaze to Rolf's dwelling.

"'Tis fit for a king," she murmured.

Calla's eyes glowed over her strangely. "'Twas an abbey. Vikings slew the monks and stole the treasures stored here and claimed it for themselves."

Sunniva blinked. "Mean you," she whispered, "that Rolf did that?"

Calla shook her head. The maid was a total innocent. "'Twas over two hundred years ago when Ballageay was first seized. It has been a Viking stronghold here on Ballaugh Beach ever since. They fight amongst themselves for it. Hedeby took it three years ago."

"I—did not know." Sunniva was shamed. What had her people been thinking to do such a thing? Oh, why had they not stayed at home in Norway where they belonged?

"'Tis said the monks in abbeys near the shore prayed for storms at sea so they would be spared the hordes of Norsemen who came without end."

"I—I grieve for your people . . ."

Calla studied Sunniva's pink face. She believed her and vowed to say no more. "Have you broken fast yet?"

"Nay. And I ate but little last night."

Calla's mouth tightened. "I hear 'twas an exciting evening."

"'Twas horrible. The most horrible I ever spent. Not only were the men—"

"Hush, you, Rolf comes."

When Calla saw the glitter in Rolf Gunnarsson's eyes as he looked on Sunniva, she feared for her young friend. She herself had been through it all. She had been strong enough to survive, but would this maid live through it? She doubted anyone so soft and beautiful had the necessary strength to withstand Hedeby's cruelty and lust. It filled her with unexpected sadness.

"I would speak with you, Sunniva," Rolf declared.

"Ay, my lord Hedeby." Sunniva was disgusted to find herself trembling. He had but to speak her name to make her feel like a thrall. She forced herself to stand tall and straighten her shoulders.

"I will be gone for a time and I have instructions for you."

"Ay, sire."

"You will not consider escape. Ballageay is well guarded, and all around us are similar villages inhabited by men such as you saw last night. Know you what I am saying, wench?"

Sunniva murmured, "I understand, my lord."

"Nor would it go any better for you if the Celts were to find you unprotected."

"Ay, sire." She gazed at the turf so he would not see the rebellion flaming in her eyes.

Calla stoically watched Sunniva's discomfort, yet what Hedeby said was true. It would not go well for her if she attempted escape. What man would not want to ravish such a beautiful maid? And unless she herself were there to intercede, the girl would fare no better with Celt than with Viking.

Rolf regarded Calla with hostile eyes. "See that the priest is here when I return so that we may wed immediately."

"Ay, sire."

With no further word, he left, striding toward the bay where his men were boarding the Landwaster.

"I hate him," Sunniva said softly, for there were others about. "Never have I hated anyone as I hate him."

"There are two of us now," Calla answered. "Come, I will show you where we break fast."

"I have no hunger now."

"Then let us walk and talk. I will show you the fields and gardens which supply our food. If you will, tell me how he came to enslave you. I would hear it. . . ."

Calla's ears were the first to hear the tale, and Sunniva's grief and rage were as great in the telling of it as when it had actually occurred. Calla shook her head.

"So, 'twas your wedding day. . . . Well can I see that you would hate the scut."

"What of you?" Sunniva asked. "How came you to be his thrall?"

"His Vikings surprised Crow Creen, my own village, when many of our men lay ill with the throat-sickness. Most were slain, and Hedeby claimed me before my father's eyes. When the macLir broke free and would have skewered him, Hedeby slew him first." Calla's handsome face was masked. "My father was chieftain, so it served the bastard well to declare me in thrall and band me before all. Rather would I have died by his hand in battle than to shame them so."

"O, Calla. . . ."

"He and his Vikings took our homes and farms and women for their own."

Sunniva murmured, "I trow you will see him dead."

"Ay."

"As will I."

They walked toward the manor that had been an abbey with Sunniva brooding on what had happened there as well as to Calla's village. To villages all over the land.

"How long have you been captive?" she asked.

"'Twill soon be two winters. Shortly after he took Crow Creen, he brought me here to Ballageay."

Sunniva's hopes for her own escape went crashing. "Have you not tried to escape?"

Calla snorted. "Does not a falcon try to fly? Many times have I tried and failed."

"Were you—punished?"

"Ay. But that never stopped me."

The two had walked behind the abbey where there was an enclosure fenced in by tall timbers pounded into the earth. The tops of the timbers were filed to points and Sunniva marked two armed men stalking the perimeter from opposite directions. The looks the two women received from them were menacing.

"It seems a prison," Sunniva whispered. "Who is in there?"

"Celts," said Calla, softly, "including one that I cherish. 'Tis why I no longer attempt to flee. He would be tortured and slain."

Sunniva shook her head. "My people have brought you naught but grief!"

Calla felt a stirring of warmth, a feeling she had almost forgotten.

"'Tis no fault of your own, Sunniva. See you," she

pointed toward the Irish Sea. "The great lord is gone; his purple sail fades in the distance."

"Has he gone a-viking, think you?" Her heart shriveled, thinking of yet more destruction wreaked on this land and her people.

"Nay, he's gone a-trading. 'Tis almost certain we will not see him again for nigh onto ten days or so. Methinks 'tis time I show you Clagh Burroo."

Sunniva laughed, so odd was the name. "What is Clagh Burroo?"

"Yon moor." Calla pointed to the cliff that looked like a hatchet buried in the sea. "Come. I will show you."

Seeing the mysterious look on Calla's face, Sunniva sensed an adventure ahead and hurried to match her new friend's long-legged stride. She had not felt so carefree since that day when she and Raven had ridden off into the woods and made love.

"Hold, you two!" An armed Viking was suddenly blocking their way. "Whither go you?"

Calla was as tall as he. She poked his chest with a stiff finger. "To the witch-field, oaf. Would'st go with us?"

The Viking stepped back, his face dark red against his pale hair. He made the sign of the Hammer. Sunniva herself was uneasy. Witchfield? She did not like the sound of that at all. As they climbed a hill abloom with unfamiliar yellow and purple flowers, she marked that lyngwort grew there also. She would pluck some on the way back for it was always good to have. But as they gained the moor, her thoughts were not on lyngwort or the beauty spread out before them.

"Why did you call this a witchfield?" she asked. "Do witches live here?"

"Nay. Only fynnoderee." As they walked, Calla

fastened her wind-whipped hair into a long braid, which she thrust beneath her tunic.

Sunniva looked about. She swallowed. "What be a fynnoderee? Is't a troll?"

"Never have I seen a troll. These be neither fairy nor human and while none have seen them, they come down to work our farms at night. Oh, ay, and the buggane haunt this place nights, too. You can hear them moaning and roaring." Calla's broad mouth tilted at one corner. "Or so 'tis said. . . ."

Sunniva's eyes narrowed. "Calla macLir, I don't believe a word of it."

"Good. Nor do I." There was a lilt in her speech. "But the others do. And I have your Vikings believing it."

"They are not my Vikings."

"All right, they are not. The main thing is, they believe this headland is haunted. 'Tis all that matters."

"Why? 'Tis almost as if you are hiding something."

Calla's green eyes glowed. "That I am. Come, I'll show you." She swung through the knee-high grass to where a pile of boulders stood heaped up.

"What is't?" Sunniva asked.

"'Twould seem to mark a burial place, but if we roll these two boulders away. . . ." It took a large effort but Calla would accept no help.

As Sunniva stared down into the black opening in the earth, Calla slid into it and disappeared. Sunniva gave a small shriek. She knelt at the edge and peered in.

"Calla? Are you all right?"

Calla's grave face appeared. "Ay. Come down."

"In an eyeblink." Sunniva got to her feet, removed her kirtle, and bound up her chemise as though she were about to ride Sooten. "'Twould be unwise to rouse gossip with a dirt-spattered dress."

"You're right. Do you need a ladder?"

"Nay."

Sunniva easily leapt the distance down to the earthen floor. She looked about, her eyes quickly adjusting to the dimness. It was a cave, yet far more than just a cave. It was a long narrow room shored up by timbers and with one end looking out onto the rolling sea. The sea-window was curtained by a veil of greenery that bathed all with a greenish glow. She was awed.

"'Tis unearthly. 'Tis like—being beneath the sea. Oh, Calla, 'tis wonderful."

"So I thought when I found it," Calla said.

But what was truly wonderful, Calla mused, was having a friend and ally after all this time. There was none among her own countrywomen whom she could call friend—and not for lack of trying, for she had been lonely.

"Know you who made this place?" Sunniva asked, walking about exploring. There were sleeping benches on the long walls, and a sturdy table and many chests at the far end.

"Mayhap 'twas monks who dug it as a hiding place in the beginning, but fighting men used it last."

"How know you that?"

Calla strode across the hard-packed earth to where several chests sat. She began lifting off lids to reveal a shining trove of weapons: daggers, spears, battle-axes, swords, bows, arrows.

Sunniva gazed down on them, astonished. She moved from chest to chest, running her fingers over the smooth polished wood and thin blades. She could scarcely believe their good fortune. She threw back her head and laughed.

"If Rolf but knew . . ."

They were not without hope after all. With weapons, she and Calla had a good chance at escape—but first, first they would slay Rolf Gunnarsson. A cold thought struck her. Did Calla know how to use these? Weapon-play was not a womanly skill, and while she was tall and strong, perhaps it was too much to ask that she throw a spear, too. She had said nothing of it, only that she was a chieftain's daughter.

Even as Sunniva brooded, Calla lowered a large sheepskin attached to one of the ceiling timbers. It hung down before the chests, and on it was a red circle no bigger than an apple. Sunniva brightened. She knew a target when she saw one. Calla chose a bow and collected several arrows and returned to the sea-window end of the cave. Sunniva followed her.

"Now must you learn to use one or another of these weapons, Sunniva. I hope you have some small talent." She held up the bow. "I trow you know what this is."

Sunniva bit her lip to keep a grin from spreading across her face. "'Tis a bow for shooting the arrows, of course. I have seen men use them."

"Very good. Many maids know not that these things have a name even." Calla strung the bow, nearly as tall as herself, notched the arrow, raised it, sighted down the shaft. "Mind how I hold my left arm, else the returning string will bruise it." There was a twang, a hum, and the arrow whistled into the red circle on the skin. "'Tis Hedeby's heart, that," she muttered.

"Ay." Sunniva took the proffered bow. "Thinking that will make it easier for me to learn." Placidly, she allowed Calla to position her hands and cluck over her.

"'Tis very hard to pull, Sunniva, so don't be discouraged. And mind your arm, Hedeby would recognize a string burn. There, that looks good. Now try to pull it back . . . tch, mayhap you should stand closer this first time and—"

Sunniva drew the arrow back to her ear, sighted briefly and let fly. The arrow nicked Calla's so that both hung from the exact center of the scarlet circle. She heard Calla's gasp of surprise followed by an oath.

"Was't an accident, Sunniva?"

For answer, Sunniva notched another arrow, aimed, and the arrow sang. It knocked the other two to the earthen floor.

Calla's laughter rang out, a great exuberant whoop almost like a man's. To think, she had hoped for some *small* talent!

Sunniva was pleased. "I thought never to hear you laugh nor see you smile," she said.

"'Tis little I have had to laugh or smile about 'til now." Her eyes glowed green as the cave itself. "What other weapons, Sunniva?"

Sunniva glanced over them and shrugged. "All of these."

After that display, Calla had no cause to doubt her, but—all of them?

"Is't the way maids are raised in Norway then?"

"I was playmate to a—a chieftain's son."

For some few moments, she had been happy there in the cave with Calla, but now reality had returned. She was far from home, and while Raven would find her eventually, perhaps it would be too late for her. How could the two of them possibly hope to slay the Hedeby lord when his berserkers were always there and ever wakeful? She sank to the cave floor and sat, chin in hands. The spirit was gone from her.

Calla sat down beside her, cross-legged. "The chieftain's son," she said quietly, "was he this Raven to whom you are betrothed?"

"Ay, 'twas Raven. He taught me all I know."

Seeing her sadness, Calla said sternly, "Hear you, Sunniva, the two of us together will do what one never could. 'Tis my promise I give you—we will escape. And the one behind that stockade will go with us. He and his men."

Sunniva gazed at her sadly. "Mayhap the two of us could succeed, but to help the others—'twould seem impossible."

Calla got to her feet. "I will not go without him. I would die for him, and he for me. I have told you, 'tis why I have not fled before now. Con Cory's life would end in torture. But now that you are here, Sunniva, all has changed. We have much planning to do these next few days."

Sunniva said nothing of it, but it was plain to see that Con Cory was Calla's beloved. She saw it in her eyes.

CHAPTER 14

SUNNIVA WISHED THAT SHE FELT AS CONFIDENT ABOUT their escape as did Calla, but she did not. Too clearly she saw all that could go wrong in such an undertaking, but Calla's eyes burned with such hope and eagerness that she kept silent.

"How long has your friend been captive?" she asked, her fingers stroking the smooth wood of the bow.

"Since last harvest-time. He had made a successful sea-strike against a Viking camp, but as they left, Hedeby happened by. He rammed their vessel and seized all thirty men on it."

"Your friend is a chieftain?"

"Ay."

"Then Rolf does not always slay his captives?" She would have thought that surely he would slay a dangerous chieftain.

"Hedeby knows 'tis worse than death for such as

181

Con Cory to see his land and her women in chains and be helpless to do aught about it."

"I understand."

Sunniva imagined Raven with his wings clipped, raging, helpless. For him, too, it would be worse than death. He had told her once that a man without his ship is a man in chains. She shivered in the cool wind gusting through the sea-window. Calla rose, fetched the ladder, and leaned it against the opening above their heads.

"'Tis time we left, Sunniva. Never do I stay here long nor do I come when Hedeby is about."

"'Tis a marvel you are allowed to come at all." She bent the bow, unstrung it, and carefully laid it in the chest with the others.

"Rather would they have me prowling about this headland than the stockade. Here they think I can do no harm—'tis patrolled all around the base so there is no escape. At the stockade, I stalk the perimeter and glare at them and mutter. They fear I am putting a spell on them."

Sunniva gave her a level gaze. "Are you?"

"Would that 'twere so, but nay, I know naught of spells and incantations. I am a warrior-woman, Sunniva, not a witch-woman."

She mounted the ladder, Sunniva after her, and then toppled it backwards onto the cave floor. Sunniva helped her roll the boulders back in place, then followed her to the cliff's edge.

"'Tis Ireland across the sea on our left," Calla said, pointing, "and straight ahead in the mist lies Scotland. England is to our right, Cambria behind us, Maun all about us, and up above, 'tis Heaven. Atop our highest mountain, all can be seen on a clear day. Is there anywhere in Norway's land where you can see six kingdoms from the same spot?"

Sunniva knew her own land was larger by far than

this small speck of earth in the Irish Sea, but not for the world would she have hurt Calla's pride.

"If there is, I know naught of it."

Calla's tanned skin had gone colorless. "'Tis easy to forget most of this be Viking land now."

"Nay, Calla, surely not."

"Ay. Much of it. But 'twon't be forever. The Norsemen had best enjoy it while they can. . . ."

In silence they descended, striding through the lyngwort and the purple and yellow blooms to the base of Clagh Burroo. A second scowling warrior had joined the first. Both swaggered toward them, chainmail agleam and swords drawn.

"What is't you do up yonder, Celt bitch?"

"Pray to Manannan, Viking bastard. He is going to send such a mist that your chieftain will never find this isle again."

The two looked at each other uneasily before covering their fear with more bluster. "Why went lord Hedeby's future bride with you?"

"So she would not have to look at your ugly faces." Calla lifted two fingers and hissed, *Kione ny h'eaynin!* They jumped back as if struck.

As the women continued on their way, Sunniva asked, "What said you to them? Was't a curse?"

"Nay, 'twas the first stupid thing that flew to mind."

"Who is this Manannan that has mist at his command?"

Calla gave another of her rare laughs. "There are those who believe he is our sea-god."

"But not you."

"Nay, not I. Surely you are hungry by now," Calla said. "Come, we will eat, and then must we work."

In the longhouse, others already sat eating. It minded Sunniva greatly of the planting and harvest times at Lilleby when her mother and the serving-wenches cooked the day long for the fieldfolk. Except here the men looked on her with appraising eyes while the eyes of the women burned with hostility. She felt their gazes on them both as she and Calla put barley bread, cheese, and boiled eggs into wooden bowls, ladled milk into wooden cups, and carried the food to a table.

"I trow you will lose all your friends if you tarry long with me," she murmured as they sat down.

"Already we are unfriends, these wenches and I." Calla glowered back at their sullen faces. "Never have they liked me."

"Are they not your countrywomen?"

"Ay, but never have they liked me." Calla cracked open the boiled egg and smeared it onto her bread.

"Perhaps 'tis jealousy. You are the bravest woman I have ever known."

"Nay, I am not," Calla said gruffly.

The maid had not seen her weeping in the night for her father and her land and people. And for Con. And well she knew how strong Sunniva herself was to have survived a sea-voyage with Hedeby and his scum.

"I say you are," Sunniva insisted gently. "And you are beautiful. 'Tis small wonder these crones are jealous. Never have I seen hair the color of yours."

Calla's mouth formed the ghost of a smile. "'Tis strange, that, for I trow your mane is the most wonderful I have ever seen. 'Tis like the sun shining on wheat."

Sunniva laughed. "'Tis grand we have each other."

"All such silliness aside, Sunniva, this jealousy of theirs is an ugly thing. Always have they resented Hedeby's attention to me. Now they will now resent his wedding you. They themselves covet him."

Sunniva frowned. "They covet Rolf? Why?" She could scarce believe such a thing.

"They are naught but low-born wenches who have

gone from drudgery under Celt husbands to drudgery under Norsemen. The fools think their lives would be changed were the great lord but to notice them."

"Ay. So they would."

"You know and I know 'tis not for the better."

"He never—asked to wed you?"

"I trow he thought 'twas greater dishonor to use me without marriage." Calla's mouth tightened. "Yet rather would I be his thrall than his wedded wife."

"Ay." Sunniva's heart was heavy as she finished the last scraps of her breakfast. "'Tis my thinking. . . ."

Seeing her change of mood, Calla muttered, "You will not wed him, Sunniva, for the priest will not be found. The old fellow will wander in the mountains to cleanse his spirit after he leaves Rushen. We will have fled long before he returns, you may depend upon it."

"I still don't see how we will do it," Sunniva whispered.

"I do not speak idly. Each trip to the cave, we will carry back as many daggers as we can hide beneath our clothing. We will choose a misty night—there be many such—to free the others. I will take one of the guards, you the other, and—" She broke off to stare stonily at a woman who had come to their table.

"'Tis time you thralls stopped your yarning and got to work. You act as if there is naught to do."

Calla answered sharply, "We have but finished our food this instant, Ena."

"'Tis about time, for there is wool to be combed and spun, barley to be ground, and bread to be made." She gave Sunniva a special hard look. "Know you how to do any of these things, wench? You may be my lord Hedeby's future lady, but until such time as the priest is found, you are naught but a thrall to me."

Sunniva got to her feet; she towered over the

troll-woman. "All of those chores have I done on my father's manor," she answered coolly.

The woman laughed. "Ah, your father's manor, is it? How grand. Well, hie you to the trough yonder and get to kneading the dough then. Next you can grind. You, slut," she addressed Calla, "are needed in the fields."

She spun, her wadmal skirt swirling, and marched back to the others who waited and watched. All laughed then.

"Witch!" Calla hissed. "She has a face like a plate. I will go now, but only so they will suspect naught. We will talk later, Sunniva." She gathered up her bowl and cup.

"Calla?"

"Ay?"

Sunniva whispered, "'Tis glad I am to have you. . . ."

"And I you. 'Twill go well with us, Sunni."

Sunni. It was Raven's pet name for her, and Inge's. Sunniva's heart was warmer and fuller than it had been for a long time as she went to the trough. She rolled up her sleeves and plunged her hands into the barley dough. It felt good, familiar. She was glad to be doing something to keep her mind off that coming misty night when they would flee. But she could not dismiss the worry that Rolf would return before then.

Always had Raven said that a warrior must secure his retreat before the battle ever began. She was not a warrior, but she, too, could secure her retreat from Ballageay. If Rolf came, then she would give him and his berserkers lyngwort. This very eve she would begin drying the leaves she had gathered earlier.

The next day was a frightening one for Sunniva. It was after evening food, and she was behind the

longhouse grinding grain when she heard shouts
from the shore. Though she was curious, she remained at the hand quern. Sooner or later she would
learn what all the excitement was about. Suddenly,
the woman, Ena, was beside her waving her arms.

"'Tis the lord Hedeby!" She was out of breath. "He
is returned and asks for you."

Sunniva's blood turned icy. "So soon? I
thought—"

"Go! He is wroth. Wait at the manor until he
arrives." Ena clutched Sunniva's arm in her thin
brown fingers to hasten her.

Sunniva looked about for Calla, but she was nowhere to be seen. Doubtless she was in the fields still,
and even so, what could she do to help? But what was
Rolf doing here when he was supposed to be gone
nigh onto two weeks? Did he expect the priest to be
here already? She lifted her skirts and ran. Frightened as she was, she gave thanks that she and Calla
had not been atop Clagh Burroo. What if Rolf had
stormed up there to find her? What if he had surprised them in the cave? It was too awful to think on.
From now on, they would have to keep a more careful
watch from the sea-window. Reaching the manor,
she saw that Rolf and his berserkers were already
there.

"Greetings, my lord Hedeby." Sunniva was pink
and breathless. "I am sorry to keep you waiting, I was
at the—"

"Bring her," Rolf growled to Bjork. "I would have
privacy."

"My lord, wh-what is't?" Sunniva asked, as Bjork
grasped her arm and marched her hastily to the rear
of the manor.

They entered the kitchen room and mounted the
narrow stone steps, first Rolf, then Sunniva, then

Bjork. Helgi remained on guard below. Down the dark passageway they went until Rolf stopped at a door, unlocked it, and flung it open.

"Wait here," he commanded Bjork.

When the door closed behind them, Sunniva's heart stood still. It was Rolf's bedchamber. It was four times larger than her own small cell and in one corner stood a box-bed heaped with sheepskins.

"What know you of Brother Asmund's whereabouts, wench?"

Sunniva was taken aback. "I know naught, my lord. I never met the man nor heard his name before coming here."

"It doubts me not the macLir witch knows more of this than she has let on and has filled your ear with it. I hear you two already have your heads together."

"'Tis not so, my lord. 'Tis only that I was lonely and she is k-kind."

Sunniva's heart pounded, for Rolf Gunnarsson looked murderous.

"Asmund will not return to Ballageay for weeks. The macLir knows it."

"I had not heard, but if that is so, I—"

"Silence. I have no time for woman-talk. The tide and my men await me. But know you this, wench— when I return, you will lie in my bed as my wife, priest or no, until such time as he can be found."

Sunniva's eyes were drawn to the box-bed. It stood in the corner of the bedchamber and was wood-paneled on all four sides except for the opening through which she saw the heaps of skins. Always had she loved her own box-bed at home, where the paneling kept out the bitter drafts that swept through the room in winter, but Rolf Gunnarsson's bed would be a cage for her. Once she was in it, there was no way for her to leave unless he wished it.

"Understand you what I am saying?" He gripped her jaw, forcing her to look at him.

"Ay, my lord Hedeby, I—understand. I will be ready." *With a dagger* . . .

But then she remembered Calla's promise. How quickly she had forgotten that she would not even be here when he returned.

Rolf wasted no further words on her. He left his chamber, Sunniva following. Bjork closed and locked the door. They traversed the dark passageway, descended the stone steps, and then the three men strode down to the bay where the dragonship waited. They were gone as suddenly as they had come.

During the two days that followed, Sunniva worked harder than she ever had in her life. Not even the drudgery aboard the Landwaster compared as Ena, in a position of command, drove her from morning until night. Learning that Sunniva disliked spinning and weaving, it was that which Ena bade her do, saying there was a great need for cloth. Not only was there clothing to be made for winter, there were always tents to be made, and wagon covers, and above all, sails for the ships, both large and small.

Sunniva saw Calla only during the twice-daily meals, when there was little time and even less privacy to talk. When they broke fast the third day, Sunniva marked that Calla was near to exploding with anger.

"That plate-face is doing this to vent her wrath on you, and it must be stopped," she said. "I trow your hands are being damaged. Hold them out."

Sunniva did. Calla cursed, seeing that they were cut and blistered and stained with dye. The damned crone had the maid doing that which no one else wanted to do—preparing the dyes and shrinking and fulling the fabrics. She rose and stalked over to where Ena sat with her friends.

"Witch!" Calla snapped. "Think you to please your lord by bidding his new lady ruin her hands with your damned cloth-making? Know you he will lie in the bridal bed with her when he returns, priest or no?"

When Ena blinked up at her, mouth agape, Calla saw that the she-toad had not known. She plunged on, her rage towering. "Think you he wants her soft white skin to be brown and parched like yours and reek of dye? Best had you set her down to some tablet weaving and embroidery and let her hands recover, else I would not walk in your shoes for any money when he returns."

The very next day, Sunniva was put to boiling seawater for salt and helping prepare the food for cooking. After evening-food, she and Calla walked on the beach in the sunset.

"'Twas a fine performance you gave at break-fast yester morn," said Sunniva, laughing. "I'm grateful. Not because I fear for my hands—'tis just that I detest spinning and weaving."

Calla gave her a scornful look. "Mayhap you fear naught for your hands, but I do, my sister. And not so they will be white and soft for Hedeby." She gave a derisive snort. "Nay, you need them strong and limber for weapon-use." She looked about her and even though they were alone, she lowered her voice:

"I have news."

The last time Calla had looked so, she had shown Sunniva the cave on Clagh Burroo. Sunniva felt a shiver of anticipation. "News about what?" she asked.

"My people are nearby," Calla said. "A message-arrow fell near me in the field yesterday." She was pink-cheeked and her green eyes resembled those of a cat with prey in sight. "They are planning an attack to reclaim Ballageay."

Sunniva's skin prickled. "When?"

"Soon. They are awaiting more men. Only with sheer numbers can they hope to overpower a stronghold the size of this one. 'Tis close to four hundred here."

Relief spread over Sunniva. Although the two women had been carrying weapons down and concealing them, never was she confident that they could free Con and his men. Now it would be done.

"Oh, Calla, 'tis glad I am for you. For all of us!" She gave a little skip. "I feel like jumping and shouting it to the sea and the sky!"

Calla gripped her wrist and said sternly, "But you will not." The maid was eight winters younger than herself, but at times she was like a child. "Not in any way will you call attention to us or act as though aught is different from usual."

Sunniva bit her lip. "Of course I will not. None will learn it from me."

"Good. Now we will go back to the village and go to bed, but before we break fast, we must go up Clagh Burroo again."

"'Tis none too soon for me."

Calla's blood stirred with thoughts of the revenge to come, yet part of her feared greatly for Sunniva. What would become of her when Ballageay was reclaimed by her own folk? She was so fair, and she was Viking. Calla doubted her own influence was strong enough to keep the maid from harm.

The next morn, the sun was just peeping over the eastern hills of Ballageay when the two women started up Clagh Burroo. The sentries eyed them insolently, but did not hinder them. Neither wanted a Celt curse upon his head.

Sunniva's lavender kirtle, the only dress she possessed, was dew-drenched when they arrived at the cave, but Calla had a surprise for her. Beneath her own tunic were hidden leggings and a similar tunic for her friend.

"Oh, Calla, 'tis wonderful! Oh, a thousand th—"

"Nay, Sunniva," Calla said brusquely. "I'll not hear thanks. 'Tis time you had clothing befitting a warrior."

The leggings were butter-soft and ended in boots that laced to the knee. They were fawn-colored as was the coarsely woven tunic. Sunniva quickly donned both. She was delighted.

"'Tis like they were made for me! From whence came they?"

Calla shrugged, unwilling for Sunniva to know she had worked long and hard to make them for her.

"I made them for myself a while back. I had but to shorten them a bit for you. Now must we stop our prating and get to work." She went to the chest of spears, chose one with a short blade, and lowered the sheepskin target. "How long since you used such weapons as are here, Sunniva?" She let fly, easily hitting the red circle.

"Months, I trow."

Sunniva, too, chose one, tested its point and weight and balance, and then drew back her arm for the throw. It shot forward and hummed sweetly into the bull's-eye.

Calla's eyes glittered, seeing the maid's ability. "Which weapon suits you best?" she asked.

"Always have I liked the bow," Sunniva murmured, retrieving the spear and examining its point. "I confess, I have used weapons only for sport."

"So I suspected."

Sunniva raised worried eyes to Calla. "I suppose when your people come, there will be great bloodshed. . . ."

"'Tis only to be expected. Never has Hedeby spared

enemy blood, nor that of his own men."

Sunniva nodded. "That I know."

She sat down cross-legged, elbows on knees, chin in hands, remembering Rolf's wounded, and especially the one with whom she had walked to Valhalla's gate. She moistened her lips.

"I know not that I can slay a man, Calla. I know not if I can slay Rolf despite my bold talk. I can put an arrow through a man's shoulder or thigh and I can do great mischief with any weapon you choose. I know the points of a man's body to strike with my hands or feet or elbows to fell him, but slaying . . ." She shook her head.

"I ken 'twill be hard for you."

It was ironic, Calla mused. Sunniva's skills outshone her own, yet never would she put them to good use. Her heart was too gentle.

"Mayhap you should escape before my people come, Sunniva."

Sunniva's beautiful dark eyes widened. "Why? Where would I go?"

"There are other Viking settlements."

Sunniva rose. "You were not at the feast to see the way those men looked at me. I would as lief enter a snakepit. Nay, Calla, I stay."

"Listen to me," Calla's voice was stern, her lilting accent more pronounced. "Celt men are no better than Vikings. You are the enemy, Sunniva. You are booty. I cannot promise you safety."

"I will stay with you, no matter." Fright gripped her as she remembered Haftor Kol's black eyes burning over her, and then scorn overcame her fright. The damned scut-pig. "I stay."

"So be it. But know you, there are several Viking villages where the women, too, are Norse. 'Tis certain they would treat you well."

"Norse women are here? On Maun?"

"Ay. Which minds me, there is more to discuss before we return to Ballageay."

"I trow we must plan on Rolf's returning before your people strike."

"Ay. 'Tis ever in my mind."

"And mine." Sunniva returned the spear to the chest and found a dagger she favored. She sat on the table, weighing it first in one hand and then the other. She gave Calla a grin. "I have already secured my retreat, just in case."

"I would hear it," Calla said, thinking that this was a woman after her own heart.

"I am drying lyngwort leaves. Mind those silvery gray plants I pointed out 'midst the gorse and heather? Next I will powder them."

"I don't understand."

"Were I forced to bed, or to drink wedding ale with Rolf Gunnarsson, there would be lyngwort in his horn."

Calla's green eyes flickered. "How does lyngwort affect a man? I know naught of such things."

"'Tis a lovely cure for sleeplessness—or an easy death for those folk who are hopelessly pain-wracked and want to die. A pinch in a horn of ale will put a man to sleep for a day. A thimbleful will put him to sleep forever. . . ."

Calla's eyes were slits. "Which will you give Hedeby?—and, I trow, his berserkers."

"Ay, definitely his berserkers," Sunniva said softly. "I have told you I cannot slay them, nor would I dream of cheating you and your people of the revenge you crave. I will put them to sleep."

Calla nodded. "'Tis good you have thought ahead —as have I." She drew from her tunic pocket a piece of cloth with markings on it. "'Tis a map I have drawn. 'Twill get you to a village in the south where live the Norse women. Later this day, I will bring you a wallet to carry your belongings, and a helmet. 'Twill help disguise you."

"Will I flee on foot or horseback?"

Calla's mouth twitched. She might have guessed that a woman skilled in arms would also know how to ride a horse. "You must go afoot. The terrain is treacherous because 'tis unfamiliar to you. Now we had best get down to break fast. That plate-face Ena will wonder what we are about."

CHAPTER 15

When Sunniva came down off Clagh Burroo, seven dirks were bound to her body by a belt beneath her loose-hanging kirtle. Calla had ten, their cold sharp points slipped under the waistband of her leggings. In addition, Sunniva's new leggings and tunic were once more concealed under Calla's tunic. Only after their booty was hidden in their rooms did the two meet to break fast, and not until bedtime did Sunniva have a chance to study the map Calla had given her. Until the last light of day was gone, she pored over it, seeing that to reach the Viking encampment containing the Norse women she must go southeast and eventually cross a river. It was fortunate that she knew how to swim.

As Sunniva lay in the dark on her cot, she felt excitement crackling in the very air. Many things were afoot, but which of them would happen first? Would the Celts attack or would Rolf return first? Or

197

would Raven come before either of them? If he did, there was little she herself would do except stay out of the way of the fighting. And she would stay out of the sight of the Ballageay Vikings lest she be taken hostage. If she found herself in the hands of Celt warriors, she would defend herself as best she could, but in the end, much would depend on Calla. She sensed that Calla would prevail. On the other hand, were Rolf the first to arrive . . .

Sunniva grimaced at the thought. Rather would she face a horde of howling Celts with only her bare hands and feet as weapons than to be in Rolf Gunnarsson's power again. Already the man's insane craving for her had left five good men lying in the dead-straw. Perhaps there were more. She shook her head. She did not want to think about him, wanted never to think of him again, but she must. This was a thing in which none could help her. Once she was in his power, she had only her own wits to save her. Long and long into the night she lay awake, wide-eyed, heart thundering, planning how she would get Rolf and his berserkers, should they come unexpectedly, to drink lyngwort-tainted brew. And then she prayed to Odin and Mary-Jesu-Holy Ghost that the need for it would never arise. She prayed Raven would come first.

Sunniva's prayers were not answered. Early the next morn, she was bread-baking behind the longhouse when the purple sail of the Landwaster was spotted on the horizon. Calla, who had been in the fields, was suddenly at her side.

"So. 'Twill be Rolf for me," Sunniva said tonelessly.

Calla's face showed nothing. Neither the sorrow nor sympathy she felt for the maid would busk her for the ordeal that lay ahead of her. She must give her heart.

"Your plan to use lyngwort is a good one, Sunniva. You will win through."

"Ay, I intend to."

"If we do not talk before you make your escape, know you that I will be about after dark. If I can draw eyes from your leave-taking, 'twill be done."

"Have thanks for that—and for everything."

Sunniva felt her throat closing, burning with the tears she would not shed. For the first time, she realized that she loved this tall, fearless woman who had befriended her in this strange land.

"A fair wind be at your back, Sunniva, and may your gods go by your side." Calla grasped her hand.

Sunniva's handclasp was no less heartfelt. "May Ballageay soon be Celt again. May all of Maun be in the hands of your people again one day."

There was a flash of appreciation in Calla's green eyes and then she was gone, as swiftly as she had come. Seeing that the bread loaves, on their long-handled iron pans, were baked, Sunniva removed them from the embers. She rolled them onto racks to cool, filled the pans with more loaves to bake, and thrust them into the embers. She sat down on an upturned keg. Here she would stay, she thought stubbornly. She would mind the bread as Ena had bade her, and if Rolf wanted her, he would have to summon her.

Strange flickerings darted through her body. It was fear, she knew, yet it was mingled with excitement. She knew now which fate lay ahead of her, and she knew what she had to do. And she was going to win. This night she would leave Ballageay and the lord of Hedeby behind her forever.

Rolf Gunnarsson had seen no need to prolong his journey to his customary trading places. Five days ago when he had left Maun, his hold had contained skins, furs, dried fish, tallow, and several choice slaves he had been saving for a discriminating buyer. Now both the Landwaster and his burden-ship bulged with trade-goods: cured meats, bolts of English wool and linen, wheat, honey, wine, wax, and kettles.

While it was a rule that places of trade and the merchant ships that came and went to them were inviolable and safe from all attack, Rolf's eyes and ears were ever open. As he returned to Ballageay, he knew exactly when and where his next strike on Maun was going to be. It was time he strengthened his already considerable hold on the isle.

But for these next few days and nights, he would put warfare from his mind. He meant to give his full attention to the delectable wench he would have in his bed this night. Having waited an uncommonly long time for her, five damned years, he meant to make the bedding of her an exquisitely delicious event. When the anchor was dropped and the ramp thrown down, he went ashore, his loins already athrob at the prospect of it. He did not wait for the unloading of the two vessels to begin, but strode with Bjork toward his manor.

"Fetch my woman," he commanded Helgi. "I will be in my chamber."

Shortly, he was relaxing in his fur-draped chair and drinking ale from a horn filled to the brim. He had removed his sea-clothes and was garbed in narrow silken breeches and a sleeveless silk shirt when Sunniva was brought before him. Helgi then returned to the corridor with Bjork.

"Greetings, my lord," she said, eyes downcast.

"You will kneel before me henceforward."

"Ay, my lord." Sunniva went to her knees.

"Has the priest come?"

"None have found him, my lord."

"Meaning the macLir wench has not done her job," Rolf said.

"That is not so. Daily Calla has sent men to every part of the isle. 'Tis thought now that he may be in the mountains communing with his god."

"The troll will have need of his god when I lay hands on him." Rolf's eyes, pale blue in his tanned, scarred face, slid over her. "You have not forgotten, I trow, that you lie in my bed this night."

"I have not forgotten." Sunniva continued to gaze at the floor, fearful that he would see the thoughts of escape in her eyes.

"But still you think Raven Trondsson will come for you in time." He drank from his horn.

"I—I no longer know, my lord." The lie tasted bitter in Sunniva's mouth, but it was time she put her plan into action.

Rolf gave her a low-lidded look and laughed. "He will come, wench, you may depend upon it. He will not give up such a treasure as you all that easily. And you can depend upon me to slay him, but not before he sees that you are thrice mine. My thrall, my wife, and bearing my seed. When that is impressed upon him, then will I slay the bastard."

Seeing the blanching of her beautiful face, he said softly, "I will slay him before your eyes, Sunniva. 'Tis a pity, that, but 'tis necessary for a wench such as you who believes Raven Trondsson is invincible."

Sunniva raised her eyes, surprised to find that she was in command of herself. "Have you never noticed, my lord Hedeby, that wanting a thing is oft times better than having it?"

At that, Rolf threw back his golden mane and laughed. His throat minded Sunniva of a smooth dark column of oak, so broad and strong was it. All of him was lean and strong, she conceded, and there was no denying he was handsome. But why could he not vent

his desire for woman-flesh on one of the silly Celt
wenches who craved him?

"'Tis a deep thought for a wench to have grasped,
Sunniva. Always are dreams better than reality." He
studied the swells of her body beneath her coarsely-
made kirtle. "But 'tis not true where you are concerned. Too long have I waited for you, and I expect
—nay, I demand perfection from you. I trow you will
quickly learn what pleases me."

"Ay, my lord."

Sunniva moistened her dry lips and tried to calm
her breathing. It was behaving strangely, and her
knees were aching and beginning to stiffen from their
being bent so long in a kneeling position.

"You will bathe daily, unlike these others—"

She flared: "My lord, I always bathe daily!"

"—and you will be available whenever I require
you."

She felt her entire body turn pink with embarrassment. "Mean you," she muttered, "that I am to be
here waiting for you the livelong day?"

"If I say it, ay," he said.

She smothered an insulting retort. There was no
need to get herself maimed or killed when this night
she would be free. She said only:

"My lord, I fear my legs will break if I must remain
kneeling thus much longer. . . ."

"You may sit, Sunniva. Here, at my feet." He
snapped his fingers as though she were a dog. "Rest
your head against my leg." His big hand went to the
back of her neck and caressed it. "I trow you can
receive a man this night. . . ."

"Ay." Again her body burned. If she had lied, she
knew he would demand proof.

"I have a garment for you to wear."

He bent his head toward her, raised her face for his
kiss and grasped a breast with his other hand. Long

he kissed her, the kiss deepening and his hand growing so cruel and demanding on both her breasts that Sunniva struggled to be free.

"You are ungentle, sire."

"Never am I gentle, Sunniva, nor will I hear any prattle on the subject. Go you now—wait, first I will give you the garment."

She rose as he went to his sea-chest and drew forth a gray bundle. He thrust it at her.

"Wear this tonight. Helgi will come for you after sunset. Be ready."

Traversing the dark corridor, Sunniva held the hated bundle by two fingers as though it were a dead rat she had by the tail. She stopped by her own small cell, tossed it onto the floor, and hurried down to where the bread was still a-baking on the iron pans in the embers. None had noticed it there and she saw that the loaves had long since turned hard as rock. Good. Let them break their teeth on it at evening-food as a remembrance of her.

Sunniva was there for the preparation of evening-food, but she did not stay to partake of it. She had no hunger nor did she want to face the women's stares and the men's knowing eyes. All knew what was going to happen that night—or thought they knew. Never could they have suspected that she planned to flee, or known that earlier that morn, after she had finished the baking, she had taken an unburned loaf and some cheese and secreted it beneath her bed alongside the weapons hidden there.

Back in her tiny cell, she wondered where Calla was. She had not seen her since morn, and she doubted now that she would see her before she left. But it was all right. She had time only to prepare for what lay ahead. She knew exactly what had to be done and she set about doing it. With the bone handle of her dagger, she ground the dried lyngwort leaves until they were a fine golden powder. She then brushed them into a fresh leaf, tucked in its ends and rolled it into a cylinder. She hid it under her pillow. There. The most important thing was done. And one dagger would she take on her journey. Only one. The other weapons Calla would retrieve another time.

She withdrew Calla's cloth map from its hiding place beneath her mattress and studied it one more time. Since there would be no light when she left except that from a small crescent of waxing moon, she impressed each mark on it upon her mind. Next she stuffed the wallet Calla had given her with the bread, cheese, carrots, and turnips. Last she tucked in the map and her dagger. Her travel-clothing she would don after Rolf and his two wild boars lay sleeping like babes.

Sunniva smiled, thinking on what a sight it would be when Rolf awakened and found her gone. She was tempted to savor the thought, but not now, for soon the sun would set and she would be summoned. Instead, the image would warm her in the night as she made her way across the unfamiliar countryside.

Sunniva picked up Rolf's bundle from the floor and frowned at it. At first, she had thought it was an awful gray wadmal kirtle, but now she saw that the wadmal was but a bag. She opened it, drew out its contents, and held it up, her eyes widening. It was a cloth of sorts, a gauzy plum-red with a wide band of purple bordering it, and it was aglitter with the thread of gold woven through it. It was exquisite, ay, but what was it?

It was like no gown or kirtle Sunniva had ever seen. Rather it was like a table-covering or a wall-hanging excepting it was so fragile. She could see her hands through it. Perhaps she was to wear it like a shawl, she mused, draping it over her head and shoulders. Or was it the bridal veil of women in some distant land? There was no more time to ponder, for it was dusk and soon the berserker would come for her.

Quickly Sunniva neatened her cell, for all must be where she could lay hands on it in darkness—the wallet under the foot of her cot, the leather helmet beside it, her clothing beneath the mattress. Next she dipped water from the soapstone bowl, rinsed her mouth and bathed her face. She unbraided her hair and had just finished combing it when there was a thumping on her door. She jumped, even though she had been expecting it.

"My lord awaits you, wench," Helgi growled.

Sunniva drew in a long breath. "One moment, please."

She slipped the soft cylinder of lyngwort inside her shoe and settled the shimmering cloth over her head and shoulders. She drew back the bar, opened the door, and met Helgi's eyes unafraid.

"I am ready," she said.

Rolf Gunnarsson had bathed and dressed with care, his one regret being that he did not have a tub of water in which to see his own magnificence. His strong dark arms were bare in a blue, sleeveless, fur-lined kirtle usually worn over his mail. Gold bands glistened on his forearms, matching the forehead band that tamed his lion's mane of tawny hair. He wore tight-fitting silken breeches of navy blue, and matching skin stockings that resembled high boots. For this night, he had removed the spurs attached to them. His narrow waist was accentuated with a showy gold belt and buckle, but his sword, Battle Fiend, and his dagger he had put aside. They lay on the floor next the fur-draped, throne-like chair where he sat awaiting the wench.

The wench. Holy Thor, his blood had been roiling

and racing ever since he saw her that morn, but he was certain none had guessed. He had calmly gone into the village, talked to his men, mended his weapons, done his daily war-play with his berserkers, and seen to the macLir wench.

It was past time she was punished, for always did she grow overbold when he was gone on cruise or a-trading. Well had the slut known the troll of a priest was gone a-wandering somehwere up on Snaefell, and she had chosen not to tell him. And why there was only one damned Norse priest on this whole accursed isle, he knew not. No matter. His enjoyment of his future bride would not be lessened by an absense of vows. He raised heavy eyes to the door when it opened and scowled as his betrothed entered.

"Greetings, my lord Hedeby," Sunniva murmured, dropping to her knees as he had demanded.

The room was dimly lit, oil burning in but one soapstone bowl suspended from a rafter. She saw that he looked as she always thought a god might look—lean, powerful, wondrously fair of face and form and with bands of gold glistening on his hair and arms. His clothing was rich and fitted him like a glove. He was magnificent—but for his hard pale eyes and the unsmiling mouth that showed his cruelty.

Rolf glowered at Helgi. "Out," he growled. To Sunniva he snapped, "What prank is this you play on me, wench?" He leaned forward and snatched the fragile veil from her head and shoulders.

Sunniva blinked, shocked. She had not meant to anger him in any way. "Prank? Wh-what mean you, sire?"

"You were to wear this." He gave the veil an angry shake.

"I did wear it, sire. I—I knew naught else to do

with it. Never have I seen such a garment before. . . ."

Her fright pleased him, made him wonder if her backbone were not as stiff as it used to be. The thought mellowed him considerably. He rose and drew her to her feet, one corner of his mouth lifting in an almost-smile.

"In the land whence this came, Sunniva, certain women wear naught but this veil."

Nothing but that flimsy thing? It was hideous to think on. She would die first, Sunniva thought, but nay, nay—for now, death was not to be thought of.

"Mean you that you want me to—wear it so now?"

"Ay. Take off your gown, Sunniva."

Still holding the veil, Rolf sat down again. He lounged back in the furs, one long leg thrown across the other, and lifted his drinking horn from the stand. He studied her with narrowed eyes. Soon would he command her to eat one of the small cakes with the friggja-grass in it, and then would he have her writhing beneath him. No woman could withstand the instant aphrodisiac effects of the friggja-grass.

"The wench who wore this veil lived in a Turk harem," he told her. "She displeased her master and he slew her. Know you what a harem is, Sunniva?"

"Ay, lord." Sunniva hated it that her voice sounded so small and trembling, but he was frightening her.

"Come, wench, remove the rag you are wearing."

Sunniva drew her kirtle down over her shoulders and stepped out of it, her whole body flaming with embarrassment.

"Know you, Sunniva, I have sold many women to Kemal Attibak and I will not hesitate to sell you to him if you displease me."

"Ay, lord."

She next removed her chemise and her shoes and carefully laid them to one side. She stood before him then, naked but for the slave band on her ankle, and saw his icy eyes move over her, assessing every inch of her. Perhaps she would kill him—kill all three of them. It would be so easy, just a pinch more of the lyngwort and they would never again see the light of day.

"Come here, Sunniva."

When he pointed to his feet, she knew she was to kneel again. She obeyed. He lifted the veil above her head and then she felt it shimmering down over her body, soft as a whisper.

"I would have you walk about," he said gruffly.

"Ay, my lord."

When she rose, she heard his sucked-in breath. Feeling like a fool, she moved about the room, knowing he wanted to see the movement of her breasts and legs under the clinging, diaphanous folds. She obliged him, raising an arm to touch her fingers to the oil lamp, stroking the heavy tapestry that hung over his windows by night, putting her small pile of clothing and her shoes next to the keg of brew. . . .

"May I serve you more ale, my lord Hedeby?"

"Ay."

She was superb, Rolf mused, as she came for his horn and returned to the keg—soft-voiced, regal, those full swaying breasts, her entire body soft, silken, and graceful. Her skin gleaming whitely, her nipples were red as her pomegranate mouth beneath the veil; her hair was like thread of gold, her eyes as deep purple as a Northland tarn at dusk. Holy Thor, she was exquisite. Exquisite and treacherous. He felt it in his bones. On an impulse, he rose, took up the Battle Fiend and his dagger, and laid them both atop a rafter far over Sunniva's head. Next he took a long chain from his sea-chest.

Guessing what he was about and knowing this might be her only chance to drug him, Sunniva quickly removed the rolled-up leaf from her shoe. As his attention focused on fastening one end of the chain to her ankle-band, Sunniva tapped a pinch of lyngwort into his empty horn. As he locked the other end of her chain to his wristband with the small key he wore about his neck, she ladled out a stoup of ale for him. She held it, watching coolly as he returned to his throne-chair. He reeled her in like a sleek, colorful fish.

"Have I displeased you, my lord, that you must chain me?"

Rolf gave his cold laugh and pulled her down onto his lap. "I mistrust you, wench. Methinks you would as soon slit my throat as look at me."

It was but half the truth. The other half was that he enjoyed seeing a chain bite into a woman's soft flesh. They were all bitches, starting with that mad wench who had spawned him, and followed by the cruel serving-wench his father had taken to wife. That one had been his first taste of woman and his hunger had been more for vengeance than for pleasure. He had slain her after, and none ever knew. He had been but a boy, after all. He took a great swallow of ale and then wrapped the chain tightly about Sunniva's body, binding her in her silken cocoon from her ankles to her neck.

Sunniva was truly frightened. What if he did not finish his ale? But he had to! He had to or all was lost. She gasped, "My lord, can we not—go to the bed and drink our wedding ale there?"

Rolf got to his feet and, blessedly, unwound the chain from around her body. He lurched toward the bed, but changed his mind and returned to the throne-chair. He sank into it and growled at her:

"Sit you on my lap again"—Once more he lifted

the horn to his lips—"and take one of those cakes."
He indicated the tray beside his chair.

"Ay, lord." Her relief made Sunniva weak. He was
drinking the lyngwort and he had unchained her. He
drained over half of the horn before offering her any.
She took but a sip before taking one of the small
cakes from the tray.

"You be my wife, Sunniva Mellby," he muttered,
repeating, "you be my wife. You be my wife."

Three times he said it. Sunniva had heard of such
pagan practices of marriage, but witnesses were
needed, and their witnesses were outside. None had
heard them—nor would they now, for the lord of
Hedeby sat on his throne fast asleep.

Sunniva tore off the veil, hurriedly unlocked the
chain from her ankle-band, and donned her chemise.
She then added a fine touch to her thirst for vengeance. She wound Rolf's chain about his slumped
body and the chair, thus binding the two tightly
together. Both ends of the chain she locked to his
wrist-band before she hung the key about her own
neck. Bastard! And now for the berserkers . . .

She poured the remainder of the lyngwort into the
drinking horn and ladled ale into it. She then remembered the veil—it might seem odd if she were not
wearing it. She quickly covered herself with it before
unbarring and opening the door. Helgi and Bjork
were instantly on their feet.

With a bowed head and bent shoulders, Sunniva
murmured, "My lord Hedeby bids you share our
wedding ale. Drink all you can hold, and knock on
the door when this is gone."

Helgi took it, giving her a respectful look. "Ay. Our
thanks, my lady Hedeby."

Sunniva sat herself on a stool in the flickering light
and waited, heart thumping. Rolf slept deeply, heavily. She had not poisoned him. Much as she hated him,

she could not, nor had she poisoned the berserkers. Soon they would sleep as deeply as their master. Perhaps they already did. When no knock came and when she could stand it no longer, she opened the door widely, as though to offer more ale. They had fallen like two oaks, sleeping where they fell. None of the three would awaken before the next eve, but nonetheless, she had no time to waste. She hurriedly caught up her kirtle and shoes, and found the door-key on Rolf's chain. She must be on her way.

CHAPTER 16

SUNNIVA WAS TEMPTED TO TAKE THE OIL LAMP TO HER chamber, for it would help her to move more swiftly, but she dared not. Any of the guards who saw a light where no light should be might suspect that something was amiss. With one final scornful glance at the sleeping Vaaga king, Sunniva moved to blow out the flame. But wait—it would infuriate Rolf beyond measure to waken, not only chained with his own chain, but with the Turk harem veil draped over him. Eyes aglimmer, she seized the lovely floating thing, thinking betimes of the woman whose only garment it had been. It was for her, poor thing, and poor revenge it was, that she settled the veil over Rolf's cruel, handsome face and beard, his lion's mane of thick, tawny hair and down over his long, powerful, slumped body in its silken trews and fur-lined kirtle.

Her eyes went then to the weapons he had thought beyond her reach. She smiled. So easily could she leap up, snatch them, and plunge a steel point into his heart or throat. But nay, his mortification was enough; the Celts could have him. Perhaps they would strike even as he slept. But possessing his sword, Battle Fiend, tempted her. He would be as enraged by its loss as by her escape. She would take it, ay. She crouched, sprang, caught the rafter with one small, strong hand and cautiously, silently, retrieved the weapon before dropping to the floor like a cat. The whole had taken but an instant. She looked out the door again. Satisfied that the berserkers still slept the sleep of the dead, Sunniva blew out the flame and stole to her chamber.

In the blackness, she tore off her chemise and donned the tunic and soft leggings Calla had given her. She braided her hair, tucked it under her tunic, settled the helmet on her head, and slipped the wallet on her back. After stuffing her clothing under her cot, she was ready. The Battle Fiend in her right hand, her dagger stuck in her waistband, she crept down the narrow stone steps, through the kitchen-room, through the door, and out into the damp night.

Panting, she stood in the shadows watching the two hulking guards prowling the boundaries of the stockade like hungry bears. It was in that direction that lay her destination and she had but to slip by them to be on her way. She waited, her breathing soft and shallow, sweat beading her body, heart flying—not with fear but with excitement. Soon would Ballageay be behind her.

Her eyes slitted. It was easy to see the men as they approached each other in the moon's faint light. When they made the same approach on the opposite side of the stockade and out of her sight, then would she make her move. She was a fast runner, and never would she run as fast as this night. She crouched, waiting, waiting for them to turn the corners, the sword under her arm, her breath rasping now in her throat and lungs. Any instant now . . .

"Hold! Who goes?" came the distant shout.

Sunniva froze, thinking it was herself the one guard had seen and hailed until she saw the figure shuffling toward him, arm out-thrust, fist shaking, a curse ringing out. She recognized the wild mane of hair. Calla! Holy Odin, it was Calla drawing their attention from her. But that shuffling gait. Why did she limp so? What had happened to her? Sunniva hesitated, ready to fly to her friend's aid—but nay, Calla had known she was there and had seen she was ready to make her move. She had jeopardized herself on purpose and would have nothing but the greatest scathe for Sunniva were she not to take advantage of her sacrifice.

As the second guard came running and the angry voices of all three were raised, Sunniva flew. She ran low, looking neither to the right nor the left, and she thanked Odin and holy Jesu that her feet seemed to have wings. She was beyond the stockade and out of sight of the entire village almost before she knew it. Not until she thought she would drop with weariness and breathlessness did she stop. She crawled beneath the low leafy branches of a large bush and lay panting, the blood roaring in her ears. As soon as her heart and her breathing were calm again, she was on her way. And although she knew Rolf and his berserkers would not awaken until the next eve, she knew she must be ever wary on her trek. There were others she did not want to meet.

When Helgi awakened, he knew not where he was and scarce knew who he was, his head ached so. It was dim in the corridor, and pale sun struggled through the slit windows at either end, as though it were setting. Setting? Hel's death! He sat up, and the movement made him moan aloud. Why would the sun be setting? What had happened to morning? He looked over at Bjork, who was flat on his back. The bastard's snores sounded like the roar of the monster that was said to swim in the sea here. By the gods, he hated this creepy land. He gave Bjork a kick in the ribs.

"Who goes?" Bjork muttered, bolting to his feet. He held his head then and groaned. His eyes were glazed. "Methinks I drank too much last night." He looked confused. "Did I?"

"Nay, I mind we had but a half-horn each."

"Ay. But 'twas too much. Hedeby will skewer and roast us if he knows we slept the night long."

"There's no sound from within—mayhap he sleeps now, too."

"If he gored the bitch the livelong night, mayhap they both sleep now. Or else she is dead. . . ."

"If so," Helgi muttered, "well did the wench deserve to die in such a way. Ah, Thor, my head . . . and I'm like to burst. . . ."

"Go you down first then, but don't take all day."

"Day?" Helgi growled. "Look without, man. 'Tis eventide. The day is long gone."

Heller Orm awaited Helgi as he stumbled out from the bushes. "Has your master not asked for food?" he said, blocking the oaf's way. "The women have prepared a great quantity, thinking he would wish to feast this eve."

"He has asked for naught," Helgi blustered. "His hunger is for other than food."

Orm fixed him with a steely eye. He had no love for either berserker. "Methinks a discreet tap on the door would be appropriate."

"Then 'tis you who can do the tapping," Helgi

muttered. "Never would I disturb my lord Hedeby when he is with a woman, least of all his betrothed."

Orm liked it not. His cousin was besotted with the wench, ay, and for good reason—Orm himself craved her as did every man in the village—but for Rolf to show such weakness as this was odd. He had a sudden strong feeling that something was amiss. He turned and made for the back door, Helgi at his heels.

"If you disturb him, 'tis on your head, man," Helgi said, following him up the steps and down the darkening passageway.

"What is't?" Bjork demanded, seeing Orm coming hell-bent. He drew his sword and braced himself before the door of his master's bedchamber.

"Stand aside, fool," Orm's voice cracked like a whip. "Something may be amiss." What, he could not say, could not begin to imagine, but he felt a black gloom descending upon him.

"What think you?" Bjork gave Helgi an uneasy look.

"Let him do what he will, but 'tis on his head."

Without waiting for them to agree, Orm tapped on the door with the butt of his dagger. There was no answer. Again he tapped. "My lord?" he called.

"'Tis like that they are asleep after a vigorous night," said Helgi. Both berserkers laughed and began jesting.

Orm tapped louder. "My lord Hedeby? Is't well with you, kinsman?"

When no answer came still, Orm banged on the door with the dagger. From within there was nothing but silence. At that, all three began pounding and shouting for Rolf to answer.

"Shall I fetch the ram, sire?" Helgi asked.

"Ay," Orm muttered. To Bjork he said, "Stay you here. I will look in the wench's chamber."

Finding nothing there, he returned to Rolf's chamber as Helgi came with the short ram. With much effort, the door was downed. The three stepped over it and entered the cold, dark room.

"My lord?" Orm whispered. He heard Rolf's heavy breathing but nothing else.

He rolled up the tapestry covering the windows so that the waning sunlight illuminated the room. The three stared, hammer-struck, at the sight that greeted them. There, on his throne-chair, lolled the Vaaga king, head fallen forward on his broad chest. He was covered from head to toe with a shimmering cloth.

"By the gods," Orm growled, "what is't draped over him?"

Helgi sniggered. "'Tis the wench's veil she wore when I fetched her to him."

Bjork laughed outright and Orm gave him a terrible look. "'Twould seem you two have allowed her to escape," he said.

"Nay!"

The three moved swiftly about the room looking for Sunniva, but she was neither in the boxbed nor in the great carved chest that stood on one wall.

"The bitch is gone," Helgi muttered. He and Bjork gazed at each other, white-faced.

Rolf forced open his heavy eyes. He wanted to sleep, and he was wroth that he had been awakened. Thor, his head felt as if it was cleaved by an ax and his eyes swam and could not focus. All was misty and blotched. Red, purple . . . By the gods, what had happened to him? Through the mist, he saw Orm's horrified face and staring eyes. He made to leap up but he could not.

"M-my lord," Orm gasped, "what has happened?"

Rolf opened his eyes wide, though it pained him to do so. Such effort brought more blood to his head and he feared it would burst like a ripe plum. Now he saw why everything was misty, and why he could not rise from his chair. His head grew tighter still as the blood was pumped to it by his raging heart. He was shamed. Mortified. He, a king and chieftain, a leader of strong dangerous men and conqueror of a people —he, bested by a soft, slender white maid he could break in half with one hand.

"Get this damned rag off me," he said, low, to Orm, "and get the key that hangs about my neck and unlock this chain."

"Chain?"

"Damn you, you bastard, I am chained to this chair!"

Gingerly, Orm took hold of the veil and unswathed his lord's mighty body. He saw then that a chain had indeed been wrapped tightly round and round the throne-chair, confining even his legs, before the two ends were locked to his wristband. By the gods . . .

"Hurry you," Rolf snarled.

Orm fumbled, trying to find the key under his cousin's luxuriant beard. "There is no key," he said finally.

Rolf was wont to roar, but seeing the faces of the three, their damned mouths twisting as though they were holding back laughter, he held on to such dignity as he had left. Soon enough they would feel his wrath. And the wench—by the Hammer, she would suffer. There was no need to ask if they had found her. He knew she was gone.

"Use your axes to free me," he commanded his berserks.

"Ay." They moved toward him, drawing the weapons from their belts.

"Mind you don't take off his hands," Orm snapped.

When at last the lord of Hedeby was freed, he rose to his feet, glaring, his face flaming. He swayed. His hands clasped his roaring, aching head; his guts were hot and sick. Was he dying? Was this how he was to meet his end, not on the field of battle but in his bedchamber, poisoned by a thrall who had cheated him of a hero's welcome in Valhalla? He had no doubts now that the ale she had served him was drugged.

"What day is't?" he muttered to Orm. "How long has she been gone?" His head swam with his fury and angry questions.

"You claimed her last night, my lord." Orm doubted that such was the case, but he deemed it wisest not to say so. "After that, she left as these two slept." He looked at the berserkers coldly.

Rolf's pale eyes, ice and fire, moved over his giants. "How come you to explain such a thing?" he asked softly, his voice filled with menace.

"My lord, the sun was gone when she came to us with a brimming horn and—"

"Since when do you take my ale from any but me unless I command it?"

"She said you bade us share the wedding ale," Bjork muttered.

"And of course you did."

"Ay, my lord Hedeby."

He would kill the bastards. When this was over, he would cut the blood-eagle on both their hides and mount their heads on poles for all to see.

"We will say naught of this to any, understand you?" he said grimly.

The three nodded, their faces ashen. They saw well his rage and mortification and knew this tale was far from over.

Rolf brooded. What damned story could he tell the village, which doubtless waited for them to come a-feasting? Could he say she was confined to his bedchamber? But nay, that meant his staying there pretending to be with her whilst she fled farther afield and went unpunished for the outrage. It was certain she would be caught by someone eventually, ay, and Celt or Viking, her fate would not be a pleasant one.

But he wanted to be the one to capture her and bear her back to Ballageay in chains. He wanted Raven Trondsson to see her humiliation before he slew the bastard, and then—then would he sell her to Kemal Attibak to live out her youth and beauty in his harem. And in the future, when he brought women to Kemal, then would he enjoy the treacherous wench day and night for as long as his visit lasted. Ay, it was the way he would work it. He could not be troubled to have another such damned, untamed bitch under his roof. She and the macLir were cut from the same cloth.

"We will leave to seek her immediately," he said, although his head and his stomach were nigh to killing him.

"Lord, what will we tell the others?" Orm asked, stroking his black beard, for he could foresee much embarrassment.

"Naught. We say naught. Have the women prepare food-packs. You two"—he snapped at the berserkers —"choose ten men skilled in tracking to accompany us. And any who speak of what happened in this room last night will feel the kiss of the Battle Fiend. 'Tis clear the wench is an enchantress who worked her spells on us all. Go now."

Minded of his sword, Rolf reached up to the rafter for the precious, silver-chased weapon with which he had been blooded in battle as a young lad. His hand did not find it. He grasped the beam and lifted himself up, looking up and down its dusty black length, but the Battle Fiend was gone. He groaned. The unspeakable bitch.

Never had Rolf Gunnarsson dropped to his knees

in supplication to any god, but now he did. He cursed Sunniva Mellby before them all, and asked for strength not to slay her when he caught her. Slaying was too clean, too easy for such a diabolical female. He prayed that his hand would spare her for a much worse fate—the vast impenetrable harem of Kemal Attibak.

In the great military camp of Aggersborg, Raven Trondsson had learned much. Those based there remembered well when the Landwaster arrived early in July. They recalled she had stayed for repairs until dawn the third day, and never had her crew stopped their brawling and drinking except when they slept. Never had Rolf Gunnarsson cracked a smile, but had remained so black and scowling that none went near him. It was said he now owned the most beautiful maid in Norway's land, a high-born wench he had stolen in the westland and was taking to Maun as his thrall. But none knew where on Maun. He had many strongholds on the isle, and looked to take even more, for he craved to be king there.

Hearing this news, Raven had commanded his men to remove his scarlet sail and banner. It was replaced with one that none would recognize—the purple and white striped sail given his father by King Olaf. This was done in great haste, after which they weighed anchor. While it was good to know finally who held Sunniva and where he was taking her, Raven's heart was heavy. No chieftain was more feared and despised than Rolf Gunnarsson. When Raven thought of his treasure being in thrall to such a man, his blood ran cold. All had heard the horrifying tales that came out of Hedeby concerning Rolf and his father and their thrall-women, and all feared that the devil was abusing Sunniva. But none could speak of it to Raven, not even Ulf. Instead, they clasped his shoulder to give him silent support and to give him heart.

Well they knew, these Solby Vikings, that other men fought for their chieftains because they loved booty and adventure. These fought for Raven Trondsson because him they loved and would die for. All were equal in his eyes, and he himself claimed no chieftain's privileges. Only in a crisis did he assume command and then it was evident to all why he, not they, was chieftain. It was Raven, therefore, who decided their plan of attack after listening to their suggestions.

Maun was but a small island. A man on a fast horse could traverse its breadth in little over a day, and its length, double that. Starting at the northernmost tip, Raven sailed east, putting men ashore near all the key Viking strongholds to listen and keep their eyes open. The second day, he retrieved them, but none had any news. And then, as they passed Ballaugh Beach with its red cliffs and approached Jurby Head, his sharp eyes spied what they had not seen earlier because of mist—the Landwaster anchored deep in a cove. They sailed on by, put into the next cove and dropped anchor. Two men stole south to Ballageay. They reported back to Raven before sunset, saying that the place was in turmoil. Sunniva had indeed been there, but she had escaped. None knew how or where she had fled, but it was on every tongue. The lord of Hedeby and thirteen men had left to find her.

Raven laughed at the news. He could expect no less from a Valkyrie like Sunniva. But while he was relieved that she was out of Gunnarsson's clutches, she was not out of danger. By the gods, where would she fly to? In discussing it hastily with his men, all concluded that she had needed help to escape such a well-guarded place. And since no man who saw her would give her up, a Celt woman must have befriended and helped her. Doubtless she had been sent to where other Norse women dwelt, which meant the northern areas—Andreas, Bride and Jurby. Or the southern area of Malew. Something told Raven it was Malew. Long ago he had learned to listen to the small inner voice that told him such things.

"We'll round Point Ayre again and head south," he told his helmsman. "Half of us will go ashore in Malew and trek north. The rest of you return to this cove, fan up north and then back here to wait for us."

Sunniva had fled southward the night long, stopping to rest briefly only when it seemed she might drop. Ever did her eyes dart in all directions and her ears listen for every sound of the night. But always in her mind was the thought that she was free. Free! And when she reached her destination, perhaps a smith would remove Rolf's band from her ankle. And perhaps the folk there would have a waif word of Raven and could help her send word to him.

Her spirits were so high, they gave wings to her feet. Over gorse-covered moors she flew, and glens forested with firs and rowans. Hastening across vast grazing lands under the waxing moon, she marked that the cattle and sheep were still up in the highlands just as they would be at Lilleby. It brought a sudden lump to her throat, thinking of her folk going about their work while they grieved for her, not knowing whether she lived or lay cold in the ground. She thrust the thought from her mind. All her attention must be on the present, not on any brooding imaginings.

The sun was but a pale gray lifting of darkness in the east when she began to think of where she might sleep during the daylight hours. She was on a beach cleft by many ravines and small valleys, each with a rushing stream pouring into the sea. It was in one of these, thick with firs and bracken, that she decided to shelter. When she spied a broad outcropping of rock roofing a thick carpet of moss beneath, she smiled. She had found her bed.

After a supper of rock-hard bread, cheese, and a raw turnip, she drank from the small, clear pool that broke the stream's headlong rush to the sea. Never had food or water tasted so good. She curled up on the moss then, her head on her wallet and the Battle Fiend and her dagger by her side. She slept instantly. Not until twilight did she awaken, to eat and begin her trek again.

Once she lost her way, coming upon a great peat bog that was not on Calla's map. Painstakingly she retraced her steps, ever on the lookout for danger. By the time she was on the right path once more, it was near dawn and she was too weary to seek out a secret sleeping place. Besides, she had not seen a soul on her trek except from a great distance—those folk haying in their fields. She dropped to the thick grass beneath a tree and tucked her wallet under her head. Sleep came as soon as she closed her eyes.

A noise made her stir—a jangle of metal, a twig snapping underfoot. Sunniva awakened instantly, her eyes widening as two armed men approached her. She saw they were Vikings. They wore leather helmets and mail under their brown-green tunics. She seized her weapons and leapt up, her back to the tree.

"If you would live," she spat, "move on!" Her sword was up and the dagger raised to strike.

The two laughed, but not with malice. It was happy laughter. Their eyes danced. One held up his hands, yielding.

"Hold, mistress," he said. "We mean you no harm."

The other cupped his hands to his mouth and bawled, "She is found. Ho! Everybody! She is found!"

The sweat started out on Sunniva's body as more and more men appeared from the fir forest and came toward her. Who were they, and how did they know she was missing? She did not recognize them at all. Seeing their smiling faces, the truth dawned. They were home-folk!

She gasped, "Be you Solby men?" When their grins broadened, she cried, "Raven's men?"

They made no answer for at that moment, a tall, black-haired warrior, his berserkers at his side, came breaking through the thick foliage. It was Raven. In his glowing eyes and on his dark bearded face was a look that Sunniva had never seen before. Wordlessly she went into his arms and wordlessly he lifted her and cradled her against him. Long and long he kissed her as his happy men looked on.

CHAPTER 17

Perhaps it was only a dream, Sunniva thought, feeling Raven's strong, protecting arms about her and his warm mouth on hers. She had had so many dreams. When their kiss ended, she looked up at him, almost fearful.

"Is't a dream?" she whispered.

Raven laughed. His relief at having found her was enormous. "Ulf, feel you like a dream?"

"Ulf!" Sunniva cried, seeing her brother. She ran to his open arms, and stroked his wild blond hair and wiry beard. He gave her a kiss and a bearhug. "Oh, tis glad I am to see you! All of you! How go our parents, Ulf?"

"'Tis long since I saw them, but I trow they are making do. They knew we would find you."

Raven watched Sunniva closely. He was heartened by her glowing face and eyes and good spirits, but his concern for her was great. He led her apart from the others.

"Sunniva, did the bastard harm you?" he asked softly.

Sunniva blinked and turned pink. "Nay, Raven."

He gave her a little shake. "Sunni, know you what I mean?"

"Of course I know what you mean." She lowered her voice. "And nay, he did not harm me."

She felt very young of a sudden. Never could she tell Raven those disgusting words Rolf had forced from her lips and the cruel way his hands and mouth had moved over her, purposely bruising her. She had been so very shamed. It shamed her to think on it even now.

Marking her pink face and downcast eyes, Raven said no more, but his thoughts raged. So. It seemed he had made her his. No woman was safe from the bastard, especially one who looked like Sunniva, but she was making a brave front of it, not wanting to hurt him. By the gods, he would have the devil's heart in his hand before this was over! But for now, he must let it pass. Later they would talk of it in private. He put his arm over her shoulders and took her back to the others.

"Are you ready to trek now?" he asked, his grave eyes moving over her long legs in the doe-colored leggings and the golden braid hanging down her back. She was more fair than ever, if such were possible.

"Ay, I'm ready."

"Even though we interrupted your sleep?"

"'Twas a silly place to sleep," Ulf teased her. He gave her shoulder a gentle buffet, not unlike when they were small.

Sunniva gave him no argument. "I knew it even as I lay me down there. I was just too tired to move."

"'Twas fortunate, that," Raven added, "else we

might have walked on by and not seen you. Were you headed for Malew, by chance?"

"Ay."

"We thought you might." They had reckoned her movements well.

Sunniva stood on tiptoe and wrapped her arms tightly about his neck. She kissed him. "You came," she whispered. "You once said that if I was lost, you would search the earth to find me and you did. You came. . . ."

"Ay, and you said you would be waiting."

"And I was. Until the night before last, I was waiting, but then—then 'twas no longer safe to wait."

"We will hear it all, but now we must move on. My ship is north of Ballageay and we have a stiff trek ahead of us."

"Wait, where is my wallet and my sword?"

"Eiliv will carry them. 'Tis a mighty weapon you have there, little troll." His laughing eyes moved over her. Never would he understand how her slender arms and small white hands could even hold it.

Sunniva smiled. "Ay. You will hear it all."

Raven brooded that he had much dealing to do with Gunnarsson and little time in which to do it. The weather had been fair, but it would not last. They must push forward as hard as they could. He slipped his wallet off his back, got out bread and smoked meat, and offered it to Sunniva.

"You can eat as we go along, and now let's move." To his men, he said, "Fan out, but stay away from the coast. Speak low if speak you must, and no crashing through the brush. We will rest every two hours. Questions?"

When there were none, they set off, Sunniva between Raven and Ulf and Raven's two berserkers ten paces on either side of them. The others, more than forty men, spread out and moved so silently through the countless glens and ravines of Maun that only forest noises could be heard. When the path was wide enough, Raven walked beside Sunniva, their arms linked.

"Tis only fair that you know my plan," he said softly. "We will reach the ship later this day and I will then take you to Dublin. You will be safe there until I return for you."

"Return from where? Can I not go with you, wherever you are going?"

"I am coming back here to slay Rolf—unless he should happen to fall into my hands this day."

"Raven, you need not!" She raised her voice.

He put a warning finger over her lips. "But I do, Sunniva. Never will I have peace until he dies by my hand."

Remembering Rolf's terrible strength and his deep hatred for Raven, remembering his giant berserkers who were so eager to kill, Sunniva began to tremble. "What if you are the one to die?" she whispered and caught his hand. "Raven, he is heartless. He thought naught of having his men slay the convent guards when they stole me, and he—he slew Eirik Paalsson. . . ."

Raven scowled down at her and back at Ulf. He motioned Ulf closer to hear their low talk. "How know you he slew Paalsson?" he asked.

"He told me. And he told me he would slay you when you came for me. He knew you would come. Please, Raven, can we not just leave for home right away?"

Again Raven and Ulf exchanged looks. "Nay, Sunniva. 'Tis more urgent than ever now that I take him first."

"But he may already be dead!"

Raven's gray-gold eyes narrowed. "How so?"

They were moving rapidly over bracken-covered hillsides and leaping narrow streams as they traversed the ravines that sliced through the coastline. Noting that Sunniva had grown breathless, Raven called a brief halt. He leaned against a tree trunk, arms crossed over his chest as he gazed down at her. She sat on the ground rubbing her doeskin-clad feet.

"What mean you, Sunniva, he may already be dead?"

"The Celts were about to attack Ballageay when I fled." Sunniva quickly explained about Calla and how she had helped her escape the guards. "So you see, 'tis possible he is slain already."

"Nay, Sunni, he is not. When my men scouted Ballageay, he was already gone seeking you. The devil lives still, and I am glad. Slaying him is a pleasure I have promised myself."

Sunniva stared at him. The face of her beloved was that of a stranger. His ebony hair was long and shaggy and his skin was burned by the wind and sun. He was handsome, ay, always would he be handsome; it was the beard that made him look like a fierce stranger. His beard and the way his mouth was twisted into a bitter half-smile. She reached up to stroke his lips, and he caught her hand and kissed it.

"Calla has as large a grievance against Rolf as you," she murmured. "More so, I trow. When he returns to Ballageay, he will learn too late 'tis no longer his. He is a dead man, Raven, I promise you."

"That must I see for myself, Sunniva. Come, 'tis time we moved on."

Sunniva remained planted on the ground where she was. She was glaring at Raven's broad departing back when Ulf came from behind and lifted her to her feet.

"Up, you!" He grasped her arm and marched her beside him. He had listened to the two, saying nothing, and now his blue eyes, so like Sunniva's, were frosty. "'Tis Raven's decision to make, not yours. You are a grown woman now, not some sulky maid who must have her own way. Pouting and glaring will gain you naught from our chieftain but his irritation."

"But 'tis stupid," she murmured, "and it frights me. Rolf has vowed to kill him. He has those two awful berserkers."

"Raven's own berserkers will take them as easily as they took his others," Ulf said, his voice a whisper. "'Tis a natural thing for Raven to seek out the man who stole you. Gunnarsson must pay, and who better to take him?"

Sunniva blinked back the tears that wanted to flow. "If aught happens to him, then will I die, too, Ulf. Think you that a maid can go to Valhalla? I—I would be there with him to care for him. . . ."

Ulf was touched beyond words. It was moments before he could trust himself to speak.

"For such a maid as you, Sunni, I trow there is a place in Valhalla, ay."

His heart grew full suddenly, thinking how fair she was and how loving. He could see in her still that rosy-cheeked, sturdy little maid she had been not all that long ago, but those days were gone. She was a grown maid. In fact, he doubted much that she was a maid still. Never had Raven spoken of it, but Ulf had seen in Sunniva's eyes as she looked on him that she was a woman. The two were one. She was a woman who matched Ulf's own steps as they strode along, her long legs moving in easy unison with his. But the roses were gone from her cheeks. Her face shone white against her green tunic, and her eyes were large and frightened. Ulf caught her hand.

"Raven will be safe. Odin himself watches over him."

Sunniva nodded bravely. "Ay."

"And know you that Rolf Gunnarsson will not take it kindly that you have escaped. No power on this earth will keep him from tracking you down and seizing you again, and well can you imagine his fury and his thirst for revenge."

"Ay." Ulf did not even know the worst of it!

"'Tis Raven's decision that we seek him out and slay him before he can harm you. Henceforward, you will say naught against it. Hear you, little sister mine? He must die. Only death will stop the devil's hounding you."

"Ay," Sunniva murmured. She knew he spoke the truth.

It was late afternoon and they had made good time. Every so often, birdcalls from their right and left assured them that all was well with the men on both sides of them. As long as Sunniva did not allow her thoughts to rush ahead, it gladdened her to stride along with Raven and Ulf pointing out to her things of curiosity and interest—the little white roofless church in a field where it was said fairies lived; glens that were beautiful beyond anything she had ever seen; lovely shallow rivers filled with trout. Through rich farmland they went, and they were following beside a marshland paradise for birds and waterfowl when the first drops of rain began to fall. Mist swirled through the air. Raven halted their column.

"Think you we should whistle them in?" he asked Ulf.

"Ay, this rolls in fast."

Cupping their hands to their mouths, they whistled, Ulf to the right and Raven to their left, a weird high warble which Sunniva had never heard before.

"What is happening?" she asked.

"'Tis bad weather coming in," Raven answered. "'Twill be upon us in no time. We had best wait it out in the village that lies ahead." He caught Sunniva up in his arms and gave her a hungry kiss as Ulf and one of his berserkers continued whistling.

Sunniva returned his kiss, her hunger as fierce as his own. Slipping her arms about his narrow waist, she drew him closer, pressing her breasts against him, reveling in his hard strength.

"I love you, Raven Trondsson."

Raven's arms tightened. "And if my men were not here, little seductress, I would demonstrate my feelings for you."

"You have. You came for me."

Even now, after trekking with him these many hours, Sunniva was still in a daze of disbelief that he had found her. She wavered between euphoria over her dream's coming true, and fright that a new nightmare was about to begin, for she could not forget Rolf Gunnarsson's vow to slay Raven. She was brooding over it when Ulf said low:

"The men are all called in."

"Single file then. I will lead." Raven glanced about, frowning at the thickening mist. "Methinks this is as bad as I have seen, so stay close to the man before you—there are bogs about. Asla and Hauk," he addressed his berserkers, "go you on either side of my lady. Ulf, bring up the rear of the column."

"Ay. Fall in, men." Ulf moved among them, whispering. "Fall in and move along. Swiftly now, and go you softly. No talking. We will shelter at Magher 'til this passes."

They moved like shadows, an arm's-length apart. Sunniva felt small and safe with Raven before her, Asla and Hauk on either side, and the man called Eiliv who bore her sword and wallet directly behind. The top of her head came but to their shoulders, and she knew that were Rolf Gunnarsson to come upon them, a great shield-burg of forty men would be thrown around her. He would not even see her.

"We are close," Raven's low voice broke into her thoughts. "All of you wait whilst I go and talk to the sentries." He was gone but a short while before returning with four of them. "These are my men," he told them, "and this is the lady we are protecting. We seek shelter only until the fog passes."

The stranger-Vikings moved up and down their column, glumly counting and assessing Raven's men before disappearing into the mist.

"Think you their chieftain will let us stay?" Sunniva whispered. She was wet, weary, hungry, and more than ready for a rest.

"Ay, I think he will. These guards are being cautious, as well they should. They go now to tell him who we are. We have met, he and I. He has as little love for Gunnarsson as do I."

Their band stood quietly in the curling mist and fine drizzle until the four reappeared. "Come you, Raven Trondsson of Marvik," said the leader. "Bring your men and the lady, and welcome to Magher. Our chieftain has bade us take you to his manor. He has room for the lot of you."

Raven nodded. "We give him thanks for that."

When Sunniva saw the large stone dwelling, she suspected it had once been a church. Not as grand as the abbey in which Rolf dwelt, but grand nonetheless. The great hall had benches on all four walls, a fire roaring on the hearth, tapestries, and a shield-wall with shields agleam. And then she saw the chieftain striding toward them in welcome, a bear of a man, tall, and with long black hair tucked under his gold-embossed belt. Haftor Kol! She stood taller, her eyes icy.

"Trondsson of Marvik, by all the gods!" he roared.

"Methought you were home for the winter. Welcome to Magher."

"Thanks for the shelter," Raven answered. "My ship lies northwest of here but in this fog—" He ceased his explanation, noting that Haftor Kol was staring rudely at Sunniva and hearing none of what he said.

"Did you buy this thrall from yon Gunnarsson?" the Magher chieftain asked. "He told me she was not for sale."

Sunniva opened her mouth to protest, but Raven gripped her arm. "This lady is my betrothed," he said quietly, but his gray eyes glinted dangerously.

"So said Gunnarsson." Kol's own eyes were hungry. They remained on Sunniva. "How many betrotheds does the wench have?"

Raven's heart thundered as he strove not to slay the fellow then and there. "Gunnarsson took her by the stronghand on our wedding day. I have just found her again."

Kol's lips twitched. "Ah. You have stolen her from him then?"

"Nay. I escaped on my own!" Sunniva was outraged at being discussed as though she were not even there. "I drugged him and his berserkers, bound him with his own chain and stole his sword." She crossed her arms and glared at both men.

Raven chuckled. He knew she had a tale to tell but this—drugging and chaining the devil? But then, why had he expected anything less?

Haftor Kol threw back his head and his laughter filled the hall. Sunniva thought he had recovered only too well from his wounds at Rolf's hands—he had forgotten why he had been dealt them. "Bound him, you say? And with his own chain? And you stole the Battle Fiend? By the gods!"

Now the whole hall rang with the men's laughter until Kol held up a hand for quiet. As he gazed down at Sunniva, all merriment was gone from his eyes.

"Lady, I salute you," he said.

Sunniva was about to make a crisp retort when Raven put his arm around her and pulled her close. "She thanks you, Kol, and now if she might rest a bit. . . ."

"Ay. She may have my own bedchamber—I will have a wench fetch fresh straw. And we will feast this night. A celebration is in order." Again his eyes glittered over Sunniva. He shook his head, admiring. "Bound with his own chain, by the gods, and the Battle Fiend stolen. This is quite a wench, Trondsson."

After he strode off, Sunniva faced Raven, her cheeks fiery. "I hate it when you act as though I am not even here. 'She thanks you. . . .'" she mimicked.

"The less you say to that bastard, the better."

"'Tis demeaning. 'Tis as if I had no mind or thoughts of my own. As if I were naught but a—a possession!"

"And so you are in his eyes," Raven said curtly. "Be she wife or thrall, a woman is owned by such a man. 'Tis of the greatest importance, therefore, that he knows you belong to me. You will not resist me in this, Sunniva, hear you? You have just escaped one bastard, and damn me if I will lose you to another before I can get you to safety."

Sunniva's triumph over Rolf Gunnarsson had caused her memory of Haftor Kol to dim—his leaping atop the board in Rolf's great hall and claiming her for his wife, his berserkers bearing her off. His eyes said he craved her still. Raven had marked it instantly, and were he to learn of the other while they were here, there would be bloodshed.

"I am a troll-woman," she said softly. "You must do as you will. I promise not to sulk. Forgive me?"

"Ay. But not here and now." Raven's mouth lifted at one corner; his eyes danced. "I will forgive you properly when we get to your bedchamber, imp."

CHAPTER 18

AFTER THE FEASTING, THE MAGHER CHIEFTAIN CALLED for his skald and another keg was opened. He sat in the high seat on the north bench and Raven in the seat of honor on the south bench. Sunniva sat close by Raven's side, glad that she had not been relegated to the women's bench, where she would have sat alone. But then, never would Raven have permitted it, she thought, sliding her hand into his and feeling his fingers close tightly on hers.

She sipped her beer and kept a polite smile on her lips as the skald launched into a tale of old. She had heard enough songs and stories of war and bloodshed to last a lifetime these past weeks. If only she could just fall into bed now. The great hall had grown over-hot and smoke-filled from the ill-tended fire spitting on the hearth and the many torches guttering on the walls. And the noise was ear-splitting. In addition, Haftor Kol's great hounds were slavering and nosing about, paws and muzzles on the tables, begging food as the men laughed and encouraged them. She felt her head nodding, too heavy to hold upright, and her eyes closing. She was so tired.

"My lady is weary, Kol," Raven spoke to his host over the skald's chanting and the babble of voices. "I ask that you excuse me while I take her up and settle her for the night."

"Of course." The Magher chieftain smiled and raised his horn to Sunniva. "Again, I salute you, lady."

"Have thanks for your hospitality, sire," Sunniva answered coolly. Never would she forget how he had humiliated her.

Raven, his arm about her, led Sunniva firmly through the smoky hall, past the hounds and the hearth and the up-raised horns in the hands of both the Solby and Magher Vikings. A serving-wench, flaming fir-root torch in hand, guided them up narrow stone steps to a chamber that had been freshened for Sunniva. After lighting a lamp, she left.

"Lie you down and sleep now, beloved," Raven said. "I will return after I accept further hospitality." He watched as Sunniva lowered herself to the fresh straw pallet. She stretched and yawned.

"I wish you would stay," she murmured, holding out a hand to him. "I—feel unsafe. . . ."

"You are safe. My berserkers will remain here to guard your door, and I will be back shortly."

Sunniva drew his hand to her lips and kissed it. "I love you. . . ."

"Sunniva—"

"Ay, beloved?"

"'Twould seem that you know this Haftor Kol." When he saw her eyes turn guarded, he asked gruffly, "Well? Do you?"

"I—met him once."

Knowing her moods as well as he knew his own, he

saw that she was frightened. "How do you know him, Sunniva?"

Sunniva's heartbeat changed from the slow, heavy measure of fatigue to pounding like Sooten's flying hooves. She did not dare tell him the truth when they were on the man's own manor and outnumbered by his warriors.

"Can we not talk of it later, Raven? I am so sleepy. . . ."

"Has he harmed you in any way?" Raven's eyes glittered in the half-light.

"Nay." She shook her golden head, her own eyes wide and serious.

Raven knew she spoke the truth. If he had thought otherwise, he would have confronted the scut as he sat swilling his beer. He smiled down at her then and bent to kiss the top of her head. How like a lad she looked, lying there in the shadows. But in the light of day, none would make such a mistake, seeing the soft delicate curve of cheeks and chin, the tender white throat and satiny skin, the tantalizing hint of her breasts and slender rounded arms and legs beneath her leggings and tunic.

"Promise you will come back after you talk?" Sunniva whispered, responding to the heat in his eyes despite her weariness. She yearned to lie close to him again.

"I will be back. I have waited long for this night, my Sunniva."

"I love you," she murmured again.

He chuckled. "I will show you my love when I return. Sleep, now. My berserkers will guard you well." He saw her smile, watched her gold-lashed eyes close. She slept even before he left the chamber.

Raven's mood was black when, after the feasting, he returned to where Sunniva lay sleeping still. His time spent with Haftor Kol had proven what he already knew. The bastard lusted for her and wanted her for his own. The only reason he had not tried to seize her was simple—he feared having Trondsson of Marvik as an enemy. But it had not prevented his offering to buy her. Raven had growled a refusal, declaring yet again that she was his betrothed, but Kol had been too drunk to understand. The matter, therefore, was not ended. By Odin, just as soon as this damned mist lifted, they would be on their way.

Quickly, quietly, Raven removed his clothing and crawled onto the pallet beside Sunniva. In the flickering lamplight, he saw that her lips were parted and her long sable-soft lashes brushed her pink cheeks. His heart brimmed with such love and longing for her that his body ached with it. He slipped his arms about her slender form and his lips sought hers. How sweet and fresh her mouth was, he marveled, even in sleep. He gave her lips a gentle kiss and saw her eyelids flutter open. Her eyes widened.

"Is't really you, or am I dreaming again?" Sunniva whispered, snuggling closer. She lifted her lips for another kiss.

Raven laughed, pressing her closer so that she could feel his need. "'Tis no dream, Sunni. I am here. . . ."

She ran her fingers over his bare shoulders and arms, loving how hard and strong they felt. She traced his dark eyebrows and the chiseled lines of his cheeks and nose, the familiar curve of his mouth, now smiling at her. She stroked the dark fur on his chest, his thick raven-black hair, his beard—ay, even his beard she loved. Haftor Kol would think long and hard before angering such a dangerous-looking chieftain as Raven Trondsson of Marvik.

She slid her arms around him, melting against him,

feeling his urgent hands moving over. She laughed then. "Methinks I have on too many clothes. . . ."

Raven helped her to sit up. He then untied the laces on her tunic and pulled it over her head, cupping, caressing, tenderly kissing each full white breast in turn. How fair she was. How shining and perfect and glorious. But beneath his joy ran the dark thought of what she had endured before he found her. Gunnarsson had not let her go unscathed, that he knew, and how did the Magher chieftain figure into it? What had he done to make her fear him? He would find out, damned if he would not. But not this night.

"My treasure . . ."

His gray eyes were gentle as he pulled down her leggings, kissed the sweet mound of her belly, her thighs and the down-soft triangle between them. He kissed every precious part of her as it was revealed to his starving eyes . . . her dimpled knees and firm shapely calves, her ankles . . .

Sunniva heard his breath catch, felt his hold on her tighten. She saw then that his gaze was fastened on the band about her ankle. He had not seen it until now.

"That bastard . . ." Raven muttered a string of curses, his voice thick with fury as he stared at the abomination cutting into her flesh—a wide bronze band with HEDEBY pounded into the metal.

"Shhhh, 'tis all right," Sunniva said. "'Tis over and now I am here with you. I am safe. 'Tis all right, Raven." Seeing that he had paled in his rage and that he shook, she cupped his face in her hands, kissed his mouth, soothed him as best she could. "Shhh . . . shhhhh, beloved. . . ."

She drew him toward her breasts, felt the fury draining from him as she comforted him. He nuzzled her then, touching his tongue to her hardened nip-

ples. Fire streaked through her as his hands and
mouth began moving over her, coaxing, teasing her,
possessing her. . . .

She loved him more than life itself, Sunniva
thought afterwards, lying in his arms, stroking his
chest, playing with his beard and his long eyelashes
and his fingers. And she meant the same to him. Had
he not searched for her far and near just as he
promised he would? She sensed that without her, he
was not complete; just as without him, she felt
nothing but emptiness. He was her beloved, her
childhood's dearest friend. She smiled, closed her
eyes, and treasured her memories of a young Raven
—tall, slender, immensely strong as a lad even, his
gray eyes laughing, teasing, but always caring. She
raised his hand to her lips, inhaled its familiar male
scent, pressed a kiss on it. Whoever would have
thought that their best-friendship would catch fire
and he would become her husband? Even now she
could scarcely believe it.

Raven's own thoughts were on a different path.
Sunniva was his. He loved her, and she loved him.
Never had he felt such a way about a woman before.
Never had he known such a woman before, and the
thought of her being abused by Gunnarsson—a slave-
band on her ankle, by all the gods!—and now this
thing with Haftor Kol, whatever it was. He ground his
teeth. With his passion now abated, his anger
mounted. He was ready to slay both men, but of this
Magher chieftain, he was uncertain. She said he had
not harmed her. The Vaaga chieftain was a different
matter. The arrow had gone out on him. He was a
woman-stealer and he had caused men to be slain.
Rolf Gunnarsson was fair game and Gildor thirsted
for his blood. Raven himself thirsted for it.

"You seem far away," Sunniva murmured. "What is't, Raven?"

"I am thinking of Gunnarsson."

Sunniva had been so happy and now she felt only a sick fear in the pit of her stomach. "Can we not just leave for home when the fog lifts? Please? I do not want to go to Dublin." Her eyes seemed as deep and glistening as a forest pond.

"He must pay for what he has done."

"Leave him to the Celts. Please. I am unharmed."

Raven sat up. "Nay. There is not a man on this isle or in Norway who does not know of his hunger for women and his cruel treatment of them. This damned band on your ankle—" He lifted her foot, examined the shackle again and scowled at her. "I would hear everything, Sunniva. Now. Beginning to end."

"Nay." Sunniva, too, sat up. She pulled on her tunic. "'Tis over and I want to forget it."

She was ashamed to repeat those words which the Hedeby lord had forced her to say; shamed to describe his plans for her and his cruel treatment of her. If Raven knew, he would go after him for certain. It was a danger she still hoped to avoid.

"Damn it, Sunniva—"

"Nay!" Sunniva's eyes flashed.

Raven studied her pale, defiant face in the guttering light. He knew her every mood, the meaning of every glance and tilt of her mouth. Always had he known where he stood with her; she was completely open and candid and without guile. Now there was something she was not telling him. A thought so terrible struck him that it was like a blow beneath the belt. His first instinct was to crush it, but that would make two of them being secretive. One was enough. And he had to know. . . .

"Did you let him bed you willingly then?" he asked gruffly.

Sunniva stared at him in total disbelief. His face and mouth were stiff as granite, his eyes like gray stone. "How could you even think such a thing?"

"There are those wenches who call him fair. Some even like to be manhandled by him, although never would I have thought it of you."

She found her leggings, angrily thrust her feet into them, and pulled them on. She bound the ties about her legs, knotted them, and tied the laces of her tunic, her cold eyes on Raven all the while.

"You can stay or go as you choose," she snapped, rising to her feet. "I am too angry with you to care."

Raven stood. He grasped her shoulders and gave her a shake. "Think you that I am not angry? Damn me, Sunniva, you expect me to believe the bastard did not touch you all those weeks when he killed five men to get you?"

Sunniva twisted away. "I don't care what you believe."

Had they been at Lilleby, she would have marched from the room and taken Sooten on a wild ride. Or she would have taken out her wrath in weapon-practice or in running or in the many chores that always awaited her on their steading. Here, she could do nothing. Fog without, drunken men within . . .

Raven sat down on a chair and watched as she paced the chamber, cheeks flaming, eyes burning, not looking at him.

"Sunni." When she made no answer, he said gently, "'Twas my anger speaking. I thought, wrongly I see, that you would be eager to tell me all and that you might need comforting." He shook his head. "Damn me, I know you did not bed with the devil willingly." He added gruffly: "I know that. Forgive me."

When Sunniva spoke finally, her voice was high and tight. "'Tis clear you thought it, else you would never have said it."

"Nay, 'twas my anger. My worry is that the bastard raped you, and you are silent for fear I will be killed avenging you." He stood and pulled her roughly into his arms. "And while I am glad for your concern for my safety, it says little for your confidence in me as a warrior."

"That you don't believe me says little for your confidence in my love for you."

She pulled free and flung herself onto the straw pallet where they had just made love. Panic swept over her. Was that lovemaking their last? Oh, what was happening to them? He had always been so sympathetic and understanding but now, now he could actually ask if she had bedded with that brute willingly! She yearned to tell him all, to pour it all out, but she could not. Not now. He would go wild. When they were safely at home, then would she tell him. . . .

Raven said gruffly: "This is getting us nowhere. Go you back to sleep."

Furious as she was, Sunniva did not want to see him go. "You can sleep here. . . ."

"Nay. I will be with my berserkers in the passageway. You will be safe, so sleep well. We will talk more tomorrow on our way to the ship."

The next day, the mist had worsened. It was so thick that none could venture forth without a rope attached to some solid object. When Sunniva heard the Magher men muttering, worrying about Manannan, the Celt sea-god who had the mist at his command, she was minded of Calla. How was her friend, she wondered, and had her people come yet? Raven himself was not worried about Manannan—

he trusted Aegir and Ran to protect him in matters pertaining to the sea. What he worried about was Sunniva. While he did not expect an attack from Rolf Gunnarsson when visibility was so poor, he was wary of Haftor Kol. There were few women at his encampment, and the Magher Vikings stared at her so hungrily, as did the chieftain himself, that Raven bade her stay in her chamber with his berserkers ever on guard. When the mist still clung to land and sea by the end of the second day, the tempers of all his men were on edge. After seeing Sunniva safely to her bedchamber after evening food, he said:

"We leave tomorrow, Sunni, mist or no. We can waste no more time in this place."

"I will be ready." She was not unaware of her danger and of the great strain borne by the Solby men on her account. She, too, was under a strain. While neither she nor Raven had spoken further of their disagreement, things were amiss between them.

"Until tomorrow then." Raven kissed her lips lightly and turned to leave.

"Raven—" Sunniva caught his hand. "Will you not stay?"

He smiled, a glow in his pewter eyes. "Though you want to slay me?"

"Only when you say stupid things," she whispered.

He cracked the door, murmured to his berserkers, and then closed and barred it. He slid his arms around her, molding her body to his.

"Then we will not talk."

"What will we do?" Sunniva teased, twining his dark hair about her fingers and drawing his face toward hers. She kissed his lips, kissed them again and again.

"This . . ." Raven murmured, placing his own long hungry kiss on her soft mouth.

He untied the laces of her tunic and pulled it up over her head. His breath caught. Her breasts were the most beautiful he had ever seen. High, exquisitely full and symmetrical, the white skin satiny, her pink nipples thrusting out from them like the small perfect buds of a rose. He dipped his head, taking first one in his mouth and then the other, circling each in turn with his tongue, nipping them gently with his teeth, seeing them pucker in her excitement.

"Don't stop," Sunniva gasped, for he was sending ecstasy raying throughout every part of her body.

Raven laughed at her innocence. He could not have stopped had he wanted to, not even had Sunniva begged him to. Her beauty aroused in him a primal hunger that would not be denied. As his hands stole over her, stripping off the rest of her clothing, he commanded himself to be gentle, for she was but a tender maid. She was his treasure. Yet he heard a growl rumbling in his throat, felt the heat of desire flaming through him, the urgency to claim her flooding his loins, stiffening him. He could wait no longer.

As carefully as he could, he laid her on the pallet and parted her legs. Sunniva, as eager as he, helped him, opening herself to him, stroking and guiding him, and as he thrust within her, all gentleness forgotten and his possession of her all that mattered, her own hot rush of passion crowned the head of his shaft.

Afterwards he lay spent, Sunniva still in his arms. She was a queen, a goddess, an enchantress . . . yet still was she his little Sunniva, that wide-eyed, inquisitive child he could never deny. Holy Odin, how he loved her, but try as he might, he could not quell the black jealousy that raged within him whenever he thought of Gunnarsson. It was jealousy that could destroy all reason, all common sense. He would slay the devil, there was no doubt in his mind on that matter, but Haftor Kol, too, stood in grave jeopardy. If he made but one more mention of buying Sunniva, the words would be his last. . . .

CHAPTER 19

THE NEXT MORN, RAVEN ALERTED HIS MEN THAT THEY would be on the move to the coast no later than midday, mist or no. As it fell out, the fog lifted long enough for an early start, and while Haftor Kol's hungry gaze slid over Sunniva as they took their leave, he uttered no further word about buying her. The Solby men departed in peace, Raven at the head of their column and Ulf guarding the rear. Sunniva walked between Raven's berserkers. She was in men's clothing still, but she wore mail beneath her tunic. Once more, her hair was braided into a shining gold rope and was hidden by helmet and tunic.

Raven mused gratefully that she looked much like the others in his band. Though she was smaller, she moved with a long confident stride, a dagger at her belt and bow in hand for instant use. Her face was dirtied to hide its smoothness and fairness. Were they to pass others out tramping, none would ever guess that a beautiful woman was among them. Nor would any guess, were his men apprehended, that he was their leader. They had orders to say that they were on their way to meet him. It would not be a good thing for the Celts to know they had captured a Viking chieftain.

They maintained a tight, silent column as they moved across the countryside, for their enemies were many—both Viking and Celt—and a misstep in the mist, still thick over the ravines and bogs that riddled the area, could result in injury or death. When Raven caught a glimpse of sun through the fog, he reckoned they were near the bay north of Ballageay where the remainder of his men waited for them on Odin's Raven. He yearned to get Sunniva aboard his vessel and to Dublin, for only then would she be safe.

Con Cory and his men lay in ambush in the thick mist north of Ballageay. It was cold and damp, yet he was warmed by the flow of jubilation that pulsed through him. It had been two days since a great army of Celts had overrun Ballageay and had immediately freed him to fight in the reclaiming of it. While the dead were many, Viking and Celt alike, the stronghold was in Celt hands for the first in his memory.

Con was thirty winters old, and never had there been a time when he and his brother, Finn, sons of a Jurby chieftain, had not known the sting of Viking raids and heard of the Viking ravages and plunderings of old. Both had been blooded in battle in their early days, and both had fought under their father, hitting Viking settlements frequently but never once impeding the progress of the marauding enemy bands that swarmed over their land without end. His father had been slain in one of those raids, and now Finn, too, was dead. Rolf Gunnarsson had

slain him that day last October when he had taken
Con himself captive. The devil had much to answer
for, Con mused, and soon, very soon, he was going to
feel Celt iron at his throat.

Not only did Con intend to slay Gunnarsson and
nail his head to a post, he was now about to capture
the highest prize of all, that chieftain held in highest
esteem by every Viking on Maun—Raven Trondsson.
Con laughed, a low, soft sound more growl than
laughter. After Ballageay fell to them, he and his own
band had gone on to reclaim other villages in the
area and had come upon unexpected treasure—
Trondsson's longship. He had taken her at a high
price on both sides and now, hidden by fog, he
awaited the Viking chieftain himself.

Con gazed in satisfaction at the mist swirling so
thickly about them. His men swore Manannan had
summoned it to confound and confuse the enemy
these past two days. Not so Con. Even though he had
once seen Manannan in battle, he was not one to put
his trust in the whim of any god. He trusted only that
which he could see—his strong right arm and these
faithful men of his who had been imprisoned with
him and now waited in ambush with him.

Hearing a strange, muffled sound in the distance,
his questioning blue eyes moved over his men. Ah,
they, too, heard it, the faint chink that came when a
man walked in chain mail. Con nodded. His band
hunched lower behind bushes and rocks, waiting,
waiting, hardly daring to breathe.

Raven, out in front of the column, brought it to an
abrupt halt. Something was amiss. They were so close
to the beach that the land underfoot was sandy and
he could smell the sea. When the mist thinned
momentarily, he glimpsed his vessel. She was where

he had left her and seemed unscathed, ay, but he sensed that she was taken. She had fallen into Celt hands. He ran back to his berserkers and Sunniva.

"Take cover!" he shouted to his men, the time for quiet and caution gone. "'Tis a trap!"

As his eyes sought a safe place for Sunniva to hide, he saw that already it was too late. A host of armed men had appeared on every side of them—men with metal under their tunics like his own crew, swords in hand, archers and slingers behind them. Holy Odin, Celts! And so many! He raised a war-shout and brought his sword hissing out of its sheath. Gildor blazed right and left, and his shield took blow after blow as his frantic gaze roved over the scene. Sunniva. Where in the name of all the gods was she?

Sunniva had instinctively sought cover. As the men attacked, she flitted unseen into a clump of tall bushes. Seeing how great was the number of the enemy surrounding them, she trembled. Raven and his men needed her help, not for her to cower unseen, doing nothing. She rapidly pulled an arrow from the quiver on her back, sighted, and let fly. A Celt dropped, the shaft protruding from his thigh. Again and again she aimed and struck her target, never killing, only wounding.

One man in particular she wanted to stop, so certain was she that he was their chieftain. He was tall and broad-shouldered, a striking-looking man with thick, flame-colored hair and fierce blue eyes, and his voice seemed to ring from deep in his lungs. Sunniva could not understand his shouted words to his men, but it was clear that he was urging them on to slay her people. Some Vikings already lay dead or wounded, and she thanked Jesu and holy Odin that Raven and Ulf had been spared.

As she used her last arrow, she saw that yet more of the enemy were arriving. The battle was ended. The

Solby men were throwing down their arms. Four Celts came toward her, menacing, and Sunniva, too, tossed down her bow and dagger and faced them, eyes a-blaze. She was pushed roughly toward the Solby Vikings and forced into a line where they were surrounded by jeering Celts and prodded with spears. Her heart pounded and her mouth was so dry she could scarcely swallow. She was even more frightened when all grew quiet and the jeering and prodding ceased.

The flame-haired chieftain had begun a slow inspection of his prisoners, stopping before each man, his ice-blue eyes moving carefully over him from the top of his helmet to his booted feet. He spoke Norse to them and his voice was low, as were the voices of the Solby men as they answered. Sunniva could make out little until he drew closer. Her legs trembled so that she was certain all could see that she shook like an aspen in the wind. But perhaps the thickening mist hid it. She drew a long breath and commanded her heart to calm itself.

By the time the Celt chieftain stood before her, his bone-chilling gaze on her alone, she had collected her courage and her wits. Raven had prepared her for this very moment, after all. Eyes lowered, she muttered: "Mellby, Paal, crew, Solby." None had said more, nor would she.

"Mellby—" said the chieftain. "Be you kin to the other named Mellby?"

"His brother." Sunniva's voice was always low-pitched, but now she feared it was not low enough. To her horror, the tall Celt reached out and stroked her chin and her downy cheeks.

"'Twould seem your chieftain is hard up for crew, to sign on such a beardless lad as you, Mellby."

Sunniva said through clenched teeth: "Look you to your men with arrows in their right thighs, Celt. My chieftain chose me for my aim, not for how full a beard I may or may not grow."

At that, his laughter boomed out over the water, but it was short-lived. His eyes pinned her again.

"Which one is Trondsson?" It was the same question he had asked them all.

"He was to meet us here," Sunniva gave the answer she had been instructed to give. She was happy beyond words that he had not recognized Raven.

Con Cory said nothing further. He moved on down the line, and when all had been questioned, he addressed them coolly.

"I have claimed Odin's Raven for my own. Now will you sail her to our destination under the command of my men. Of those who were aboard her, know that half are slain, half lie bound in the hold." When an angry mutter arose from the Solby men, he growled, "Silence! Shackle them." His blue eyes moved up and down the line as his orders were obeyed. They came to rest on the figure before him.

Sunniva's return gaze was defiant but she grew more fearful with each passing moment. There was such mockery and amusement on his face that she was certain he had seen through her disguise.

"Step forward, Mellby." A long bronzed arm shot out, his finger pointing to a spot before him where she was to stand.

Sunniva obeyed. She held herself straight and proud as he removed her helmet. A murmur of surprise arose from his men as they saw her golden hair. Next he lifted the thick flaxen braid that was tucked beneath her tunic. He laid it on her breast, a smile playing over his lips.

"You are indeed fair, Paal Mellby. You will come with me." Con grasped his prisoner's slender arm. The next thing he knew, his own arm was being twisted in its socket and he thudded heavily to the earth. There was not a sound from the men who looked on in astonishment. Celts and Vikings alike held their breath.

Sunniva, too, held her breath. She blinked as he rose quickly and easily to his feet. He scowled down at her, but she did not miss the laughter in his eyes. Whether it was meant for her or for himself she did not know.

"There will be time enough later to teach you some manners, wench. For now we move on." He bent, grasped her about the thighs and threw her lightly across his shoulder. "Get these devils aboard," he instructed his men, "and guard them well. They're not to be trusted any more than this one." He gave his captive a hearty thump on her backside and started off with her. "We will see you there," he called back.

Sunniva bore in silence the indignity of being carried like a bale of hay across the Celt's broad shoulder. But she gave it little thought after the first few moments; her worries were for Raven's men who had been slain. Ever were men being slain on her account, she brooded, yet Raven himself had left the battle unscathed, as had Ulf. For that she was thankful. And soon she would be reunited with them. Even as she thought it, she was transferred to the back of a small, shaggy brown horse and her ankles tied beneath its barrel.

There was complete quiet as the men mounted, quiet as they rode south along the beach with the sea lapping at the horses' hooves. Sunniva's eyes widened when eventually she saw red cliffs in the distance. She was confused. Could this be Ballaugh Beach where Ballageay was located? She grew more anxious still as she saw the break in the coastline. That would be the bay, ay. There was no doubt in her mind. This was Ballageay and it meant they were in grave danger. She turned to the chieftain who rode on her right, the reins of her mount clasped firmly in his big hand.

"Celt, listen to me," she whispered. "We are in danger, all of us. 'Tis Ballageay ahead. 'Tis the stronghold of Rolf Gunnarsson of Hedeby."

Con Cory looked over at her with narrowed eyes. "Ballageay is no longer in Viking hands," he said. "How know you, Mellby, that 'twas held by Gunnarsson?"

"I—lived there for a time." That the Vaaga Vikings no longer held it was good news to her ears. As they reached the bend in the shoreline, she marked that the bay was filled with strange vessels, and running toward them was a great crowd of people. She picked out Calla immediately.

"Sunniva!" Calla's long legs and wine-red hair were flying.

"Calla! O, Calla!" Sunniva was near to weeping as Calla's angry green gaze took in the fact that she was bound to her mount.

"How come you to have this woman captive, Con Cory?" Calla demanded as more and more folk—women, armed men, and children—crowded about to stare.

Sunniva turned shocked eyes on the tall chieftain. Con Cory? This was Con Cory, the beloved of Calla? She was filled suddenly with such astonishment and relief that she wanted to laugh aloud, but discretion held her back. It seemed they were safe, all of them. Was not Calla her sister? Surely she would not allow any harm to come to them.

"Why should I not have her captive?" Con answered Calla in their native tongue. "She is Viking and she was with the men we took in Jurby. I trust their vessel is here by now?"

Calla's lips tightened. "Ay, 'tis hidden in Caitlin Cove. The men are in the stockade. But this one is my friend." She took her dagger and slashed the rope that bound Sunniva's ankles so tightly.

Con frowned, but made no move to stop her. He said gruffly, so that Sunniva could understand. "'Twill be your problem to find and return her to me when she flees."

"She will not flee," Calla answered. "When she goes, it will be with your blessing."

Con's eyes were icy. "We will talk of this later, woman."

Calla flashed him one of her rare smiles. "So we will, Con Cory. And now, Sunniva, come—if you can still walk, that is. Your bonds were damnably tight."

When Sunniva slid off her mount, her feet were so numb they would not support her. She sank to the sandy shore, murmuring, "If I could but sit a moment. . . ."

"Ay, sit you, girl, and let me rub the blood back into your feet." Under the ministrations of Calla's strong fingers, her friend was soon able to flex her toes. "Can you feel them now?"

"Ay." Sunniva got to her feet, uncomfortably aware that she was the focus of all eyes. The women, many of whom she now recognized—Ena was there—stared at her coldly, the men, hungrily. "I am unarmed," she told Calla, low. "Think you 'twill be a problem?"

"Nay. You are under Con's protection. They'll not touch you. Come with me now." Calla started toward her small hut; she lowered her voice. "I am eager to hear everything—especially how you came to be in Jurby when you should have been south in Malew!"

"And I want to hear what happened to you," Sunniva whispered. "A thousand thanks for your help as I was leaving. I would surely have been noticed but for you. I saw that you limped. Was't Rolf's doing?"

"Ay."

"The bastard!"

Calla shrugged. "'Tis of no import. We are free now, and Con will slay him one of these times—or I will." They had reached Calla's thatched hut. She drew Sunniva into a room that was damp and shadowy and bade her lie on her pallet. "Rest now. Take off your shoes. I will massage your feet some more if you wish."

Sunniva sank to the pallet but waved off the other. "Tell me what happened after I fled."

"'Twas the next eventide before any suspected that aught was amiss." Calla poured water from a jar into a small cup and handed it to Sunniva, who drank it eagerly. "Orm went up finally to tell Rolf the women had prepared a feast. A short time later, the four of them left with several others. . . ."

Sunniva's eyes danced. "Mean you that naught else was said—about anything?"

Calla shook her head. "Naught was said, except 'twas clear you were gone and they sought you." Calla's mouth twitched. "Did you chain him to the rafters?"

Sunniva laughed. "Nay, 'twas more devilish than that. I bound him with his own chain to his throne chair and draped him in the silly veil he bade me wear. I trow he was a fine sight for Orm and his two wild boars to find. Oh, and I stole his sword. . . ."

Calla's green eyes were admiring in the dimness. "'Twas better than slaying, that—the bastard's own men seeing him helpless as a babe. And to steal the Battle Fiend! Wait 'til Con hears."

"'Tis glad I am that you all are free, Calla," Sunniva said gravely, "and that your beloved is safe. . . ."

Calla stared. "What mean you—beloved?"

"Con," Sunniva said, uncertain now. "Con Cory. Did you not tell me once that you cherished him?"

Calla frowned. She said quietly, "I cherish him, ay."

"But he is not the one you love?"

"I love no one," Calla said crisply. "Con knows I would die for him, as he would for me. I would do anything for him. We grew up together—our tribes were friendly. We have mated, he and I, but never could I give myself to any man for all time." Seeing her friend's confusion, she added, "'Tis all right, Sunni, no more could Con could give himself to any woman. We belong to ourselves. 'Tis our freedom we love."

"I—I see," Sunniva murmured, not seeing at all. All she wanted in the world was to belong to Raven Trondsson and never be parted from him again.

CHAPTER 20

"WHEN DID YOUR PEOPLE COME?" SUNNIVA ASKED.

"'Twas the day after Hedeby left to seek you." Calla sat down cross-legged on the mossy, hard-packed earthen floor beside the pallet. Her face was grave. "Your people were overwhelmed, Sunniva. I fear many were slain, as were many of mine."

Sunniva said quietly, "I grieve for the slain, but know you, Calla, Rolf Gunnarsson's men were not my people. My people are those Solby men being brought here by ship."

Calla nodded. "Ay. I regret that." Now was not the time to tell her the vessel already had arrived and the men imprisoned. She herself knew no more than that. "How came you to find them? How came you to be in Jurby in the first place?"

"To begin with, Raven found me and—"

"Raven? Mean you that Raven is one of the prisoners?"

"Nay, not Raven." Sunniva suppressed the sick

feeling swimming over her. She gave Calla a candid gaze, thinking how accustomed to deceit she had become. But none, not even Calla, must know Raven had been captured. "He left us shortly after he found me, he had things to tend to, and we were to meet him at Jurby Head where he left his ship . . ." She went on to tell Calla the whole story. At its conclusion, Calla shook her head.

"By all the saints, you did not need this, Sunni. You have been through enough. Would that you were on your way home right now."

Sunniva gave a wistful smile. "And would that every Viking on Maun returned whence he came. . . ."

"Ay. We will drink on that later, I promise you," Calla said.

"We will drink on it now." The tall chieftain stood in Calla's doorway. He stooped to enter the small, dim room and handed Calla a jug. "'Tis a while since I had mead." He spoke in Gaelic.

Calla rose, her eyes cool. "I have told you, Sunniva is my friend. 'Twould please me if you spoke so she could understand." Or don't speak at all, she wanted to snap but held her tongue.

She could not remember being so annoyed with Con ever before. After Ballageay had been wrested from the Vaaga Vikings at a stiff price, he had immediately led his men on a continuing rampage to other enemy strongholds. He was like a wild thing let out of a cage. She understood his need for vengeance, ay, but for Sunniva to have been caught because of it was intolerable.

Con leaned against a beam, his narrowed gaze on the Viking maid. "So, 'tis Sunniva, is it?" His Norsk held the same lilt as Calla's. "Methinks the lad's name suits you better, Mellby."

Calla gave him a beaker of mead and poured some

for herself and Sunniva. "What mean you? What lad's name?"

"This wench called herself Paal when we seized them. She downed ten of my men with her accursed arrows and near twisted my arm out of its socket." He drank deeply of the mead, wiped his mouth on his sleeve, and returned his gaze to Sunniva. "Methought no woman in the world other than yourself was such a warrior, macLir."

Calla nodded. "So thought I myself 'til I met Sunniva."

Sunniva had sat up on the pallet to sip the mead. She felt a sudden resentment recognizing its familiar flavor. It was brewed at Marvik and had come from Odin's Raven. She met Con Cory's appraising eyes with defiance.

"Are my people here yet?"

"Ay."

When he offered nothing further, she said, "What will you do with them?"

"Mayhap I will slay every man fit for war. I trow that would mean the lot of them."

Sunniva got to her feet. She shot a look of appeal at Calla, but Calla's face was masked. "But you will not!" Her heart beat in her throat. "You are not a cruel man—I see it in your eyes."

Con laughed at that. He poured himself more mead and then lowered himself to the mossy floor. "Sit you, Mellby, and I will tell you what you see."

Sunniva obeyed, seating herself on the pallet once more. She grew cold as she sensed that she had been wrong about him. Now she saw the grim hatred that lay behind the ice in his eyes; she felt the fierce animal magnetism emanating from him.

"You see patience, Mellby," he said softly. "You have mistaken it for kindness, mayhap, but 'tis naught but patience. I will slay your Vikings, you can be sure of it. But not just yet. I will hold them until their chieftain comes seeking them, for seek them he will. He will gather men and come to free them, and when he does, I will have him."

"You are over-confident."

"Nay. 'Twill happen, and then I will have him, this Trondsson. And if he has tricked me, if he be in my stockade already"—his mouth smiled, but his eyes did not—"that will I learn soon enough."

Sunniva's heart beat faster, but her face remained serene. It was Calla, seated on the floor beside Con, who scowled. "No torture," she ordered.

Con gave her a long look. "'Tis all right for them to torture us, but I may not torture them? When did you turn soft?"

"I have not turned soft," Calla said. "These are not Hedeby nor Kol men. These be here for one reason, to fetch Sunniva back to Norway. They did not come to raid."

"Oh, ay, mayhap this time they did not." His eyes burned. "But if it suited their purpose, then would they raid. Know you, Mellby, your people have carried off everything of value and beauty in this land of ours. Our soft, lovely girls and blooming young women and strong young boys, our gold and silver and jewels and treasures. Know you they have slain our men and burned our towns and left behind naught but ashes. Our houses and our halls have been black-draped for an eternity. Of Maun and all the lands about, your damned Vikings have made spoilland and sword-land. Conquered land."

His blue eyes held a light so terrible that Sunniva flinched. "I—I grieve for you. . . ." she whispered.

His mouth twisted, mocking. "Oh, ay. . . ."

"She speaks the truth," Calla said. "Do not judge this one by the others."

"I would hear how you came to know this wench," Con growled in their own tongue.

Calla bit her lip. She knew this mood of his, and knew better than to anger him further when he was so wroth, just as he would yield to her were it she who raged. She answered in Gaelic.

"She was stolen from her folk by Hedeby, who brought her here to Ballageay as a thrall." Seeing Sunniva's wide frightened eyes fastened on her, Calla said to her in Norsk, "He asks how I come to know you and I am telling him. 'Tis easier for him in Gaelic."

Sunniva nodded. "'Tis all right. I don't mind." But her worried eyes never left the chieftain as he listened to Calla's words and drank Raven's mead.

"On the night Hedeby forced her to drink the wedding ale without a wedding," Calla continued, "Sunniva drugged him and his berserkers and fled. I had supplied her with clothing and weapons." She told Con all she could remember—Sunniva's journey aboard the Landwaster, their own plans to free Con himself and escape, their weapons-practice, the women's cruelty to her. She saw the fury gradually leave his eyes. His mouth relaxed. He poured more mead for himself and Calla, held out his hand for Sunniva's small cup.

"Let me give you more, Mellby, 'tis good brew, this."

"Ay . . ." Sunniva lowered her eyes, misliking the way his gaze was now moving over her, as though he were seeing what lay beneath her tunic and leggings.

Calla, too, saw the heat in his eyes and knew that he wanted the maid. She had known from the moment she saw Sunniva riding at his side why Con had brought her to Ballageay. She felt no jealousy, only regret that Sunniva was already betrothed to another.

For if ever a woman was born to be the mate of a chieftain like Con, it was Sunniva. And Con—blooded in battle at his father's side when he was but a babe, spending his youth, his young manhood trying to wrest his land from the enemy—deserved the best. Sunniva was the best. She would not have him, nor did Con want a wife. Yet Calla knew, better than did he himself, that such a woman would fill a great void in his life. She would make him complete. But how to bring such a thing about . . . ?

Three days passed before Calla knew what course she must follow. She must leave Ballageay for a while, making Con fully responsible for Sunniva's protection. But the first thing was to speak honestly with Con. Never had either of them been anything but truthful with the other. Knowing that he slept lightly at all times, she went to his hut that night and scratched on his door.

"Who goes?" His deep voice came instantly.

"Calla. Let me in."

The door creaked open and Calla entered the familiar, shadowy room. The small windows in the thatched roof let in moonlight enough so that she saw the concern on his handsome face as he gazed down at her.

"Is aught wrong?" he asked.

"Nay. All is well—or soon will be."

His frown turned to a scowl. "How so?"

"Sit you, Con." Calla pointed to his rumpled pallet. When he sat, she asked, "Have you more of that Viking mead?"

"Ay." He pointed to a corner of the room where a keg rested. He grinned as Calla filled two beakers. "You woke me for this? By the saints, macLir, I will give you a keg of your own."

"Hush, you, Con Cory." She handed him a beaker. "You know drink is not my weakness."

"Ay, well I know. So why are you here?" He took a swallow as she sank down beside him on the pallet. His languid gaze moved over her. "I hope 'tis what I think it is. . . ."

Calla laughed and pushed his hand away as he stroked her breast. "Indeed it is not. This is serious business I mean to discuss with you."

Con gave a deep sigh. "Get on with it then, wench. Don't torment me with that comely body of yours."

"You need a woman of your own, Con."

"I have no time for a woman of my own."

"If you had one, you would make time."

"Nay. I am not a man with a constant itch, like Hedeby."

"A fighting man needs a woman."

Con laughed softly. "Never have I wanted for a woman when the need arose."

"What think you of Sunniva?"

"She is fair. Near as fair as you. I would have taken her already, but for your incessant mothering of her."

Calla's eyes sparkled in the pale light. "'Twas wise of you to notice that."

"I tire of this. 'Tis not like you to jaw so much. Say what you came for, macLir."

"Methinks you should wed the maid." When Con looked at her askance, she added, "She is brave, fair, and a warrior-woman. You will never find another like her." And it had been plain to Calla that not all was rosy between Sunniva and her betrothed. She had hinted that his jealousy of her was great.

Con laughed. He caught Calla's hand and raised it to his lips. "Know you, macLir, if ever I take a wife, 'twill be you."

Calla pulled her hand from his caress. "I will not have you, Con Cory. I will not have any man, and well you know it. I belong to myself and never will I change."

"Yet you ask me to change."

"You have changed already. I see it."

Con's mood turned abruptly. He rose. "I have not changed," he said gruffly, "and this woman-talk bores me. Get you home and to sleep, macLir."

Calla, too, got to her feet. He was angry, but she knew she was right. He had changed. The light had left his eyes long before he had been captured by Hedeby. The years were taking their toll on him. He was ever on guard and planning constant deadly counterattacks, springing with his men from cave and copse to ambush the enemy time and again with no loving arms awaiting him when he returned to his dark hut, wherever it happened to be at the time. He had women, ay—those wenches who craved importance by throwing themselves at the boldest chieftain on Maun. Calla spat on them; she had nothing but scathe for them. Con deserved only the best.

"You would do well to wed Sunniva, I think," Calla said.

"Woman, now you annoy me," Con growled. "Go."

"Ay, I will go." Calla opened the door. "I am leaving Ballageay for a while. I trow you will not rape her after I am gone, but will woo her and make her love you."

Con's eyes narrowed. He put his hand atop hers on the latch and closed the door again. "What nonsense is this? Where go you?"

"I crave a change. I tire of this place. Now that you are free, there is naught to hold me here. I would see my kin in Marown."

"God's bones, why now when I need you by my side to raid?"

Calla lifted her chin so that her eyes were nearly level with his own. "I have told you, I crave a change. Don't look so black. I will not be gone forever, only two weeks or so." She stroked Con's rough cheek and pushed back a heavy lock of dark-red hair from his forehead. "Methinks Sunniva was right, Con Cory. You are not a cruel man by nature. I trow you will remember she is but a tender maid who—"

Con snorted. "Tender? She is a menace."

"In ambush she fought as I would, and now I am telling you that she is but a lonely, frightened maid who craves what most maids crave. Love and gentleness."

"She will not get it from me," Con muttered.

"She will need your protection when I am gone."

"I am damned if I see why."

"Then I will tell you," Calla flared. "I helped her and sent her on her way, but 'tis you who have dragged her back again. Therefore, she is your responsibility. She is in grave danger here. The women hate her and the men lust after her."

Con glowered. "Of course they lust after her. They know I intend to bed her and pass her on when I tire of her. 'Tis the way of it. She will receive the same treatment Hedeby and Kol and the others give our fair Celt women." A muscle moved in his jaw. "You of all people know that."

"'Twould seem, then, that I should take her with me," Calla said tightly.

Con shook his head. "Anywhere in this land that you take her, she will be in danger."

Calla's eyes blazed green fire. "Very well, then. Treat her as Hedeby would, and Haftor Kol. Chisel your own name on the band she still wears about her ankle and sell her if you like. Be it on your head."

She had not expected Con to yield instantly to her plan, but now she wondered if he would ever accept it. Damn it, if only he were not so stubborn, he would see that Sunniva was the perfect woman for him. She would grow to love him if he but gave her the chance, for none other was as brave and bold and handsome as Con. And he made love like no other man Calla had ever known. He was a far better mate for the maid than Raven Trondsson. Calla blinked. It was as though lightning had struck her. Of course, why had she not thought of it sooner?

"Did I mention," she said casually, "that Sunniva is handfasted to Raven Trondsson? I trow he will attempt to seize her when he comes for his men." She turned to leave, but Con caught her arm.

"The wench is betrothed to Trondsson?"

"Ay." Calla's smile was hidden by the shadows. She turned to Con then and embraced him. "I will say goodbye now, old friend. Methinks I will leave for Marown before sun-up."

It had been but two days since Calla's leave-taking and already Sunniva missed her terribly. Her spirits had not been so low since Rolf had carried her to sea and put a band on her ankle. In addition, she knew that Raven would be as wild with worry over her as she was over him. He and his men were being held within Ballageay's heavily guarded stockade, and she had not had even one glimpse of them. What was worse, she doubted the other Vikings on Maun knew of their capture.

Each morn before breakfast, she stood in the shadow of the abbey gazing at the enclosure and wondering what Raven and his men did there. Were they shackled still? Were they being fed enough and had they pallets on which to sleep or must they lay their heads on the hard earth at night? And what did they do with all the time that crept by so slowly? She could scarcely bear to think of their being shackled and doing nothing; sitting, heads sunk in their hands, all hope gone.

But nay, never would Raven allow his men to sink into despair. They would be fired always with reciting the sagas, and they would make up poems and riddles and play chess using stones and twigs as Raven had taught her to do so long ago. In all likelihood, they would be wrestling and leaping and balancing, anything to keep fit. She was so certain of it, she felt a keen sense of relief as she started for the kitchen-house to do her chores. Once more she was helping with the breadmaking and baking, and it was time now to take the loaves from the ovens.

As she trod the log path behind the abbey, she was surrounded suddenly by a band of men. These past two nights, with Calla gone, men had come to her hut demanding entrance. When she remained silent, they had kicked the door and left, cursing. Now her heart faltered. Were these the same?

"Methinks this Viking wench looks pale," said one, laughing.

"Ay. Some kisses will put the roses back in her cheeks."

"Touch me at your peril," Sunniva muttered, crouching, prepared to grasp and toss the first man who touched her.

"Watch her, she's a tricky one."

She was caught of a sudden between two men. One held her, her back to his chest, while the other pressed his body against her and kissed her roughly. There was laughter and low talk as Sunniva struggled, her mouth sealed, arms held down.

"Let's give the wench a taste of Celt she'll not forget."

"Where?"

"In the abbey. 'Tis empty."

"What of Con?"

"What of him? If he wanted her, he'd have taken her by now, with Calla gone. She's booty, man. Come on, she's ours."

"Ay . . ."

Sunniva was compressed so tightly between the two men that she could not even move and there was blood in her mouth from the punishing kisses she was receiving. She could not even cry out. Suddenly there was dead quiet, followed by a roar and cursing. The two were torn from her and flung to the ground. Sunniva stood free but trembling, her wide eyes seeing that Con Cory was her rescuer. He had defended her with his bare hands, although a deadly-looking dagger, its hilt encrusted with gems, hung at his belt.

"You will not touch her again," he rasped. He stood between her and his sullen men, his eyes burning like blue flame.

"By all the saints, Con, you said naught . . ."

"Then I say it now," Con growled. "This woman is mine."

At that, Sunniva bristled. "Indeed I am not, I—"

"Silence." He reached out a long arm and pulled her roughly against him. "You dwell with me from now on."

"Nay, I will not," she flared. "Calla bade me live in her place while she is gone."

"'Tis not Calla who gives the orders here, I do, and I say you dwell with me." Seeing the rebellion in her eyes, he shrugged, released her. "Men, she is yours." He turned away, ignoring the fact that she was seized instantly and borne toward the abbey.

"Please, wait!" Sunniva called to him. "I—I will dwell with you, Con Cory."

"I doubt me that I want such a damned, mutinous wench under my roof after all." Seeing the fright and pleading in her eyes, he relented, muttering, "All right, then, come along. But know you, wench, I will take no foolishness from you."

CHAPTER 21

Sunniva followed after Con Cory, sizzling with anger and feeling betrayed. He had rescued her from the Celt pigs merely so he could claim her for himself. None of this would have happened if Calla were here. Oh, why had she chosen this time to see her kin? And how unfair that Con Cory had seized their band when they were so close to leaving for Dublin. It was infuriating.

Con turned. Seeing her burning eyes and tightly compressed lips, he made no comment. He said only, "Fetch your pallet and your belongings. I will be at my hut. Know you where it is?"

"Ay."

As Sunniva marched angrily away, she minded Calla pointing out Con's dwelling to her. It was an isolated cottage partly sunk into a hill overlooking the sea and the bay, rope netting securing the thatch above its low walls, small windows in the sod and thatch to let in the daylight. Calla had explained that it was always a chieftain who dwelt there so he could watch the sea both day and night. The heat of fury swept over her body again, thinking that now she herself would dwell there with Con Cory. She stuffed her few belongings into her wallet, slung it and the rolled-up pallet over her shoulder, and soon was standing at his door. It was open.

"Are you there?" she raised her voice.

"Ay. Come in."

She stooped and entered the shadowy, low-ceilinged room. It was damp and cold and smoky. He had thrown a square of peat onto a fire that was spitting on the hearth.

"Put your things down wherever you want."

"Since I have a choice," she answered coldly, "I choose the stockade. I want to be with the Solby men."

"So they can abuse you as my men would have?"

"They will not, for they are my people from my valley."

But Con knew men on cruise. Even if they were her homefolk, she would be safe with them only if Trondsson, too, were in the stockade. Was she so innocent that she did not know that, or was the Solby chieftain already his prisoner, as he suspected? He would learn soon, and he would use this wench to discover it.

"You will stay with me, and that is the end of it," he said. He pointed to the table. "There is bread and cheese if you are hungry."

"I am not hungry." Sunniva threw her belongings into a corner. Her eyes seemed to crackle. "Know you this, Celt, if you lay one finger on me, I will cut it off. If you lay more than a finger on me, that also will I cut off."

Con laughed. By the saints, what a sassy witch she was.

"I find nothing amusing in this," Sunniva muttered. "You can scarcely guard yourself from me day and night." She wondered, worrying, if Calla had told him she was betrothed to Raven. It could not help matters.

"Sit you, Sunniva," he said, gravely, for the moment of levity had passed. "We must have a little talk, you and I." When she remained standing, as regally aloof as any captive princess, Con sat himself down before the fire with the bread and cheese. He broke off a hunk and used his dagger on the cheese. He said: "I am going to be honest with you."

Sunniva blinked gold-lashed eyes at him. "Already have I been honest with you—if you touch me, you will suffer."

Con bit into his food, chewed and gazed into the dancing flames. "And know you, wench, that I will surely hand you over to my men if you annoy me further. You are my prisoner, and if I want to bed you, I will bed you."

He watched her sink to the hard-packed floor a safe distance from him and sit tailor-fashion, her eyes huge pools of deep blue. They were unblinking in the firelight as she glared at him. Should he tell her the truth—that he craved her body less than he craved Calla's respect and trust? Nay. He shook his head and got to his feet. She was arrogant enough without knowing she was safe in his hands. Besides, he was not all that sure that she was safe.

He had seen finally that her beauty surpassed Calla's. That skin of hers—it was as if a candle was lit within her to make it glow so. Cheeks pink as columbine, a sweet, soft mouth, breasts curving high and full beneath her tunic, hair like a cape of sunshine, a smooth white throat that he yearned to taste . . . He returned his dagger to its sheath and glowered down at her. She was a wench to drive a man out of his skin with desire, but he was damned if he would let himself be bound by her. Viking chains bound his land and it was enough. Never would a Viking witch claim his heart.

"I have said all that needs to be said for now," he muttered. "Go back to your work. This door will be open when you return. 'Tis never locked."

Sunniva rose. She hated the place, hated the damp and the chill, the thick sod walls and shadows and smoke. She was eager to flee, even to breadmaking, because then could she think on Raven and calm her thoughts. But the Celt chieftain stood between her and the door, his hooded eyes assessing her.

Con laughed, seeing her hesitation. "Mayhap I will take a kiss before you leave."

"I will scratch your eyes out!"

He was as tall as Raven, and of his strength she had no doubt, for the hard swell of muscles in his long arms and legs was evident beneath his tunic and leggings. She admitted, grudgingly, that he was comely, with his broad, handsome face, ruddy cheeks and lips, and thick, reddish hair that fell to his shoulders. It was a startling contrast to his dark skin and the piercing blue of his eyes. Never had she seen such coloration before.

"Come, wench, I will have a kiss. 'Tis time I knew what you tasted like."

Before Sunniva could protest, Con pulled her, not ungently, into his arms and covered her mouth with his. Her breasts were soft against him though she held herself stiff as a log. Her mouth was as soft and warm and sweet as he expected it to be, though she did not return his kiss. He was in no hurry to let her go and kissed her hungrily. Her nails raked several deep bloody tracks across his cheek.

"Bastard!"

Con released her, his face darker still with the

blood that rushed to it. Sunniva feared suddenly that
he would pick her up and hurl her across the room.
Worse, she feared he would cease protecting her. She
put both hands to her cheeks. What was she to
do . . . ?

Seeing her fright, Con said gruffly, "I will let that
pass this time, Mellby, but not again. I have told my
men you are my woman, but I'll not have a wench
with claws."

"I will not submit to your pawing."

He growled, "You will submit to whatever I
choose."

The bitch. He was rankled by her choice of words
—submit to his pawing—as though he were some
inexperienced clod who did not know how to excite a
woman. By holy St. Lonan, he needed her like he
needed a new horde of Vikings swarming over
Ballageay. In fact, she would be a constant reminder
of them. He was tempted to throw her out, yet were
he to do so, these men of his tribe, kinsmen all, would
feast on her without mercy. He would not do it. But
not because he cared about the damned wench, or
because Calla would be wroth. Nay, at this moment,
his main interest was in using her to trap Trondsson.

Sunniva sensed the struggle taking place in him.
She waited, tensed, almost afraid to draw breath, for
fear of what he might do to her. Would he take her
now? She yearned for the safety of Raven's arms,
yearned for his shield-burg of men to protect her.

"Go you to your chores," Con rasped, finally,
"before I decide to bed you now."

This time she did not hesitate, but flew to do his
bidding.

It was two days before she ceased to tremble when
Con Cory looked at her and another two before she
could sleep at night. Even then, she awakened and

jumped at every noise, thinking he was coming to her. And then yester-eve, he and his men had gone off in their ship and she had lain in the cottage alone. She had not slept at all for the murmurings and whispers and rustlings she heard. She knew now she was more frightened with him gone than with him there, and as she kneaded dough in the kitchen-house, she thought of the coming night with dread.

Had the night-noises been those men who had tried to rape her? If so, would they come again with Con not there? Surely they would not, they feared him too much. But then, what if they were not Ballageay men but Rolf Gunnarsson and his men? While the boundaries of Ballageay were tightly guarded, might he not come in from the sea? Con's hut was so isolated. O, holy Thor and Odin, she was so frightened and there was none she could turn to. Certainly not Ena or the other women. They would laugh at her and delight in her fear.

Hearing a sudden commotion, Sunniva looked up from the trough and saw Con Cory and his men swarming into the kitchen-house, greeting the women and demanding food. He was back! She felt a burden lift from her shoulders, for she knew she would be safe from whoever had been beyond her door last night. She knew also that she feared Con Cory less than she feared the unknown. As she continued kneading and punching the great wad of dough, she learned that they had gone a-raiding. It was as she had suspected. She learned also that there were wounded who had been carried into the great hall in the abbey. Wounded, she thought. Could she somehow use that to her advantage? Could she offer to treat them? Suddenly Con was at her side.

"I trow no harm came to you while I was gone."

"Nay, none did," Sunniva murmured. But don't leave again, she wanted to cry.

"If you be safe, why do you look so?" He tilted up her chin and studied her wide gaze. "'Tis as if you had seen a ghost. What is't?"

"I heard things all the night long and wondered if—"

"What things?"

"Rustlings and whispers. . . ." Sunniva herself whispered, seeing Ena hovering close.

"Doubtless 'twas the fynoderee," the Celt woman declared. The other women laughed.

Con shot an annoyed glance at them. "Get you back to your cooking." To Sunniva, he said low, "Pay them no heed. They like nothing better than to stir the pot and watch it boil. What you heard was the sea and wind. Always at night it sounds different."

"I hoped 'twas that. . . ." Sunniva regarded him with new eyes, realizing he was attempting to soothe her fears. Feeling a small bond between them, she acted on it. She asked:

"Have you many wounded?"

Con was instantly suspicious. His eyes, heaven-blue in his sun-darkened face, narrowed. "Why would you want to know?"

"Mayhap I could help with them. I learned to tend the sick at Solby Convent and I nursed the wounded on the Landwaster. Yon hill," she pointed toward Clagh Burroo, "is filled with lyngwort. 'Tis wonderful for treating illness."

"The offer is appreciated," said Con, his mouth tightening, "but I decline. 'Tis best you stick to your breadmaking—and stay away from Clagh Burroo."

"But Calla and I—" The words died. He had already left.

Con mulled her words as he strode to the hut. He knew all about the trips she and Calla had made to the cave. Already his men were in possession of the weapons. He knew also that it was her lyngwort that had drugged Hedeby and his berserkers. Well could he imagine his tribe's reaction if she used the unfamiliar herb on his men and they died in her care. Nay, he would not allow her to come near them, but her offer astonished him. He did not understand the wench at all, nor her willingness to help in such a dirty business as tending wounds and the fact that she had been in a convent. A Viking warrior-woman in a convent. He laughed. Calla had said nothing of that. By the gods, he had not imagined there was a church in all of that accursed pagan land of Norway, let alone a convent. And then there was her given name. Always had he thought Sunniva was a Celt name. He must ask her about that some time.

Entering his dwelling, he stopped abruptly, threw his wallet down, and looked about, a frown pulling his brows together. It was changed; changed, yet the same. And then he realized that it was clean. The dust was gone from tabletops and shelves—even he could see that—and the trash from the mossy floor. He had not minded it, he never saw it, but now his cottage was speckless. Not so much as a cobweb or a piece of lint was to be seen. The hearth had been swept, peat laid for a fresh fire, and his pallet was plump with fresh straw. The windows stood open, allowing the sea breeze and the sun to enter. His lips formed a silent whistle. Now what was this all about?

It was eventide, and Sunniva, perched cross-legged on the thatched roof of Con Cory's hut, was watching the sun melt into the Irish Sea. Con came silently and sat down beside her. He had with him a beaker of mead which he offered to her. She shook her head.

"If you look to the sea for a rescue from your chieftain," he said, "'tis a lost hope."

"No hope is ever lost where Raven Trondsson is

involved," Sunniva answered, but her voice was mild. Never would she let him forget Raven's might and importance, but also, she had determined to use honey, not vinegar, to get this Celt to do her bidding. She wanted desperately to be with Raven, but she must move slowly. Never must Con Cory guess that she was manipulating him.

Con himself sprawled out in the deep flowering thatch and narrowed his eyes against the sun-dazzle. He leaned on one elbow, quaffed his mead and enjoyed the glitter on the sea and in the woman's golden hair. God, but she was a beauty. Long, gold-tipped lashes, violet-blue eyes, a nectar-sweet mouth, skin like cream, a body as slender as a wand yet possessing the most delectable curves and mounds and valleys a man could ever hope to lay eyes on.

He drew a deep breath, took a swallow of Viking mead, and envied Raven Trondsson. Had the Solby chieftain made her his? And was he here in the stockade with his men, or was he out there some-where enlisting another vessel to replace the one chained in the bay at Ballageay? One thing Con knew for certain: If he were out there, he was planning an attack. His men and his vessel were here and never would he abandon them. And Sunniva Mellby was here. Never would he abandon such a jewel. Con felt a warm wave of contentment—and thankfulness that he himself was not in thrall to the wench—roll over him.

Were she to make the smallest move toward him, he would take her, ay. Well did he know that if such a woman beckoned, a man must follow with no heed to the consequences and no turning back. But she had not beckoned, nor did he think she would. She seemed true to the Solby chieftain, and he was not going to attempt to change her mind. He had thought things through these past few days: He was satisfied with taking a woman after battle or whenever else he chose, but as for the ties and entanglements of matrimony, he wanted none. Especially he wanted no bitterness with his people over a Viking woman. Neither did he want a quarrel with Calla. But he doubted much if she would complain of his not wooing and winning the wench if he left her unsullied.

"Believe you in the sea-god, Manannan?" Sunniva asked of a sudden, interrupting his dangerous thoughts. Her dreamy eyes reflected the sun on the sea.

"Believe you in Thor and Odin, having gone to a convent?"

"I did not 'go' to a convent. I was there awaiting my wedding day—and ay, I believe in our gods *and* in Jesu-Mary-Holy Ghost." She missed the surprise in his eyes, and in the same breath, she added: "Raven Trondsson has seen Odin, our god of war, in battle. He was tall and bearded and had but one eye. His ravens sat on his shoulders. . . ."

"I have seen Manannan," Con said quietly, not to be outdone by a damned Viking.

"I would hear it," Sunniva said.

Never had Con Cory confessed to any the remarkable sight he had seen that day when he was a lad. Calla would laugh and his men would treat him differently, for Manannan showed himself only to a chosen few.

"Please, will you not tell me?" Sunniva begged.

"I will tell you," Con said brusquely, not expecting to be believed. "Manannan had gathered in his mist-cloak from the seas to protect us from a great horde of Vikings who lay off our coast for three days. It enabled us to gather our forces and take the battle. 'Twas afterwards that I saw him. He had taken the form of a three-legged man"—His voice was low, his eyes distant with memory—"and he was rolling down the face of a steep cliff like yon Clagh Burroo, rolling, tumbling head over heels as a hoop might, and then he rolled into the sea and was gone. . . ."

Sunniva drew a long breath, imagining such a strange sight. "'Tis wonderful, that."

"Ay," Con answered gruffly. She had not laughed, and her beautiful eyes were glowing. He got to his feet. There would be no more moments like this, for he would not allow it. He would keep distance between them until he decided what he would do with her.

It was three days since Sunniva and Con Cory had talked of gods. As she did her bread-baking behind the abbey, she pondered the fact that she now felt comfortable with the Celt chieftain when he was there nights. She saw now that he was a man with more on his mind than the momentary pleasure he might receive from a woman's body. And surely he knew that she was not his personal enemy. Soon now, very soon, she would ask if she might visit the stockade. He could hardly deny her a visit.

He had been gone yester-night, and again she had heard those strange noises. This time she had hurled open the door and gone out boldly, only to find nothing. She smiled at the memory. He had been right; it was the wind whispering over the sea and the grasses rustling. No longer was she afraid.

Suddenly hearing shouts and the weeping of women, Sunniva snatched the bread-pans from the embers and ran to where a crowd was coming up from the beach. Con's ship stood there, and she saw that more wounded were being carried to the abbey on their shields. Seeing that one of them was Con, her hand flew to her lips. Holy Odin, he looked dead already. She waited until the furor was over before asking if she might see him, but the women tending the sick cursed her and drove her away.

At eventide, she went again, vowing that none would drive her off this time. Entering the great hall where she had attended Rolf Gunnarsson's feast as his thrall and his betrothed, she looked for Con's distinctive red hair. She found him, but before she reached his side, a woman hurried toward her. Ena. She carried a spear.

"Viking witch, why are you here?"

"I would see Con Cory," Sunniva demanded, as the other women drew near.

"You cannot. Go you, before I call the men."

"Nay, I will see him."

When Ena threatened her with the spear, Sunniva easily disarmed her. The woman set up such a screech, it was as if her last hour had come.

Hearing the noise, Con forced open his eyes. He could not guide them where he would. All was misty, and the room was filled with women. But only one woman he knew had that cape of sunshine falling over her shoulders. He smiled.

"Be you all right, Mellby?"

"Ay." Sunniva dropped to the floor by his bloody pallet and took his hand. "How goes it, Con Cory?"

"I trow I will die this time," he murmured.

"Nay, you will not!" Her face blanched as white as his own. She turned to the women who stood watching with pursed mouths. "What are you doing for him?" she cried. "What herbs have you used?" They gaped at her so stupidly that her heart quavered. It was clear they knew nothing and had done nothing. With trembling hands, Sunniva examined the terrible wound near his abdomen. It had not even been cleansed. O, Jesu . . .

"Bring me boiling water," she commanded Ena. "And soft rags. Clean ones. Damn you, move." She rose and stepped toward the woman, menacing, her eyes flashing. "Bring them now!" When Ena left, Sunniva again examined Con's wound.

"'Tis all right, Mellby," he muttered. "Don't look so. I do not fear death. I will but step into the next room. . . ."

"You will be all right," she murmured. "I can help you."

"Nay." He shook his head. "Me you cannot save."

"Con Cory, I will not hear such talk."

"Know you, Mellby, no man lives 'til eve whom the Fates doom at dawning." His teeth began to chatter.

Sunniva snapped to the women who stood a-gaping: "You, all of you. Fetch jars of hot water to lay about him!" As they hastened away, she caught Con's hand in hers, and spoke low. "I am going to bathe your wound, and then I am going for lyngwort."

"You will not go to the witchfield. I forbid it."

"I am no more afraid of your witchfield than you are of death, Con Cory. I am going."

"If I die, you will be blamed. . . ."

"I am going, and you will not die. Hush you, now. Sleep until Ena brings the water."

CHAPTER 22

WHEN ENA CAME WITH THE WATER AND CLEAN cloths, Sunniva quickly set to sponging away all the dried blood and other matter from Con's wound. The sight made her stomach churn, and as she dipped and sponged, her mind played terrible tricks in the leaping shadows. It was as if Raven lay there in such great peril of life. She knew panic. What if he did lie a-dying behind that high log wall? What if he had been wounded in his capture, and the wound now festered like this one? Oh, beloved! But then she caught hold of her thoughts, minding herself that Odin walked with Raven. He was all right. She gritted her teeth and continued cleansing Con's wound until it bled profusely.

"Slut!" Ena hissed. "You make him worse!"

"I am making him better," Sunniva answered coolly. "He has given me leave to treat him as I will." She ignored her further muttering. When the women returned with the hot jars, she packed them next to

Con's shivering body and covered him with a skin. The women crowded close to stare. "Get you back and give him space to breathe!" Sunniva ordered. She did not add that they befouled the air with their unwashed bodies.

"Is this your treatment?" Ena whined. "Making him bleed anew and then scalding him?"

Sunniva fixed an angry gaze on her. "'Tis but the first step. I go now to fetch lyngwort. In my land, we heal with it."

"We have no such thing here. You have made him bleed and now he is dying."

"You have lyngwort on Clagh Burroo and I am going there to fetch it, for he will surely die without it."

"Clagh Burroo?" Ena drew back from her as though stung. So did the others. "She goes to the witchfield," she cried. "Did I not say she was a witch, the way she enchanted the Hedeby lord and our own chieftain? Our own men . . ."

At that, Sunniva confronted them. She feared suddenly that they would undo the treatment she had begun. "I will return in a very short time, trollwoman," she spoke to Ena with soft menace. "I trow I will find this man exactly as I left him or you will feel my wrath. You will have boiling water waiting so I may brew the lyngwort tea he has requested, and I will require a bowl and spoon and more clean cloths. Hear you?" She left in a near-rage. Fools, all of them. Witch, indeed. It was they who were the witches, especially the plate-face.

Sunniva hurried to Clagh Burroo, filled her apron with as many leaves as she could quickly pluck in the fading light, and ran back to the abbey. The water awaited her, for there was now a fire on the great hearth and a small pot hung over it, bubbling. She tipped some of the water into a beaker and put in four leaves to steep. The rest she laid out on a lowered board. Ena picked up a leaf and peered at it.

"'Tis naught but a weed!" She held it up so the others could see and they all laughed. To Sunniva, she said, "'Twill heal nothing, you fool. More likely, 'twill poison him."

Con raised himself up on his elbow then and gazed at Ena, his eyes a-glitter in the flame-light. "Get you away from her, you damned wench," he growled. "Mellby will tend me."

Sunniva paid her tormentors no further attention, but carried the new-brewed tea to Con's pallet and supported his head while he drank. He slept immediately. As the others exchanged dark looks, she tore leaves into a bowl, added water, mashed the mixture to a pulp and then spread it onto a cloth to make a poultice. She folded it, dipped it into the water, and laid it, hot as she herself could stand it, onto Con's gaping wound. He gasped at the pain but made no murmur. This Sunniva repeated throughout the night, the tea, the ever-hot poultice, sitting by his side and wiping his damp brow with cool water, talking softly, telling him small tales of her home and the folk she knew and the way it was in Norway's land.

The next morning he was still pale and tired, but his forehead was cool. "Methinks I will live, Mellby," he said finally.

"Ay." Sunniva smiled. "I trow you will, Con Cory."

"As will you now."

She nodded. She had never a doubt that had he died in her care, especially after she had gone up on Clagh Burroo for the lyngwort, she herself would have been put to death.

"I wonder," Con said, his eyes gently mocking, "be you the one they call Saint Sunniva?"

"Saint Sunniva?" Sunniva laughed. "Methinks you're teasing me. 'Tis a good sign, that."

"Never would I tease about such a thing. I know little of the thing, only that she was an Irish princess who fled the attentions of a heathen chieftain . . ."

He looked at her so oddly that a wave of shyness swept over Sunniva. She shook her head. "Never have I heard the tale."

Raven Trondsson had not experienced a peaceful moment since he and his men had been seized and Sunniva taken from him. All knew that their plight, especially Sunniva's, was a dangerous one. None of the Vikings on Maun knew of their capture—even Haftor Kol thought they were on their way back to Norway.

"Let us have a game of chess." Ulf approached him where he sat brooding and dropped a hand on his shoulder.

"Later," Raven muttered.

"When will something happen, think you?" Ulf's own spirits were low with the uncertainty of waiting.

"I wish I knew."

It had been fifteen days since their capture and they were no closer to escaping now than they had been on the first day. Through the narrow cracks between the stockade logs, a continual parade of eight to ten armed guards was seen day and night. Raven knew there could be no leaping over the top of the wall and surprising them, for they would be picked off one by one.

Yet their treatment at the hands of the Celts had been surprisingly good, considering they had expected to be slain. They had shelter from the weather, there being many small huts within the stockade, and twice daily they were given water and food that was actually edible. Raven and Ulf had concluded that Calla, the woman who helped Sunniva escape, had intervened in their behalf. Or had Sunniva herself struck some bargain with the devil?

Raven leapt to his feet. By the gods, why was he so plagued with such thoughts? Why could he not just believe, once and for all, that Sunniva's love for him was as great as was his love for her?

"Raven, what is't?" Ulf asked, seeing the wild, despairing look in his chieftain's gray eyes.

Raven waved him off. "I would be alone, man."

"Ay." Ulf clapped his shoulder and left.

The truth of it, Raven brooded, was that Sunniva's love for him was as great as his love for her. That was the whole damned problem. There was nothing she would not do to save him. Nothing.

Con Cory healed quickly. With his strong body and Sunniva's skilled care, he was back on his feet in four days. On the fifth day, he strapped on his sword and returned to his own cottage. It was empty—Sunniva was milking the cows newly brought down from the summer pasture—but it was as he wanted it. He craved to be alone.

He sat on his thatch roof, gazing out at the misty sea and gathering his thoughts of her. Earlier he had decided that if such a woman gave him the least sign of interest, he would claim her without thought of consequences or without ever looking back. He knew now he had received such a sign. She had risked her own life that he might live, and now his thoughts burned with his memories of her beauty and intelligence and fearlessness; with his admiration and hunger for her, his respect for her. Calla had been right. She was a woman fit for a chieftain and never would he find another like her. That she was Viking mattered not at all; what his tribe thought mattered not at all. He was a chieftain and he coveted her; therefore he would have her.

"Con Cory!"

Sunniva stood frowning up at him, hands on her slender hips, her cheeks pink from running. She wore a blue kirtle and white apron and the wind whipped her hair. Con had not heard her coming as he sat there amid the thatch and the bright fall flowers dreaming of her.

"What are you doing here?" she chided. "Did I say you could be up and about?"

"'Tis past time I was up and about and learning to hold a sword again." He patted it where it lay beside him. "Get you up here, Mellby. There is something I would say to you."

Sunniva ran up the hillside and thence out onto the roof. She sat down, tucking her skirts under her legs so the wind would not whip them about.

"What is't?" She herself had something to say, but she would let him speak first. His mood seemed good, but she would make certain before asking to see the Solby men.

Con studied her eyes, such a deep, fathomless purple-blue that he could not even see their black centers. He marked that they were watchful. Did she suspect he was about to broach the subject of marriage? Perhaps he should wait until he had chosen the exact right words to say—he did not want to act a tongue-tied fool. But then, what did fancy words matter? It was not as if they would affect her decision. She would say ay, certainly. And if she did not, it mattered little. It was not as if she had a choice in the matter.

"Mellby"—He did not look at her, but gazed out at the mist rising from the Irish Sea—"We will wed, you and I. I have decided it."

"Wed?" Sunniva could not believe she had heard him aright. Wed. They had grown closer when he lay ill and she nursed him, ay. She had seen his appreciation, but wed . . . ? Had not Calla said Con Cory would never wed, no more than she herself would? Had she not said both cherished their freedom too deeply? This could not be happening. Before she could collect her thoughts to protest, she was pushed backward into the thick fragrant thatch and Con was atop her, pressing his body onto hers, his mouth on hers.

It was a thing she had not felt for long and long, a man's big hands moving over her, his lips teasing hers, his tongue tasting, his teeth nipping. She struggled as she felt his hands on her breasts and belly and thighs, felt him seeking all of her secret places. He turned on his side then, pulling her rigid body against him, his hands on her buttocks lifting her, pressing her into him so she could feel his hardness thrusting against her. Sunniva was shocked suddenly into reality. He was going to take her! She had struggled, ay, but not as fiercely as she might, for she was minded of his unhealed wound. And now he thought she was accepting him.

A hot current of exuberance roared beneath Con's passion. He had had women without number. He had begot his first son on one of his father's serving wenches when he was thirteen, but never had he possessed a woman such as this one. Such beauty of flesh and bone, such spirit and purity and bravery all in one slim, fearless female. By the gods, hers was the power to smite him so he would fall to his knees—and so he had. He was in her thrall. Eyes closed, Con lifted her skirts and caressed one long silky leg.

Sunniva smote his hand. "Stop you right there, Con Cory!"

"I am going to make love to you, Sunniva."

"Nay, you are not."

He opened his eyes. "Why not?" He had expected to see excitement on her beautiful face; instead he saw fury.

"Con, free me." He did. She sat up and covered her legs with her skirts. "'Twas wrong of me to allow you to kiss me so. . . ."

"Allow?" Con laughed. "Methinks you had little choice, wench. And it seemed to me you enjoyed it."

Sunniva did not laugh with him. "Hear me well, Con. I did not fight as I would had you been well." She saw his face and mouth stiffen. He was angry with her, but she could not stop there. "Remember you, I am handfasted to another."

"And remember you, Mellby, you are my woman now," he answered gruffly.

She stared at him. He was big and brawny and comely, this Celt chieftain with his heaven-blue eyes and his hair flaming to his broad shoulders. But the only man she craved was Raven Trondsson. It was him she loved and would love forever. Even as she gazed at Con, Raven's dark, tall image filled her thoughts, heating her blood and making her heart race. They would be together again. All these weeks, that thought had sustained her, and she would not abandon it now.

"I am not your woman, Con, and well you know it," Sunniva answered crisply. "I belong to none but my betrothed and he to me. We are promised to one another before men and all our gods."

Con said, "You should know by now how I feel about your men and your gods."

"Ay, but methought you had some respect for me and my wishes. I cannot go to a man I don't love."

"Love? You said aught about love? I covet you, I desire you."

"You would not dishonor me so," Sunniva whispered, remembering how she had virtually brought him back from the dead.

Dishonor her? Con was stung to the heart. Any other woman would have held it an honor to wed him. "If your betrothed were any but Viking, then would I yield you. But to a Viking, nay. Him will I slay." Sunniva shook her head and covered her ears, but he went on brutally. "Your damned Vikings have taken our land and our women and you ask that I surrender you?" His eyes burned over her. "Nay. You are mine. Who deserves you more than I?"

How naive she had been, thinking that her nursing him to health might make him bend himself a bit to please her. Instead, he was more unwilling than ever to give her up—and threatening to slay Raven. She was fury-filled. She grasped the sword lying by his side, rose to her feet, and unsheathed it in one swift movement.

"Nay, Mellby," Con growled, but it was too late. She held the point surely and steadily at his throat.

He cursed himself for his carelessness, knowing he was a dead man if she so desired. He told himself that if he were in his full strength and power, this would not have happened, but he remembered well his men downed by her precisely placed arrows. She could have slain them all. She was a formidable adversary. He gave her a tired smile and raised his hands in surrender.

"I yield me, Mellby. I trow you will want to cut the blood-eagle on me." He saw the glimmer of tears in her eyes.

"Methought we were friends, Con." As she held the point unwavering against his throat, Sunniva's own throat was so closed, the words were scarcely audible. "Never did I trow you would treat me so. Wedding me against my will, as would Rolf Gunnarsson. Threatening to slay my betrothed as did he. 'Twould seem I should have let the Fates take you."

This was insanity, she thought, tears spilling down her cheeks and onto her gown. What earthly good was it, holding him at swordpoint? She could no more slay him than she could slay the Hedeby lord, a man whose evil was boundless. And Con was not evil. She understood his hatred and the fury that drove him to venge himself against her people. She hurled his sword from the roof down to the field where it landed upright and stood quivering in the tall grass. Herself she threw onto the thatch, sobbing.

Con gazed down at her, surprised. Why had she not pressed her advantage? And never had he thought to see her cry, no more·than Calla would cry. Her body shuddered but she made no sound; her sobs were silent. He said gruffly:

"Come, Mellby, you are not the first woman to be a prize of war." She made no answer but continued to weep. "'Tis not as though I mean to harm you. By the saints, 'tis honor I am offering you. To share my name and all that I own. . . ."

"I—do not want to share your name nor all you own," Sunniva's voice was muffled. "I do not love you."

Con gritted his teeth. It would be easy to forget all she had done for him and think only of how he yearned to destroy Trondsson. He was certain that with the Viking chieftain out of the way, she would come eventually to forget her love foolishness for him. Doubtless it would take time, but for Sunniva Mellby, he was willing to wait. He sat down beside her, stroked her trembling shoulder. She rolled beyond his reach and glared at him.

"Don't touch me."

He said gravely, "I trow you are worn out to weep so easily. Nursing me, doing your chores . . ."

"Weep so easily?" Sunniva sat up. "You grind my hopes and dreams under your heel and then tell me I weep easily?" Her laughter was bitter. What a fool she had been to think him a kind man. He was as cruel as Rolf in his own way.

Con sighed. The truth was, he would rather see an enemy slain than a woman cry. "Mayhap you would like to visit your Solby folk this afternoon."

"What?" Sunniva wiped her tears and stared at him. Perhaps she had not been wrong after all.

Con shrugged. "'Tis time, I trow, that you saw them. I know 'twould make you happy, and despite what you think, I want you to be happy."

"'Twould make me happy, ay." But now was not the time to speak of dwelling in the stockade. It would only anger him. "How long may I stay?"

"The whole afternoon if 'tis what you want."

"'Tis what I want." Sunniva got to her feet, wiping the last of her tears away with the edge of her apron. "Have thanks, Con."

Con made no answer, but buckled on his swordbelt and jumped from the roof to the ground. He pulled his sword from the earth, slid it into the scabbard and walked down to the sea. He did not want her thanks. Twice now she had given him his life, yet before this day was over, he meant to use her to discover if the Solby chieftain was one of his prisoners. If he were there, Con knew he would find Sunniva in his arms.

CHAPTER 23

RAVEN DID NOT BROOD OVER SUNNIVA FOR LONG. ULF took matters in hand.

"Come along, man, you've gloomed enough for one day. We're going to wrestle, you and I. Or mayhap chess would suit you better."

"Nay, we'll wrestle." He needed to use his body more than his brain, to let out his fury and frustration in a harmless way. He froze suddenly, seeing the gate swing open. "Ulf, by the gods, look!" It was Sunniva running toward him. The others had seen her and were crowding about, greeting her.

"Raven! Ulf!" Sunniva kissed her brother's cheek and then went into Raven's outstretched arms. The two kissed long and hungrily. Afterward, Sunniva wanted to fall on him weeping with her joy, but she did not. He was a chieftain and a chieftain's woman did not weep over him before his men. Instead she asked, "How goes it with all of you?"

"We are well." Raven held her tightly in the crook

of his arm, his gray eyes moving over her anxiously. She looked healthy and in good spirits and as fair as ever. Did nothing ever drag her down? He said, "'Tis you we have all been wondering and worrying about."

"I'm unharmed. I wanted to see you sooner, but 'twas forbidden. In fact, I wanted to dwell here in the stockade with all of you, but he—would not hear of it." She saw that familiar angry glitter in Raven's eyes.

"How long can you stay?" he asked.

"He said all afternoon, but then mayhap he will change his mind."

So. The devil was granting her favors. And what was he receiving from her in return? The thought was like a kick in Raven's gut. He said to his men: "I would be alone with her for a while." There would be no lovemaking, but he craved to hold and taste her, inhale the fragrance of her sweet flesh and her lips, feel her soft body pressed against the length of his.

"Stand watch," he ordered. "If you see through the cracks that any come near the gate, give the signal." He then led Sunniva into one of the small huts and lifted her into his arms.

Sunniva smoothed back his hair, stroked his face, traced his lips with trembling fingers. "Oh, beloved, how I have missed you. Are you really well? You have not been mistreated?"

Raven's answer was to take her mouth in a deep possessive kiss, one hand slipping beneath the neck of her kirtle to caress her breasts. He heard her small gasp of pleasure and then her arms went about his neck, pressing his lips ever more closely to hers. Their tongues met, teasing, searching; she twisted her slim body so that her breasts thrust eagerly against his chest; his breathing grew labored. But then, that part of him that remained ever dispassionate in battle took over. He wanted to make love to her, ay, but from the first he knew they must not. It was too dangerous.

Sunniva was tingling all over, that hot, unbearably sweet pressure growing and spreading deep within her. She yearned, she craved for Raven to love her, to take her quickly, for it was the only way she knew to find relief. When he lowered her to her feet, she began immediately to unpin her gown. He covered her hands with his.

"Nay, Sunni, not this time," he said low. He pulled her close, breathed in the fragrance of her shimmering hair. "You know I want you, but we must not. 'Tis too dangerous."

"Ay," she whispered. "I trow you are right." Her disappointment was great, but if Raven Trondsson sensed danger, it was there. She trusted him completely.

"I would talk with you during this time," he said, gently. He lowered himself to the hard-packed earth floor and sat with his back against the wall. He pulled Sunniva down beside him so that their bodies touched, her small hands cradled in his.

"Where do you dwell, Sunniva?"

Having guessed it would be one of his questions, she had decided he must not know the truth. She answered, "With my friend, Calla."

"Know you what Con Cory means to do with us?"

"He waits for you to come for your men and your ship and me. I trow he wants to slay you."

"And he grants you favors."

She said quickly, "Ay, but only because of my friendship with Calla." How easily she lied to him now, Sunniva thought, hoping her guilt did not show. Never did she think she could lie to Raven. "Calla begged him to let us go, knowing 'twas only because of me that you all were here, but he would not. She continues to intercede for us, and I trow she will succeed eventually." She added lamely, "Con thinks highly of her."

Raven's eyes narrowed. So she called him Con. He marked the rosy flush sweeping over her milk-white skin. She was lying about something—but what? He felt an ugly swell of jealousy.

Seeing his face etched in such harsh lines, Sunniva felt a stab of worry. He looked older, more tired than when she had seen him last. And so grim. "Are you sure you are all right, beloved?"

"Ay," Raven muttered. "But 'tis damnable, this being cooped here and worrying about you and none of our comrades knowing we are here. 'Twould be preferable if the bastards made to slay us, then at least we would have a chance at battle and escape. This way there is none. They bring food and water with ten armed men looking on, and then they leave. But enough of that—I need information. How many men are here? How many are left when they go raiding?" He plied her with questions, and Sunniva answered as best she could. He said finally: "I trow you have not told him I am here."

"Never!"

"Does he know you are betrothed to Raven Trondsson?"

"He knows I am betrothed, ay, but I gave him no name." She fretted that perhaps Calla had mentioned it to Con before she left, but why would she? She sighed. She would not burden Raven now with her own worries, nor tell him that Calla had left Ballageay to visit kin. It would only worsen matters.

She looked so upset that Raven pulled her back into his arms. He brushed kisses over her face and throat and caressed her breasts. "'Twill all work out to the good, Sunni," he said, low.

"I hope so. . . ."

"Always have I trusted that within me which guides

and guards me. 'Tis what I must do now." He would not tell her how very difficult it would be.

"Ay," she murmured. She clasped both his hands and held them cradling her face, felt his warm, firm lips on hers. He would trust that wisdom within him, ay, but it was Raven himself she would trust and cling to.

Raven kissed her, a long, hungry kiss that she returned eagerly. Afterwards, he could only gaze at her, taking in the beauty that never failed to dazzle him. His little Sunniva. His beloved enchantress. It was beyond his ken that she could still love him after all he had allowed to happen to her, those damnable things he had been helpless to prevent. He bent to kiss her lips again when he saw her eyes widen. He looked toward the door where her frightened gaze was fastened and saw the Celt chieftain.

Con Cory laughed as a dark red flush touched his enemy's face. "Do not blame your men, Raven Trondsson. They would have met a quick death had they warned you."

Raven got to his feet. He thrust Sunniva behind him. "'Tis glad I am they did not, Celt. 'Twas time you knew I was here."

Con's blue eyes measured the Viking's impressive height and gauged his strength. "Long and long have I heard of Trondsson of Marvik," he said. "Methinks we might have been friends had things been different between our lands."

Raven was unmoved by his words, but having nothing to lose, he said: "Then for what might have been, free us so I can take my betrothed back to Norway. We came here seeking her, not a fight."

"Nay, I will not free you," Con drawled. "I consider you the most dangerous of enemies. And 'tis time you learned that this woman is no longer your betrothed. She is mine."

Joan Van Nuys

"I am not yours!" Sunniva cried.

Raven felt his body tense. Sunniva had said nothing to him of this. He marked that not only was the Celt tall and in prime condition, he was a man that women would be attracted to. Even as he damned his surging jealousy, he wondered if Sunniva had succumbed to the bastard's virility.

"You have naught to say about it, wench. 'Tis my decision to make." To his men, Con said: "Take her out."

As they moved to obey, Raven moved swiftly, downing the Celt chieftain before he himself was surrounded and his arms wrenched behind him. Spears were held to his throat and heart.

Con climbed to his feet. He rubbed his jaw and gazed on Raven with approval. He laughed. "Ay, 'tis certain we two would have been friends in another time."

Sunniva's eyes blazed her contempt. "'Tis better by far he have you for an enemy—one expects treachery from an enemy. And you have just destroyed any friendship between us, bastard." She was furious with him as well as frightened. He had known of Raven and her, and known she would go directly to him if he were here. It was a cruel, sly trick he had played on her.

Con's own eyes were mocking. "Did you tell him you dwell with me, Mellby?" he asked. "'Tis a thing he should know."

Raven's disbelieving gaze shot to Sunniva. Seeing her lovely face turn pink, and the guilt in her eyes, his heart turned to ice. So. It was that which she had lied about—telling him she dwelt with Calla when all along she lived with this bastard. His earlier ugly suspicions about her and Gunnarsson leapt afresh to torment him. Had the sweet child, the innocent maid become a lying, treacherous woman then?

"Is't true, Sunniva?"

"Not the way he says it!" Sunniva cried. She would have broken away from those men forcing her toward the door and fled to Raven's arms, but they held her fast. "I lived with Calla 'til she left to visit her kin. Con then bade me dwell with him. When I refused, he—would have given me to his men. There was naught else to do, Raven, but dwell with him. . . ." She bit down hard on her lower lip. She would not weep before these scuts.

Raven read in her eyes that she spoke the truth. By the gods, he had done it again. How could he mistrust her so? When would he learn that her love for him was real and abiding?

"'Tis all right, Sunni," he said, gently, "'tis all right." He turned to the Celt chieftain. "'Tis lucky for you, Celt, that I stand here hampered by your men, else you would lie in the dead-straw this day." Even as he said it, he knew that he would do nothing so foolhardy and put Sunniva in still greater jeopardy. But he wanted to trounce the devil within an inch of his life.

"'Tis certain one of us would die, Viking," Con answered, his anger mounting. "Remove the woman," he ordered his men.

"Don't touch me!" Sunniva snapped. "I know the way." She looked back at Raven. "Odin guide and guard you. . . ."

Raven watched her leave, Celts on either side of her. Always had he known she was brave and strong, but never more so than at this moment. He gave Con a wry smile. "You may think she is yours, but as long as we both shall live, she is mine. She is faithful. Her love, her very soul belongs to me."

Con nodded. "Methinks what you say is true. Therefore 'twould seem you must die, Trondsson. In time she will forget you."

Raven's laughter filled the small hut. "Think you she would give her love to the one who slew me? By the gods, you are innocent—or stupid. If I die by your hand, you will surely die by hers. Never will you sleep again in peace unless you plan to keep her under lock and key as Hedeby meant to."

Con's low chuckle had chilled many an enemy. "'Tis good to hear of such love in a woman," he said. "I trow she will do anything to save the life of the man who holds her heart."

Raven's rage flared. He charged past his captors to smash a clenched fist at Con Cory's head. The Celt responded swiftly, blocking a second blow with his forearm. When his abashed men again subdued Raven, Con growled:

"Nay, stand back. 'Tis between the two of us." He unbuckled his swordbelt. As he threw it to the earth, his foot shot out to catch the Viking's belly.

Raven twisted away from the blow, lunging for his enemy's windpipe with stiffened fingers. The Celt was ready. He crouched, slapped Raven's wrist away, only to be jerked forward and a steely shoulder rammed into his heart. Raven heard his harsh gasp, then gave a gasp of his own as Con Cory countered with a chop to his right biceps with the hard edge of his hand. Long and long they fought before the watching Celts, sweating, bleeding, silent but for an occasional muffled groan or oath.

"Yield you, Viking?" Con muttered as they rolled on the hard-packed ground.

"Nay. Yield you?"

"Nay." Con was tiring. His wound throbbed and his muscles burned with fatigue. He rasped, "I trow you are the finest foe I have ever fought."

"I trow the same of you." Raven's breathing was labored. Despite a rigorous regimen of exercise within the stockade, he was not fit. Captivity had made him soft.

"Since we be so evenly matched," Con muttered, "'twould bring no dishonor to either of us if you craved to call a draw." He feared he would drop before his men.

"Only if you crave it—" Raven was panting.

"We must both crave it, damn it."

"So be it."

"So be it."

They climbed to their feet, sullen, watchful, each expecting a trick from the other, but there was none. Con strapped on his swordbelt and, with no further word, left with his men.

Ulf and the others hastened to Raven's side as the Celts departed. "We are shamed, the lot of us, that we did not warn you, but they fair swarmed over us. 'Twas a trap, right?"

"Ay." Raven's eyes burned; his fists clenched. "He knew of our betrothal and suspected I was here."

"Damn the bastard. . . ." Seeing Raven's fury, his swollen eye and puffed lips, Ulf turned to the men. "I would speak with our chieftain alone." When they had dispersed, he said, "They took Sunniva out some time ago. . . ."

"Cory says she is his."

"Then he has a tiger by the tail." He added, "I see you fought."

"Ay. Would that I had killed the devil, but I dared not. Not with Sunniva in their hands." Raven ran his hands angrily through his hair. "Methinks I have made a bad mistake, telling him of Sunni's love for me."

"How so? It should discourage him."

"Nay, he will use it to his advantage." He smashed

a fist into his palm. "How could I have been such an ass? He will use us to gain her."

Ulf laughed. "She will slay him first."

"She is no fool. Then would his men take her and slay us. Nay, he will bargain with her, I see it. Our lives for her hand. And once she is his by the laws of the land, then he will be free to slay us all." Raven sank his face into his hands. "Ulf, what have I done in my pride that she loves me?"

"Damn me, Raven, think you that yon Celt devil cannot see with his own eyes how she feels about you? Think you for one instant that she would not tell him with her own tongue of her love? Why take all the blame on your own shoulders?"

"Damn me, I am responsible for all of this. All of it. I knew from the beginning that chieftains and kings would crave her. I should have guarded her more closely. A woman who looks like Sunniva"—he groaned, his eyes wild—"Ulf, the gods themselves would kill for her."

Ulf gave him a stiff buffet. "Nay, man, get hold of yourself now. Sunni is a fair enough maid, but there are others equally fair. I trow any other you might have chosen could have set this damned thing in motion."

Raven had not heard him. He was striding about the compound, death on his mind. His list was growing. Gunnarsson, Kol, Cory—he knew not how many more before this damned thing was ended and he had Sunniva safe on Marvik-land where he would guard her night and day. But he did not see the path leading there any time soon. Something would turn the tide eventually, ay, but for now, there was nothing. Damnation, he could not let his men see his agony. It was up to him to see that they did not lose heart and stayed fit for the battle that would eventually come. He ceased his pacing.

"Summon the men, Ulf. 'Tis past time we stretched our legs and practiced our war-play."

Con Cory was in a grim mood. He had found Raven Trondsson, and now he almost wished he had not. As he strode from the stockade to his cottage, he wondered if Sunniva would be there. He hoped not; he did not want her to see him looking so bruised and battered. It was a forlorn hope. She was sitting on the thatched roof gazing at the sea. When she saw him, she jumped down easily to the ground. The wind lifted her flaxen hair and billowed her blue kirtle around her long legs. She seemed not to notice or care that his eyes were on them. Her own gaze widened as he drew closer. She gasped.

"You fought with Raven?"

"Ay."

She put her hands on her hips and laughed, seeing his cracked lips and the black swellings around his eyes. Blood streamed freely from a cut on his temple.

"'Tis a pity he did not kill you," she said.

"'Tis not for lack of trying," Con admitted. "Nor did I succeed in slaying him."

Her laughter left. "You—gave him a weapon?"

"Think you I gave the bastard a broad-sword?"

Sunniva blinked. She knew he could have slain Raven with any weapon he chose and no Celt would have raised a finger to help the defenseless Viking. Ballageay was Con's land, his stronghold, his men, and Raven was his captive, to do with as he would. And instead of slaying him outright, he had fought him bare-handed and been bloodied and bruised. Gratitude warred with her fury, but she did not thank him. Not after the despicable trick he had played on her.

"We will battle again," Con said gruffly, "you can be sure of it. With weapons." He liked it that the devil

313

was as big and strong and skilled in war-play as he himself was. He craved the challenge of pitting himself against Norway's best, and there was no doubt in his mind as to the outcome. "Know you, Mellby, he will lose."

"Nay, Celt, 'tis you who will lose." But Sunniva did not want them to fight. She prayed that Calla would return in time to put all things to rights. "Raven's skill with weapons is great. Odin himself fights by his side in battle."

"Doubtless because Trondsson cannot manage alone," Con snapped. He was growing more and more annoyed with the wench.

Sunniva saw it, and marked she had gone too far. She added quietly, "He is a good man. All say he is as fair and just on cruise as on his own estates."

Con's mouth tightened. "Oh, ay. 'Tis why he comes to my land twice yearly to demand tribute."

Seeing her look away, pink with embarrassment, Con felt desire and jealousy sweep over him. He remembered Trondsson's arrogant declaration that Sunniva Mellby would be his own as long as they both would live; that slaying him would only make her hate him. He deemed the devil was right, which meant he had a decision to make. Which was the greater prize—gaining Sunniva's love and gratitude by freeing the bastard, or ridding his land of one of its greatest enemies and having her lifelong hatred? He was at an impasse. He craved Sunniva grateful and unresisting, ay, but he also craved Trondsson's death. By the saints, why should he not have both?

Sunniva had spoken to Con Cory boldly, but she was afraid. As he strode into his hut to tend his wounds, trembling seized her. Her thoughts were like leaves in a maelstrom. He was a fitting opponent for Raven when it came to size and bravery and heart. Of his weapon-skills, she knew nothing, but he was a chieftain. A man did not get to be chieftain without proving his supremacy over other men, and his Viking-hatred frightened her most of all. He would face Raven with a white-hot blood lust, for Con wanted him out of his land and out of her life.

What could she do to help? Plead for Raven's life and that of his men? Offer herself in exchange for their freedom? Nay, she was not so foolish as to think she mattered that much. Her one hope was Calla. She had been gone nigh onto twelve sunsets now, and surely she would return soon. And when she heard of Con's outrageous plan to wed her, she would point a finger at him, and her green eyes would glitter and she would make him see reason. Ay, she would certainly make him see reason. Sunniva's heart lifted at the thought.

CHAPTER 24

IT WAS THE SUNSET HOUR, AND SUNNIVA WAS GLAD TO have been called to the byre to help with the milking. Its quietness and the dim light there helped to calm her turbulent thoughts. It minded her of the cow-barn at Lilleby. The sounds—the creak of leather, the cattle's lowing, the whisking of their tails against flies—and the smells of straw, fresh hay, and milk foaming into the bucket. She loved it all, but as she hiked up her kirtle and sat in close to the swelling cow-flank, her peace fled. What was going to happen to them all? To her and to Raven and his men?

Her mind roved restlessly, endlessly over all the terrible possibilities. Would Con slay the Solby Vikings, including Raven? It was his right, after all, and what purpose did it serve for him to keep them there eating his food and taking the time of his warriors to guard them? Or would he sell them into slavery? She quaked at the thought, for she still bore Rolf's band on her own ankle. Or would Con use them, the Vikings, for bargaining with her and forcing her to do his bidding? But that was ridiculous. She was already in his power.

Quietly, competently, she went about her chores, helping the maids strain the milk through rushes into shallow tubs where the cream would rise. She then carried the wooden pails to the creek for scouring. She had just reached into the water to remove those pans soaking there since morn when a noise startled her. Ever aware that Rolf Gunnarsson sought her still, Sunniva leapt to her feet. A tall, handsome woman in leggings and tunic stood there.

Calla nodded sober approval. "'Twas very good, that, Sunni. You are as quick on your feet as ever."

"Calla!" Sunniva flung her arms about her friend's neck. "Oh, Calla, 'tis glad I am to see you! When came you?"

"This instant," Calla answered, smiling at the other's genuine joy and thinking that never had she received such a welcome from Celt women. "Tell me, how goes it, Sunniva?"

Sunniva laughed, for now all was well. Her problems were near solved. "Let me put these buckets in to soak, and then will I burn your ears." Calla helped. They filled the buckets with stones and lay them on their sides in the rushing creek to scour overnight. "'Tis a good place to talk, so sit you, Calla." Sunniva sat down beside her friend in the deep grass. "'Tis the answer to my prayer that you have come—everything has gone agley. . . ."

Calla frowned. "In what way?" She had expected Sunniva by now to be fully enthralled by Con Cory. Wedded to him even. Con's charm with women, when he put his mind to it, was legendary. His lovemaking was unforgettable.

"I am in terrible trouble." Sunniva lowered her voice and looked about to make sure they were alone. "Con Cory has taken it into his head to wed me. Calla, is there aught you can say or do to make him see reason? I cannot wed the man. I am handfasted to Raven."

Calla was relieved; this was no problem at all. She said easily, "Yet I mind you were hurt by Raven's mistrusting you. Mayhap he is not the man for you."

Sunniva shook her head. "But he is. 'Twas just his jealousy. Never did he mean it."

"I trow he has not come in force yet or you would have said so." She much doubted the Viking chieftain had had time to gather men enough to attack a stronghold the size of Ballageay.

"That is one of the problems. Raven is here."

Calla stared. "Here?"

"In the stockade. He has been here from the beginning. I saw him today for the first, and 'twas naught but a cruel trap Con sprang on us. He suspected that Raven was among his prisoners, but had no way of knowing which was he. Today he said I could visit the stockade, and then—he found us together." Her angry words tumbled out breathlessly. "Methought he was grateful for my tending his wound and that we had become friends. Fool that I was."

"Wound?" Calla muttered an oath and sat up straighter. It was she who had told Con the two were betrothed, ay, but not that Raven was captive! "What mean you? What wound? Sunniva, methinks you had best begin at the beginning."

As Sunniva's tale unfolded, Calla saw that nothing had happened the way she had intended. Nothing. It was clear that Sunniva loved Raven more deeply than ever, and her resentment of Con was fierce. Damnation. Why had she herself not allowed things to go their own way instead of attempting to match the two of them?

"Calla, Con regards you highly, 'tis plain to see. Will you not put things right for me? I am so afraid . . . what if he sells them into slavery?"

"Rather would he slay them," Calla answered grimly. When Sunniva gasped, she added, "But he will not, I promise it."

"And promise I will not have to wed him. Oh, Calla, you can surely make him see reason. 'Tis an impossible thing he asks. Promise you will help."

Long and long Calla gazed at Sunniva as the sun set behind her golden hair, golden skin, gold-tipped lashes. "I doubt I can," she said finally.

Sunniva gave a low cry. "Why not? Calla, what is't? What have I said to make you look at me so?"

"You have done naught. 'Tis all my doing, this," Calla muttered.

"I—don't understand."

Calla made herself meet Sunniva's astonished eyes. "'Twas I who told Con to pursue you. I was certain Raven did not deserve or appreciate you."

"What?"

"'Twas wrong of me, I know that now."

Sunniva sat very still, the darkening fields seeming to spin about her every which way. She put her fingertips to her pounding temples. "Is't why you left? You wanted us to be alone?"

"Ay," Calla answered quietly. "Know you how I cherish Con, and more and more I have seen that he needs the love and support of a good woman. I trow you are the finest I have ever met. He is worthy of you, Sunniva—and you of him."

Worthy? Folk married for love, or they married for money or to extend their influence through an important family. But worthy?

"Calla macLir!" She could scarcely speak, she was so wroth. "You got me into this, now you get me out of it!"

"'Twill take some doing. When first I broached the subject to Con, he was balky. He didn't like you. Now 'tis different. I trow that when you nursed him, he came to care for you deeply. Now he sees in you what I have seen all along."

"Then you had best make him see me differently," Sunniva said hotly. "Now I must go to him, otherwise he will turn the village inside-out looking for me."

Con Cory sat on his roof gazing out at the last rays of sun glimmering on the pewter sea. He had reached a decision. He wanted the woman more than he wanted his enemy dead. Calla was right. There was none other like her, and he did not want her as an enemy. He wanted her as a lover, wanted her by his side sharing life with him, sharing laughter and sorrow, giving him sons. That he did not love her was of no importance. It was a boon, considering the fact that she did not love him. She loved Trondsson. That he could live with, since she was going to forget the bastard completely. He would make her forget him when he took her to bed. And he wanted the Viking to know it. He wanted Trondsson of Marvik to know that he, Con Cory, had stolen her love from him.

Trondsson. Con pulled a stem from the thatch and chewed on it, his eyes thoughtful. He was minded to slay the bastard now, slay all of them, but he had a use for them. He would offer Sunniva their freedom if she wed him. There would be mutterings from his tribe, ay, but then, any who disagreed could bring their grievance to him and he would settle it with a sword. He smiled, knowing none would disagree— except Trondsson. But he had planned for that.

Hearing a rustling in the grass, he turned and saw Sunniva coming across the field.

"I would talk with you, Mellby. Come up here and sit with me."

Wordlessly, Sunniva obeyed. She walked out onto the roof and sat, her eyes on the gray sea, mutiny on her face and in her very bearing. Con's anger leapt.

"We will wed, woman, never doubt it."

"'Twill take brute force."

"Nay, 'twill not. In fact, you yourself will tell your Viking that you no longer love him, but want me. In my magnanimity, I will then free the lot of them."

Sunniva threw back her head and laughed. "Never would he believe I could love you, nor that you would free him." But she saw his trap closing. The bargaining was about to begin, just as she had feared it would.

"'Twill be your job to make him believe it," Con answered quietly, but she heard the underlying menace in his voice. "In your hands lies his fate." He took both her small hands, but she angrily snatched them away.

"What mean you?"

"I mean that you will be convincing. You will act such a fickle witch, the man will be happy to be rid of you."

"'Tis madness. He knows me—he knows I love only him."

"His life depends on you, Mellby," Con said grimly. "You will deceive him if you love him enough. If he roars and threatens, then will I slay him where he stands, as well as his men. It depends on you."

"You bastard. . . ."

Con grinned. "Actually, my lineage is quite distinguished—more than yon Viking's, I trow." He grew serious then. "Do we have an agreement?"

Sunniva got to her feet. "Nay, we do not." She

jumped to the ground, Con following, and entered the shadowy hut where a lamp burned low. She thrust her few belongings into her wallet and took up her pallet.

"Where go you?" he demanded.

"To Calla. She has returned."

"You will remain here." Con blocked her path of retreat.

"Will you chain me?" Sunniva taunted. She lifted the skirt of her kirtle. "The slave-band is on my ankle still, awaiting my next master. Go ahead, chain me!"

"I will not chain you," Con growled, cursing himself for not having the smith remove the damned thing. He had forgotten it completely. "Never have I taken a woman in thrall, nor will I. But you will stay, Mellby."

"Nay!" She struggled as he lifted her and carried her to his own pallet. He lowered her to it and sat down beside her.

"You stay or Trondsson dies this night. If you don't believe me, walk out that door and see what happens."

Sunniva's hand shot out and cracked against his cheek. The blow sounded sharply in the small room. "I hate you!"

"Ay, methinks you do. But 'twon't last—not after you taste my lovemaking." He pushed her onto her back and stretched out on top of her.

As he sought her lips, she screamed, clawed, twisted her face from side to side, but there was no stopping him. His mouth took hers. He had kissed her only once before and the tantalizing memory remained. She tasted the same—fresh, sweet, succulent, even as she tried to bite him. Remembering her in the Viking's arms, her face and lips rosy from his kisses, Con's jealousy flamed. Damn the bastard.

Long and long he kissed her, crushing her mouth, her body beneath his, until she ceased to struggle. His hands moved over her, gently questing, seeking the soft curves beneath her kirtle. He realized finally that she was weeping. His lips and hers, too, were wet with her tears. He raised his head, his heavy body still pressing her into the pallet. He scowled down at her.

"I have not hurt you, woman."

Sunniva's tears flowed freely. It was not for herself she wept, it was for Raven. He was going to die.

"He will not believe me," she whispered. "Con, you cannot do this . . . and you are . . . so heavy . . . ."

Con remained where he was. "He had better believe you. In seven days, you will return to him. You will tell him you dwell with me now because you want to dwell with me. You will tell him you crave my lovemaking and plan to wed me."

Sunniva shook her head. "He will never—"

Con's long fingers gripped her jaw like an iron vise so that she cried out. "Listen well, Mellby," his voice rasped and his icy eyes were those of a frightening stranger. "I am minded to slay your beloved this night. 'Tis because of my feelings for you I give you this chance. Hear you?" His fingers tightened. "Or mayhap you prefer that I slay him here and now."

"I—I will do it," she wept. Her voice shook; her entire body shook. Calla had to help, she thought, she had to, but for now, she would agree to anything. Anything. "I will—make him hate me."

"Good." Con rolled off her and sat, his back against the wall, gazing at her in the dimness. She was the loveliest thing he had ever laid eyes on.

Sunniva, too, sat up. She dried her face on her skirt and wrapped her arms about her to stop her shivering, but she could not stop. Con bundled her in a skin, and still she shivered. Through clenched teeth, she said:

"Celt dog, I don't trust you."

He laughed, savoring her boldness. "Nor I you, Viking bitch." But he had not forgotten the night she had gone to the witchfield for lyngwort to heal him. She had risked her life that he might live. He added, gently, "'Tis a problem, that, Mellby. Trust."

Sunniva's gaze was defiant. "There would be no problem if you would free us all." Her eyes widened. "Con, I will make you a promise—free us, and Raven and his men will never return to Maun."

"I have but to slay them to assure that, Mellby." Seeing her face turn pale, he said, "Methinks you will do as I ask."

"And after, when he is gone, then what? Am I to believe you will actually let him go unscathed once he is out of my sight?" He smiled briefly. Sunniva caught but a glimpse of the Con Cory who had been her friend.

"You feel I am without honor then?" he asked.

"You have not so much as a shred of honor. Know you, Celt, that if I must send my man away at your damned bidding, then will I insist on proof of his safe passage."

Con's eyes danced over her. She was a queen, a goddess, a mate fit for a chieftain. "What is your command?"

"Your men will escort his vessel till he reaches the open sea. And by that, I mean men on all of your vessels. I will not have any lying in ambush for him. And if any one else attacks him, then will you defend him."

"By the saints, you ask much, wench."

"'Twould seem I am worth much." She was not sure why, but it appeared to be so. "Do we have an agreement?"

Until that moment, he had seriously considered slaying the Vikings after Sunniva was his. He had meant to wait until the last to make a final decision but now, in the space of an eyeblink, all was changed.

"Ay, Mellby, we have an agreement," he said.

Sunniva nodded. "I will accompany you. I will be in the lead escort-vessel to make sure you play no further tricks."

"Ay," Con said gravely. "'Tis what I would have suggested myself. . . ."

The precious days slipped by, and the help that Sunniva had begged from Calla never came. It was not that Calla did not attempt to change Con Cory's mind, it was that he was like granite where Sunniva was concerned. Again and again she went to him, reversing the very arguments she had made before leaving Ballageay, but to no avail. He wanted none but Sunniva. On the morn of the seventh day, he stopped Sunniva as she left his cottage.

"You will see Trondsson today," he stated.

"If I must . . ."

"You must." He marked that she was prepared for it. She wore a violet-colored gown he had not seen before, and her hair was new-washed and lay on her slim shoulders like a cloak of gold. He steamed with worry and resentment, hating it that she needed even to go near the bastard again. "My men will take you when you are ready."

Sunniva did not let him see her anguish. Ready? Never would she be ready to tell Raven Trondsson that she no longer loved him and would wed another. She was sick to her stomach thinking of what lay ahead. But she had to convince him or he would be slain. She thought suddenly of that other Sunniva, the Irish princess. They shared the same name and they both feared the attentions of a heathen chieftain, ay, but there the resemblance ended. The princess had been able to escape. Sunniva herself was unable to flee and would wed the heathen. And the princess was a saint. Sunniva drew a deep breath. Well she knew she was no saint.

"I am ready," she said coolly. "I forgot to tell you—I would be alone with him."

"Nay," Con angrily waved her words aside. "'Tis out of the question."

"Think you he will harm me?"

"Nay, methinks he will charm you. He will bed you."

"Nay, he will not. I go alone, Con Cory, or I do not go."

"Then you forfeit his life, you stubborn wench."

Sunniva put her hands on her hips and glared at him. "Then will you lose yours. Never doubt I will avenge him."

Con drew a deep breath of exasperation. He was out of his mind to desire such a contrary, blood-thirsty bitch; out of his mind to turn those damned Vikings loose in his land again in order to have her. By the saints, he was mad. He glared back at her.

"Go, then, but never doubt, Mellby, you are mine."

"Never will I lie with you until we are wed."

Con glowered at her. Never had he known such a demanding wench—except for Calla. He shook his head and muttered, "Granted." He then summoned two men and ordered them to take her to the stockade and leave her there. Before they left, he took Sunniva's arm. "You will return when the sun is overhead, Mellby," he warned. "No longer. Remember, I would just as soon slay those bastards as look at them."

"Ay."

Over and over, Sunniva had repeated the words she

must now say to Raven. There could be no mistake. If he doubted her, if he raged and refused to yield her when the guards came for her, then he would die. All of them would die. She did not doubt Con Cory's sincerity.

Oh, bright elves, help me this day, she prayed as the gate was opened and she walked into the stockade. Holy Thor and Sif, holy Odin and Frigg and Brage. Holy Jesu-Mary-Holy Ghost, help me. Help me. . . .

She saw him then, Raven. Raven was coming toward her. He was running, and how big and strong he was, how much a chieftain. Bearded, broad-shouldered, sinews standing forth on his long, sun-darkened arms and legs, his hair as it was in her dreams—thick, black, glossy as a raven's wing—his eyes gray-gold, sun and shadow, eagle eyes, and holding such gladness, such love for her as she had never before seen. Oh, Raven, beloved, forgive me for what I must do to you. . . .

Before she could say a word, Sunniva was lifted into his arms, cradled against his hard body, crushed as if he would never let her go. When his mouth took hers in a fiercely hungry kiss, she responded just as hungrily, just as fiercely. Forgotten was her terrible reason for being there.

CHAPTER 25

Raven had been thinking of Sunniva constantly, worrying over her, yearning for her, and suddenly, he thought he saw her. But nay, it was a vision. He was imagining things. Why would she be here at this hour, unguarded and looking as though she had just stepped out of one of his dreams? She wore a blue-violet gown the color of her eyes, and her long silky hair was like spun gold spilling, gleaming, down her back and over her shoulders. A smile lit her beautiful face as she caught sight of him. Holy Odin. She wasn't a vision, nor was he imagining her. She was real.

He didn't care how she came there or why or for how long. All that mattered was that she was there and he was hungering for her. Dying for her. He broke into a run, and an instant later, Sunniva was in his arms. Her face, her eyes, the way she returned his starving kiss, her body melting against his, told him that her passion raged as fiercely as did his. He carried her to the hut he shared with others, knowing it would be empty, knowing his men would not let any Celt enter. This time, even were death the result, they would bar the enemy. All knew that hell might lie ahead, but first their chieftain would know paradise.

Gently, Raven set Sunniva on her feet. Their lips still sealed, pressing her soft body to his, he began stripping off her gown and chemise. Sunniva helped when she could tear her own hands away from his hair, his face, his broad shoulders and strong arms. She yearned to caress his dark polished skin, to taste him, hold and press him to her. She loved him. She loved him more than her own life, yet she was sounding his death knell by returning his kisses and revealing her hunger. How could she have been so thoughtless and selfish? She stiffened in her fear.

"What is't?" Raven murmured, his hands roaming over her naked body. He held her at arm's length, gazing at her luminous white skin and pink-tipped, thrusting breasts, her slender rounded limbs and parted lips, so red and full and soft he wanted to bite into them. "Sunniva, you are the fairest thing. . . ." He felt a stab of anger, seeing the hated band on her ankle.

"Raven, I would talk with—"

His greedy mouth sought hers, stopping her words. He cupped her breast, took one perfectly-formed nipple between his teeth and then the other, nipping, suckling her until she whimpered.

"Raven, please, I must—"

"Later, Sunniva. Later . . ."

His hungry kisses consumed her, but even as the fire raced through her body, she ordered herself to tell him. Tell him that she no longer craved him but had grown to love another . . . tell him that she dwelt with Con now because it was her desire . . .

tell him that she and Con would wed soon. *Tell him, tell him*! It was a silent shriek as her lips parted for yet another kiss that was deeper still and he lowered her to the earthen floor. It was not too late, she could still pull away, still break his heart and make him hate her. . . .

"Raven, nay—" Sunniva put both hands on his chest and tried to push him back. She turned her face to the wall. "I mean it, we must talk," she said sharply.

"Temptress," Raven breathed, pinning her arms above her head. His tongue circled her hardened nipples and made a glistening trail across the soft swell of her belly to where the golden down shimmered.

Sunniva felt him part her thighs, delve into her cleft with gentle skillful fingers, so gentle. She gasped; she heard his breathing quicken and grow harsh. His eyes glittered. Well she knew she could not stop him now to save either of them. She could not. His body and his hunger were too strong, and her will was too weak. She had forgotten that deep, enticing warmth that was spreading, burning within her now. Consuming her.

"Oh, Raven." She wept softly. She had wept before with the joy of it, the sheer ecstasy of it, ay, but now she wept because she was condemning him to death.

"Shhh, 'tis all right, Sunni. Open your legs just a bit more, little enchantress."

Sunniva obeyed, trying to put from her mind everything but the moment, his love and tenderness, his great arousal, her own hunger and love for him. She watched his eyes as they burned over her, watched his long, supple fingers, so dark against her breasts, molding them and stroking her thighs, opening them to him wider, wider, his dark head dipping to her there. Her breath caught. Never had she felt such a thing. Fire streaked through her, and then came the gout of moisture, like honey, as Raven slid himself into her waiting sheath. He filled her totally, yet he lay there quietly, allowing her to get accustomed to him.

Raven, Raven, Raven. How dear he was. Sunniva slipped her arms around his hard torso, her hands on his buttocks, pressing him against her ever more tightly, for even now, lying within her, he was not close enough. He began to move, at first imperceptibly, slowly, so slowly, rubbing, teasing her, his eyes beginning to show his primitive hunger as his shaft penetrated her more deeply still. And then his stroke lengthened, growing more demanding with each great thrust. Suddenly she felt his manhood thudding, thudding ever more rapidly against the very walls of her womb.

Sunniva cried out softly, not in pain, but with the deliciousness of it. It was torment, sweet, hot, throbbing, growing torment. She could scarcely bear the ecstacy of it and yet she wanted it to stay with her forever. She squirmed beneath him, arching against him, drawing their bodies closer still, her hungry mouth searching over his face and throat, kissing, savoring the salty male taste of his flesh, her hands caressing, loving the feel of his silky hair and beard, the smooth, taut skin on his back and shoulders. And then, then, as he claimed her completely, she was aware only of his mouth on hers in a deep possessive kiss, and his seed flooding into her in such a hot violent rush that her own desire peaked.

Long and long they lay unmoving and wordless in each other's arms, their damp skin sealing them together. Sunniva's body was completely without strength, but her thoughts churned. Never could she follow Con's orders now. It would have been difficult enough to tell Raven earlier that she no longer loved him; now it was impossible. He knew she loved him. And he loved her. Her heart sang even though his peril was great, as was her own. His long fingers tightened about her hand.

"What were you going to tell me?"

Ay, what was she going to tell him? There was only one thing she could think of that rang even slightly of the truth. Calla. She must convince him that Calla was involved.

"I came to tell you that—you are going to be freed. All of you." She felt the instant alerting of his body and his senses.

"And you?"

"I, too, of course," she lied, and smiled. It would be far easier, this, than trying to convince him she loved Con Cory. His gray eyes were on her, narrowed, watchful, as she rose and began to pull on her clothing.

"I would hear this wondrous tale," he muttered, donning his own garb. He suspected his fears were about to take shape. Had the devil bargained for their lives with Sunniva and won?

"'Tis Calla's doing," Sunniva said promptly, but she saw the skepticism in his eyes.

"When did she return?"

"Seven days ago."

"And how is she planning this miracle? Will she call on Manannan to fog up the damned place and blind the men and then unlock the gate?"

"Nay," Sunniva answered quietly. "You—we are to walk out." When Raven gave a bark of disbelieving laughter, she hurried on. "'Tis true. Mind, I told you—she likes me. We are sisters. She has convinced Con Cory that you were here only to find me and take me home." Again he laughed. "Raven, 'tis true! She cherishes our friendship, and Con cherishes her. He craves to please her.'' Would that it were so, she brooded, studying his taut face.

"Con you call him, do you?'' Raven muttered.

" 'Tis his name.''

" 'Tis the same Con, I trow, who told me you were his woman and that you dwelt with him? Sunniva, that devil craves only to please himself and now you tell me he will allow me to walk out of here with you?''

Sunniva had to look away. She bit her lip to keep it from trembling.

"Come, Sunniva, methinks not.''

She sighed. Never could she tell him an untruth. "Ay. 'Tis a lie. . . .''

His arms went around her. "Since when are there lies between us?'' he asked, gently, and stroked her hair. "I would hear it, Sunniva.''

Sunniva drew a deep breath. " 'Tis partly the truth. You will be allowed to leave.''

"My men? My vessel?''

"Ay.''

"But not you.''

"Nay. I will stay.''

Raven held her close, her head on his chest, his lips touching her hair. "Will stay—or must stay?''

"Must.'' Her voice was small.

"Why?'' he asked gruffly.

Sunniva made no answer. But if Con did this thing for her, if he freed Raven and Ulf and the others, she meant to honor her part of their agreement. She would wed him. She could do no less.

Raven felt the old familiar rage flooding through him. She had told him more by her silence than if she had tried to deny it. The bastard wanted her in his bed. Looking on Sunniva, he did not see the grown maid, the treasure of his heart and the object of his passion. She was the small Sunniva who had always come to him for comfort and protection, to be taught the things no one else would teach her—the golden, laughing child catching snowflakes on her pink tongue and with her red-mittened hands. He gripped her arms.

"I will slay him."

Sunniva cupped his face, stroked back his hair. "Shhh, you will not. You will leave quietly and safely and not look back."

His fingers tightened. She winced, but he did not notice. "Think you I will leave this place without you? What sort of man do you think I am?"

"Methinks you are a chieftain, a man responsible for the lives of his crew. You will all be slain if you protest, but if you raise no fuss, Con will let you leave in peace."

Raven's mouth curled. "'Twould seem the bastard has you believing all he says."

"I believe he will slay you if you resist, ay."

"Then believe he will slay us in any event," Raven said sharply.

"Nay!"

"Listen to me, little wench." Raven spoke softly but his eyes flamed. "That devil has charmed you. He wants you and he has taken advantage of your innocence. 'Tis one of the things about you I treasure, but this is too much. You will see us leave and be assured of our safety, ay, but never doubt he will slay us after he has you."

Rarely had Sunniva seen him so angry. It roused her own wrath. "I may be innocent, Raven Trondsson, but I am not simple! I have given—"

"Never have I thought you were simple," Raven growled, "'tis that you are so beautiful, so special, that he covets you." He held up a hand, not allowing her to deny it. "I cannot blame him, nor can I fault him for making sure we do not return for you. He must slay us. If I were him, I would do the same."

"Raven, hush you and let me speak! I have given him an ultimatum."

"Oh, ay, and what might that be?" Seeing her beautiful eyes swim in sudden tears, he said gruffly, "The truth, Sunniva. I will learn it in any case."

"To have my goodwill, he must give you safe escort to the open sea and defend you if any attack you."

Raven swore. "By the gods—'tis exactly what I mean. They will sink us, not defend us." He hoped the devils had not discovered the extra weapons hidden beneath the half-deck planking on his vessel.

"Nay, they will not sink you. I will be in the lead vessel to make sure of it."

"And he will have you in bed on the way back to Ballageay." Raven shook his head. "Nay, Sunniva, I will have none of this plan."

Her relief was great that he had not guessed the truth—that she had promised herself in marriage to Con—but his stubbornness frightened her. She said gently:

"He will have me no matter, Raven. He could have forced me long before this, but he has chosen to please me. I trow he has some small speck of honor."

"So you defend him?"

"Nay, I do not defend him, 'tis merely the way of it." Seeing his anger was building, she murmured, "Raven, if you refuse to leave and are slain because of me, I could not bear it. 'Twill be hell as 'tis. . . ."

All thoughts of himself, his own hurt and rage and jealousy fled as Raven saw suddenly what life would hold for her. She loved him—she had the world to choose from, but she had chosen him—and now she was being torn from him and claimed by another.

How would he feel in her place? How would he feel if he were a helpless woman, a prize of war, forced to yield to a conqueror?

His blood turned icy. He could think of nothing worse, but then, he was a man, not a woman. Always had women been treated so, always had they been the property of men to do with as they chose, even in his own land. But not Sunniva. Not his brave, proud, fearless maid who threw a spear and shot an arrow with the best of his warriors. Not Sunni. He held her so close, kissed her so deeply, he left her breathless.

Sunniva laughed. "'Twas just what I needed. . . ."

"'Tis going to be all right," he said, gruffly. He knew now what course to follow. "Never will I let you go. That promise still stands."

She tried to pull away. "It cannot. I—I must leave now." She could not stay another moment, else she would want to make love again. "Raven, please, let me go."

"Listen to me, Sunniva." His hold on her tightened. "We are going to play the game he wants."

"What?" The hair rose on the back of her neck, seeing the glitter in his gray eyes. "Raven, what mean you?"

"He offers us freedom in exchange for you," Raven said, "so I accept. Tell him you are his. We will play his damned game, but we will return. He will expect it, ay, and he will be waiting, but never will he expect the horde I will bring. We will overrun this accursed place and make him regret the day he ever cast eyes on you." He would sail down and up the east coast of the isle sounding the lur horn at every Viking encampment. It would be like the old days—a horde of Vikings such as only Con Cory's forebears had seen before.

Sunniva felt a welling of hope. Was rescue possible or would she be wedded by then? She thrust the doubt from her mind. Now must she think of the ways she could forestall Con.

"How long will it be," she asked, "from your leavetaking 'til your return?"

"From dawn 'til dawn or sunset to sunset. Know you when we will be released?"

"Soon, I trow."

"The sooner the better. I want to see this place in flames. I trow you can hold the bastard off?"

"Ay." But she was thinking of Ballageay in ashes, the bloodshed, Calla slain, and Con. So many slain. And these people had suffered so much already. "Raven—" His hard arms were still around her; his mouth sought hers. "Let us think on this further. Mayhap no blood need be shed. Mayhap Calla can help me to meet you somewhere. . . ."

Raven smiled down at her. She was as tender-hearted as she was fair, and much as he hated the enemy, he loved Sunniva more.

"Ay, we can think on it further." He brushed her lips with his. "When must you return?"

"When the sun stands overhead." Already her breathing was coming quickly.

"Then there is time yet. Come, Sunni," his eyes danced, "we will lie down and talk. . . ."

CHAPTER 26

THE SUN HAD JUST REACHED ITS ZENITH WHEN CON and his two guards arrived at the stockade. Sunniva was still limp and glowing within, still in a daze from Raven's lovemaking, but she held herself stiff. Never would Con guess it. She watched him stride past her to where Raven stood, but—what was all of this? She stared as a great band of armed Celts suddenly swarmed over the stockade. Orders were called, and the Solby men were backed against the wall, spears pointed at the heart of each. Sunniva ran to Con.

"What mean you by this!" she cried.

"Keep her back," Con said. As two men took her arms and held her at a distance, Con's cool gaze went to Raven. Blue eyes narrowed, hand on hilt, a slight smile playing over his lips, he studied the Viking. Ay, this was a good man. The devil stood there tall and without fear, victorious almost, his strange gray-gold eyes hooded. What was he thinking? Con brooded, but the Solby chieftain said nothing.

"The woman has told you her decision?" Con asked.

"Ay."

"And what say you, Viking?"

Raven met the other's gaze coolly. "'Tis her choice. Never would I force a woman to do what she would not."

Con laughed. Ah, the other was stung despite the diffident mask he wore. "She has told you she loves me then, and she dwells with me now because 'tis her desire?"

Raven's eyes flickered briefly before shuttering, and Sunniva thought she would fall through the earth. Oh, no. No. She had not told Raven that silliness, for it was bootless. Never would he have believed her after such wonderful lovemaking. Now, hearing it from Con Cory in such an arrogant way, she dreaded what would happen next. She held her breath. She could scarcely believe it when Raven gave a lazy blink and drawled:

"Ay, so she says. I trow there is no accounting for women's peculiar tastes."

When Con's mouth tightened, Sunniva thought she might swoon. She could not listen to this. She would think of home, of Lilleby-land, and of riding Sooten. Suddenly she was jumping creeks and flying across meadows; she was helping her mother prepare evening-food for the serving-folk; she was laughing and talking with Inge and helping her father with the milking. Oh, holy Odin, how she missed her family and her home. . . .

"Then all is settled," Con said gruffly. "She is mine. Tomorrow at sunrise you leave." Con's eyes held a deadly light. "Know you, she will be well guarded. Don't plan on returning for her."

Marking the sadness in Sunniva's eyes, Con knew that she had accepted her fate. It did not concern him, her sadness. He would make her forget Trondsson. What surprised him was that the Viking had surrendered her so easily. Was it a trick? Damn, it would be the wiser thing by far to slay them all here and now, no matter what Sunniva thought or felt. But he had promised her, and never would she forgive him if he reneged. He went to her, put a possessive arm about her, and drew her toward the gate.

"Hold, Celt," Raven shouted.

Con turned, as did Sunniva. "Ay? What is't?"

"I would have your woman know why 'tis I surrendered her without a fight." Raven's chilly gray eyes were on Sunniva alone. "Comely wenches are easy enough to find—the world is filled with them—but not so good men or a vessel like mine. Know you that, wench."

It was Sunniva who looked away first, her cheeks a-flame. Raven appeared so furious and his words were so cruel, she was crushed. But she was being silly to take it so. It was but part of the game. Or was it? Surely he had not believed Con, surely he did not believe she loved the Celt . . . !

Con Cory lay on his pallet in the darkness. He stared at the pale stars through the open windows in the thatch, listened to the murmur of surf and wind and to the soft steady sigh of Sunniva's breathing. She slept on her own pallet on the other side of the room; he could barely make out her form. He sucked in a deep breath, released it, stretched the taut muscles in his long arms and legs, and felt the heat between his legs. Soon he would wed her. First came the jaunt north to get the damned Vikings to the open sea, then the journey back. He would have a Celt priest waiting, and then—then she would be his. By tomorrow night she would sleep in his arms.

Over and over he recalled the events of the day and how ravishing she had looked when he had gone to fetch her. Shimmering golden hair, lips full and pink as though she had just sipped nectar, skin glowing and rosy, her beautiful breasts curving above the neckline of her kirtle. She had looked soft. So soft. He shook his head. It must have killed the devil, no matter what he said, to hand over such a woman to another.

Con sat up, his eyes wide, a hammer pounding suddenly in his head. By the gods! He had been so filled with his own triumph, he had not seen it until now. The wench pink and dewy, softer looking than ever, and Trondsson, tall and cold and unafraid. Victorious. The bastard had had his woman. He stared at her shadowy form, allowing his anger to beat its way through him. But then, the deed was done; it was bootless to fume over it now. It was what came of yielding to such a headstrong wench. But changes would be made. Soon she would learn that in this land, it was a wife's place to please her husband. And if yon bastard had begot a Viking brat on her, he would not accept it.

Jaw clenched, eyes aglitter, Con foresaw it—the mewling newborn on the rush-covered floor awaiting his acknowledgment. If it were fairhaired, then would he wrap his cloak about it and claim it as his, ay. But if it had coal-black hair, even be it a man-child, then would it die. None such could be his son, and it would not be the first babe in this land cast out to perish by exposure.

He rose and trod the dirt floor on silent feet, his wrath growing. Damn the wench. The so-pure Sunniva, refusing to lie with him before they wed, yet she had lain with Trondsson. Did she think he was not as hungry? Not as deserving? Why should he not make her his when she was his? By holy St. Lonan, he was a chieftain, and when had he not taken any woman he craved? When had he ever craved one more than this one? She was twice his; she was booty and he had gotten her by fair trade. His loins flamed for her. He stripped and knelt by her pallet.

Sunniva lay on her side, and as he stretched out close to her, facing her on the packed earth, her soft breath, warm and sweet as a spring morning, fanned his hot face. His manhood stirred and grew. He slipped both arms around her and, as she slept, pulled her hard against him.

When she cried out, he murmured, "'Tis me, Con." He began kissing her face and lips. She pushed against him, but he held her closer. "Mellby, you are mine, remember?"

Sunniva had been dreaming of Lilleby and at first did not know where she was. Seeing Con, she gasped, "You promised we would not lie together until we wed."

"I have changed my mind."

"So this is how you keep a promise!"

She struggled to free herself, but his arms and legs were wrapped about her tightly. She felt his hard shaft thrusting against her belly and his hands claiming her breasts, his tongue expertly exploring her mouth. When she twisted her head to escape it, his lips found her cheek and throat.

"To think I told Raven you were not without some honor. 'Twould seem I was wrong."

"'Twould seem we were both wrong. I said he would charm you, and you promised he would not. I believed you. Now methinks he bedded you this morn. I trow 'twas not the first time, though you two were not wed." When she made no answer, he murmured, "Why should I, too, not have you beforehand?" As he spoke, he pulled up her nightshirt and began to caress her leg.

Sunniva struck his hand away. "I will tell you why, Con Cory," she said, her teeth clenched. "'Tis because I love Raven Trondsson. Him I have known since I was but a tiny maid. He was my dearest friend long before I ever knew I loved him. Now, here are you, a man I scarcely know, an enemy of my people and my betrothed who has won me through unfair means—here are you demanding that I yield myself to you without marriage." She had grown breathless. "Well, I will not yield me. You will have to force me every inch of the way. I cannot imagine 'twill give you much pleasure."

Ah, God. Con held her, his face buried in her fragrant cloud of hair. He could not bring himself to free her, but he ceased fondling her leg. Grimly he pulled down her nightshirt, covering her nakedness, and wondered what was happening to him. Where was the abandon, the satisfaction that had always come with the hunt and a conquest? Wenches he had had aplenty, some a-weeping, ay, but there were more who craved him than those who wept. But never before had their tears turned him aside. Now he found he could not lay a hand on the damned wench.

He rose, wordless, furious with himself, and went to his own pallet. He did not understand why he craved her trust and respect as much as he craved her body. It was the way he felt about Calla. Always had he been ashamed of such feelings, for he deemed it a grave weakness. It was not the way of men in his tribe, and now here it was again. By the saints, it was a damned nuisance.

Rolf Gunnarsson was a man raging inside, but never did he allow his men to see it. His gut burned with the desire to venge himself on Sunniva Mellby for the humiliation she had dealt him. If ever he found the wench, he vowed he would take her to Kemal Attibak for his harem. And during the long voyage there, he intended to gore her bloody, for his lust for her burned as wildly as ever. Long and long he had considered keeping her, a thrall chained constantly to his bed, for he yearned to break her spirit. But in his heart, he knew he could not defeat her, nor could he abide a defiant female. Were she to remain in his hands, he knew he would kill her, and he wanted worse than death for her. She would suffer more deeply at the hands of Kemal and his many sons and his constant visitors from foreign lands. Certainly no one deserved to suffer more than she did. He had learned that the damned wench had caused him to lose Ballageay.

For more than three weeks, he and his small band had combed this accursed land afoot, battling mist and ravines, tangled vines and bogs, traveling day and night in stealth and snatching what quick sleep they could. They had visited openly three of his strongholds scattered about Maun, but in secret they had spied on Celt and other Viking encampments. Rolf knew well that any Viking chieftain who held the wench, even be he a comrade, would not willingly surrender her. But their seeking had been fruitless. She was nowhere. She had disappeared from the isle as if she never existed.

And then yester-eve, approaching his stronghold near Peel, they had found the Landwaster at anchor and heard of the Celt attack on Ballageay and its surrender. Had he been there to rally his men, Rolf brooded, never would it have been taken. He placed the blame for its fall squarely on Sunniva Mellby.

In his first heat, he craved to gather his men, sail the Landwaster up the coast, storm the stronghold, and take back what was rightfully his. But he would not. He had not become chieftain and king through acting heedlessly and hastily. First the area must be scouted. He himself would go with a band of carefully chosen men. Ballageay was to have been the seat of his kingdom on Maun, so it seemed a reasonable thing for the Hedeby lord himself to go. None knew how reasonable, for Rolf had a growing suspicion that he would find his escaped thrall at Ballageay. He had looked everywhere else. This very eve they would trek there.

It was dawn and the sky was as fiery as Con Cory's temper. He waited impatiently at the shore for his armed men to march the Solby Vikings to their vessel tied in the shallows. His own vessels were in readiness, as were their crews. Sunniva, too, was ready. He had commanded her to keep distant until they cast off. She had obeyed. She leaned against a boulder, Calla by her side, and her eyes on the red-tinged Irish Sea. She wore the boy's clothes in which he had first seen her. Paal, she had called herself then, Con thought blackly, and wished to St. Lonan she really had been a lad. Then he would not be feeling such ugliness as now surged through him, and never would there be such friction between him and his kinsmen. It was wrong, he knew, allowing those devils to leave, only to return and plant more of their damned seed in Celt women.

Likely Sunniva herself was filled with it. That, more than anything, angered him now. He had been mad to let her go alone to Trondsson in the stockade. At the same time he fumed at himself for resenting his feeling of betrayal. She cared nothing for him, not yet, so what did it matter? Seeing the tall Norsemen coming down over the hill with armed Celts on either side of them, Con moved to meet them. He faced Raven Trondsson with hostile eyes.

"Board your vessel, Viking, so we can have this

over. There is a storm brewing and I would be back before it strikes."

Raven turned to his companions. "Get her into deeper water," he ordered. His men immediately waded into the shallow surf, several of them boarding Odin's Raven and manning the oars, the rest pushing her.

Con watched the Norse chieftain gazing on his crew as they did his bidding. Not once did those cool gray eyes shift to Sunniva, yet he must have seen her as they approached the shore. Con marked also that Sunniva did not look toward Trondsson. The two had made love, but they did not look at each other—and the Viking had hurled the cruelest sort of insult at her as she departed. It was strange behavior indeed if she loved him as much as she said. Too strange.

"Viking, I will be waiting if you return for her."

Raven laughed. "She is yours, man. Too many crave her and now I know why."

For the space of an eyeblink, Con wanted to slam him to the earth. But he held his tongue and clenched his fists at his sides.

"She is not a slut. Never would I take a slut to wife." Seeing the widening of those gray eyes, the quickly hidden shock, Con smiled. By the gods, Trondsson did not know he meant to wed her. "I trow she has told you," he said smoothly, "that we will wed this eve. Would that 'twere even sooner, but then, she has insisted we first escort you women safely to open sea. . . ."

Raven ignored the deadly insult. All of his attention was on one word. Wed. Sunniva had said nothing of it. He had been playing the game and was well-pleased with himself, sensing the Celt's confusion and uncertainty over his easy surrender of her, but now he was caught completely off-balance. Wed? He knew instinctively that it was the truth. How could he have been so blind? He roared and sprang for his enemy's throat, but this time Con Cory he did not throw down his arms. Raven felt the point of a dirk at his throat and saw Sunniva flying toward them.

"What is't?" she cried, knowing that Raven was an instant away from death. "Nay, Con, don't harm him! Put it away!"

"Get her away from here," Con growled to his men.

"Nay, don't touch me!" Sunniva looked to Raven. His face was dark-flushed, his eyes murderous. "What has happened?"

"You mean to wed this bastard?"

He was so accusing, Sunniva spoke sharply. "He gave me but a thin choice—wed him or the lot of you die."

An angry murmuring arose from the Solby Vikings. They had splashed ashore to aid their chieftain, but the Celts, spears at the ready, surrounded them, overwhelming them by sheer numbers. Sunniva stood frozen, remembering Con's words—if Raven roared or threatened, then he would slay him where he stood. As she plead to Odin for help, Raven's hand shot out. Con's dirk dropped to the sand.

"Viking bastard . . ."

"Raven, nay!"

Sunniva's cry went unheard. Raven sent one fist crashing into Con's belly, the other to his head. The Celt chieftain dropped, taken unaware. His men swarmed over Raven, downing him, as Sunniva stood, hands to her mouth. Raven had doomed himself. She felt Calla's hand on her arm.

Con was smoldering as he climbed to his feet. His voice was thick with anger. "Get up, and then go you, Trondsson, before I change my mind." But he had already changed his mind. This devil could not live.

Raven was yanked to his feet by rough hands, but he remained where he stood. His molten eyes burned over the Celt.

"Raven, go," Sunniva cried. "O, Ulf, make him go!"

Ulf and the others formed a shield-burg around their chieftain and shoved him toward the drekkar, now afloat in deeper water. As they boarded her, the Celts made to board the escort vessels.

Con shouted, "Hold! One ship only goes, and only as far as the North Channel."

There was momentary surprise before its crew climbed in. The others milled about, watching, laughing, calling advice to their comrades.

Sunniva cried to Con, "'Twas not our plan!"

Con said tersely, "The plan is changed."

"Then I will be on the one ship, I demand it."

"Nay." Danger glittered in his blue eyes.

"Then neither will you," she flared. "You I cannot trust!"

"Calla, teach this wench that my wrath is not to be encouraged," Con said. "I am minded to throttle her."

Sunniva was ready to fly at him, but Calla's hand gripped her wrist.

"Sunni, nay," she whispered. "'Tis bootless—you will only hurt yourself. Come with me."

Con watched as Calla drew Sunniva off. He then boarded the vessel readying for departure. "I will remain," he lowered his voice, "for this be my wedding day and there are things I would attend to. As for yon bastard and his crew, they will not reach open water." He looked toward where the blood-red sail was being hoisted. "Send the lot of them to their Valhalla where we sent the others of their crew. Questions?"

"Do you want his vessel?"

"Nay. Fire her." He wanted no reminder of Raven

Trondsson for Sunniva to brood over. "Go you now, and if you should crave some amusement after, 'tis understood. I will not expect you back this eve. . . ." He knew they would want women after their job was done. He waded ashore then, thinking of his own woman. After the two vessels left, he would ride to Kirk Michael and fetch a priest.

CHAPTER 27

After the red sail of Odin's Raven took the wind, and the oars began a rhythmical plying of the water, Raven Trondsson gazed back at the shoreline. His eyes went to the tall figure standing there. He scowled. Nay, it was two figures that looked like one, for Con Cory stood behind Sunniva. His chin rested atop her golden head and his long dark arms were wrapped around her, binding her to him. Seeing the Celt laugh and lift one arm in farewell, Raven turned his face to the prow. He did not look back. There was work to be done—their extra weapons dug out of hiding, an attack planned . . .

Seeing Raven turn away from her, Sunniva died inside. She had not struggled against Con, knowing he would subdue her forcibly. It would have hurt Raven too deeply. But more deeply than this? Standing here with his arms about her as though she were perfectly content to be his? Anything she did would have been wrong. It seemed this was the end. Raven and his crew were without defense and by the time he gathered more men and arms, she would doubtless be wed. Even though this plan was not the one agreed upon, Con would remind her that the Solby men had been allowed to sail off. But how would she know if they were safe? Oh, nothing was right. She wondered now if Raven even wanted her any more.

"Now we will get on with our lives," Con said, when the sails had disappeared from sight. His voice vibrated through her body for his arms were about her still, his chin resting on her head.

"My life has just sailed away," she said dully.

He turned her around. "I will make you forget yon Viking, Mellby." He knew how to give women great pleasure. In addition, he would be kind to her. "I promise, before many sunsets, you will have forgotten him."

"Think you that all it takes is prowess in bed?" Sunniva snapped. "I have heard tell of your legendary lovemaking, and to me it means naught."

So. Calla, he thought, and kept a grave face. It was true that he and Calla had a certain magic together.

"Tonight I will change that, Mellby. You will wonder how you ever lived without me."

"I will think of naught but Raven," she muttered, wanting to hurt him. "Nor will I lie with you unless we be wed. And why should I wed you at all? What proof have I now that the Solby men are safe?" She shook off his hands. "Nay, I think not to wed you, Con Cory."

Con laughed. "But I will wed you, Mellby. 'Tis all that matters. I will take you for my wife before the priest that I go now to fetch."

"I will hate you all my days."

He was in great high spirits. "'Tis possible, that. Yet my lovemaking you will crave. I will carry you to the very heavens, Mellby." He turned, scanned the figures still milling about. "MacLir, I would talk with you."

Calla's long legs carried her swiftly across the sandy beach to where the two stood. She marked that Con was flushed and his eyes glittered, while Sunniva stood a-glowering, arms folded across her breasts.

"Ay, Con, what is't?" Calla asked.

"I ride now to fetch the priest at Kirk Michael. I trow we will be back by noon. I will wed this wench then." He shot Sunniva a glance to see how she took this and was met with a sullen glare.

Calla raised an eyebrow. "So soon? 'Twill give the women no time at all to prepare."

"Prepare what? 'Tis Mellby I wed, not those witches."

"Know you, Con, you are special to—to us all. They will want to cook a feast for you. I trow they will also want to deck the bridechamber with flowers."

Con shrugged. It was all unimportant. What mattered was to claim his woman with the authority of the church before any other tried to carry her away. He wondered, as he did often, if Gunnarsson still searched for her.

"Tell the women they can cook and deck all they want," he answered curtly, "but first we will wed. We can feast tonight or tomorrow. 'Tis unimportant. As for the bridechamber"—he gave a slow smile that only Calla saw—"well you know, macLir, that the flowers in a meadow are beyond compare. . . ."

Calla's sun-darkened face flushed darker still. Her green eyes flickered. "That escapes me. Else I have just forgotten."

Con nodded. "Ay, 'tis likely you have. Well, I am off now." He looked at the red sky turning pewter. "'Twill storm soon, but no matter. Make sure the Valkyrie is here when I return."

"She will be here," she called to his departing back. She would also see that Sunniva was garbed and brushed, but there her help must end. She could not force the maid to remain docile while the vows were read. She was aggrieved that Sunniva was so set against Con Cory, aggrieved at her own part in the whole disaster. But then it seemed that Sunniva's troth to Raven was doomed from the beginning. Rarely was a woman given to a man she cared for. Damnation, if only she could make her friend see how special Con was. She turned to Sunniva, met her blazing eyes.

"You are a great help and comfort, Calla macLir."

"I know your hurt is deep, Sunniva." Calla lowered her voice. "We must talk, you and I, but not now. First I would speak with these witches."

"Doubtless they will be as overjoyed about the wedding as I am."

Ena and her friends had come to see the excitement of the Viking departure. Now they milled about in a festive mood still, and loathe to go back to their chores. Calla approached them.

"Con Cory has bade me tell you he will wed his woman today at noon," she said, having decided on tact. "He is riding to Kirk Michael for a priest."

"She has bewitched him," Ena said, sourly.

"If she has, 'tis because he allowed it."

Ena's plate-face twisted into a grin. "What a slap for you, this. 'Tis known you wanted him yourself."

Calla yearned to thrust the wench into the sea and sit on her, but she said, calmly enough, "I'll wed no man."

"Ay, so you say. And as for this madness at noon,

'twill be impossible to get things done. 'Tis all too hurried. . . ."

"Con bade me tell you he will enjoy feasting tonight or tomorrow night or whenever you say. Tradition means naught to him, as you know."

"Ay, or never would he marry a Viking witch." She scowled at Sunniva, who was gazing glumly toward the sea. "Tell him we will feast tonight. I trow he will at least wait until afterwards to bed her."

"Ask him if you dare," Calla answered sharply. She returned to Sunniva as the others started for the kitchen-house. She took her friend's hand. "Sunni, come along to my place. Methinks you will like a gown that was given me, and—" Seeing the mutiny in Sunniva's eyes, she held up a hand. "Nay, Sunniva, I will not hear your moan. This must be, and I trow you are woman enough to realize it. You are a prize of war, yet Con Cory has not taken you before all his men, nor does he call you slave. 'Tis honor he gives you. He cares for you." Sunniva made no answer.

As the two walked silently to her small dwelling, Calla told herself that all was well. Sunniva was the perfect mate for Con, and in time the maid herself would know it. As for Con, it was plain to see he was wild about Sunniva. She doubted much that he could wait until after the feasting to claim her. Ay, that was the way of it. For the man, hunger came first. Love followed, if it ever came at all. But Con would be kind to her, that much she knew. What she did not understand was the strange hollowness in her own stomach. Never had she felt such a thing. . . .

Rolf Gunnarsson knew Ballageay like the palm of his hand; it had been his foremost stronghold for three years. His men knew it as well, so that long before dawn each had settled in hidden spots surrounding the village. Heller Orm was in the tunnel that had been carved as a safeguard their first year there. It stretched from the woods to the cowbarn, so that one could hear all that was said yet be hidden by a great straw-heap. Rolf himself was at a prime vantage point with his berserkers. The three lay hidden in thick brush atop a gentle hill; it was around the bend north of the docking area.

Rolf made a grimace meant to be a smile, for he had just seen an amazing thing—Odin's Raven sailing north, wind billowing her blood-red sail. He was not surprised Trondsson had been here; he had expected him to come seeking Sunniva Mellby. What did surprise him was his peaceful leavetaking from what was now a Celt encampment. It made no sense. Seeing the position of the sun through the black, scudding clouds, Rolf judged that soon his men would be arriving. Ay, there was the signal now—a faint whistle. He waited, watched, as one by one they arrived, blending into the brush and earth in the brown-green garb they wore.

"Report," Rolf ordered, his cold gaze on his kinsman.

"She is here," Heller Orm said, and swallowed. Always was he the bearer of bad news regarding this damned wench. "Con Cory has gone to fetch a priest and they two will be wed as soon as he returns."

Rolf's face was impassive as his eyes moved to the next man. "Report."

"'Tis said she has bewitched him. . . ."

The next said: "She was with Raven Trondsson when Con Cory took him and the Solby Vikings captive. . . ."

The others reported seeing great activity, men being taken from the stockade and marched to they knew not where. Perhaps to be slain. Their spying had been from such a distance, little else could be discerned.

Rolf Gunnarsson spoke then. "What you saw was Trondsson and his men being escorted to their vessel. They sailed shortly after dawn. I trow the Celt gained from it, and the Vikings will be sunk farther north. 'Tis inconceivable he would let them go unscathed." He frowned up at the sky. The clouds were gray and roiling now, pressing in on them. Soon it would storm. "We will do naught until dark," he continued. "If they wed today"—damn the bastard, he would skewer him for that—"then will there be great feasting and revelry tonight. 'Twill be an easy thing to seize her, for I trow the Celt will be drunk. But first will we slash their sails and smash their longboats, saving but one for ourselves."

"Where does he dwell?" Orm asked.

"Not in the abbey, I trow. 'Tis too holy for ordinary mortals. Nay, he will be in that miserable isolated hut sunk into the hillside overlooking the sea. 'Tis his duty to live there and keep watch to guard his flock." He smiled his wolf-smile. "In the abbey, he might have lived the night."

Raven stood on the tilting deck of his vessel, braced against the steer-board rail, his big hands steady on the steering oar. Above his head, the red sail creaked against a fast-darkening sky. It was filled near to bursting with the rising wind, and in addition, the oars were at work. Odin's Raven fairly flew through the growing gray seas. The men had lengthened the distance between her and the Celts while Ulf and another worked feverishly to uncover those weapons that lay hidden. With so many of his crew slain by Con Cory, Raven mused, there were now pikes, battle-axes, and spears enough to arm them all. His mouth tightened. There were many things for which he would pay back the Celt chieftain. Through his mind flashed that terrible last memory of him: Sunniva pulled back against his chest, his long arms around her, his damned red beard resting atop her golden head. Her face had been ashen and her eyes revealed her anguish and fright. Odin damn the bastard.

"'Tis time we turned about," he called to Ulf.

"Ay."

Raven had discussed his plan with his men, and all had agreed upon it. Now they would put it into action. Ulf laid hands on the thick steering-oar, helping Raven to swing the ship around, and then, catching the wind again, they headed straight for the enemy. By the time the Celts realized what was happening, it was already too late. Their shouts and cries rose to their gods as the massive iron prow of the dragonship rammed their vessel, slicing her in two. Their cries turned to screams for help.

"Shall we slay them?" Ulf asked, fingering a pike.

"Nay. Land is not too far. Let the devils sink or swim."

Ulf nodded. It was not in him to slay a defenseless man, even a Celt, floundering in the water. "Now what?" he asked.

Raven saw again Sunniva's terror-filled eyes and the tall chieftain holding her. "Full speed back to Ballageay," he muttered.

"Full speed," Ulf called to the rowers. His eyes narrowed. "By all the gods, look out there. Is't the damned mist rolling in?"

Raven grinned. "Ay, 'tis mist. Mayhap we can put Manannan himself to work for us this time. . . ."

"I see naught to laugh about, man. What will we do when we get back to that damned place? 'Tis crawling with Celts."

"We go by stealth, for certain. 'Tis not the time for the lur horn and a grand attack with but forty of us."

"Methinks you are in rare high spirits of a sudden, and I'm damned if I know why."

"'Tis just a hunch." His blood fairly sang through his veins. A hunch, ay, but it told him that all would be well. He had learned to trust such feelings as this.

"I suppose next we try and stop the wedding," Ulf said.

Raven shrugged. "If we knew where 'twould be, then we might take them by surprise and hold Con hostage 'til we escaped. But who knows where the damned ceremony will be—or when?"

"By Odin, Raven, methinks you don't see how bad this is. Sunniva could be wed to the bastard by the time we get to her."

"Ay, so she could."

Ulf's anger flared. "And you grin! Damn me, man, I could knock you down!" He grabbed Raven's arm just as the sky opened and the rains poured down.

"Hold, old friend," Raven gave Ulf's shoulder a friendly blow. "Think you, now. How serious can such vows be? A Celt chieftain, a pagan most likely, saying 'I wed you' three times? I cannot worry over gnats buzzing around my head. So she is wed. So? There is naught to worry us."

The wind keened; rain streamed down their faces. Ulf blinked. "Never had I thought of such a thing. But—what if the bastard takes her?"

"That I cannot control," Raven said softly, "but if he does, I will kill him. I will kill him in any event. But Sunniva knows we will return. She is clever. I trow she will give him the same brew she gave Gunnarsson."

"I wonder. Your words to her were harsh— mayhap she will not be waiting for you this time."

"She knew I was playing the game," Raven said,

but his heart was gripped suddenly in an iron fist. His high spirits fled. "At least, methought she knew 'twas but a game." Now he wasn't sure. Minding how stricken she had looked, he wanted to rage in his sudden confusion, but there was no time for that luxury. He glared at the leaden sky and teeming rain. "Reduce speed," he said. Ulf relayed the command. Raven continued: "We will drop anchor soon and lay low till nightfall."

"Till all are dead drunk."

"Ay, I am counting on it."

"But won't the devil be expecting us? Won't he be on guard?"

"Did you not see him board the escort vessel and talk to his men?"

"Ay. They but laughed and yarned a bit."

"Did you not see their faces?" When Ulf scowled and looked at him askance, Raven shook his head. "I know death when I see it. There was laughter, ay, but when I looked across at them, none would meet my eye. We were doomed, man."

Ulf shook his head, amazed. "You notice more than I, old friend. More and more do I see why you are a chieftain and I am not."

"Never mind that. Listen to this and tell me what you think. We shelter in a cove north of Ballageay until nightfall, and then sail her down to Con's dwelling."

Ulf scowled. "Do we know where 'tis?"

"Ay. As we left this morn, I marked a hut sunk into the hillside to the left of the bay. 'Twill be his. 'Tis the same everywhere in this land; the chieftains dwell on the coast. Once there, several of us will swim ashore, slay the devil and his guards, get Sunniva, and make off before any are the wiser."

"If the mist and rain hold," Ulf said, grinning at

him through the downpour,. "and if they are as drunken as we hope, and if your hunch is right . . ."

"Ay. If all the *ifs* work, then 'twould seem our chances are good."

"I see now why your spirits were high, man. She is as good as ours."

CHAPTER 28

SUNNIVA HAD ALWAYS HATED THE MIST THAT COVERED Maun so often, but now it seemed a blessing. The noon hour had come and gone without any sign of Con Cory or the priest. She and Calla were in Calla's hut still, where she had looked at the gown with no enthusiasm. It was pretty enough, being a fine, soft white linen with decorative stitching in thread of gold, but Sunniva's heart had been heavy as she gazed on it. She could not be wedded in it—she could not be wedded at all. This was madness. It was a bad dream and she prayed to the White Jesu that she would awaken. She stared glumly at Calla, who sat hemming the skirt in the dim light.

"You do that for naught. I told you I will not wear it."

"You will wear it." Calla rose, opened the door and closed it as the mist swirled in. "This fog be damned."

She was worried. There were hazardous spots aplenty between Kirk Michael and Ballageay, and in Con's haste to return to his bride, he might have taken one chance too many. But surely not with the old man along. Doubtless he was late because he was being careful. Perhaps the priest was not used to riding. Calla returned to needle and gown.

"Mayhap Con and his priest have fallen into the sea," Sunniva said calmly. "Or a peatbog. Or off a cliff . . ." In truth she wished for no such calamity to befall them, but she would not have minded if either broke a leg.

"Con did not become a chieftain by falling into the sea or a peatbog," Calla answered, equally calm. "He will come, never fear."

"You regard him so highly, methinks 'tis you who should wed him," Sunniva snapped. "I have thought it all along."

Calla drew a deep breath. She tired of this, all thinking that she herself wanted Con Cory. She cared for him deeply, ay, but never could she be his wife nor any man's wife. Not in this land or any other where a man had but to command and his woman obeyed— bearing as many brats as he wanted, cooking his meals, sewing his garb. It fair turned her stomach to think of it, for she was a chieftain's daughter, raised as a son, and always had she been as free to come and go as any man in her tribe. She rode, fought, lay with whomever she chose, sewed no garb but her own, and cooked no food for any but herself— except those times she helped in the kitchen-house. She belonged to no man and it was as she wanted it.

With Sunniva, she saw it was different. Already had the maid been betrothed in Norway, so she knew full well all that she would be surrendering to a husband, the most important being her freedom and her body.

Calla had marked that most women, especially the fair ones, lay in the birthing straw yearly, whether it was to their liking or not. Sunniva could not help but mark that. And if she had been willing to make such a sacrifice for Raven, why should it be any different with Con? Con was as gentle and virile and strong as Raven. And as comely. More so, she thought. She looked up from her stitching and studied Sunniva's angry face.

"You are a warrior-woman, Sunniva. I have seen your great skill with weapons and heard of your bravery. You have been staunch in battle and risked your life to save Con's—and I have seen how you dealt with Hedeby. But methinks the bravery needed to face the inevitable, that which cannot be changed, is the greatest of all. You have such bravery, and now you must use it." When Sunniva made to protest, Calla shook her head. "I know you would not wed Con had you the choice, but of choice you have none. I regret I put the thought in his head, but I see now 'twould have happened anyhow. He craves you and none other—and he has freed Raven. 'Tis an unheard-of thing he has done. It means he cares for you deeply. You will wed him, Sunni."

"I will never even like him, let alone love him."

"Methinks you will. You cannot see it now, but I promise, 'twill be a good thing for you. For both of you."

"I know 'tis what you think."

Calla did not understand love, Sunniva brooded. Never had she felt it, so how could she possibly understand it, this woman who had wanted them to wed because they were worthy of each other! How could she imagine that hot, sweet current that vibrated between herself and Raven even when they were far apart?

Calla finished her sewing and rose. "'Tis musty

here with no windows open. Let us go to the abbey and see what they are about."

"I trow they are building a scaffold to hang me."

Calla smiled. "Nay. If Con loves you, so will they in the long run. They will want to please him."

"He does not love me. You yourself said he craves me. There is a difference. They think I have enchanted him."

"Mayhap you have. . . ." But it was all to the good, Calla thought, as they trod the log path to the abbey. Con's eyes were alive again. He looked more as he used to.

Sunniva was torn. With such a mist as this, ghostly white fingers wrapped about trees and barns and dwellings alike, mayhap she could elude Calla before Con returned. She could flee toward the south as she had when she fled Rolf—but then Raven would come for her and she would be gone. And she might get lost in the mist and fall into enemy hands. Much as she yearned to flee, she deemed it best to stay where she was. Besides, it was not as if she were going to marry Con Cory. She was not. She simply would refuse to accept him as her husband.

As they neared the abbey, the smell of baking bread and crisping swineflesh teased her nostrils. And she was shocked when she looked upon the great-hall. She knew it had been scrubbed and virtually purged when Ballageay was reclaimed from the Rolf-Vikings, but this was special. This the women had done for Con. The floor was strewn with fresh rushes and all the boards had been lowered from the walls and waxed until they gleamed. Already were they decked with flowers and candles. And at the far end of the hall was a great mass of autumn flowers, gold and purple and rusty red.

Seeing the two low benches placed there, Sunniva knew it was where she and Con were to kneel as they were wed. Several men wandered in laughing, drinking horns already in their hands. The revelry had already begun. No matter that the groom and priest had not yet appeared.

It was late afternoon when Con arrived finally. The mist had lifted, but the rain still fell in a gentle drizzle. Con himself was in high spirits, but the priest, a man long in years and seeming short in health, was ready to faint away from hunger and weariness. The women fed and dried him, and then there was nothing to do but let him sleep until he recovered. He stretched out on a wall-bench in the great-hall and lay there a-snoring while Con left to change into dry garb.

Calla hurried a reluctant Sunniva back to the hut, bullied her into the white-gold kirtle and a hair-brushing. When they returned to the abbey, Con was waiting. He wore familiar forest-green garb, trews and tunic, and his sword hung at his side in a jewel-encrusted scabbard. Around his neck was a great silver medallion. Sunniva had to admit that he looked every inch a chieftain, tall, strong, undeniably handsome with his ice-blue eyes and flaming hair and beard. He grasped her arm.

"Come, Mellby." He led her through the great oak doors into the great-hall. It was jammed with all who dwelt in Ballageay, and when the folk saw the two, a roar rose to the vaulted ceiling.

"'Tis madness," Sunniva murmured, pulling back. "I—I cannot do this, Con."

"You will," Con commanded her. His fingers tightened around her arm, and she was propelled forward. "'Tis time. Even the priest has waked, I see."

The great-hall glittered with candles and torches reflected against the wall-shields. It was so warm with the crowd there, and it reeked so of flowers and the fumes of the wedding ale that Sunniva's head swam. Con's strong arm had gone about her waist. He drew her inexorably toward the far end of the hall, where the priest stood.

It was a nightmare, she thought, and if she bit her lip she surely would awaken. Or she would look up and see it was Raven by her side, his gray-gold eyes moving over her hungrily, lovingly. She bit her lip and looked up. Oh, Jesu-Mary, it was not Raven. It was not a dream. It was Con Cory looking down at her, just as she knew it would be. His hair and beard were the color of angry flame, and his blue eyes roaming over her held many things—jubilation, amusement, curiosity, hunger. Ay, great hunger, but there was no love in them that Sunniva could see.

She wished she did not feel so strange. She was so warm, and that sickening-sweet odor made her head swim. There was a blue haze a-gathering as though the smoke-holes were not drawing. She swayed and felt Con pull her closer. She allowed herself to lean against him. It was either that or fall.

"Kneel," intoned the priest as they stood before him.

Sunniva was grateful to obey. She could not have remained on her feet another moment. She lifted her eyes to the stranger, wondering if indeed he were a real priest. He looked like one—gaunt and grim and holy from fasting, his eyes burning as though he communed long and faithfully with his gods. She felt a shiver shoot through her body, wondering what he would do when she refused to take Con as her husband. It was what she meant to do; she would say nay when that time came. She blinked, realizing suddenly that she had not understood one word the priest was saying. Was it Latin? She had learned many Celt words since coming there, enough to get along, but this tongue she did not know at all. She gazed up at Con, stricken. She was trapped. . . .

Con was not pleased. When would this old fool cease his prating? What mattered all this endless reading and chanting and reciting when the only words he wanted to hear were the ones that declared Sunniva his. When she had gazed up at him but an instant ago, his heart was touched. She seemed terrified, like a netted swan. He had wanted to pick her up, carry her to his hut, cover her with kisses, and show her how gentle he could be . . . But nay, here they were with this damned ass going on and on and on. Con grimaced. His damned knees were beginning to ache, and Sunniva was ready to keel over. The day be damned when he had ever decided he needed a priest. Why had he not just claimed her as his wife? It had been good enough for his own father.

"—and so, Con Cory, take you this woman to be your wedded wife?" the holy voice rang out.

By the saints, finally. Con glared, ready to throttle the old fool. "Ay," he snapped. At least the fellow had remembered to say the most important part in Norse, as he had ordered.

"And you, Sunniva Mellby, take you this man to be your wedded husband?"

When Sunniva did not answer, Con looked down at her. He had been supporting her, his arm about her and her slim body leaning against his. Now he saw that she slumped. Her skin was pale and moist and her beautiful eyes glazed. She was ill. It was all this damned holy-yapping. Con's heart lurched, but he kept his wits. He put his mouth to her ear, whispering so that only she could hear:

"Be you ill, Sunniva?"

"Ay," Sunniva murmured. She felt dreadful. Dizzy

. . . her breakfast sitting in her throat still . . . the smokiness . . . all those odors. It took every bit of her strength to remain on her knees.

"Now be you man and wife," said the priest, "in the holy eyes of Father, Son, and Holy Ghost."

Only when Con lifted her in his arms, kissed her lips, and sent a jubilant shout to the rafters did Sunniva realize she was wed. The cheers were deafening. She stiffened, stared at him with disbelieving eyes.

"Never did I agree to wed you!" she choked. "We are not wed!"

"But we are," Con laughed and kissed her again.

Sunniva's frightened eyes sought Calla. "Did you hear me say I would wed him?" Her heart raced. She had not heard Con's vow either.

Calla frowned. "Ay, 'tis what I heard. 'Twas put to you in Norse, even."

"I—I don't believe this. Never did I say it!" She began to tremble.

"Never would I lie to you about such a thing, Sunni."

"You tricked me, Con Cory!" Bitterness overwhelmed her. Sunniva still felt dizzy and sick, but this great peril was clearing her head of its cobwebs.

Con laughed. "Nay, I did not. No tricks. Methinks that in your heart, you wanted me to make you mine, Sunniva Cory."

Sunniva Cory . . . Sunniva stared at him. His cheeks were deep-flushed and his eyes sparkled like sun on the Irish Sea. He was the most comely man in the hall, but she hated him. Had she a sword handy, she would have slain him.

"Let the feasting begin," Con shouted to his men and their women. "Feast and drink and make merry."

"Put me down," Sunniva's low voice was frigid.

"I may never put you down, Sunniva. You are mine, hear you? You are my wedded wife."

He gave her a deep, primitive kiss before them all, mortifying her thoroughly, but she did not struggle. Let him think what he would, but this night, she vowed, she would give him lyngwort and she would flee. Raven she could not worry about; he had found her once, he would find her again. For now, it was going to take all her effort to get through this feast and this eve without revealing what she meant to do. She remained docilely in the high-seat when Con put her there and sat down beside her. Calla was on her left.

"I see you are wroth, Sunniva," Calla said in a lowered voice, "but never would I lie. I swear by whatever gods you find holy that you took Con for your husband."

Sunniva was too hurt to answer. She knew full well it was a lie. She had been betrayed. The hearth-fire leapt and crackled and the blue haze thickened as the evening wore on. She sat quietly in the midst of talk and laughter, the clashing of cups and horns as the mead and ale and beer and wine flowed without end. Never had she seen such drink or such food at Ballageay—swineflesh, sheep, fish, lobster, bread and butter and cheese, sausage, leeks and cabbage and fruits and nuts. . . .

The talk and songs rose in a crescendo about her. She could not eat. She took a sip of wine but could hardly force it down. She was sick. Sick at her stomach, sick at heart, sick all over. Until this day, she had never doubted she would be with Raven again or that he would take her back to Lilleby. Now she was wed. And by a priest. When Raven returned for her, he would learn that she was gone, and that she belonged to Con in the eyes of god. And while it was no god Raven himself believed in, her father was prime-signed. He honored and believed in the White Jesu-Mary-Holy Ghost as well as the gods of old. To Arn Mellby's thinking, she was now a wed woman. In Norway's land, her long hair would go under the coif. She closed her eyes and tried to sit tall though she wanted to die.

What would Raven do when he heard? Con had boasted that they would wed, ay, but this morn it had been nothing but a boast. Raven would have trusted her to forestall it until he returned, and she had meant to. Instead, she had failed him miserably. Oh, how had this ever happened? She recalled only that she had felt sick and faint, close to swooning, and that the priest had spoken a strange tongue. Surely there was a mistake. She turned to Calla, who sat as silent as did she herself. She whispered:

"You swear 'tis the truth, Calla? You heard me accept Con for my husband?"

"Ay. Never have I had a friend like you, Sunniva. Never would I lie about this."

Marking the grief in her eyes, Sunniva knew that she told the truth. She squeezed her hand. "I believe you. 'Tis my own doing, I trow. I felt faint for a bit. Doubtless that was when 'twas done."

Still Calla looked stricken. "Know you, Sunniva, I want only gladness for you and Con."

"Ay . . ."

Con's arm went around Sunniva. "We have stayed long enough, wife. 'Tis time we took our leave." He swayed as he got to his feet and smiled down at her. He had drunk overmuch, but no matter. This night he was not going to spend on his feet, but in bed. He took his bride's arm and drew her out of the high-seat.

Sunniva yielded without protest, for the lyngwort waited. She had had more time to think, sitting there amidst the babble. She knew she would not murder him, though he deserved it. Nay, he would sleep, and she would be long gone when he awakened finally. She began to wonder then if they ever would get to the hut and the bridal bed. They were surrounded by folk, well-wishers who would not let them go until yet another toast was drunk. Con, his spirits mellow, could not resist.

"Sit you, Sunniva Cory. Soon will we go. . . ."

Sunniva sat while he drank yet one more beaker and sang one more song. Those at the board sang also, but from somewhere behind her, she heard a man talking. His voice was low, but it reached her ears easily. At first she paid little attention, for it was one voice among many, but certain words stood out.

". . . Trondsson and his men."

Laughter came. ". . . You haven't heard?"

"Heard what, man?"

"Con's final order . . . slain . . . ship sunk . . ."

The voice went on, but Sunniva's thoughts reeled. Had she heard it aright amidst all the laughing and music? Slain? Raven slain? And after Con had promised his safety? Con's arms slid around her; he bent and kissed her.

"'Tis time we left," he said. When Sunniva remained seated, her eyes burning through him, Con gripped her arm and none too gently forced her to her feet. As the laughing and jesting began, Con whispered, "Unless you want to be carried out of here like a sack of flour, come along, Sunniva Cory. This be our wedding night, and I have waited for you long enough."

CHAPTER 29

FROM HIS AERIE OVERLOOKING BALLAGEAY, ROLF Gunnarsson watched the mist rolling onto the land again. He was well-pleased that it had chosen to return, making the moonless night foggy—perfect for the task that lay ahead of them. But he was annoyed with waiting. Nothing could be done until the Celt dog brought the bitch back to his miserable hut by the sea. And only after the devil's guards called out to him that all was well, could Rolf's plan be put into action. As the two lay lovemaking, his men would slay the guards and secure a longboat for their sea-flight to the Landwaster. The other vessels they would damage. Rolf himself would slay Con Cory and seize his thrall. He moistened his lips, smiling at the thought of the pleasure awaiting him.

Sunniva walked at Con Cory's side, her small hand grasped tightly in his. She did not understand how he could move so quickly in such fog and find his way.

375

She kept stumbling, but then, she was leaden. She could scarcely lift her feet to put one in front of the other as the voice she had heard at the feast droned on in her head. Slain, it said. Slain . . . slain . . . slain. Raven was slain by Con's orders.

"I know 'twas hard for you, this day," Con said, "but by and by, you will like being mine. I will be good to you."

Good? Such words deserved a scathing retort, but Sunniva was too crushed to make it. She wanted only to lay herself down in some quiet place and close her eyes and sleep; forget all that had happened. But there would be no sleep for her tonight; Con would demand that their marriage be consummated. The sound of waves crashing on the shore told her they were nearing his hut.

"You seem weary," he said. "Let me carry you."

Sunniva jerked her hand from his. "Nay. I will walk."

This man had betrayed her completely. He had made first one promise and then another which he had never intended to keep. Raven had seen his slyness. He had seen the Celt chieftain's intentions from the beginning and warned her, and fool that she was, she had defended Con. She had insisted that he had some honor. But he had not, and now it was too late. Her beloved was dead. Warring with her grief was a growing fury. Had Calla known his plan? It would explain her strange mood during the feasting.

Seeing they had reached the cottage, Sunniva busked herself. Not for the bridal bed, but for revenge. This night she would slay Con Cory. After he drank the lyngwort, he would not awaken. She was startled when a dark shape loomed out of the fog. She recognized one of Con's men.

"All is well, Con. The others have reported in. I trow you are firmly wed?"

"Ay. Before man and god."

The other laughed and clapped Con's shoulder. "Enjoy her. And may a son come from this night."

"Ay—and tomorrow will I drink with you, old friend," Con called after him. He then swooped Sunniva up into his arms.

"Put me down!"

"Listen and listen well, wench," Con said, gruffly. "I have borne your surliness all this day, for I knew 'twas hard for you. But this be our wedding night and now I will see you behave as a wife should."

"The trolls take you, you bastard!" Sunniva struggled to free herself.

"Well they might if I lower you here on my threshold." He wrapped his arms about her more tightly and jumped across the doorsill. "'Tis a dangerous place for a new-wed woman. Spirits could be lurking here to bear you off."

Sunniva's lip curled. "Better the spirits than you!" She hated him.

Con looked about the room in amazement as he stood Sunniva on her feet. The Ballageay women had done themselves proud. Never would he have thought this old shack could look so good. The women must have come and gone just ahead of them, for the soapstone lamps were newly filled and lit, and the floor covered with fresh rushes. There were flowers everywhere. Sunniva would have no fancy bride-bed here by the sea at Ballageay, but there were purple and golden flower petals strewn across his pallet. He smiled.

"'Tis a fair bridal-bower they have made us, wife."

Sunniva went wordlessly to her own pallet, sank onto it, and glared up at the tall chieftain. Lamplight shone on his red hair and beard and on the gold-chased hilt of his sword. He was as comely as ever, but now she marked the treachery in his eyes. She steeled herself, thinking that he was a dead man. Some of the powdered lyngwort she had used on Rolf and his berserkers was still in a pocket of her trews. There they hung, along with her other meager clothing, on the peg by the door. Somehow, she had to get it, and get it into his drink.

Con marked her sullenness as he gazed down at her, but he was unconcerned. Soon he would have her aroused and hungry for him. He removed his swordbelt; his sword he unsheathed and stuck into the earth beside his pallet. He next stripped off his dark-green tunic and then bent and caught Sunniva's hands. He pulled her to her feet. He said softly:

"You be the fairest woman I've ever seen, Sunniva Cory."

It was like a knife in her heart. The words were the very ones Raven had whispered when last they made love—except then she had been Sunniva Mellby. Now her very name was gone as well as her beloved.

Con's passion was such that he could have claimed her then, but he held himself under tight rein. Already she hated him. He would not rape her. He would coax and tease and fondle her. Let her see that Trondsson, damn his heart, was not the only one who knew how to make love to a woman. He craved to see her warm and pink and glowing. Satisfied. Begging for more. He took the pins from the shoulders of her gown, kissed her stiff lips, moved lazy, teasing fingers over the curves of her breasts. But she was rigid in his arms. Unmelting.

"Methinks you need some ale, wench."

"I trow 'tis the only way I can bear your touch, if bear it I must."

Con laughed. "You will more than bear it, you will crave it, wench. 'Tis a promise." He released her, sloshed the ale that the women had provided into a horn and held it to her pale lips. "Drink, Sunniva."

She took a sip, barely wetting her lips, and turned her head. "Drink it all," he commanded.

"Nay. 'Twill make me dizzy."

"So I would hope," he muttered. "You are stiff as a pike." In forcing more into her mouth, a quantity of it spilled onto her gown.

"Now see what you have done!" she cried, but it was exactly what she had hoped for.

"Take the damned thing off," Con said. "Better still, let me do it." He pulled it and her chemise down, baring her shoulders and then her breasts. Seeing how they thrust out, so white and full, from her chest, he pulled her hard against the dark fur on his own chest. He groaned and kissed her mouth. His manhood swelled, stiffened against the confinement of his trews. The saints help him. It was going to take all the restraint he possessed to hold back, and then make love to her gently, not in the wolfish way he craved.

He forced himself to loose his tight hold on her and, her kirtle slipped to the floor. He blinked, seeing her naked form in the flickering light. Her hair a golden veil not quite hiding those exquisite breasts and small, taut red buds . . . the long, rounded arms and legs . . . her perfect little rump and the soft white mound of her belly. His loins throbbed, ached with wanting her. He sat down to tug off his leggings and trews and saw her move toward the door.

"Where go you?" His gruffness froze her where she stood.

"To hang up Calla's gown," she said icily.

Con marked that she shivered. Her hands shook so that when she tried to place the kirtle on the peg, it fell to the ground, as did the garb that already hung there. He watched, narrow-eyed, as she picked up the things and replaced them, all but one that she clutched to her breasts.

"'Tis chill," she whispered. "I would—wear my nightshirt. . . ."

Con threw back his head and laughed. "Woman, 'tis my hunger that will warm you this night." His eyes were on her nipples, standing out on the white mounds of her breasts like rubies. He lowered his head, took one in his mouth, and teased it with his tongue. It aroused him beyond measure but Sunniva was unmoved.

"I crave some wine," she said.

Con drew a deep breath. Damn the bitch. He was going to pour it down her throat if she did not soon respond to him. He refilled the horn and handed it to her.

"'Tis not to my liking, drinking alone," she murmured.

"Then will I share yours."

"Nay!" As soon as she spoke, Sunniva knew she had protested too much. She cursed herself. "I—will fill a horn for you also. . . ."

Con lowered himself to his pallet and sat with his back against the wall. He watched his wife fetch the horn and pour the ale. She brought it to him then, her plump white breasts swaying, tantalizing him as she bent to place a horn-rest beside him. She returned and sat herself on his pallet also. Eyes lowered, she took a sip from her own horn. Con did not drink. Long and long he gazed at her before he spoke:

"I will have your ale, Sunniva. You take mine."

Sunniva's heart sank. She did not look at him. "What silliness is this? 'Tis all the same."

His arm slid around her slender neck and closed on it, clamping her in a vise. One long powerful leg was thrown over hers, pinning her down. He held the horn to her lips. "If 'tis all the same, then drink you, Sunniva, or I will pour it down your throat."

"Con, nay!" She struggled but he held her fast.

"It holds lyngwort, I trow. Was I merely to sleep or did you mean to kill me?" Her nails raked his cheeks. He tightened the vise about her throat. The little bitch, he was minded to squeeze the life out of her. "Answer me."

She choked, "You deserve to sleep the same sleep as Raven. . . ." Even so, she had not given him enough of the drug to poison him. At the last, she could not do it.

Con released her. He hurled his horn and its contents to the floor. "What mean you—the same sleep as Trondsson?"

Sunniva sat up, her arms crossed over her breasts. "At the feast—before we left, I—heard talk. 'Twas said you ordered Raven and his men slain and his ship sunk. . . ."

But then, she had felt so strange and dizzy all day, perhaps she had imagined it. She searched his face, hoping to see some sign that she was mistaken. He looked astonished as well as angry, but was it because she had found him out, or because he had been unjustly accused? Now she was so befuddled, she didn't know what to think. She wanted more than anything to believe he would not do such a terrible thing.

"What say you, Con? Is't so?" she asked, tonelessly.

Con tried to calm his wrath, but it was simmering. For her to have heard such tidings on this of all nights was not to be believed. Was there no limit to the obstacles thrown before him? It was ridiculous, this defiance of hers. She was only a woman; he was a chieftain. And in the eyes of the church, she was his. He had made sure of that. He said crisply:

"Methinks you misheard or misunderstood."

"Methinks I need proof of that before you touch me," she answered stubbornly.

"I am your husband, wench." Con lay back on his

pallet and pulled her down beside him. "If I say you misheard or misunderstood, 'tis all the proof you need." He forced her arms behind her and fondled her breasts.

"Raven was not so trusting or gullible as I," she said hotly. "From the very first, he knew you for the treacherous scut you are. He warned me not to believe you."

Con lowered his head and kissed her right nipple and then sucked on it. Marking the spasm that went through her soft body, he laughed. "I see you liked that, wife." He kissed her other breast.

"I mind that Raven pleased me more." Sunniva's eyes held nothing but scathe for him. "He will return for me, I promise you." Suddenly she believed it herself. She had to. She could not go on living otherwise.

"Even were the bastard to return," Con said, "which he will not, I promise you—you are wed."

"Mayhap I will soon be widowed," she taunted him.

The little witch surely knew how to hurt him, but he saw that she was more fair than ever in her anger, this Viking of his. And was not her courage one of the reasons he craved her? He cupped one breast again. They were so round and ripe he could not keep his hands and mouth off them. Nor did he have to now. Not any more.

"'Tis not the time to talk of such things, Sunniva. 'Tis our wedding night." His other hand roamed the silky length of her body. When she tried to knee him, he imprisoned her legs between his. "Nay, wife, that I will not allow."

He had been patient long enough. He took her mouth in a bruising kiss and his hands were no longer gentle. Now he must show her that it was not a woman's place to decide how and when things would be. It was for him to command, her to obey. He had wanted their first togetherness to be one of gladness for her, but he saw now that it would not. He must force her. Nor did it matter. There would be pleasure for her later. Most important now was for her to understand that she was his. He rolled her onto her back.

"Celt scut!" She spat at him and missed.

Con forced her legs apart and knelt. Damnation, it was not an easy thing when a woman did not yield. Now the wench had begun screeching.

"Hush, you!" he snarled. "Behave you like a wife!"

"Oh, Con, behind you!" Sunniva cried.

Even before her warning, Con sensed danger. The lamps had flickered and brine filled his nostrils. It meant his door had been opened. He leapt to his feet and crouched low. A cold sweat covered his skin as he saw Rolf Gunnarsson standing there in chain-mail and helmet. In his hands was a two-edged sword.

"I hear you have wed my thrall," Rolf said coolly. "I have come for her. Prepare to die, Celt."

CHAPTER 30

SUNNIVA HAD CRIED OUT THE WARNING TO CON, BUT IT was some moments before her horrified mind could assess the situation. These tall, powerful men were both in the prime of their manhood, yet she saw that this battle could not be an equal one. Con Cory was crouched, naked, at the far end of the room, his only weapon a stool he had snatched from the hearthside. Rolf Gunnarsson stood just inside the threshold holding sword and shield. Chain-mail glittered on his broad chest, and on his head was a steel helmet with nose and eye guards.

His was the victory, Sunniva thought, numb with fear, but even as she sensed it, she saw what had to be done to help Con. She moved quickly to his sword where it was stuck in the earth beside his pallet and tugged it out. She tossed it to him, hilt first.

"Brave lass," Con said. His blue eyes glowed.

As Sunniva watched his sword thrust out, flashing, to clang against Rolf's shield, she knew she was not brave. It was that a terrible fate awaited her at Rolf's hands. He had vowed to carry her to a harem if ever she displeased him, and that she had surely done. She had rejected him, drugged him, put a woman's veil over him, chained him to his throne-chair, stolen his sword . . . Any one of those would have been enough to warrant his slaying or selling her, and she had done them all.

Rolf Gunnarsson was thrown off guard. None of this was as he had expected. He thought to find the two deep in lovemaking, thus enabling him to skewer the bastard easily. Instead he had interrupted a rape. Had he waited a few moments more before attacking, the Celt would lie dead now. Instead, his fury had made him a formidable opponent. Damn the wench, throwing him the sword—and her nakedness was a deadly distraction. His life depended on his alertness, yet too often was his gaze drawn to her white body. The fact that he himself had never possessed it sent a fresh river of rage flooding through him. His sword-tip left a scarlet stripe on the Celt's glistening shoulder. First blood.

"Bitch, you are mine still, hear you?" Rolf shouted to her. It gave him satisfaction to see that she wore his slave-band still. Through the eye-slits of his helmet, he saw her rush suddenly to one side of the dim chamber. What in damnation? She threw a white cloth to Cory—a gown? He saw the Celt rapidly twist it about his left forearm for protection. Rolf lunged, thrust viciously, and was surprised to feel a fiery sting in his upper arm. Never had he seen that coming. It was this damned helmet. Sweat poured into his eyes, and in these shadows, the eyeguard hampere ! his vision. He tugged the helmet off and hurled it to a corner. The woman was crouched on a pallet nearby. He noticed only her breasts. Soon would they be under his hands and his mouth again.

Sunniva had not missed his hate-filled glance at her. She began to tremble, thinking of what lay ahead for her were Rolf to win this victory. But there was nothing more she could do to help Con. As the men circled, parrying the other's jabs and thrusts, she was minded to dart in and crash a bowl over Rolf's head. But it could not hurt him and what if he caught her? And she dared not run out into the night for help. His berserkers would be nearby. She decided to bar the door. At least she could keep them out. She was shocked to hear Con laughing.

"'Twas a mistake, Gunnarsson, wearing such heavy gear for such a simple task," he said. "To slay but one man who might have been asleep or making love to his wife."

"She will be your widow, Celt." Rolf's deadly sword drew another clean-etched vermilion stripe across Con's chest.

Again Con laughed. "Nay, for 'tis not my time to die. 'Tis you who will go, Viking. I see in your bleary eyes that you be death-fated. Even now you tire, old man."

Rolf roared. Hurling his shield to the side, he gripped his double-edged sword with both hands and came on like a whirlwind, slashing from side to side. Con side-stepped. His own sword was lighter and longer than that of the Viking. He himself was lighter, taller, and more agile. He danced around him, harrying, tormenting, each small jab drawing blood. He continued to taunt him, for well he knew that the other's rage could be his undoing.

"You will die here tonight, Gunnarsson. Not on a bloody battlefield where you would go to Valhalla, but here—in the bride-bower of the woman you are too old and too feeble to wrest from me. You will die for naught but a woman, Viking."

Sunniva huddled on the pallet. She feared to watch, yet she could not look away from the terrible scene. Lamplight flickering over the two tall, bearded warriors and their gleaming weapons, their shadows twisting, leaping on wall and floor as they themselves twisted and leapt and lunged, the clang and rasp of steel on steel, the blood-hunger and cruelty in their eyes, blood streaming from their wounds, the grunts and curses. She could not look any more. She hid her face in her hands, and thus did not see Con's savage attack.

The Celt pressed home a fierce charge, relentlessly driving the Viking back, lunging again and again in rapid succession at his sword arm to weaken it. At the same time, he had loosed Sunniva's white kirtle that protected his own arm. Without warning, he flung it over his enemy's head. As the Norseman tried to disentangle himself, Con's point found his throat.

Hearing a choked scream, Sunniva's eyes flew open. She could scarce believe what she saw: Rolf Gunnarsson stretched out on the floor and Con Cory gazing down at him.

"'Tis over, Sunniva. He is dead." Blood streamed from Con's own wounds.

"Are you sure?" It had happened so quickly, yet she saw that the Viking's tall form lay motionless. Over his face was the white kirtle in which she was wed. It was blood-soaked.

"I am sure." Con bent, wiped his blade upon the kirtle, and began to don his clothing.

Sunniva's heart would not stop thudding. She whispered, "What if the others are outside the door?" She was thinking of the berserkers, of how they would rampage when they learned their chieftain was slain.

Seeing her white face, Con said easily, "Mayhap they are not."

He did not let her see his concern. He knew nothing of the number of men the devil had brought or what damage was done. He knew only that he feared greatly for his men who lay in drunken revelry. If Gunnarsson had come with a great horde to retake Ballageay, all was lost. He could not have chosen a better time, and Con cursed himself for not having foreseen it. He stood on a stool and, reaching overhead, raised the horn window-pane in the roof just a crack. He held his breath, listening. There were no sounds of battle, no cries nor clashing of arms, only a distant, irregular noise he could not place.

Con closed the window, climbed down, and unbarred the door. Sword in hand, he opened it a crack. Nothing. He opened it further. Still nothing. Had his men taken the remaining Vikings? He took a wary step out into the darkness. A sliver of moon had appeared and was riding high, and the mist had lifted enough for him to spy instantly the forms lying on the ground. Celt or Viking, he could not tell. He smelled danger and retreated. He hurriedly closed the door, but before he could bar it, there was a crash and it was kicked open. A near-naked Viking stood there with drawn sword and blazing eyes. It was Raven Trondsson.

Raven's plan had gone smoothly. In a shallow bay north of Ballageay, they had lain hidden in mist until nightfall. When the fog did not lift, they rowed Odin's Raven south to where they deemed Con Cory's hut stood. Raven, Ulf, and eight others stripped down to loincloths and dagger-belts, slipped quietly into the water, and came ashore slightly north of the hut. Raven bade them lie in hiding while he reconnoitered.

As he neared the dwelling, the fog chanced to thin. He saw a man lying on the ground. A Celt. Raven crept close and bent to the fellow's chest, listening for a heartbeat. There was none. He hastily fetched his men, whereupon all returned stealthily to the hut. It was then they spied other bodies, both Celt and Viking.

"What think you?" Ulf whispered. "'Twas not a raiding party on such a night as this, surely."

Raven held up a hand. "Listen—what is that sound?"

"'Tis south of here," Ulf said. "Something being smashed."

"Stay by me, Ulf. You others, go quietly and see what is happening."

As the eight men disappeared silently into the darkness, Raven took a sword from one of the dead Vikings, as did Ulf. The two turned back to Con Cory's dwelling. Raven busked himself, fearful of what he would find there. Seeing the door open and a thin shaft of light fall across the ground, both men froze. As it closed, they rushed it. Raven smashed it open with his foot. Con Cory spun to meet him. The two glared at each other.

In the space of an eyeblink, Raven saw all in the flickering shadows: a warrior lying dead, the room that was a bridal bower with petals strewn on the earthen floor, Sunniva pulling on a kirtle to cover her nakedness, her eyes widening as she saw him. He exhalted that she was alive, alive and pink-cheeked and bright-eyed. He wanted to sink to his knees and give thanks, but his fears for her were still too great. His gaze locked onto the Celt chieftain.

"Methinks you are surprised to see me, Celt."

"Raven! And Ulf! I knew you would come! Oh, Raven, Rolf is slain. . . ."

"Stay back," Raven warned. To Ulf, he said, "Stand

guard without." He stooped and entered the room through its low door, his sword raised. When Con made no move but stared, Raven muttered, "I am waiting, Celt."

His blood was boiling. A bridal bower, by the gods. And Sunniva had been naked; she had been tugging on her kirtle as he entered. What had gone on here before Gunnarsson came? Could she not hold Cory off, or had she not tried? Why had she not drugged him? Or had Ulf been right? Were his own words to her so harsh that she had believed them and yielded to the devil? His heart thumped wildly, thinking of the fellow's trickery.

"Come, Celt, I tire of waiting." He took a step forward, crouching, on guard.

"Stay, Viking." Now Con's sword went up. His limbs ached and his wounds streamed blood. He was unfit for battle. And how in damnation did this bastard come to be alive still? He reached around suddenly and caught Sunniva, pulling her in front of him. He pressed his blade to her throat.

"Con, you are hurting me. . . ."

"Hush you, wench."

"'Tis clear why you wanted her." Raven's voice was thick with fury. "You needed a woman to hide behind. What manner of man be you, Celt?"

"Three times I have given you your life, Con Cory," Sunniva said. "Is this how you repay me?"

"Ay, for each time it has bound us closer. None other can have you, Sunniva. I will slay you first." Con was astonished by the words coming from his mouth. He had no intention of slaying the wench, but he doubted Trondsson would put him to the test.

"Have you gone mad?" Sunniva tugged at his forearms with both hands but he held her tightly.

"She is my wife now, Viking."

Raven's heart was in his throat, yet he could not let

Sunniva see his fear for her. "Sunni, are you wed to this devil?"

Sunniva wanted to shriek that she had been tricked, but Con's blade was icy against her throat. She murmured: "I don't know. 'Tis said we are wed. There was a holy brother who talked of the White Jesu, but never did I take any vow, Raven."

Ulf came to the door. "There is news."

"Report," Raven said, his deadly gaze remaining on Con Cory.

"The Vaaga Vikings were damaging the Celt vessels in the bay. When we approached, they fled in a longboat."

Con heard and laughed. "Frighted sheep without their leader."

But he was concerned. Not over the Vaaga men or his damaged ships but about these damned Solby Vikings. There were but forty or so of them, yet they could wreak havoc among his reveling men if Trondsson were so minded. All that prevented the slaughter was his own blade on Sunniva's throat.

"Take your men and leave, Trondsson," he growled. "Now." He saw well that the Viking chieftain was in torment. To emphasize his command, he made one small movement with his sword. Sunniva shrieked as a thin line of blood appeared on her white throat.

Raven's face grew pale, so great was his rage and his fear for her. She had not been badly hurt, and he could scarce believe the Celt would slay her, but how could he take the chance? "Sunniva, there is naught to do but go. I trow you can see that. . . ." His eyes told her that there would be another time, and she must not despair, but she did not see his silent message.

"Nay! Don't go. You cannot. He will not slay me.

Oh, Con, if you have any mercy in your heart, let me go."

"Of mercy, I have none, Sunniva. Say no more of it."

Sunniva was frightened. Con's hold on her was brutal, and her throat stung where he had drawn blood, but she could not contain her fury and disgust. "Slay me and be done with it then, for without Raven, I don't want to live. Slay me!"

"Hush you!" Con's grip tightened. It was the blunt edge of his blade that now grazed her throat.

If only she could get him to battle Raven as he had Rolf, Sunniva thought, frantic, Raven would win. But Con was wounded and weary and with her as hostage, why should he fight? Unless she could make him so angry, so jealous. . . .

"Coward!" she lashed.

"Sunniva, nay," Raven warned, seeing the dangerous glint in the Celt's eyes.

"Is he not hiding behind me?" She made a scornful snort. "An old woman fights better than he."

"Watch your tongue," Con growled.

"I will not. You're a coward, Con Cory. The only reason you fought Rolf was because you had no choice. You could scarce run, for he stood between you and the door!"

Con's handsome face flushed. He was shamed for her to speak so before these Vikings. He said sharply, "You know 'tis not so."

"And when you saw he was no match for you, you grew brave," Sunniva persisted. "He was heavy with mail and older than you. Had it been Raven who appeared, I trow you would have hidden behind me as you do now. . . ."

"Now you have gone too far, wife," Con growled. His arm tightened about her so painfully that she cried out. "Nay, Viking, not a step closer or she tastes my blade again. In fact, it wonders me why I crave such a sharp-tongued witch in the first place." He laughed. "But then, I always did like a challenge."

"Then should we fight for her," Raven said, softly. He had seen where Sunniva's taunts were leading. She was amazing. There she was, a Celt blade at her bleeding throat, and she had seen the only way out of this deadly quandry—make the devil think she doubted his manhood. He held his breath as he waited for the other's reply.

"Ay, 'tis time we fought again, you and I, Trondsson," Con Cory said finally. "At dawn tomorrow. And may the gods help whoever 'tis wins this wench."

Raven's relief was so great, he was swept by magnanimity. "Methinks you are too bloodied from battle to fight in the morn."

"By morn I will be fit," Con muttered. Perhaps this was the best way after all. Now she would see who was the stronger of the two and the more deserving. There was no doubt in his own mind that he himself would take the battle. And her.

"Your choice of weapons," Raven said.

"Double-edged swords," Con replied. "A fight to the death."

"Ay, a fight to the death."

Sunniva gasped. Never had she meant for either of them to die over her. "Can you not just dr-draw blood?" she quavered.

"It shall be as I say," Con said, still holding her close in front of him. "We fight to the death. If I be slain, Viking, you take her and go peaceably, but Ballageay you will leave untouched."

Raven said gravely, "I did not come here for Ballageay. It doubts me I could take such a stronghold with but forty men in the light of day. Nay, Celt, I want only Sunniva. But if I be slain in my quest, you will allow my men to depart in peace.''

"Ay.''

"Then 'tis agreed on.'' They struck hands, but not for one moment did Raven believe Con Cory. He fully expected to win tomorrow's battle, ay, but he was certain his leavetaking would not be a peaceable one.

"Go you now,'' said Con, his sword still at Sunniva's throat.

Raven did not move. "She will not stay this night with you.''

Con's eyes narrowed. "She stays. I tire of this, Viking. Go before I change my mind.''

"Beloved, go,'' Sunniva said. "'Tis all right. He will not harm me.'' She tried to smile.

Raven felt no such confidence, seeing the thin, glistening scarlet line on Sunniva's soft throat. Yet there was nothing to do but leave. For years he had seen Celts in battle. They were wild-tempered, fierce, tenacious warriors who fought like Norse berserkers. He was not about to provoke a Celt chieftain while Sunniva's life lay in the balance.

"I will go,'' he said. "I will return at dawn.'' His eyes assured Sunniva that all would be well. She must trust him.

CHAPTER 31

AFTER THE VIKINGS LEFT, CON FORCED SUNNIVA TO the door ahead of him, his sword at her back.

"Bar it," he ordered.

She obeyed. "How valiant and fearless you are."

"More than you obviously think I am, wench. And smarter. 'Tis clear yon damned Vikings are not to be trusted. 'Twould be like them to come crashing back in here to catch me unaware."

With Raven there in the same room with her, Sunniva had been brave for him. Now that he was gone, she was brave no longer. All seemed hopeless and she could think only of the awful things that had happened: Con's forcing her to wed him, Rolf's attack, and now a fight to the death. She sank onto the small stool Con had so recently used as a weapon and covered her eyes.

"Sunniva . . ."

Con saw that she wept. He scowled. If this wasn't the damnedest wedding night he had ever heard of—two men trying to steal the bride. There lay Gunnarsson still, and by the saints, there he would stay until morn. He was not going to open his door 'til dawn with all those damned Vikings lurking about. He started at the loud thumping on his door. Sunniva raised her head, her eyes like drowned violets.

"Con, be you all right, man?" a voice bawled from without. "Con, open up, there be bodies out here!"

His kinsmen, having come to carouse outside his door and cheer him on in the bridal bed, listened somberly to his remarkable tale and left with the body of Rolf Gunnarsson on his shield. When all was finally quiet again, Con said softly:

"Never did I want to hurt you, Sunniva. 'Tis just that you are mine, and I go wild when any want to take you away."

"Never was I yours, Con Cory." Sunniva was huddled on her pallet. "From the beginning, you knew I was betrothed. And when you learned 'twas to Raven and 'twas him I loved, still you went your own way, forcing this marriage between us." She shook her head. "Never will I love you. If I could, I would—for my own sake I would, but I cannot. 'Tis Raven I love."

Seeing her fall a-weeping again, Con felt a heaviness within him. Never would he admit it to any, but he wondered now if he had done the right thing. He poured a bowl of water and found a rag and salve and carried it to her pallet.

"'Tis all right, Sunniva, cry," he said, gruffly, "but betimes, let me cleanse your wound. 'Tis not good to let it go too long without treating it."

Sunniva knew he was right. Her wound needed cleansing, but she ceased her weeping. She dried her eyes and allowed him to bathe and salve the fiery ring on her throat. He had inflicted it, after all. As he tended her in silence, she saw that his own wounds still bled.

"I will tend you after, if you wish," she said coolly.

He nodded. "'Tis a good idea."

His wounds were ugly, deeper than her own, and as Sunniva bathed them, she thought of the coming morn. Would he die at Raven's hand? Or would it be Raven who went to Valhalla? She wanted to throw the water and salve against the wall, to scream and rage at the unjustness of it. She did not want either of them slain, but whoever died, it would be because she had sent them off into that dark night; she who had goaded them into fighting for her. How could she live with that the rest of her days? She patted dry Con's wounds and spread a thin coating of salve on them.

"You had best get some rest now," she murmured. He was going to pull her down to his pallet, she knew he was, and she was too sick at heart, too weary to fight. She did not resist when he took her hand.

"You be my wife, Sunniva—"

She sighed. "So you say."

"—but I see your unhappiness. 'Tis not the night I had planned for you. I wanted to carry you to the heavens. . . ." Seeing her confusion and disbelief, he added brusquely, "Now 'tis too late. It has been a damnable wedding night, and the rest of it I give you, just for yourself. Get you to bed now."

Sunniva blinked. "Without you?" she asked stupidly.

Con laughed. "I will join you if you insist."

"Nay!" She saw that his eyes were pain-glazed. He was hurting far too much to make love, and she was glad. She wondered if he would be able to fight come dawn. Damn, if only the whole terrible thing could be called off.

* * *

Raven and his men swam back to their vessel. After they dried themselves and donned their clothes, Raven and Ulf sat in the prow drinking mead and talking softly while the others slept.

"Tell me your thoughts," Raven said.

"He will not change his stripes before dawn. I smell treachery," Ulf answered.

"'Tis my feeling. But now he has no fleet to send out to sink us. All his vessels are damaged."

"Thanks be to Gunnarsson for that. Think you he will fight tomorrow? His wounds looked bad."

"He will fight."

"And what of the so-called wedding? Was't real, think you?"

"Ay," Raven answered glumly. "He's more clever than I thought. But then, it matters little—she will be his widow."

"Man, they will go crazy when you slay him, agreement or no. You have seen Celt wildness."

"Ay, I have seen." Raven drained his horn and poured more for both of them from a small keg.

Nor would his own men take to the agreement kindly. None knew of it yet; they would not know until dawn. And if, the gods forbid, he were slain, they would go as wild as any berserker. They would slay as many Celts as they could before they cast off, agreement be damned. And this proud vessel of his would be his funeral pyre.

Raven dismissed the thought. He was not ready yet for Valhalla, and the only Valkyrie he wanted to attend him was Sunniva. Nay, he would not die tomorrow and leave her so far from home among these wild strangers. With Odin's help, he would win the battle and after, he would trust to Odin to get them to safety. He didn't finish his mead. He emptied his horn into Ulf's, yawned, and crawled into his sleeping bag.

"You mean you can sleep?" asked Ulf, scowling.

"Can you think of aught better to do?" Raven closed his eyes. All was in Odin's hands. As sleep overtook him, he saw that Ulf scowled at him still.

It was the middle of the night when Con Cory added more oil to the lamp. He wanted light if any started breaking down his door. He returned to his pallet and lowered himself to it painfully. He stifled a groan, not wanting to waken Sunniva. Gunnarsson's sword had sliced deeper than he had thought, but by morn, he would be better. He willed himself to be better. Nor did he doubt that he would be the victor. Had he not skewered the great Hedeby? But then the fellow had been at a disadvantage. Sunniva was right in a way. He had been weighted with mail, and it was possible his older eyes had not seen so well in the shadows, and then having that kirtle thrown over his head. . . .

Con sighed. He had heard that all was fair in love and war—except he did not love Mellby, nay. He coveted her. He desired her. Mellby? Ay, she was Mellby still. He had tricked her during the ceremony just as he had tricked Gunnarsson during their battle. He felt a twinge of guilt, for never before had he stooped so low. It was these damned Vikings who had turned him from an honorable man to one he would not want to know.

But it was more than that. He had battled Vikings ever since he was a lad and always had he been honorable about it. Sometimes it had near killed him, but he had been honorable. So what was this thing that had turned him to scheming and breaking promises? When had he ever broken a promise or blinded a man during battle? It was as bad as stabbing him in the back. What had happened to him?

He looked over at Sunniva curled up on her pallet. Golden hair in a wild tumble over her shoulders, soft lips parted, flaxen lashes brushing her pink cheeks, her slender body drawn into as small a spot as possible. She was cold. He rose and gently, not disturbing her, covered her with a sheepskin. As he stood looking down at her, a pang of loss hit him. He thrust it away as if it were poison. He had not lost her, not at all. He was going to win this coming battle.

Strangely, he felt regret that his people would never allow the Vikings a safe leavetaking. It was yet another promise broken, another reason for Sunniva to be unhappy with him. He shook his head. What was this strange power she had over him? When had he ever wanted a woman's happiness before? But he had. Long ago, he had craved Calla's happiness. That woman he would have died for. And still would. He might have shared his life with her, but she would not have him, so why was he even thinking of the cantankerous witch? It was with Sunniva that his future lay, Sunniva whom he loved. . . .

He sat very still. There was that word again. Love. Damnation, he did not love her. He craved her. There was no love involved. Besides, she loved Trondsson. Loss stabbed him again, a sword in his gut; the knowledge that he might possess her body but never her heart. It belonged to another and always would.

When Sunniva awakened, Con's pallet was empty. Remembering what day it was, she leapt up. Had he gone? She hurried outside and called his name. Nothing. Were he and Raven battling already? she wondered. But nay, it was not dawn yet. Not quite. Heart pounding, she walked out onto the damp thatch and sat down. She saw that Odin's Raven rode at anchor, empty, her sail furled. The sky was a soft pink-gray and the tide rushed in from the Irish

Sea—just as the tide of her own terrible thoughts rushed into her mind. She instantly swept them out.

She would hold only good thoughts. Raven and Con both would be unharmed; all of them—Raven, the Solby men and herself—would be allowed to leave Maun in peace; Con and Calla would discover that it was each other they had wanted all along. . . . Over and over and over she said it. It was her wish, her prayer to all the gods.

As the sun rose over Clagh Burroo and its pale rays touched the hard-packed sand at the water's edge, Con Cory and Raven Trondsson faced each other. They were naked but for loincloths and leather helmets, and in Raven's hand Gildor glinted, long and silver-gold and deadly. Con held a Celt weapon of formidable length and appearance. Both carried shields. Raven's Vikings stood grim and uncertain as to what was happening. Not even the folk of Ballageay knew why they had been called together until their chieftain's voice rang out:

"We will fight, Trondsson and I, for we both claim the same woman as our own."

Every eye swung to Sunniva where she stood on a rise at the edge of the crowd. Calla was with her. At the angry rumble of protest, Con held up his hand.

"'Twill be a fight to the death," he shouted, his stern gaze moving over his tribe, "and if I be slain, these Vikings and the woman will be allowed to leave in peace. Hear you? I trow you will not dishonor my vow."

Raven next spoke to his men, his deep voice soaring over the uneasy assemblage: "If I be slain, I have said you Solby men will go peaceably, leaving behind the woman to the victor. I trow you will not dishonor my vow."

There was quiet. Sunniva heard only the sound of

the sea as the life drained from her body. She swayed, felt Calla's arm go around her to steady her. . . . *leaving behind the woman to the victor . . .* Imagining such a thing, being left to the victor, she wondered if she would be brave enough to kill herself.

"Take the Viking woman to your dwelling, macLir," Con said. "She will await the victor there."

"Calla, nay! I—I cannot leave here . . ." But neither could she stay and watch them chop each other to pieces.

"Come, Sunni, 'tis best." Calla took her hand. "Come away with me."

Raven watched, his sword-point resting lightly on the sand, as the women departed. He felt strangely detached, having placed all in Odin's hands, not only the battle but their leavetaking as well.

Con was annoyed, seeing how heavily Sunniva moved as Calla pulled her away; her golden head and slender shoulders bowed as though she had lost the very will to live. Damn the wench. But he could not think about that now. Eyes narrowed, he raised his sword, circled, and made a rapid thrust that was met with steel. He marked that Trondsson had a cold smile and a distant gaze that chilled him suddenly to the bone. It was as though the Viking himself were not even there, as though some other held his glittering blade. He grew aware of the crowd-noise then, the cries and mutterings, the urgings of his men for him to make short shrift of the bastard. And why should he not? Was he not the winner of untold battles and the conqueror of untold women? To him would go this battle.

"You will go to Valhalla this dawn, Viking," he shouted. He sprang and then feinted, driving for Trondsson's throat instead of his shoulder, but the fierce lunge met the other's shield with the black raven on it. His enemy's next stroke was unexpected.

It knocked off his helmet, and the impact drove him into the sea. He charged back, alert, cunning, using trick after trick, seeming to yield, pretending weariness, only to slash out like a streak of lightning. Twice he drew blood on Raven's dark, glistening torso as the battle wore on. The Celts cheered.

Raven, too, had drawn blood. When he had sent Con's helmet sailing, Gildor had creased the side of his scalp and now blood streamed into the Celt chieftain's eyes. The Vikings' hoarse cries, calling for Con's death, spurred Raven on. He downed Con with a fierce body blow from his shield, aimed for his throat and thrust with Gildor.

Con rolled aside and was on his feet instantly. But even as his own sword seared out like a tongue of fire, slashing Raven's chest from shoulder to navel, he was thinking of Sunniva's grief, her gentleness and bravery. Three times she had given him life, and he was battling to keep her although it would break her heart.

From the beginning, Raven had sensed that this was no ordinary battle. What a strange thing that he had been able to drive the Celt into the sea, and now, by the gods, his guard was down again. What in the—? Raven took instant advantage. He charged swiftly, furiously, shield to shield, face to face, forcing Con back into the sea once more, further and further, until with one furious shield-blow, he downed him. Suddenly, astonishingly, it was over. Con was on his back in the water. Raven lowered his point to the Celt's broad throat and the Vikings howled. He gazed down at his enemy, not showing his bafflement. What had happened to the fellow? The battle could have gone on indefinitely. They were evenly matched and neither had tired. It was as though Con Cory had suddenly lost heart.

"Yield you, Celt?" Raven asked, gruffly.

Con's eyes held flames of defiance. Yield? Him? He laughed. "Never. But for the hole in this damned sea-bed that threw me off-balance, I would have skewered you." But what was he doing in the sea in the first place? It was as much a mystery as was Trondsson's downing him so effortlessly. What had happened?

Raven's men were calling for Con Cory's death as the Celt chieftain's people muttered and moved closer. Raven saw no fear on his enemy's face; his eyes had gone steely. He was a worthy foe and a fine warrior and Raven meant to make his death as swift and painless as possible. His fingers tensed on Gildor's hilt as he raised his arm, busking himself for the downward thrust.

Con waited for the blow to fall, every muscle taut, his eyes on the glittering blade suspended above him. He muttered, "Why do you wait?"

Raven was frozen. Never before had his hands been thus stayed. His mind told them to move, but his body disobeyed. By Odin, what a strange thing. Raven's eyes narrowed. But then, perhaps it was not strange at all. He had put himself in the hands of his god and now his sword, his very body refused to obey him. It seemed it was Odin they obeyed. He suspected that if he slew the Celt, they all would die.

"Get it over with," Con growled. "'Tis not the most pleasant thing, lying in the damned sea awaiting your damned blade to fall."

Raven was remembering the Celt's earlier words: In another time and another place, they might have been friends. He deemed he was right. Reluctantly, he lowered Gildor to his side.

"I see no death in your eyes, Con Cory. Methinks 'tis not the day for you to die. . . ."

CHAPTER 32

Ever since Calla brought her to Con's hut, Sunniva had sat atop the roof, legs crossed, elbows on knees, her face buried in her hands. Calla herself prowled the field behind them like a restless cat. The shouts and cheers in the distance caused Sunniva's heart nearly to falter every time she heard them, for she knew what caused such enthusiasm. Blood was flowing. But whose blood? She raised her head finally, forcing her eyes to where Odin's Raven tugged at anchor in the blue-green sea. Her red sail was still furled, but now Raven's banner whipped in the stiffening breeze atop the mast, a black raven on a red background.

The sight sent a thrill coursing through Sunniva's body, countering her terror. How could she have doubted for one moment the outcome of this battle? Raven was a great warrior, and he had come all the way from Norway to find her and take her home. Of course he would be the victor. As for Con . . . She felt deep sadness, watching Calla's constant pacing, the sea-wind whipping her thick, dark-red mane of hair about her worried face. It was not going to be an easy thing for her to lose him. Sunniva reckoned she loved him though she had denied it. She herself even cared for the man despite the grief he had brought her.

She stiffened, noticing of a sudden that no sound was coming from the bay where the battle was being fought. She got to her feet, her skin prickling. What did it mean, such quietness? Did one of them lie dead already? Surely not. Not enough time had elapsed. She marked that Calla, too, was motionless, listening.

"What is't?" Sunniva called. "Why is't so still?"

"I trow 'tis over. . . ." Calla answered.

A sick feeling crept from Sunniva's stomach to her throat and into her head, where it clung like a cobweb. While they fought, she had had hope, but now, whatever the outcome, it had happened. It was over. She was frightened. She saw that Calla, too, was frightened, yet they did not draw near each other. Neither could comfort the other. Calla walked down to the shore, waiting, watching, for whoever would come. Sunniva could not. She sat once more, crossing her legs tailor-fashion, her back straight, her eyes closed. She did not hide her face in her hands. It was too late to pray or worry.

It seemed forever that she sat there, trying to calm her thoughts, telling herself that she would be brave, no matter what the outcome. Hearing a sound, she busked herself and opened her eyes. It had been a muffled cry from Calla. Sunniva watched as her friend, like a startled doe, sprang forward to race down the beach. Who was coming? Was it Con?

Sunniva rose. Which man would stride up that beach to claim her? When she saw him coming, her legs went weak. She managed somehow to leap down from the roof to the ground, weeping, laughing, as he waved and called her name, the tall warrior whose black hair gleamed in the morning sun. Sunniva flew to meet him.

"Raven! Oh, beloved!"

Raven swooped Sunniva up into his arms and, cradling her against his chest, twirled her around in the joyous abandon she remembered so well. He kissed her tear-streaked face and rosy lips again and again before throwing back his head and uttering a piercing cry.

Sunniva shivered. Once before she had heard that frightening shout of victory and never did she want to hear it again—not even if it meant she had been stolen and found. Her eyes widened then as she saw that he was wounded. One long slash across his chest was bleeding freely, and glistening stripes criss-crossed both arms. Blood dripped from a gash on his left temple.

"You're hurt!"

Raven grinned. "I'll live."

Ay, he would live, she thought, grateful beyond words, but it meant that Con was dead. Dead or dying. Calla had gone to be with him.

"Fetch your wallet and anything else you would take with you," Raven said, setting Sunniva on her feet. "The men are boarding and we will be leaving soon."

"For home?" Her eyes were wide.

Raven laughed. "Where else, little troll?"

Home. She could scarce believe it. But then, no longer was it necessary for her to stay in Dublin until Raven slew Rolf Gunnarsson. And there was no reason to stay here on Maun. She was going home to Lilleby. To wed Raven. And Calla would be burying Con Cory. All of Ballageay would be mourning him, she brooded, and they would be filled with hatred for Raven. She fetched her wallet and stuffed her few belongings into it. As they walked toward the bay, she murmured:

"I fear they will not let us leave."

"'Twas the agreement," Raven answered easily. "If I were victor, you and my men and I would be allowed to leave peaceably."

"I know 'twas what they said, but I saw how wroth they were at the thought. 'Twas Con's idea, not theirs. Now that he is—is gone, they will want to slay you. They will want to slay all of us." Seeing the twin devils dancing in Raven's gray-gold eyes, she grew wary. "Raven Trondsson, what aren't you telling me?"

It was then that she spied a familiar figure on the beach. Tall, fiery-haired, bearded; a handsome, scowling face. Sunniva blinked. Con? Con Cory was alive? He was! And Calla was by his side. Sunniva's head whirled. It meant she herself had a husband still! It complicated things horribly, but no matter—Con was alive. He was alive.

Con Cory was in a murderous mood. He could not believe what had happened to him during those last moments of battle, nor did he know how it happened. Never had he experienced such a thing before. He minded that he had been brooding over Sunniva, those times she had saved his life, and the damned poor way he had chosen of paying her back—when *boom*, he had fallen into a damned hole in the shoreline. Just like that, he had lost her. He was a disgrace. Shamed beyond belief. A beardless, unblooded boy could have slain him as he lay there in the shallow sea like a turtle on its back. Seeing his kinsmen and friends hanging about and staring at him with long faces, he waved them off sharply.

"Go you!" he bawled. "Have you nothing better to do than to stand here loafing and gawking?" Damnation.

Calla crossed her arms and gazed at Con with placid eyes. She herself did not know what had happened between him and Raven Trondsson, nor did she care. All that mattered was that he was alive. Her heart soared, for she had been certain that he was slain. Seeing Sunniva and Raven coming, seeing the gladness on their faces, she rejoiced for them, too. All had worked out for the best. So Con Cory was in a rage. So he would recover. She herself would see to it. Too long it had taken her to discover what she now knew: She loved and wanted this man. Him she was going to wed—but some small, wise voice inside warned her that it would not be for a while. And it would be best for him to think that it was his idea. Calla shrugged her slim shoulders and hid the smile that tugged at her lips. So be it.

Sunniva saw that the Solby men already were aboard their vessel. The Celts stood in small scattered groups, glumly watching all that was happening. Con and Calla stood alone on the shore. In her gladness, Sunniva was minded to throw her arms about both of them. Instead she greeted them gravely and then stood quietly, waiting for the men to say whatever had to be said. Seeing the tension between the two chieftains, she was uneasy. Raven had won her, ay, but she was still wed to Con Cory. She could not imagine how that would be resolved.

"Go elsewhere, you wenches," Con grumbled. "This is between us men." Seeing the concern in their eyes, he added, "Nay, the fighting is over. Now we must talk. Go you." After they left, he glared at Raven. "Why did you not slay me, Viking?"

Raven said quietly, "Never would I slay a man whose mind was not on the battle at hand."

In fact, never had he encountered such a thing before. A man so far off in his own thoughts in the midst of a sword-fight that he could be driven into the sea. It was a mystery. From all he had heard, Con Cory was a great warrior. Vikings without number had fallen at his hand, and without question, he had craved Sunniva. Yet this morn, he had been driven into the sea. Only one explanation satisfied Raven: It was Odin's doing. Seeing how the Celt bristled at his words, Raven added:

" 'Twas clear to me you could not give your all . . ."

"Could not?" Con eyes narrowed. Had the other seen his brief touch of madness during the battle? That sudden weakness that made him brood over Sunniva's happiness. Happiness? It was a bitter taste in his mouth. Who in this world had happiness? There was no such thing. "What mean you, could not?"

"Suffice it to say I know of what I speak," Raven said curtly. Never did he talk of those things that transpired between him and his god in battle. Least of all to a damned Celt.

Con gripped his arm. "You will tell me, Viking, or we may well fight again, here and now." It was bad enough to be thought weak, but he would not have the other thinking he was mad to boot.

Raven understood Con Cory's distress. He was a great chieftain, shamed in battle through no fault of his own, and it would be great scathe if he never held up his head again because of this. "Unhand me, man," he said, without anger. "I can tell you one thing only: I walk with Odin—'tis he who wields my sword in battle."

Con sneered. "You think you be invincible?"

"Odin is invincible."

Con studied his enemy. He remembered that Mellby said Raven Trondsson had seen Odin in battle, just as he himself had seen Manannan. All knew the gods revealed themselves only to a chosen few.

"Man," he whispered, "are you saying 'twas Odin who wielded the sword that defeated me? 'Twas Odin who clouded my mind so I would flounder into the sea?"

"Draw your own conclusions, Celt. I have told you too much already."

Con nodded. He stood taller. "'Tis enough." He could accept losing a battle to a heathen god. What he could not accept was losing a battle because his wits were addled by memories of a woman. As Sunniva's beautiful face leapt to his mind, it was like a fist to his heart. "'Tis time you left, Viking. Take your wench and go."

"Methinks you're forgetting something," Raven drawled. "You have wed her."

"Believe me, she is yours," Con muttered. "Take her and go."

"Does this mean you tricked her?"

Con eyes were mocking. "Now 'tis I who know of what I speak."

"Damn it, I would know how—"

"Viking," Con raised his voice, "go you while I still allow it." He motioned for Calla to bring Sunniva. As they neared, he thought them the two fairest women he had ever seen. Calla glowed, and he knew it was with gladness that he lived. Sunniva gazed at him with worried eyes.

"Can we leave?" she asked.

"Ay."

"Are we not married still?"

Seeing Trondsson's arm slip around her waist, Con felt a flare of anger. When the Viking had broached the subject, he had been testy as a wild boar, content to let him stew and brood over it. Sunniva was a different matter. He wanted to smooth her life for her.

"Never were we wed, Mellby."

"Never wed!" Sunniva was shocked. She turned to Calla. "You lied to me!"

Calla glared at Con Cory. "What mean you, never were you wed? When the priest asked if you each took the other, I heard you both say ay. We all did."

"Never," Sunniva protested again. "I never heard the question, never gave an answer."

Con's lips brushed her ear. "Mind you, Mellby, when I asked if you were ill?"

"Ay," Sunniva nodded. She looked up at the chieftain's grave face. Oh, no! She had been deathly sick when Con had asked that, and she answered then just as she had now. She had said ay. She shook her head, realizing finally what had happened, shamed that she had not seen it for the trick it was. How could a man so likeable be such a scoundrel? "The trolls take you, Con Cory." She meant it.

Con laughed. He was safe from the damned trolls. A Norse enchantress had taken him first.

"Calla, forgive me." Sunniva threw her arms about Calla's neck. "I should have known 'twasn't you who deceived me . . ."

Calla returned her hug. "I'll miss you, Sunni," she whispered. "May your gods sail with you."

Con's gruffness returned. "Take your wench, Trondsson, and go you now. If you venture to these parts again, I suggest you leave her at home." The next time, he vowed, he would not give her up.

Sunniva stood in the stern and waved to Calla until she was but a speck. Con had not watched their departure, but had gone off with his kinsmen. Despite her joy at being with Raven and going home, a weight was pressing on Sunniva. She regretted that her last words to Con Cory had been bitter ones. But he had deceived her, and he had been treacherous in his dealings with Raven. Why should she be sorry? Perhaps it was the fact that he cared for her. She knew he did. There had been something about him, something in his eyes before they had departed that nagged her. Well, it was over. She would never see him again if she was lucky, and it was time to think of other things. She turned to Raven and Ulf. The sea was choppy and both were at the steering oar.

"How may I help?" she asked.

Raven laughed outright. "There is no need, Sunniva."

Ulf scowled. "You? What could you do to help?"

Sunniva's eyes flickered over the two, always a sign that a storm was brewing. "The lord of Hedeby found me indispensable. On the Landwaster, I bailed, mended sail and clothing, served food and drink, aired sleeping bags . . . " She could have gone on, but she spied that tell-tale muscle working in Raven's jaw.

"On this vessel, 'tis you who will be served, Sunniva," he said quietly. "I trow you labored enough for that bastard to last you a lifetime."

He pushed from his mind those ugly thoughts of what other ways she might have been forced to serve Hedeby, thoughts that both crushed and enraged him. But she was so stubborn, so brave, never would she let him know what really happened. And to think that he had never avenged her for it. It was Con Cory who had had the pleasure. Pleasure . . .

Into Raven's tortured mind crept the image he had brooded on a hundred times: that room in Cory's hut, deep in shadow and strewn with flower petals; Gunnarsson stretched out on the floor; the Celt's blue eyes aglitter; Sunniva, hastily covering her nakedness. What had happened before Gunnarsson broke in on them? It was bootless to ask, for she would never say, yet she had thought Cory, damn the devil, was her husband. How could she rightly refuse him? He gave his head a violent shake. By the gods, he would go mad if he dwelt on such things so constantly. Why could he not rejoice that she was safe in his hands once more and they would soon be wed?

"Raven, what is't?" Sunniva lay a hand on his bare arm. "You look so—so wild . . ."

Her hand was so small and white against his dark skin, and she was so fair, so precious. She was his own handfasted maid, his little Sunniva, and she was safe. The trolls take him for not giving thanks for what he had and ignoring all else.

"Take the helm, Ulf," he said.

Ulf gave a wicked grin. "Ay, captain."

Without another word, Raven's arms went around Sunniva. This was all that mattered, he thought, pressing her slender body tightly against his and kissing her mouth. They were together, and never would he lose her again. She was warm and soft and the fragrance of her white skin and sweet breath intoxicated him. He felt her melting into him, arching against him, rosy lips parted, her small velvety tongue giving, taking hungrily, her hands stroking his face, his hair, even his beard which he knew she hated. Knowing his need would soon overwhelm him, Raven freed her lips. Her beautiful eyes pleaded with him to take her below. He whispered, "Nay, Sunni, not now. Before long we will make love, I promise you."

"'Tis Ballacolum ahead," Ulf said.

Raven nodded. To Sunniva, he said, "We will be taking on supplies near there."

Soon the stone anchor was dropped over the side and Sunniva watched as longboats came from shore, took on their empty water-barrels, and returned them filled with fresh water. Kegs of mead and beer were rapidly hauled aboard, as well as all manner of food: smoked fish and beef and flatbread and cheese, even fresh vegetables. And then they were on their way, little time having been spent. A crewman served their food and drink—all would take their turn at the chore, Sunniva learned—and after they had eaten their fill and laughed and yarned together and drunk many toasts to their freedom, Raven rose and pulled Sunniva to her feet.

"I would talk with you in private, Sunniva Mellby."

His men roared their laughter. Sunniva, too, laughed and felt her face turning pink. "Long have I wanted to talk with you, Raven Trondsson . . ."

Ulf said: "Just make sure you're talked out before we reach the Hebrides, man."

"What is in the Hebrides?" Sunniva asked.

"'Tis stormy this time of year," Raven drawled, "but then 'tis stormy everywhere this time of year. Give a shout if you need me, man. Come, wench, let's not postpone our talk further . . ."

The jesting began, but Sunniva marked that it was good-humored, not coarse. She gave Raven her hand and he drew her toward the trap, through the ranks of his smiling men, their horns raised in further toasts to cheer them on. They went below. As Sunniva lowered herself to the skin-covered mattress, the trap overhead was discreetly closed except for a narrow crack. Enough light entered for her to see Raven dimly as he stretched out his long body beside her. He snuggled her up against him, her head on his shoulder. It was wonderful, his hard arms around her and the whole length of him pressed against her. She buried her nose in his neck and sniffed. He smelled like the sea and leather and the sun and some exciting undefinable aroma that was his alone. Her blood stirred.

He kissed the end of her nose. "Hello, imp." His deep voice sent a vibration rumbling through her.

Sunniva giggled. "Hello . . ." Shyly she put the tip of her tongue to his lips. He tasted of sea-spray and mead. Of Raven. It was so like the dreams she had when Rolf held her captive that she knew panic. Was it but a dream?

Feeling her tremble, Raven wrapped his arms about her. He held her as tenderly as a babe. "What is't, Sunniva?"

"Tell me 'tis real, Raven," she whispered. "Tell me 'tisn't a dream." She clutched him, fearful that he would slip away if she released her fierce hold on him.

He kissed her face, her lips and hair, each slender white finger. "'Tisn't a dream, Sunni, nay. I'm here, and we're on our way home." He kissed her again, more deeply this time, and felt his loins move with passion. It was time he showed her, beyond any doubt, that this was not a dream.

CHAPTER 33

RAVEN BEGAN A LEISURELY EXPLORATION OF Sunniva's body. Never had they the luxury of so much time, and now it stretched out ahead of them. He was going to make up for all the days lost; those months before he realized he loved her and all the agonizing weeks he searched for her. He kissed her lips and slipped his hand under her clothing, caressing each breast before pulling up the tunic to expose them to his hungry gaze. His manhood leapt. White snow-peaks upthrust for him alone to see and to taste. He lowered his head and took one hardened nipple between his teeth, biting it ever so gently before taking it in his mouth and teasing it with his tongue.

It was as if lightning burned through Sunniva when he nipped and suckled her like that. He took her other nipple and fluttered his tongue-tip against it. She gave a small moan and arched against him. It was as it had been before—she was frantic suddenly to get closer to him. She had on too much clothing. Raising her arms to remove her tunic, she felt them pinned firmly above her head and the tunic covering her face. She was trapped, her breasts and nipples bared to Raven's voracious kisses. She heard his deep chuckle.

"You're in my power, wench."

As Sunniva giggled and squirmed and tried to free herself, Raven rained kisses on her breasts, all the while cupping and stroking and tasting them, inhaling her tantalizing fragrance. She minded him of roses on a summer morn. Helping her finally to pull off her tunic, he saw that she was pink and glowing, her eyes alight with excitement. He stared. She was more beautiful than ever when she was aroused: her lips and breasts fuller and softer, that sensuous gleam of invitation in her eyes. . . .

She was his treasure, his life, and when she was finally his, he was going to grant her every wish and whim. Never would she have to lift a finger. She would have serving-folk aplenty to wait on her hand and foot, and he would give her every luxury. And never again would he leave her unguarded, nor would he assume, as he had at the convent, that the men guarding her were skilled and their numbers sufficient. Never again. His own Viking warriors would stand watch over her always.

He drew down her leggings, stifling a curse as he saw the slave-band on her slim ankle. The first thing he would do when he got her home, certainly before her folk saw the damned thing, would be to have his smith cut it off. But for now—he slipped his hands up and down her cool, silky legs, then turned her toward him. He stroked her shoulders and back, his fingers tracing the delicate line of her spine. Suddenly, he sat up, pulling her face-down across his lap. Sunniva gave a small yelp as he began playfully kissing and nipping her buttocks, first one delectable white mound and then the other. By the gods, what an enchantress. He could not keep his teeth and mouth and hands off her. And if he could not, how could any other man?

He tensed, thinking of Kol who had demanded to buy her and of Gunnarsson and Cory who had had her in their power for so long. He imagined her opening her legs to them, not because she desired them, nay, but because they had desired her. And being in their power, she had to obey. He heard the growl in his throat, knew his angry bite into her soft rump hurt even before she rolled off his lap and smacked his hand.

"Beast! I'll bite you where you'll know it if you're not more careful. . . ." But she was laughing as he pulled her back into his arms. He cradled her, kissed her breasts again and her sweet mouth as they sank backwards into the furs.

"Enchantress . . ." Her lips parted for his kiss as his long fingers found her cleft and gently separated her. She was moist, ready for him, and as she opened herself to him, caressing and guiding him into her, he murmured again. "Enchantress . . . beloved enchantress . . ."

Afterwards, they lay clinging to each other long and long. They were far from Norway still, but there in Raven's arms, Sunniva was home. Always had he been her haven in a storm, her best friend and teacher and confidant. Now he was much more. He was her beloved, her betrothed, soon to be her husband. Her eyes grew damp as her mind flew over those many things for which she was grateful: Raven . . . their love . . . going home . . . Calla . . . the fact that Con was alive.

Raven stirred. He had been dozing, dreaming of

lovemaking still. He lifted a strand of Sunniva's golden hair, inhaled its fragrance, kissed it, stroked her white arm, turned her face toward his and kissed her full mouth. Seeing the distance in her eyes, he said:

"You're far away."

"I was thinking of Con Cory," she murmured.

Raven felt a stab of anger, yet he answered easily, "And why would that be?"

"Calla heard 'twas a strange battle you two fought. 'Twas whispered that Con did not fight like himself, and 'twas strange, too, that you spared him. She wanted me to thank you."

Sunniva's voice murmured on, but Raven did not hear. He was seeing that flower-strewn room again, and Con Cory's eyes agleam with triumph, Sunniva so soft and beautiful and vulnerable in her nakedness, trying hastily to pull on her kirtle. He clenched his teeth. He did not want to be jealous, but could he ever forget all that had happened to her? Would he ever know all that had happened to her? She was so fair, neither Gunnarsson nor Cory would have spared her. What man would, especially a chieftain? He sucked in a deep breath. Damnation, it was hard enough for himself not to behave like a rutting stallion when he was near her. If only she would confide in him so he could face the horror and conquer it—but she would not. And so it would sear through him, red and festering, forever. Nor would he forget that look in her eyes when she saw that Con Cory lived. There was something between those two.

"Raven . . ." When he did not answer, Sunniva whispered: "Now 'tis you who are far away." She drew his hand to her lips and nibbled the tips of his fingers. Still he said nothing. His eyes were closed and she marked the small movement in his jaw. "Beloved . . ."

"Why do you think of Con Cory as we lie here together?" he asked finally.

Seeing his anger, Sunniva stared at him. She was crushed. "Here I am, naked in your bed, filled with you—is it not obvious I am yours?"

Raven muttered, "'Tis true you are mine now, ay."

"Now?" Sunniva's own anger leapt. She sat up, her eyes a-glitter in the half-light. "Always was I yours, Raven Trondsson." Her voice was low so none would hear, but it was sharp. "'Twas not easy to save myself for you and keep my honor, but I did. I thought you would be happy, instead you refuse to believe me." She shook her head. "Never were you this way before. . . ."

"Why do you not answer my question? Why do you think of Con Cory now, here in my arms? Did you lie with him last night when you thought you were wed?"

"Nay, I did not!" she cried, "but if I had, 'tis clear you would love me less. I had forgotten this awful jealousy of yours! Will you lock me away when we are wed so I need never see another man? I trow you will leave that slave-band on for your own chain. . . ."

It was as if she had struck him. But he saw with terrible clarity that she was right. His love for her, his fear for her safety were turning him into a stranger he scarcely recognized. He was planning to lock her away. He meant to take away her independence and spirit and deny her the use of her abilities—and over and over he had accused her of lying to him. Ay, she was right. Never had he been this way before. He caught her slender naked body, pulled her down beside him and held her close. As she wept silently, he flayed himself. Had she not been through enough? Was she to have no peace with him either? This could not go on. He kissed her damp face and eyelids, stroked her hair, cradled her.

"Forgive me, Sunni." He continued to kiss her, soothe and comfort and caress her. "Shhhh, 'tis all right. Forgive me. 'Tis all right."

"Never did I let them have me, Raven. Never. They tried, but 'twas my dreams of you that gave me the strength and the courage to resist. I knew you would come for me, but never did I think you would not b-believe me."

Raven groaned. What a bastard he was. He did not deserve her.

"Raven!" It was Ulf's voice from above, followed by a banging on the trap. "Get on deck, man. Hurry."

"Coming!"

Raven yanked on his trews and was gone before Sunniva could pull on her own garb. When she stepped on deck, the foamy seas were hurtling by, gray and heavy, and the blood-red sail was dragging them westward rather than northward. As she watched, it was quickly furled and every man on board was put to the oars. Raven and Ulf, the muscles in their backs and arms bulging, braced themselves against the massive steering-oar to return the course of the dragonship to the north.

Sunniva clung to the trap opening. She cried to the men nearest her: "What is't? What is happening?"

"Hafvilla!" they shouted over the wind.

Hafvilla. She was ice-cold suddenly. Lilleby was on a fjord, an arm of the sea, and always had she heard the terrible tales of hafvilla—of fisherfolk and merchants and those men gone a-viking who were carried to sea and lost—who suffered hafvilla. Some were swept off by fierce winds and currents, others claimed by fog, others by the lack of any wind at all, but the results were the same. They disappeared and were lost forever.

Was that to be the fate of Odin's Raven? she wondered, her frightened eyes on the wild seas. All of these brave men who had come with Raven seeking her, were they to join the ones slain by Con Cory? And she and Raven, were they never to wed after all? Surely she had not endured those hardships thrust on her these many weeks in order to perish on her way home to Lilleby. Surely not.

She looked about her frantically for some way to help. She saw that the wind was driving the waves overboard and the water, sloshing underfoot, grew ever deeper. None could be spared from the oars to man the buckets—so she would. She would bail as she had on the Landwaster. Doubtless Raven would not like it and would order her below, whereupon she would refuse and they would have yet another battle. She marked that he had seen her, and waited, defiant, for his roar.

"Sunniva!"

"Ay?"

"We're getting her back on course," Raven shouted, "but 'twill be bootless if we sink betimes. Grab you a bucket and bail." When she stared, he bellowed, "Now, girl! Move!"

"Ay."

Sunniva had been prepared for an argument, but he had taken her completely unaware. She was dumbfounded by the change in him. What had happened? Her spirits soared as she hurriedly caught up two buckets, and as she began dipping, throwing the water over the side, dipping again and again, she met his approving, laughing eyes. They told her that all was well—not only with his vessel but between the two of them. The Raven she had always known had returned to her.

Sunniva was not mistaken. Raven was his old self. She saw his pride in her as she helped with those constant chores that faced a Viking longship on the high seas. The days turned cool and shorter and the nights longer. Sunniva, curled up under a sheepskin by Raven's side at sunset, listened happily, drowsily, to the men's yarning and to their tall tales and oft-told sagas. She shared Raven's mead from his horn, and when darkness came, she shared his sleeping bag and his ever-hungry body. They drifted off to sleep sealed together and always, when she awoke, Sunniva wondered if a babe had been started by their lovemaking. The thought filled her with excitement and gladness, although she could not imagine that her folk would be overjoyed. But surely they did not expect her to be a maid still. Even before she was stolen, she had belonged to Raven.

When Odin's Raven took on fresh water and supplies in the Shetlands, Sunniva learned that their next landfall would be Norway. Her thoughts were alive with her homecoming until night came and she crawled into the sleeping bag beside Raven. Feeling his big, gentle hands moving over her bare flesh, she soon forgot all but the way her body felt—hot and weak and hungry for him.

"I trow you will want to wed as soon as we get back," Raven murmured against her mouth.

Sunniva returned his kiss eagerly. "Ay. And you?"

"Ay. I want no doubt in any man's mind that you are mine." He stroked her soft belly, and patted it. "Know you, Sunni, there may well be another reason for haste in drinking our wedding ale. . . ."

She grew warm. So he, too, was wondering. Suddenly shy, she whispered. "Would't please you?"

"You need even ask? Of course 'twould please me. I crave many sons from you." His mouth curved in the darkness. The gods forgive him, but he couldn't resist teasing her. He waited, but not for long.

"Sons!" Sunniva hissed.

Raven kissed her mouth again and pulled her against him tightly. "Ay, sons. What else, wench?"

"Raven Trondsson, I was a girl babe once! Dare you to tell me that you—" She felt his body shaking. His deep easy laughter filled the black hold and then she, too, was laughing. Their lips met and clung. "Beast," she breathed, "'tis not a teasing matter."

Her fingers twined in his thick hair as she pulled his face closer. She thrilled to the primitive kisses he placed on her throat and breasts, and to the way he possessed her, his tongue and shaft claiming her doubly in sensually rhythmic unison. Oh, Raven, Raven, never would she love another as she loved him.

When Odin's Raven, her fiery sail billowing, reached the mouth of the Strandefjord, the lur horn was blown. Sunniva thrilled to the sound as it echoed up and down the Solby Valley and folk came running from fields and dwellings to see what was happening. Seeing Sunniva and Raven in the prow, they ran along the shore, shouting and waving in great excitement. All knew the vessel would beach at Marvik, where the best bay was situated. As the vessel passed Lilleby, Sunniva saw her own folk run to the water's edge where they stood staring.

Sunniva shrieked to them, laughing, crying, waving. Her father raised his hand and shouted a greeting, her mother dropped to her knees, overcome, her face in her hands. Inge was there, hopping up and down, and Sooten, frightened by the clamor, galloped about his paddock rearing and pawing and snorting. And then the drekar's great sail was furled and her shallow bottom scraped the sandy shore of Marvik. Raven leapt over the footboard onto the sandy shore. Ulf lifted Sunniva and handed her carefully into his arms. Seeing the wonder, the joy lighting her beautiful face, Raven kissed her.

"Welcome home, Sunni."

"Ay."

Home. She could scarcely believe it. And here came her mother and her father and Inge and such a great crowd of folk as she had never seen.

"Mother . . . father . . ."

"Oh, child, child. Oh, Sunniva. Precious precious babe. Oh, my treasure . . ." The words came from both her parents as Sunniva was enfolded in loving arms and wept and laughed over. Raven and Ulf, practically unnoticed, looked on and beamed.

"I, too!" Inge cried. "I, too! Let me hug her! I can't even get near her! I, too!"

Hearing her young cousin's outraged cries, Sunniva reached out for her and brought her into the circle where she was nigh smothered, but happily so.

"Inge, how you have grown!" Sunniva marveled. Seeing her rapt gaze, she asked, "What is't, honey?"

"You look different," Inge said.

Sunniva laughed. "But I am not. I have the same color of eyes and hair and I'm no shorter or taller . . ."

"You're prettier," Inge declared. She added, for all to hear; "Is't because you and Raven are wed? 'Tis said when a maid turns woman, she glows. Methinks you look like a jule candle, Sunni. I wish I glowed."

Sunniva's eyes met Raven's. She laughed, blushed.

"Inge!" Anna Mellby, her face red, caused her niece to be hurried away by neighbors. "Now then, daughter, come along home—you can greet these folk on the way—and I will feed you. Come along, Ulf, and you, Raven, and your men. Come and take food with us, too." She raised her voice above the excited babble, "Hear me, all of you. We feast here tonight. Spread the word. Raven, I near forgot, your mother is away for the day. She will be home this eve, I trow." She held out her arms then for her son and for Raven Trondsson. Both men went into them, grinning.

"Methinks I have lost my manners, you brave lads." She gave them each a kiss. "Have thanks for what you and your men have done, bringing our daughter back to us."

"Ay," Arn said, clapping a big hand on each of their shoulders. "A thousand thanks to you both and to your men." He caught Sunniva close again and kissed her cheeks, the top of her head, her hands, and hugged her until she giggled.

"I'm home, papa. I'm home!" Her eyes shone.

"Ay, my treasure." Arn gazed on his daughter lovingly. As they made their way back to Lilleby and he watched her greet those folk flocking about her, he marked that Inge was right. Sunniva was more fair than ever, if such was possible. Next he looked at the tall Solby chieftain whose glittering gray eyes had never left her. He laughed, and whispered into Anna Mellby's ear:

"Wife, methinks these two had best drink the wedding ale in all haste."

Anna Mellby nodded. "Methinks 'twould be wise. Mayhap they will want to announce it at the feast tonight." She caught the hands of the two and pulled them toward Lilleby. "Come along, children, and you, too, Ulf. 'Tis time you had a bit of real food—and we have much to plan."

EPILOGUE

SHE WAS WED. AND AS SHE SAT IN THE HIGH-SEAT BY Raven's side, revelry bursting about her, Sunniva mused that all had been every bit as wonderful as she had dreamed it would be. She still wore her mother's beautiful scarlet robe, and many precious chains and brooches adorned her. Raven's wedding train with the banners flying had been magnificent, the grandest ever seen in the Solby Valley, and the wedding mass had been both solemn and beautiful. Coming home to Lilleby, they had feasted and drunk the wedding ale and her father had declared before all that he had given her to Raven Trondsson of Marvik. The gifts had then poured in, and the many deeds and settlements between the two had been unrolled and read, and wild dancing around a great bonfire had followed. Sunniva had danced so much and laughed so hard she could scarce stand on her feet.

Now they were at the boards again for more

feasting and drinking and singing. She was growing quite dizzy, what with all the music from the harpers and fiddlers and the ale she had consumed. Suddenly she spied a small band of women approaching—her mother and aunts, Raven's mother and Inge and Sister Hildigunn. Her pulses quickened. They were coming to take her to the bridal bed.

Raven muttered: "At last. Methought they would never get here."

Marking the hunger in his eyes, Sunniva said, teasing, "'Tis lucky you are, Raven Trondsson. Your eagerness can show whilst I must pretend to struggle . . ."

He kissed her mouth. "Don't struggle too hard, wench." He rose from the high-seat and stood to one side as the women pressed in on his bride.

"'Tis time, Sunniva." Anna Mellby laid a hand on her daughter's shoulder. "We have come for you."

"Nay, I will not go!" Sunniva cried, clinging to the arm of the high-seat, but it was bootless to resist. The women pried loose her fingers and pulled her from the chair. "Nay, unhand me!"

"You are Raven's now," Inge declared loudly, proud to be part of the grand festivities. "He has bought you and wed you, and you are his!"

Despite Sunniva's cries, the women, surrounded now by Raven's groomsmen with naked swords and flaming torches, dragged her from the great-hall to the bride-house. It was a storehouse that stood not far from the manor proper and its loft-room had been made into a bridal bower for Sunniva even before she was stolen. Now, amidst hushed laughter and excited whispers, she was forced up the narrow stairs to where her bridal bed awaited. When the door was opened, she gasped. In the flickering lamplight, she saw that the old loft-room had been transformed into a bedchamber fit for royalty.

Richly-hued tapestries covered the timber walls and broidered silken pillows in all colors lined the wall-benches. The bridal bed itself was enclosed in pale, gauzy hangings as though it were a tent. Through the veils, Sunniva saw that it was covered with the broidered silken coverlid her mother had promised her, and was made soft with heaps of furs and velvet-covered pillows. Remembering those terrible days when she had been so far from home, she gazed on it lovingly.

"'Tis far more beautiful than ever I dreamed," she murmured.

Anna Mellby smiled. "Sit you, Sunniva," she said gently. "You can look on it whilst we prepare you for bed."

The women seated her in the great arm-chair, brought there for the purpose, and began taking off her bridal finery, piece by piece. She was heavy with gold and silver: rings on her fingers, chains on her bosom, the great silver brooches and golden armlets and the silver-gilt belt wound about her waist.

"Are you happy, daughter?" her mother asked, removing the last of the brooches.

Sunniva nodded, smiling. "Ay, mother, 'tis the happiest day of my life. . . ."

Many hands helped her to stand, and then Sunniva's scarlet bridal robe was slipped down about her ankles and she stepped out of it. Clad only in a sleeveless, violet-colored shift now, she sat back down in the arm-chair. Her small scarlet shoes were untied and removed and her stockings. Inge began brushing her thick, waist-length hair.

"How fair you are, Sunni," she murmured wistfully. "Your hair is like a cape of gold." She arranged it to fall down over her cousin's slender shoulders and bare white arms. "'Tis sad that in the morn you must bind it up and cover it with a stupid coif just because you are wed." She looked resentfully at the snowy pleated head-linen where it lay waiting atop a chest.

Sunniva laughed. In truth, it did not worry her. It seemed a small thing after what she had been through. She drew a deep breath, thinking that soon, mayhap this night even, Raven would hear her tale for the first time. From beginning to end. She had promised him. But for now, all of her attention was on the great golden bridal crown she had worn to be wed. It was heavy, encrusted as it was with emeralds, rubies, and clusters of tiny diamonds, and it was being fastened on her head once more with silken cords. The women then helped her to rise, and led her to the bridal bed. Inge held back the wispy bed-hangings, the coverlid was turned back, and Anna Mellby steadied the crown as Sunniva lowered herself to the bed and leaned back on the silken pillows heaped at the bed-head. The covers were then drawn up to her waist.

Anna smiled. Never had she seen a more beautiful and radiant bride. "There. You are ready. I will tell the men."

Sunniva saw in her mother's eyes her great pride tinged with sadness. She caught her hand and kissed it. "I am happy, mother. 'Tis what I want—and have thanks for all of this. 'Tis perfect. . . ."

"Ay."

As Anna Mellby left, Sunniva herself felt a touch of sadness. A part of her life had just ended, that part where she had been a treasured child living under her father's roof, and now he had given her to Raven and her new life was about to begin. Her heart was beating like an eagle's wings as Raven's groomsmen led him into the loft-room. She yearned to gaze on him openly and drink in his dark handsomeness, but she did not. It would not have been seemly for a bride to be so bold.

But from the corner of her eye through the bed-veils, she glimpsed his golden swordbelt and Gildor being removed from his waist, and then came the hiss as the long dark-green silken robe in which he had been wed was lifted up over his head. He, too, then sat in the chair in which Sunniva had sat as his boots and spurs were removed by his men. And then the guests were leaving, followed by her mother and Inge. Finally, Arn Mellby mounted the narrow stairs and himself closed the loft-room door, leaving the two alone except for the dancing shadows thrown on the tapestries.

Raven drew off his underclothing and dropped it to the floor. He saw Sunniva only faintly through the gauzy hangings. He drew them aside then, his heart thudding. She was all white and gold and slender, curvaceous softness. The glitter of the gems in her crown matched the glitter in her dark eyes. A thrill of desire shot through his body, seeing their excitement and invitation. Holy Odin, never had there been such an enchantress. He tied the veils back and reverently unbound the silken cords that held the heavy gold crown on her head. He lifted it, laid it on a table, and returned to the bed, to her open arms.

"Husband . . ." How strange the word sounded to Sunniva's ears. Raven Trondsson was her husband. She was mistress of Marvik and Nydahl, a thing she had never before given thought to.

Raven grinned. "Never had I thought to be called husband by any woman, especially by little Sunniva Mellby," he teased.

"No more am I little Sunniva Mellby." She smiled at the heat in his eyes.

"Nay, Sunniva Trondsson. You are a woman now, I vouch for it. And you are mine."

"And never doubt you are mine, Raven Trondsson of Marvik."

Often had Raven marked that her beautiful white skin glowed. It was as though a candle were lit within her, so luminescent was it. It glowed now in the lamplight, white as milk, her cheeks like roses and her mouth—but why merely look when it was time to taste and savor? He pulled her close, so close that he heard the breath being squeezed out of her lungs. He inhaled the faint, tempting fragrance of her hair and skin. Roses. He kissed her deeply, felt her hungry response, felt himself swelling, thrusting out toward her.

"Raven, Raven . . ." Sunniva stroked his dark arms and his chest and his thick hair, black and glossy as a raven's wing. She lifted parted lips and gave him a wild, hungry kiss as he stripped off her silken shift.

Soon they lay on their sides, her naked body pressed tightly against him, sealed to him. Raven lay within her, his shaft pulsing, the quiet before the storm of ecstasy that was fast approaching.

"I mind an eve long ago," he said huskily, "when I first marked your beauty and how special you were."

"Never did you notice how I looked!"

Raven chuckled and tasted her lips. "I noticed, little troll. It all began that snowy night when Ulf said you couldn't go on ski with us because you were becoming a woman. I knew then 'twould be a lucky man who got you . . ."

Sunniva laughed softly. "I, too, mind that night. I had a tantrum and stomped about throwing punches and snowballs."

"I mind it well." His eyes danced.

"Know you, Raven Trondsson, that from that night forth, I baked and broidered and sewed diligently for my bride-chest. I thought 'twas to please my folk." It was a whisper, her breathing coming faster and more shallow as her body arched against his. "Now I know

436

'twas to please you. Even then I wanted to please you . . ."

"You please me mightily, Sunniva Trondsson," Raven murmured. He began to move within her, slowly but ever more deeply, his mouth pressing soft hot kisses on her breasts and throat, on her own parted lips. He smiled at the small moan that escaped them. "Shall I tell you how much—or show you?"

He did not wait for an answer. His bride had closed her eyes and her rosy lips were parted. He covered them with his own, joining her in a headlong plunge into rapture.

GLOSSARY

Blood eagle: a method of execution in which the ribs were hewn from the backbone and the lungs and beating heart were torn out through the wound.

Busk: to gather one's courage.

Drekar: a dragonship, the finest and largest of the warships.

Extra-gift: required gift from the groom that must equal ⅓ to ½ the value of the bride's dowry.

Frey: god who rules the seasons and crops.

Freya: goddess of beauty.

Friggja grass: popularly supposed to be an aphrodisiac and named after Frigg, the goddess of love.

Gone agley: gone wrong.

Grace-deed: If a man committed an outlawry-offense, he might, on making payment to the crown, be allowed to remain at home instead of in prison until his case was judged.

Joan Van Nuys

Hafvilla: condition of being swept away or lost at sea.

Handsala: a vigorous hand-slap as sign of agreement or to seal a bargain.

Hel: goddess of death.

Manannan: Celtic god of wind, storm, and mist.

Maun: early Viking name for the present-day Isle of Man.

Morning-gift: voluntary gift from the husband on the morning after the wedding.

Mund: property or money that the suitor gave to the bride so the marriage would be legal.

Odin: god of war.

Prime-signed: marked symbolically with the cross so Vikings could live peacefully among Christians without forsaking their old gods.

Shield-burg: a wall of armed men.

Skald: one who sings and composes sagas.

Stronghand: a woman's being carried off by force.

Tarn: small mountain lake or pond.

The Thing: the popular assembly at which business was transacted, lawsuits were brought or settled, and laws were passed, among other things.

Thor: son of Odin, strongest of all the gods.

Valhalla: hall where Odin receives the dead heroes.

Valkyries: maidens of Odin who select the warriors to be slain and serve them in Valhalla.

Wadmal: tightly handwoven wool or cotton cloth.

Wergeld: an agreed-upon price paid by the killer to the kin of the slain.

I have taken the liberty of inventing the plant, lyngwort, and the place-names of Ballageay in Maun, and the Vaagaland, the Solby Valley, and the Strandefjord in Norway.